THE CROSS OF BERNY

OR

IRENE'S LOVERS

A NOVEL

BY MADAME EMILE DE GIRARDIN

MM. THÉOPHILE GAUTIER

JULES SANDEAU AND MERY

PHILADELPHIA Published by

HENRY T. COATES & CO.

MEARS & DUSENBERY, *Stereotypers.*

SHERMAN & CO., *Printers.*

PREFACE TO THE AMERICAN EDITION.

LITERARY partnerships have often been tried, but very rarely with success in the more imaginative branches of literature. Occasionally two minds have been found to supplement each other sufficiently to produce good joint writing, as in the works of MM. Erckman-Chatrian; but when the partnership has included more than two, it has almost invariably proved a failure, even when composed of individually the brightest intellects, and where the highest hopes have been entertained. Standing almost if not quite alone, in contrast with these failures of the past, THE CROSS OF BERNY is the more remarkable; and has achieved the success not merely of being the simply harmonious joint work of four individual minds,—but of being in itself, and entirely aside from its interest as a literary curiosity, a *great book.*

A high rank, then, is claimed for it not upon its success as a literary partnership, for that at best would but excite a sort of curious interest, but upon its intrinsic merit as a work of fiction. The spirit of rivalry in which it was undertaken was perhaps not the best guarantee of harmony in the tone of the whole work, but it has certainly added materially to the wit and brilliancy of the letters, while harmony has been preserved by much tact and skill. No one of its authors could alone have written THE CROSS OF BERNY—together, each one has given us his best, and their joint effort will long live to their fame.

The shape in which it appears, as a correspondence between four characters whose names are the pseudonyms of the four authors of the book, although at first it may seem to the reader a little awkward, will upon reflection be seen to be wisely chosen, since it allows to each of the prominent characters an individuality otherwise very difficult of attainment. In this way also any differences of style which there may be, tend rather to heighten the effect, and to increase the reality of the characters.

The title under which the original French edition appeared has been retained in the translation, although since its applicability depends upon a somewhat local allusion, the general reader may possibly fail to appreciate it.

ORIGINAL PREFACE TO THE FRENCH EDITION.

THE CROSS OF BERNY was, it will be remembered, a brilliant tourney, where Madame de Girardin (née Delphine Gay), Théophile Gautier, Jules Sandeau and Méry, broke lances like valiant knights of old.

We believe we respond to the general wish by adding to the *Bibliothèque Nouvelle* this unique work, which assumed and will ever retain a high position among the literary curiosities of the day.

Not feeling called upon to decide who is the victor in the tilt, we merely lift the pseudonymous veil concealing the champions.

The letters signed	Irene de Chateaudun	are by Madame de Girardin.
" " "	Edgar de Meilhan	" M. Théophile Gautier.
" " "	Raymond de Villiers	" M. Jules Sandeau.
" " "	Roger de Monbert	" M. Méry.

Who are recognised as the four most brilliant of our celebrated contemporaneous authors.—EDITOR.

THE

CROSS OF BERNY.

I.

IRENE DE CHRTEAUDUN *to* MME. LA VICOMTESSE DE BRAIMES,
Hotel de la Préfecture,
GRENOBLE (Isère).

PARIS, May 16th, 18—.

YOU are a great prophetess, my dear Valentine. Your predictions are verified.

Thanks to my peculiar disposition, I am already in the most deplorably false position that a reasonable mind and romantic heart could ever have contrived.

With you, naturally and instinctively, I have always been sincere; indeed it would be difficult to deceive one whom I have so often seen by a single glance read the startled conscience, and lead it from the ways of insolence and shame back into the paths of rectitude.

It is to you I would confide all my troubles; your counsel may save me ere it be too late.

You must not think me absurd in ascribing all my unhappiness to what is popularly regarded as "a piece of good luck."

Governed by my weakness, or rather by my fatal judgment, I have plighted my troth! . . . Good Heavens! is it really true that I am engaged to Prince de Monbert?

If you knew the prince you would laugh at my sadness, and at the melancholy tone in which I announce this intelligence.

Monsieur de Monbert is the most witty and agreeable man

in Paris; he is noble-hearted, generous and . . . in fact fascinating! . . . and I love him! He alone pleases me; in his absence I weary of everything; in his presence I am satisfied and happy—the hours glide away uncounted; I have perfect faith in his good heart and sound judgment, and proudly recognise his incontestable superiority—yes, I admire, respect, and, I repeat it, love him! . . . .

Yet, the promise I have made to dedicate my life to him, frightens me, and for a month I have had but one thought—to postpone this marriage I wished for—to fly from this man whom I have chosen! . . .

I question my heart, my experience, my imagination, for an answer to this inexplicable contradiction; and to interpret so many fears, find nothing but school-girl philosophy and poetic fancies, which you will excuse because you love me, and I *know* my imaginary sufferings will at least awaken pity in your sympathetic breast.

Yes, my dear Valentine, I am more to be pitied now, than I was in the days of my distress and desolation. I, who so courageously braved the blows of adversity, feel weak and trembling under the weight of a too brilliant fortune.

This happy destiny for which I alone am responsible, alarms me more than did the bitter lot that was forced upon me one year ago.

The actual trials of poverty exhaust the field of thought and prevent us from nursing imaginary cares, for when we have undergone the torture of our own forebodings, struggled with the impetuosity and agony of a nature surrendered to itself, we are disposed to look almost with relief on tangible troubles, and to end by appreciating the cares of poverty as salutary distractions from the sickly anxieties of an unemployed mind.

Oh! believe me to be serious, and accuse me not of comic-opera philosophy, my dear Valentine! I feel none of that proud disdain for importunate fortune that we read of in novels; nor do I regret "my pretty boat," nor "my cottage by the sea;" here, in this beautiful drawing-room of the Hotel de Langeac, writing to you, I do not sigh for my gloomy garret in the Marais, where my labors day and night were most tiresome, because a mere parody of the noblest arts, an undignified labor making patience and courage ridiculous, a cruel game which we play for life while cursing it.

No! I regret not this, but I do regret the indolence, the idleness of mind succeeding such trivial exertions. For then there were no resolutions to make, no characters to study, and, above all, no responsibility to bear, nothing to choose, nothing to change.

I had but to follow every morning the path marked out by necessity the evening before.

If I were able to copy or originate some hundred designs; if I possessed sufficient carmine or cobalt to color some wretched engravings—worthless, but fashionable—which I must myself deliver on the morrow; if I could succeed in finding some new patterns for embroidery and tapestry, I was content—and for recreation indulged at evenings in the sweetest, that is most absurd, reveries.

Revery then was a rest to me, now it is a labor, and a dangerous labor when too often resorted to; good thoughts then came to assist me in my misery; now, vexatious presentiments torment my happiness. Then the uncertainty of my future made me mistress of events. I could each day choose a new destiny, and new adventures. My unexpected and undeserved misfortune was so complete that I had nothing more to dread and everything to hope for, and experienced a vague feeling of gratitude for the ultimate succor that I confidently expected.

I would pass long hours gazing from my window at a little light shining from the fourth-story window of a distant house. What strange conjectures I made, as I silently watched the mysterious beacon!

Sometimes, in contemplating it, I recalled the questions addressed by Childe Harold to the tomb of Cecilia Metella, asking the cold marble if she who rested there were young and beautiful, a dark-eyed, delicate-featured woman, whose destiny was that reserved by Heaven for those it loves; or was she a venerable matron who had outlived her charms, her children and her kindred?

So I also questioned this solitary light:

To what distressed soul did it lend its aid? Some anxious mother watching and praying beside her sick child, or some youthful student plunging with stern delight into the arcana of science, to wrest from the revealing spirits of the night some luminous truth?

But while the poet questioned death and the past, I questioned the living present, and more than once the distant beacon seemed to answer me. I even imagined that this busy light flickered in concert with mine, and that they brightened and faded in unison.

I could only see it through a thick foliage of trees, for a large garden planted with poplars, pines and sycamores separated the house where I had taken refuge from the tall building whence the beacon shone for me night after night.

As I could never succeed in finding the points of the compass, I was ignorant of the exact locality of the house, or even on what street it fronted, and knew nothing of its occupants. But still this light was a friend; it spoke a sympathetic language to my eyes—it said: "Courage! you do not suffer alone; behind these trees and under those stars there is one who watches, labors, dreams." And when the night was majestic and beautiful, when the morn rose slowly in the azure sky, like a radiant host offered by the invisible hand of God to the adoration of the faithful who pray, lament and die by night; when these ever-new splendors dazzled my troubled soul; when I felt myself seized with that poignant admiration which makes solitary hearts find almost grief in joys that cannot be shared, it seemed to me that a dear voice came to calm my excitement, and exclaimed, with fervor, "Is not the night beautiful? What happiness in enjoying it together!"

When the nightingale, deceived by the silence of the deserted spot, and attracted by these dark shades, became a Parisian for a few days, rejuvenating with his vernal songs the old echoes of the city, again it seemed that the same voice whispered softly through the trembling leaves : " He sings, come listen !"

So the sad nights glided peacefully away, comforted by these foolish reveries.

Then I invoked my dear ideal, beloved shadow, protector of every honest heart, proud dream, a perfect choice, a jealous love sometimes making all other love impossible ! Oh, my beautiful ideal ! Must I then say farewell ? Now I no longer dare to invoke thee ! . . .

But what folly ! Why am I so silly as to permit the remembrance of an ideal to haunt me like a remorse ? Why do I suffer it to make me unjust towards noble and generous qualities that I should worthily appreciate ?

Do not laugh at me, Valentine, when I assure you that my greatest distress is that my lover does not resemble in any respect my ideal, and I am provoked that I love him—I cannot deceive myself, the contrast is striking—judge for yourself.

You may laugh if you will, but the whole secret of my distress is the contrast between these two portraits.

My lover has handsome, intelligent blue eyes—my ideal's eyes are black, full of sadness and fire, not the soft, troubadour eye with long drooping lids—no ! My ideal's glance has none of the languishing tenderness of romance, but is proud, powerful, penetrating, the look of a thinker, of a great mind yielding to the influence of love, the gaze of a hero disarmed by passion !

My lover is tall and slender—my ideal is only a head taller than myself . . . Ah ! I know you are laughing at me, Valentine ! Well ! I sometimes laugh at myself . . . .

My lover is frankness personified—my ideal is not a sly knave, but he is mysterious ; he never utters his thoughts, but lets you divine, or rather he speaks to a responsive sentiment in your own bosom.

My lover is what men call " A good fellow," you are intimate with him in twenty-four hours.

My ideal is by no means " a good fellow," and although he

inspires confidence and respect, you are never at ease in his presence, there is a graceful dignity in his carriage, an imposing gentleness in his manner, that always inspires a kind of fear, a pleasing awe.

You remember, Valentine, when we were very young girls how we were wont to ask each other, in reading the annals of the past, what situations would have pleased us, what parts we would have liked to play, what great emotions we would have wished to experience; and how you pityingly laughed at my odd taste.

My dream, *par excellence*, was to die of fear; I never envied with you the famed heroines, the sublime shepherdesses who saved their country. I envied the timid Esther fainting in the arms of her women at the fierce tones of Ahasuerus, and restored to consciousness by the same voice musically whispering the fondest words ever inspired by a royal love.

I also admired Semele, dying of fear and admiration at the frowns of a wrathful Jove, but her least of all, because I am terrified in a thunderstorm.

Well, I am still the same—to love tremblingly is my fondest dream; I do not say, like pretty Madame de S., that I can only be captivated by a man with the passions of a tiger and the manners of a diplomate, I only declare that I cannot understand love without fear.

And yet my lover does not inspire me with the least fear, and against all reasoning, I mistrust a love that so little resembles the love I imagined.

The strangest doubts trouble me. When Roger speaks to me tenderly; when he lovingly calls me his dear Irene, I am troubled, alarmed—I feel as if I were deceiving some one, that I am not free, that I belong to another. Oh! what foolish scruples! How little do I deserve sympathy! You who have known me from my childhood and are interested in my happiness, will understand and commiserate my folly, for folly I know it to be, and judge myself as severely as you would.

I have resolved to treat these wretched misgivings and childish fears as the creations of a diseased mind, and have arranged a plan for their cure.

I will go into the country for a short time; good Madame Taverneau offers me the hospitality of her house at Pont-de-l'Arche; she knows nothing of what has happened during the last six months, and still believes me to be a poor young widow, forced to paint fans and screens for her daily bread.

I am very much amused at hearing her relate my own story without imagining she is talking to the heroine of that singular romance.

Where could she have learned about my sad situation, the minute details that I supposed no one knew?

"A young orphan girl of noble birth, at the age of twenty compelled by misfortune to change her name and work for her livelihood, is suddenly restored to affluence by an accident that carried off all her relatives, an immensely rich uncle, his wife and son."

She also said my uncle detested me, which proved that she was well informed—only she adds that the young heiress is horribly ugly, which I hope is not true!

I will go to Mme. Taverneau and again become the interesting widow of Monsieur Albert Guerin, of the Navy.

Perilous widowhood which invited from my dear Mme. Taverneau confidences prematurely enlightening, and which Mlle. Irene de Chateaudun had some difficulty in forgetting.

Ah! misery is a cruel emancipation! Angelic ignorance, spotless innocence of mind is a luxury that poor young girls, even the most circumspect, cannot enjoy.

What presence of mind I had to exercise for three long years in order to sustain my part!

How often have I felt myself blush, when Mme. Taverneau would say: "Poor Albert! he must have adored you."

How often have I had to restrain my laughter, when, in enumerating the perfections of her own husband, she would add, with a look of pity: "It must distress you to see Charles and me together, our love must recall your sad loss."

To these remarks I listened with marvellous self-possession; if comedy or acting of any kind were not distasteful to me, I would make a good actress.

But now I must finish telling you of my plan. To-morrow I will set out ostensibly with my cousin, accompanying her as far as Fontainbleau, where she is going to join her daughter, then I will return and hide myself in my modest lodging, for a day or two, before going to Pont-de-l'Arche.

With regard to my cousin, I must say, people abuse her unjustly; she is not very tiresome, this fat cousin of mine; I heard of nothing but her absurdities, and was warned against taking up my abode with her and choosing her for my chaperone, as her persecutions would drive me frantic and our life would be one continuous quarrel. I am happy to say that none of these horrors have been realized. We understand each other perfectly, and, if I am not married next winter, the Hotel de Langeac will still be my home.

Roger, uninformed of my departure, will be furious, which is exactly what I want, for from his anger I expect enlightenment, and this is the test I will apply. Like all inexperienced people, I have a theory, and this theory I will proceed to explain.

If in your analysis of love you seek sincerity, you must apply a little judicious discouragement, for the man who loves hopefully, confidently, is an enigma.

Follow carefully my line of reasoning; it may be complicated, laborious, but—it is convincing.

All violent love is involuntary hypocrisy.

The more ardent the lover the more artful the man.

The more one loves, the more one lies.

The reason of all this is very simple.

The first symptom of a profound passion is an all-absorbing self-abnegation. The fondest dream of a heart really touched, is to make for the loved one the most extraordinary and difficult sacrifice.

How hard it is to subdue the temper, or to change one's nature! yet from the moment a man loves he is metamorphosed.

If a miser, to please he will become a spendthrift, and he who feared a shadow, learns to despise death. The corrupt Dor Juan emulates the virtuous Grandison, and, earnest in his efforts, he believes himself to be really reformed, converted, purified regenerated.

This happy transformation will last through the hopeful period. But as soon as the remodelled pretender shall have a presentiment that his metamorphosis is unprofitable; as soon as the implacable voice of discouragement shall have pronounced those two magic words, by which flights are stayed, thoughts paralyzed, and hopeful hearts deadened, "Never! Impossible!" the probation is over and the candidate returns to the old idols of graceless, dissolute nature.

The miser is shocked as he reckons the glittering gold he has wasted. The quondam hero thinks with alarm of his borrowed valor, and turns pale at the sight of his scars.

The roué, to conceal the chagrin of discomfiture, laughs at the promises of a virtuous love, calls himself a gay deceiver, great monster, and is once more self-complacent

Freed from restraint, their ruling passions rush to the surface, as when the floodgates are opened the fierce torrent sweeps over the field.

These hypocrites will feel for their beloved vices, lost and found again, the thirst, the yearning we feel for happiness long denied us. And they will return to their old habit, with a voracious eagerness, as the convalescent turns to food, the traveller to the spring, the exile to his native land, the prisoner to freedom.

Then will reckless despair develop their genuine natures; then, and then only, can you judge them.

Ah! I breathe freely now that I have explained my feelings What do you think of my views on this profound subject—discouragement in love?

I am confident that this test must sometimes meet with the most favorable results. I believe, for example, that with Roger it will be eminently successful, for his own character is a thousand times more attractive than the one he has assumed to attract me. He would please me better if he were less fascinating—his only fault, if it be a fault, is his lack of seriousness.

He has travelled too much, and studied different manners and subjects too closely, to have that power of judging character, that stock of ideas and principles without which we cannot make for ourselves what is called a philosophy, that is, a truth of our own.

In the savage and civilized lands he traversed, he saw religions so ridiculous, morals so wanton, points of honor so ludicrous, that he returned home with an indifference, a carelessness about everything, which adds brilliancy to his wit, but lessens the dignity of his love.

Roger attaches importance to nothing—a bitter sorrow must teach him the seriousness of life, that everything must not be treated jestingly. Grief and trouble are needed to restore his faith.

I hope he will be very unhappy when he hears of my inexplicable flight, and I intend returning for the express purpose of watching his grief; nothing is easier than to pass several days in Paris *incog.*

My beloved garret remains unrented, and I will there take sly pleasure in seeing for myself how much respect is paid to my memory—I very much enjoy the novel idea of assisting at my own absence.

But I perceive that my letter is unpardonably long; also that in confiding my troubles to you, I have almost forgotten them; and here I recognise your noble influence, my dear Valentine; the thought of you consoles and encourages me. Write soon, and your advice will not be thrown away. I confess to being foolish, but am sincerely desirous of being cured of my folly. My philosophy does not prevent my being open to conviction, and willing to sacrifice my logic to those I love.

Kiss my godchild for me, and give her the pretty embroidered dress I send with this. I have trimmed it with Valenciennes to my heart's content. Oh! my friend, how overjoyed

I am to once more indulge in these treasured laces, the only real charm of grandeur, the only unalloyed gift of fortune. Fine country seats are a bore, diamonds a weight and a care, fast horses a danger; but lace! without whose adornment no woman is properly dressed—every other privation is supportable; but what is life without lace?

I have tried to please your rustic taste in the wagon-load of newly imported plants, one of which is a *Padwlonia* (do not call it a Polonais), and is now acclimated in France; its leaves are a yard in circumference, and it grows twenty inches a month—malicious people say it freezes in the winter, but don't you believe the slander.

Adieu, adieu, my Valentine, write to me, a line from you is happiness.

IRENE DE CHATEAUDUN.

My address is,

Madame Albert Guerin,

Care Mme. Taverneau, Pont de l'Arche,

Department of the Eure.

2

II.

ROGER DE MONBERT *to* M. DE MEILHAN,
Pont-de-l'Arche (Eure.)

PARIS, May 19th, 18—.

DEAR EDGAR,—It cannot be denied that friendship is the refuge of adversity—the roof that shelters from the storm.

In my prosperous days I never wrote you. Happiness is selfish. We fear to distress a friend who may be in sorrow, by sending him a picture of our own bliss.

I am oppressed with a double burden; your absence, and my misfortunes.

This introduction will, doubtless, impress you with the idea that I wander about Paris with dejected visage and neglected dress. Undeceive yourself. It is one of my principles never to expose my sacred griefs to the gaze of an unsympathetic world, that only looks to laugh.

Pity I regard as an insult to my pride: the comforter humiliates the inconsolable mourner; besides, there are sorrows that all pretend to understand, but which none really appreciate. It is useless, then, to enumerate one's maladies to a would-be physician; and the world is filled with those who delight in the miseries of others; who follow the sittings of courts and luxuriate in heart-rending pictures of man's injustice to his fellow.

I do not care to serve as a relaxation to this class of mankind, who, since the abolition of the circus and amphitheatre, are compelled to pick up their pleasure wherever they can find it; seeking the best places to witness the struggle of Christian fortitude with adversity.

But every civilized age has its savage manners, and, knowing this, I resemble in public the favorite of fortune. I simulate content, and my face is radiant with deceit.

The idle and curious of the Boulevard Italien, the benches of the circus would hardly recognise me as the gladiator struggling with an iron-clawed monster—they are all deceived.

I feel a repugnance, dear Edgar, to entertaining you with a recital of my mysterious sorrow. I would prefer to leave you in ignorance, or let you divine them, but I explain to prevent your friendship imagining afflictions that are not mine.

In the first place, to reassure you, my fortune has not suffered during my absence. On my return to Paris, my agent dazzled me with the picture of my wealth

"Happy man!" said he; "a great name, a large fortune, health that has defied the fires of the tropics, the ice of the poles,—and only thirty!" The notary reasoned well from a notary's stand-point. If I were to reduce my possessions to ingots, they would certainly balance a notary's estimate of happiness; therefore, fear nothing for my fortune.

Nor must you imagine that I grieve over my political and military prospects that were lost in the royal storm of '30, when plebeian cannon riddled the Tuilleries and shattered a senile crown. I was only sixteen, and hardly understood the lamentations of my father, whose daily refrain was, "My child, your future is destroyed."

A man's future lies in any honorable career. If I have left the epaulettes of my ancestors reposing in their domestic shrine, I can bequeath to my children other decorations.

I have just returned from a ten years' campaign against all nations, bringing back a marvellous quantity of trophies, but without causing one mother to mourn. In the light of a conqueror, Cæsar, Alexander, and Hannibal pale in comparison, and yet to a certainty my military future could not have gained me the epaulettes of these illustrious commanders.

You would not, my dear Edgar, suppose, from the gaiety of this letter, that I had passed a frightful night.

You shall see what becomes of life when not taken care of; when there is an unguarded moment in the incessant duel that, forced by nature, we wage with her from the cradle to the grave.

What a long and glorious voyage I had just accomplished! What dangers I escaped! The treacherous sea defeated by a motion of the helm! The sirens to whom I turned a deaf ear. The Circes deserted under a baleful moon, ere the brutalizing change had come!

I returned to Paris, a man with soul so dead that his country was not dear to him—I felt guilty of an unknown crime, but reflection reduced the enormity of the offence. Long voyages impart to us a nameless virtue—or vice, made up of tolerance, stoicism and disdain. After having trodden over the graveyards of all nations, it seems as if we had assisted at the funeral ceremonies of the world, and they who survive on its surface seem like a band of adroit fugitives who have discovered the secret of prolonging to-day's agony until to-morrow.

I walked upon the Boulevard Italien without wonder, hatred, love, joy or sorrow. On consulting my inmost thoughts I found there an unimpassioned serenity, a something akin to ennui; I scarcely heard the noise of the wheels, the horses—the crowd that surrounded me.

Habituated to the turmoil of those grand dead nations near the vast ruins of the desert, this little hubbub of wearied citizens scarcely attracted my attention.

My face must have reflected the disdainful quietude of my soul.

By contemplative communion with the mute, motionless colossal faces of Egypt's and Persia's monuments, I felt that unwittingly my countenance typified the cold imperturbable tranquillity of their granite brows.

That evening La Favorita was played at the opera. Charming work! full of grace, passion, love. Reaching the end of Le Pelletier street, my walk was blocked by a line of carriages coming down Provence street; not having the patience to wait the passage of this string of vehicles, nor being very dainty in my distinction between pavement and street, I followed in the wake of the carriages, and as they did not conceal the façade of the opera at the end of the court, I saw it, and said "I will go in."

I took a box below, because my family-box had changed

hands, hangings and keys at least five times in ten years, and seated myself in the back-ground to avoid recognition, and leave undisturbed friends who would feel in duty bound to pay fashionable court to a traveller due ten years. I was not familiar with La Favorita, and my ear took in the new music slowly. Great scores require of the indolent auditor a long novitiate.

While I listened indolently to the orchestra and the singers, I examined the boxes with considerable interest, to discover what little revolutions a decade could bring about in the aristocratic personnel of the opera. A confused noise of words and some distinct sentences reached my ear from the neighboring boxes when the orchestra was silent. I listened involuntarily; the occupants were not talking secrets, their conversation was in the domain of idle chat, that divides with the libretto the attention of the habitués of the opera.

They said, "I could distinguish her in a thousand, I mistrust my sight a little, but my glass is infallible; it is certainly Mlle. de Bressuire—a superb figure, but she spoils her beauty by affectation."

"Your glass deceives you, my dear sir, we know Mlle. de Bressuire."

"Madame is right; it is not Mlle. That young lady at whom everybody is gazing, and who to-night is the favorite—excuse the pun—of the opera, is a Spaniard; I saw her at the Bois de Boulogne in M. Martinez de la Rosa's carriage. They told me her name, but I have forgotten. I never could remember names."

"Ladies," said a young man, who noisily entered the box, "we are at last enlightened. I have just questioned the box-keeper—she is a maid of honor to the Queen of Belgium."

"And her name?" demanded five voices.

"She has a Belgian name, unpronounceable by the box-keeper; something like Wallen, or Meulen."

"We are very much wiser."

From the general commotion it was easy to perceive that the same subject was being discussed by the whole house, and doubtless in the same terms; for people do not vary their formulas much on such occasions.

A strain of music recalled to the stage every eye that during the intermission had been fastened upon one woman. I confess that I felt some interest in the episode, but, owing to my habitual reserve, barely discovered by random and careless glances the young girl thus handed over to the curious glances of the fashionable world. She was in a box of the first tier, and the native grace of her attitude first riveted my attention. The cynosure of all eyes, she bore her triumph with the ease of a woman accustomed to admiration.

To appear unconscious she assumed with charming cleverness a pose of artistic contemplation. One would have said that she was really absorbed in the music, or that she was following the advice of the Tuscan poet:

> "Bel ange, descendu d'un monde aérien,
> Laisse-toi regarder et ne regarde rien."

From my position I could only distinguish the outline of her figure, except by staring through my glasses, which I regard as a polite rudeness, but she seemed to merit the homage that all eyes looked and all voices sang.

Once she appeared in the full blaze of the gas as she leaned forward from her box, and it seemed as if an apparition by some theatro-optical delusion approached and dazzled me.

The rapt attention of the audience, the mellow tones of the singer, the orchestral accompaniment full of mysterious harmony, seemed to awaken the ineffable joy that love implants in the human heart. How much weakness there is in the strength of man!

To travel for years over oceans, through deserts, among all varieties of peoples and sects; shipwrecked, to cling with bleeding hands to sea-beaten rocks; to laugh at the storm and brave the tiger in his lair; to be bronzed in torrid climes; to subject one's digestion to the baleful influences of the salt seas; to study wisdom before the ruins of every portico where rhetoricians have for three thousand years paraphrased in ten tongues the words of Solomon, "All is vanity;" to return to one's native shores a used-up man, persuaded of the emptiness of all things save the overhanging firmament and the never-fading stars; to scatter the fancies of too credulous youth by a contemptuous smile, or a lesson of bitter experience, and yet, while boasting a victory over all human fallacies and weaknesses, to be enslaved by the melody of a song, the smile of a woman.

Life is full of hidden mysteries. I looked upon the stranger's face with a sense of danger, so antagonistic to my previous tranquillity that I felt humiliated.

By the side of the beautiful unknown, I saw a large fan open and shut with a certain affectation, but not until its tenth movement did I glance at its possessor. She was my nearest relative, the Duchess de Langeac.

The situation now began to be interesting. In a moment the interlude would procure for me a position to be envied by every one in the house. At the end of the act I left my box and made a rapid tour of the lobby before presenting myself. The Duchess dispelled my embarrassment by a cordial welcome. Women have a keen and supernatural perception about everything concerning love, that is alarming.

The Duchess carelessly pronounced Mlle. de Chateaudun's name and mine, as if to be rid of the ceremonies of introduction as soon as possible, and touching a sofa with the end of her fan, said:

"My dear Roger, it is quite evident that you have come from everywhere except from the civilized world. I bowed to you twenty times, and you declined me the honor of a recognition. Absorbed in the music, I suppose. La Favorita is not performed among the savages, so they remain savages. How do you like our barytone? He has sung his aria with delicious feeling."

While the Duchess was indulging her unmeaning questions and comments, a rapid and careless glance at Mlle. de Chateaudun explained the admiration that she commanded from the crowded house. Were I to tell you that this young creature was a pretty, a beautiful woman, I would feebly express my meaning, such phrases mean nothing. It would require a master hand to paint a peerless woman, and I could not make the attempt when the bright image of Irene is now surrounded by the gloomy shadows of an afflicted heart.

After the first exchange of insignificant words, the skirmish of a conversation, we talk as all talk who are anxious to appear ignorant of the fact that they are gazed upon by a whole assembly.

Concealing my agitation under a strain of light conversation, "Mademoiselle," I said, in answer to a question, "music is to-day the necessity of the universe. France is commissioned to amuse the world. Suppress our theatre, opera, Paris, and a settled melancholy pervades the human family. You have no idea of the ennui that desolates the hemispheres.

"Occasionally Paris enlivens the two Indias by dethroning a king. Once Calcutta was *in extremis*, it was dying of the blues; the East India company was rich but not amusing; with all its treasure it could not buy one smile for Calcutta, so Paris sent Robert le Diable, La Muette de Portici, a drama or two of Hugo and Dumas. Calcutta became convalescent and recovered. Its neighbor, Chandernagore, scarcely existed then, but in 1842, when I left the Isle de Bourbon, La Favorita was announced; it planted roses in the cheeks of the jaundiced inhabitants, and Madras, possessed by the spleen, was exorcised by William Tell.

"Whenever a tropical city is conscious of approaching decline, she always stretches her hands beseechingly to Paris, who responds with music, books, newspapers; and her patient springs into new life.

"Paris does not seem to be aware of her influences. She detracts from herself; says she is not the Paris of yesterday, the Paris of the great century; that her influence is gone, she is in the condition of the Lower Empire.

"She builds eighty leagues of fortifications to sustain the siege of Mahomet II. She weeps over her downfall and accuses

Heaven of denying to her children of '44 the genius and talents that characterized the statesmen and poets of her past.

"But happily the universe does not coincide with Paris; go ask it; having just come from there, I know it."

Indulging my traveller's extravagancies laughingly, to the amusement of my fair companion, she said:

"Truly your philosophy is of the happy school, and the burden of life must be very light when it is so lightly borne."

"You must know, my dear Roger," said the Duchess, feigning commiseration, "that my young cousin, Mlle. de Chateaudun, is pitiably unhappy, and you and I can weep over her lot in chorus with orchestral accompaniment; poor child! she is the richest heiress in Paris."

"How wide you are from the mark!" said Irene, with a charming look of annoyance in the brightest eye that ever dazzled the sober senses of man; "it is not an axiom that wealth is happiness. The poor spread such a report, but the rich know it to be false."

Here the curtain arose, and my return to my box explained my character as the casual visitor and not the lover. And what intentions could I have had at that moment? I cannot say.

I was attracted by the loveliness of Mlle. Chateaudun; chance gave the opportunity for studying her charms, the fair unknown improved on acquaintance. Hers was the exquisite grace of face and feature and winningness of manner which attracts, retains and is never to be forgotten.

From the superb tranquillity of her attitude, the intelligence of her eyes, it was easy to infer that a wider field would bring into action the hidden treasures of a gifted nature. Over the dazzling halo that surrounded the fair one, which left me the alternative of admiring silence or heedless vagrancy of speech, one cloud lowered, eclipsing all her charms and bringing down my divinity from her pedestal—Irene was an heiress!

The Duchess had clipped the wings of the angel with the phrase of a marriage-broker. An heiress! the idea of a beautiful woman, full of poetry and love, inseparately linked to pounds, shillings and pence!

It was a day of amnesty to men, a fête day in Paradise, when God gave to this young girl that crown of golden hair, that seraphic brow, those eyes that purified the moral miasma of earth. The ideal of poetry, the reality of my love!

Think of this living master-piece of the divine studio as the theme of money-changers, the prize of the highest bidder!

Of course, my dear Edgar, I saw Mlle. de Chateaudun again and again after this memorable evening; thanks to the facilities afforded me by my manœuvring kinswoman, the Duchess, who worshipped the heiress as I worshipped the woman. I could add a useless volume of romantic details leading you to the denouement, which you have already guessed, for you must see in me the lover of Mlle. de Chateaudun.

I wished to give you the beginning and end of my story; what do you care for the rest, since it is but the wearisome calendar of all lovers?—The journal of a thousand incidents as interesting and important to two people as they are stupid and ridiculous to every one else. Each day was one of progress; finally, we loved each other. Excuse the homely platitude in this avowal.

Irene seemed perfect; her only fault, being an heiress, was lost in the intoxication of my love; everything was arranged, and in spite of her money I was to marry her.

I was delirious with joy, my feet spurned the earth. My bliss was the ecstasy of the blest. My delight seemed to color the contentment of other men with gloom, and I felt like begging pardon for being so happy. It seemed that this valley of tears, astonished that any one should from a terrestrial paradise gaze upon its afflictions and still be happy, would revolt against me!

My dear Edgar, the smoke of hell has darkened my vision—I grope in the gloom of a terrible mystery—Vainly do I strive to solve it, and I turn to you for aid.

Irene has left Paris! Home, street, city, all deserted! A damp, dark nothingness surrounds me!

Not an adieu! a line! a message! to console me—

Women do such things—

I have done all in my power, and attempted the impossible to find Irene, but without success. If she only had some ground of complaint against me, how happy I would be.

A terrible thought possesses my fevered brain—she has fallen into some snare, my marvellously beautiful Irene.

Hide my sorrows, dear Edgar, from the world as I have hidden them.

You would not have recognised the writer of this, had you seen him on the boulevard this morning. I was a superb dandy, with the poses of a Sybarite and the smiles of a young sultan. I trod as one in the clouds, and looked so benevolently on my fellow man that three beggars sued for aid as if they recognised Providence in a black coat. The last observation that reached my ear fell from the lips of an observing philosopher:

"Heavens! how happy that young man must be!"

Dear Edgar, I long to see you.

ROGER DE MONBERT.

III.

EDGAR DE MEILHAN *to the* PRINCE DE MONBERT,
St. Dominique Street, Paris.

RICHEPORT, 20th May, 18–

No, no, I cannot console you in Paris. I will escort your grief to Smyrna, Grand Cairo, Chandernagore, New Holland, if you wish, but I would rather be scalped alive than turn my steps towards that fascinating city surrounded by fortifications.

Your elegy found me moderately impressible. Fortune has apparently always treated you like a spoiled child; were your misfortunes mine I should be delighted, and in your torment I should find a paradise. A disappearance afflicts you with agony. I was forced to beat a retreat once, but not from creditors; my debts are things of the past. You are fled from—I am pursued; and whatever you may say to the contrary, it is much more agreeable to be the dog than the hare.

Ah! if the beauty that I adore (this is melo-dramatic) had only conceived such a triumphant idea! I should not be the one who—but no one knows when he is well off. This Mlle. Irene de Chateaudun pleases me, for by this opportune and ingenious eclipse she prevents you from committing a great absurdity. What put marriage into your head, forsooth! You who have housed with Bengal tigers and treated the lions of Atlas as lapdogs; who have seen, like Don Cæsar de Bazan, women of every color and clime; how could you have centred your affections upon this Parisian doll, and chained the fancies of your cosmopolitan soul to the dull, rolling wheel of domestic and conjugal duty?

So don't swear at her; bless her with a grateful heart, put a bill of credit in your pocket, and off we'll sail for China. We will make a hole in the famous wall, and pry into the secrets of lacquered screens and porcelain cups. I have a strong desire to taste their swallow-nest soup, their shark's fins served with jujube sauce, the whole washed down by small glasses of castor oil. We will have a house painted apple-green and vermilion, presided over by a female mandarin with no feet, circumflex eyes, and nails that serve as toothpicks. When shall I order the post-horses?

A wise man of the Middle Empire said that we should never attempt to stem the current of events. Life takes care of itself. The loss of your fiancée proves that you are not predestined for matrimony, therefore do not attempt to coerce chance; let it act, for perhaps it is the pseudonym of God.

Thanks to this very happy disappearance, your love remains young and fresh; besides, you have, in addition to the Pleasures of Memory, the Pleasures of Hope (considered the finest work of the poet Campbell); for there is nothing to show that your divinity has been translated to that better world, where, however, no one seems over-anxious to go.

Let not my retreat give rise to any unfavorable imputations against my courage. Achilles, himself, would have incontinently fled if threatened with the blessings in store for me. From what oriental head-dresses, burnous affectedly draped, golden rings after the style of the Empress of the Lower Empire, have I not escaped by my prudence?

But this is all an enigma to you. You are in ignorance of my story, unless some too-well-posted Englishman hinted it to you in the temple of Elephanta. I will relate it to you by way of retaliation for the recital of your love affair with Mlle. Irene de Chateaudun.

You have probably met that celebrated blue-stocking called the "Romantic Marquise." She is handsome, so the painters say; and, perhaps, they are not far from right, for she is handsome after the style of an old picture. Although young, she seems to be covered with yellow varnish, and to walk surrounded by a frame, with a background of bitumen.

One evening I found myself with this picturesque personage at Madame de Bléry's. I was listlessly intrenched in a corner, far from the circle of busy talkers, just sufficiently awake to be conscious that I was asleep—a delirious condition, which I recommend to your consideration, resembling the beginning of haschish intoxication—when by some turn in the conversation Madame de Bléry mentioned my name and pointed me out. I was immediately awakened from my torpor and dragged out of my corner.

I have been weak enough at times, as Gubetta says, to jingle words at the end of an idea, or to speak more modestly, at the end of certain measured syllables. The Marquise, cognisant of the offence, but not of the extenuating circumstances, launched forth into praise and flattering hyperbole that lifted me to the level of Byron, Goethe, Lamartine, discovered that I had a satanic look, and went on so that I suspected an album.

This affected me gloomily and ferociously. There is nothing I despise more than an album, unless it be two of them.

To avoid any such attempt, I broke into the most of the conversation with several innocent provincialisms, and effected my retreat in a masterly manner; advancing towards the door by degrees, and reaching it, I sprang outside so suddenly and nimbly that I had gotten to the bottom of the stairs before my absence was discovered.

Alas! no one can escape an album when it is predestined! The next day a book, magnificently bound in Russia, arrived in a superb moiré case in the hands of a groom, with an accompanying note from the Infanta soliciting the honor, &c.

All great men have their antipathies. James I. could not look upon a glittering sword; Roger Bacon fainted at the sight of an apple; and blank paper fills me with melancholy.

However, I resigned myself to the decrees of fate, and scribbled, I don't know what, in the corner, and subscribed my initials as illegible as those of Napoleon when in a passion.

This, I flattered myself, was the end of the tragedy, but no: a few days afterwards I received an invitation to a select gathering, in such amiable terms that I resolved to decline it.

Talleyrand said, "Never obey your first impulse, because it is good;" I obeyed this Machiavellian maxim, and erred!

"*Eucharis*" was being performed at the opera; the sky was

filled with ugly, threatening clouds; I sought in vain for a companion to get tight with, and moralize over a few bottles of wine, and so for want of a gayer occupation I went to the Marquise.

Her apartments are a perfect series of catafalques, and seem to have been upholstered by an undertaker. The drawing-room is hung in violet damask; the bed-rooms in black velvet; the furniture is of ebony or old oak; crucifixes, holy-water basins, folio bibles, death's-heads and poniards adorned the enlivening interior. Several Zurbarans, real or false, representing monks and martyrs, hung on the walls, frightening visitors with their grimaces. These sombre tints are intended to contrast with the waxy cheeks and painted eyes of the lady who looks more like the ghost than the mistress of this dwelling; for she does not inhabit, she haunts it.

You must not think, dear Roger, from this funereal introduction, that your friend became the prey of a ghoul or a vampire. The Marquise is handsome enough, after all. Her features are noble, regular, but a little Jewish, which induces her to wear a turban earlier and oftener than is necessary. She would not be so pale, if instead of white she put on red. Her hands, though too thin, are rather pretty and aristocratic, and weighted heavily with odd-looking rings. Her foot is not too large for her slipper. Uncommon thing! for women, in regard to their shoes, have falsified the geometrical axiom: the receptacle should be greater than its contents.

She is, however, to a certain point, a gentlewoman, and holds a good position in society.

I was received with all manner of caresses, stuffed with small cake, inundated with tea, of which beverage I hold the same opinion as Madame Gibou. I was assailed by romantic and transcendental dissertations, but possessing the faculty of abstraction and fixing my gaze upon the facets of a crystal flagon, my attitude touched the Marquise, who believed me plunged into a gulf of thought.

In short, I had the misfortune to charm her, and the weakness, like the greater part of men, to surrender myself to my good or evil fortune; for this unhung canvas did not please me, and though tolerably stylish and pretty well preserved, I suspected some literature underneath, and closely scanned the edge of her dress to see if some azure reflection had not altered the whiteness of her stocking. I abhor women who take blue-ink baths. Alas! they are much worse than the avowed literary woman; she affects to talk of nothing but ribbons, dress and bonnets, and confidentially gives you a receipt for preserving lemons and making strawberry cream; they take pride in not ignoring housekeeping, and faithfully follow the fashions. At their homes ink, pen and paper are nowhere to be seen; their odes and elegies are written on the back of a bill or on a page torn from an account-book.

La Marquise contemplates reform, romances, social poetry, humanitarian and palingenesic treatises, and scattered about on the tables and chairs were to be seen solemn old books, dog-leaved at their most tiresome pages, all of which is very appalling. Nothing is more convenient than a muse whose complete works are printed; one knows then what to expect, and you have not always the reading of Damocles hanging over your head.

Dragged by a fatality that so often makes me the victim of women I do not admire, I became the Conrad, the Lara of this Byronic heroine.

Every morning she sent me folio-sized epistles, dated three hours after midnight. They were compilations from Frederick Soulié, Eugene Sue, and Alexander Dumas, glorious authors, whom I delight to read save in my amorous correspondence, where a feminine mistake in orthography gives me more pleasure than a phrase plagiarised from George Sand, or a pathetic tirade stolen from a popular dramatist.

In short, I do not believe in a passion told in language that smells of the lamp; and the expression "*Je t'aime*" will scarcely persuade me if it be not written "*Je thême.*"

It made no difference how often the beauty wrote, I fortified myself against her literary visitations by consigning her billets-doux unopened to an empty drawer. By this means I was enabled to endure her prose with great equanimity. But she expected me to reply—now, as I did not care to keep my hand in for my next romance, I viewed her claims as extravagant and unreasonable, and feigning a strong desire to see my mother, I fled, less curious than Lot's wife, without looking behind.

Had I not taken this resolution I should have died of ennui in that dimly-lighted house, among those sepulchral toys, in the presence of that pale phantom enveloped in a dismal wrapper, cut in the monkish style, and speaking in a trembling and languishing tone of voice.

La Trappe or Chartreuse would have been preferable—I would have gained at least my salvation. Although it may be the act of a Cossack, a shocking irregularity, I have given her no sign of my existence, except that I told her that my mother's recovery promised to be very slow, and she would need the devoted attention of a good son.

Judge, dear Roger, after this recital, of which I have subdued the horrors and dramatic situations out of regard to your sensibility, whether I could return to Paris to be tl e comforter in your sorrow. Yet I could brave an encounter with the Marquise were it not that I am retained in Normandy by an expected visit of two months from our friend Raymond. This fact certainly ought to make you decide to share our solitude. Our friend is so poetical, so witty, so charming. He has but one fault, that of being a civilized Don Quixote de la Mancha; instead of the helmet of Mambrino he wears a Gibus hat, a Buisson coat instead of a cuirass, a Verdier cane by way of a lance. Happy nature! in which the heart is not sacrificed to the intellect; where the subtlety of a diplomate is united to the ingenuousness of a child.

Since your ideal has fled, are not all places alike to you? Then why should you not come to me, to Richeport, but a step from Pont de l'Arch?

I am perched upon the bank of the river, in a strange old building, which I know will please you. It is an old abbey half in ruins, in which is enshrined a dwelling, with many windows at regular intrevals, and is surmounted by a slate roof and chimneys of all sizes. It is built of hewn stone, that time has covered with its gray leprosy, and the general effect, looking through the avenue of grand old trees, is fine. Here my mother dwells. Profiting by the walls and the half-fallen towers of the old enclosure, for the abbey was fortified to resist the Norman invasions, she has made upon the brow of the hill a garden terrace filled with roses, myrtles and orange trees, while the green boxes surrounding them replace the old battlements. In this quarter of the old domain, I have not interfered with any of these womanly fancies.

She has collected around her all manner of pretty rusticities; all the comfortable elegancies she could imagine. I have not opposed any system of hot-air stoves, nor the upholstering of the rooms, nor objected to mahogany and ebony, wedgwood ware, china in blue designs, and English plate. For this is the way that middle-aged, and in fact, all reasonable people live.

For myself, I have reserved the refectory and library of the brave monks, that is, all that overlooks the river. I have not permitted the least repairing of the walls, which present the complete flora of the native wild flowers. An arched door, closed by old boards covered with a remnant of red paint, and opening on the bank, serves me as a private entrance. A ferry worked by a rope and pulley establishes communication with an island opposite the abbey, which is verdant with a mass of osiers, elder bushes and willows. It is here also that my fleet of boats is moored.

Seen from without, nothing would indicate a human habitation; the ruins lie in all the splendor of their downfall.

I have not replaced one stone—walled up one lizard—the house-leek, St. John's-wort, bell-flower, sea-green saxifrage, woody nightshade and blue popion flower have engaged in a struggle upon the walls of arabesques, and carvings which would discourage the most patient ornamental sculptor. But above all, a marvel of nature attracts your admiring gaze: it is a gigantic ivy, dating back at least to Richard Cœur de Lion, it defies by the intricacy of its windings those geneological trees of Jesus Christ, which are seen in Spanish churches; the top touching the clouds, and its bearded roots embedded in the bosom of the patriarchal Abraham; there are tufts, garlands, clusters, cascades of a green so lustrous, so metallic, so sombre and yet so brilliant, that it seems as if the whole body of the old building, the whole life of the dead abbey had passed into the veins of this parasitic friend, which smothers with its embrace, holding in place one stone, while it dislodges two to plant its climbing spurs.

You cannot imagine what tufted elegance, what richness of open-work tracery this encroachment of the ivy throws upon the rather gaunt and sharp gable-end of the building, which on this front has for ornament but four narrow-pointed windows, surmounted by three trefoil quadrilobes.

The shell of the adjoining building is flanked at its angle by a turret, which is chiefly remarkable for its spiral stairway and well. The great poet who invented Gothic cathedrals would, in the presence of this architectural caprice, ask the question, "Does the tower contain the well, or the well the tower?" You can decide; you who know everything, and more besides—except, however, Mlle. de Chateaudun's place of concealment.

Another curiosity of the old building is a moucharaby, a kind of balcony open at the bottom, picturesquely perched above a door, from which the good fathers could throw stones, beams and boiling oil on the heads of those tempted to assault the monastery for a taste of their good fare and a draught of their good wine.

Here I live alone, or in the company of four or five choice books, in a lofty hall with pointed roof; the points where the ribs intersect being covered with rosework of exquisite delicacy. This comprises my suite of apartments, for I never could understand why the little space that is given one in this world to dream, to sleep, to live, to die in, should be divided into a set of compartments like a dressing-case. I detest hedges, partitions and walls like a phalansterian.

To keep off dampness I have had the sides of the market-house, as my mother calls it, wainscoted in oak to the height of twelve or fifteen feet.

By a kind of gallery with two stairways, I can reach the windows and enjoy the beauty of the landscape, which is lovely. My bed is a simple hammock of aloes-fibre, slung in a corner; very low divans, and huge tapestry arm-chairs, for the rest of the furniture. Hung up on the wainscoting are pistols, guns, masks, foils, gloves, plastrons, dumb-bells and other gymnastic equipments. My favorite horse is installed in the opposite angle, in a box of *bois des iles*, a precaution that secures him from the brutalizing society of grooms, and keeps him a horse of the world.

The whole is heated by a cyclopean chimney, which devours a load of wood at a mouthful, and before which a mastodon might be roasted.

Come, then, dear Roger, I can offer you a friendly ruin, the chapel with the trefoil quadrilobes.

We will walk together, axe in hand, through my park, which is as dense and impenetrable as the virgin forests of America, or the jungles of India. It has not been touched for sixty years, and I have sworn to break the head of the first gardener who dares to approach it with a pruning-hook.

It is glorious to see the abandonment of Nature in this extravagance of vegetation, this wild luxuriance of flowers and foliage; the trees stretch out their arms, breed and intertwine in the most fantastic manner; the branches make a hundred curiously-distorted turns, and interlace in beautiful disorder; sometimes hanging the red berries of the mountain-ash among the silver foliage of the aspen.

The rapid slope of the ground produces a thousand picturesque accidents; the grass, brightened by a spring which at a little distance plays a thousand pranks over the rocks, flourishes in rich luxuriance; the burdock, with large velvet leaves, the stinging nettles, the hemlock with greenish umbels; the wild oats—every weed prospers wonderfully. No stranger approaches the enclosure, whose denizens are two or three little deer with tawny coats gleaming through the trees.

This eminently romantic spot would harmonize with your melancholy. Mlle. de Chateaudun not being in Paris, you have better chance of finding her elsewhere.

Who knows if she has not taken refuge in one of these pretty bird's-nests embedded in moss and foliage, their half-open blinds overlooking the limpid flow of the Seine? Come quickly, my dear fellow; I will not take advantage of your position as I did of Alfred's, to overwhelm you from my moucharaby with a shower of green frogs, a miracle which he has not been able to explain to his entire satisfaction. I will show you an excellent spot to fish for white-bait; nothing calms the passions so much as fishing with rod and line; a philosophical recreation which fools have turned into ridicule, as they do everything else they do not understand.

If the fish won't bite, you can gaze at the bridge, its piers blooming with wild flowers and lavender; its noisy mills, its arches obstructed by nets; the church, with its truncated roof; the village covering the hill-side, and, against the horizon, the sharp line of woody hills.

EDGAR DE MEILHAN.

IV.

RAYMOND DE VILLIERS *to* M. EDGAR DE MEILHAN,
Richeport, near Pont de l'Arche (Eure).

GRENOBLE, Hotel of the Prefecture, May 22d 18—.

Do not expect me, dear Edgar, I shall not be at Richeport the 24th. When shall I? I cannot tell.

I write to you from a bed of pain, bruised, wounded, burnt, half dead. It served me right, you will say, on learning that I am here for the commission of the greatest crime that can be tried before your tribunal. It is only too true—I have saved the life of an ugly woman!

But I saved her at night, when I innocently supposed her beautiful—let this be the extenuating circumstance. That no delay may attend your decision, here is the whole story.

Travel from pole to pole—wander to and fro over the world, it is not impossible, by God's help, to escape the thousand and one annoyances that are scattered over the surface of this terraqueous globe, but it is impossible, go where you will, to evade England, the gayest nation to be found, especially in travelling.

At Rome, this winter, Lord K. told me seriously that he had set out from London, some years since, with the one object of finding some corner of the earth on which no foot had ever trod before, and there to fix the first glorious impress of a British boot. The English occasionally, for amusement, indulge in such notions.

After having examined a scale of the comparative heights of the mountains of the universe, he noted the two highest points. Lord K. first reached the Peruvian Andes, and began to climb the sides of Chimborazo with that placidity, that sang-froid, which is the characteristic of an elevated soul instinctively attracted to realms above.

Reaching the summit with torn feet and bleeding hands, he

was about to fix a conqueror's grasp upon the rock, when he saw in one of the crevices a heap of visiting-cards, placed there successively, during a half century, by two or three hundred of his compatriots.

Disappointed but not discouraged, Lord K. drew from his case a shining, satiny card, and having gravely added it to the many others, began to descend Chimborazo with the same cool ness and deliberation that he had climbed up.

Half way down he found himself face to face with Sir Francis P., about to attempt the ascent that Lord K. had just accomplished. Although alienated by difference of party, they were old friends, dating their acquaintance, I believe, from the University of Oxford.

Without appearing astonished at so unexpected an encounter, they bowed politely, and on Chimborazo, as in politics, went their separate ways.

Betrayed by the New World, Lord K. directed his steps towards the Old. He penetrated the heart of Asia, plunged into the Dobrudja region, and paused only at the foot of Tschamalouri, upon the borders of Bootan. It is fair that I should thus visit on you the formidable erudition inflicted upon me by Milord.

You must know, then, dear Edgar, that the Tschamalouri is the highest peak of the Himalayan group.

The Jungfrau, Mount Blanc, Mount Cervin, and Mount Rosa, piled one upon the other, would make at best but a stepping-stone to it. Judge, then, of Milord's transports in the presence of this giant, whose hoary head was lost in the clouds! They might rob him of Chimborazo, but Tschamalouri was his.

After a few days for repose and preparation, one fine morning at sunrise, behold Milord commencing the ascent, with the proud satisfaction of a lover who sees his rival dancing attendance in the antechamber while he glides unseen up the secret stairway with a key to the boudoir in his pocket.

He journeyed up, and on the first day had passed the region

of tempests. Passing the night in his cloak, he began again his task at the dawn of day.

Nothing dismayed him—no obstacle discouraged him. He bounded like a chamois from ridge to ridge, he crawled like a snake and hung like a vine from the sharp arêtes—wounds and lacerations covered his body—after scorching he froze. The eagles whirled about his head and flapped their wings in his face. But on he went. His lungs, distended by the rarified atmosphere, threatened to burst with an explosion akin to a steamboat's. Finally, after superhuman efforts, bleeding, panting, gasping for breath, Milord sank exhausted upon the rocks.

What a labor! but what a triumph! what a struggle! but what a conquest! The thought of being able, the coming winter, to boast of having carved his name where, until then, God alone had written his.

And Sir Francis! who would not fail to plume himself on the joint favors of Chimborazo, how humiliated he would be to learn that Lord K., more fastidious in his amours, more exalted in his ambition, had not, four thousand fathoms above sea, feared to pluck the rose of Tschamalouri!

I remember that the first night I passed in Rome I heard in my sleep a mysterious voice murmuring at my pillow: "Rome! Rome! thou art in Rome!"

Milord, shattered, sore and helpless, also heard a charming voice singing sweetly in his ear: "Thou art stretched full length upon the summit of Tschamalouri."

This melody insensibly affected him as the balm of Fier-à-Bras. He rallied, he arose, and with radiant face, sparkling eyes and bosom swelling with pride, drew a poniard from its sheath and prepared to cut his name upon the rock. Suddenly he turned pale, his limbs gave way under him, the knife dropped from his grasp and fell blunted upon the rocks. What had he seen? What could have happened to so agitate him in these inaccessible regions?

There, upon the tablet of granite where he was about to inscribe the name of his ancestors, he read, unhappy man, distinctly read, these two names distinctly cut in the flint, "William and Lavinia," with the following inscription, in English, underneath: "Here, July 25th, 1831, two tender hearts communed."

Surmounting the whole was a flaming double heart pierced by an arrow, an arrow that then pierced three hearts at once. The rock was covered besides with more than fifty names, all English, and as many inscriptions, all English too, of a kindred character to the one he had read. Milord's first impulse was to throw himself head foremost down the mountain side; but, fortunately, raising his eyes in his despair, he discovered a final plateau, so steep that neither cat nor lizard could climb it. Lord K. became a bird and flew up, and what did he see? Oh, the vanity of human ambition! Upon the last round of the most gigantic ladder, extending from earth to heaven, Milord perceived Sir Francis, who, having just effected the same ascent from the other side of the colossus, was quietly reading the "Times" and breakfasting upon a chop and a bottle of porter!

The two friends coolly saluted each other, as they had before done on the side of Chimborazo; then, with death in his heart, but impassive and grave, Lord K. silently drew forth a box of conserves, a flask of ale and a copy of the "Standard." The repast and the two journals being finished, the tourists separated and descended, each on his own side, without having exchanged a word.

Lord K. has never forgiven Sir Francis; they accuse each other of plagiarism, a mortal hatred has sprung up between them, and thus Tschamalouri finished what politics began.

I had this story from Lord K. himself, who drags out a disenchanted and gloomy existence, which would put an end to itself had he not in present contemplation a journey to the moon; still he is half convinced that he would find Sir Francis there.

Entertain your mother with this story, it would be improved by your narration.

You must agree with me that if the English grow four thousand fathoms above the sea, the plant must necessarily thrive on the plains and the low countries. It is acclimated everywhere, like the strawberry, without possessing its sweet savor.

Italy is, I believe, the land where it best flourishes. There I have traversed fields of English, sown everywhere, mixed with a few Italians.

But I would have been happy if I had encountered only Englishmen along my route. Some poet has said that England is a swan's nest in the midst of the waves. Alas! how few are the swans that come to us at long intervals, compared with the old ostriches in bristling plumage, and the young storks with their long, thin necks that flock to us.

When in Rome only a few hours, and wandering through the Campo Vaccino, I found among the ruins one I did not seek. It was Lady Penock. I had met her so often that I could not fail to know her name. Edgar, you know Lady Penock; it is impossible that you should not. But if not, it is easy for you to picture her to yourself. Take a keepsake, pick out one of those faces more beautiful than the fairies of our dreams, so lovely that it might be doubted whether the painter found his model among the daughters of earth. Passionate lover of form, feast your eye upon the graceful curve of that neck, those shoulders; gaze upon that pure brow where grace and youth preside; bathe your soul in the soft brightness of that blue and limpid glance; bend to taste the perfumed breath of that smiling mouth; tremble at the touch of those blonde tresses, twined in bewildering mazes behind the head and falling over the temples in waving masses; fervent worshipper at the shrine of beauty, fall into ecstasies; then imagine the opposite of this charming picture, and you have Lady Penock.

This apparition, in the centre of the ancient forum, completely upset my meditations. J. J. Rousseau says in his Confessions that he forgot Mme. de Larnage in seeing the Pont du Gard. So I forgot the Coliseum at the sight of Lady Penock. Explain, dear Edgar, what fatality attended my steps, that ever afterwards this baleful beauty pursued me?

Under the arches of the Coliseum, beneath the dome of St. Peter, in Pagan Rome and in Catholic Rome, in front of the Laocöon, before the Communion of St. Jerome, by Dominichino, on the banks of Lake Albano, under the shades of the Villa Borghese, at Tivoli in the Sibyl's temple, at Subiaco in the Convent of St. Benoit, under every moon and by every sun I saw her start up at my side. To get away from her I took flight and travelled post to Tuscany. I found her at the foot of the falls of Terni, at the tomb of St. Francis d'Assise, under Hannibal's gate at Spoletta, at the table d'hôte Pérouse at Arezzo, on the threshold of Petrarch's house; finally, the first person I met in the Piazza of the Grand Duke at Florence, before the Perseus of Benvenuto Cellini, Edgar, was Lady Penock. At Pisa she appeared to me in the Campo Santo; in the Gulf of Genoa her bark came near capsizing mine; at Turin I found her at the Museum of Egyptian Antiquities; her and no one else! And, what was so amusing, my Lady on seeing me became agitated, blushed and looked down, and believing herself the object of an ungovernable passion, she mumbled through her long teeth, "Shocking! Shocking!"

Tired of war, I bade adieu to Italy and crossed the mountains; besides, dear country, I sighed to see you once more. I passed through Savoy and when I saw the mountains of Dauphiny loom up against the distant horizon my heart beat wildly, my eyes filled with tears, and I felt like a returning exile, and know not what false pride restrained me from springing to the ground and kissing the soil of France!

Hail! noble and generous land, the home of intelligence and of liberty! On touching thee the soul swells within us, the mind expands; no child of thine can return to thy bosom without a throb of holy joy, a feeling of noble pride. I passed along filled with delirious happiness. The trees smiled on me, the winds whispered softly in my ear, the little flowers that carpeted the wayside welcomed me; it required an effort to restrain myself from embracing as brothers the noble fellows that passed me on the way.

Then, Edgar, I was to find you again, and it was the spot of my birthplace, the paternal acres which in our common land seem to us a second country.

The night was dark, no moon, no stars; I had just left Grenoble and was passing through Voreppe, a little village not without some importance because in the neighborhood of the Grande Chartreuse, which, at this season of the year, attracts more curiosity-hunters than believers — suddenly the horses stopped, I heard a rumbling noise outside, and a crimson glare lighted up the carriage windows. I might have taken it for sunset, if the sun had not set long since.

I got out and found the only inn of the village on fire; great was the confusion in the small hamlet, there was a general screaming, struggling and running about. The innkeeper with his wife, children, and servants emptied the stables and barns. The horses neighed, the oxen bellowed, and the pigs, feeling that they were predestined to be roasted anyhow, offered to their rescuers an obstinate and philosophical resistance.

Meantime the notables of the place, formed in groups, discussed magisterially the origin of a fire which no one made an effort to stay. Left alone, it brightened the night, fired the surrounding hills and shot its jets and rockets of sparks far into the sky. You, a poet, would have thought it fine. Sublime egotist that you are, everything is effect, color, mirages, decorations. Endeavoring to make myself useful in this disaster, I thought I heard it whispered around me that some travellers remained in the inn, who, if not already destroyed, were seriously threatened.

Among others a young stranger was mentioned who had come that day from the Grande Chartreuse, which she had been visiting. I went straight to the innkeeper who was dragging one of his restive pigs by the tail, reminding me of one of the most ridiculous pictures of Charlet. "All right," said the man, "all the travellers are gone, and as to those who remain—" "Then some do remain?" I asked, and by insisting learned that an Englishwoman occupied a room in the second story.

I hate England—I hate it absurdly, in true, old-fashioned style. To me England is still "Perfidious Albion."

You may laugh, but I hate in proportion to the love I bear my country. I hate because my heart has always bled for the wounds she has opened in the bosom of France. Yes, but coward is he who has the ability to save a fellow-creature, yet folds his arms, deaf to pity! My enemy in the jaws of death is my brother. If need be I would jump into the flood to save Sir Hudson Lowe, free to challenge him afterwards, and try to kill him as I would a dog.

The ground-floor of the inn was enveloped in flames. I took a ladder, and resting it against the sill, I mounted to the window that had been pointed out to me. On the hospitable soil of France a stranger must not perish for want of a Frenchman to save him. Like Anthony, with one blow I broke the glass and raised the sash; I found myself in a passage that the fire had not reached. I sprang towards a door.—an excited voice said, "Don't come in." I entered, looked around for the young stranger, and, immortal gods! what did I see? In the charming négligé of a beauty suddenly awakened,—you are right, it was she. Yes, my dear fellow, it was Lady Penock—Lady Penock, who recognised and screamed furiously! "Madame," said I, turning away with a sincere and proper feeling of respect, "you are mistaken. The house is on fire, and if you do not leave it"—"You! you!" she cried, "have set fire to it, like Lovelace, to carry me off." "Madame," said I, "we have no time to lose." The floor smoked under our feet, the rafters cracked over our heads, the flames roared at the door, delay was dangerous; so, in spite of the eternal refrain that sounded like the crying of a bird,—"Shocking! shocking!" I dragged Lady Penock from behind the bed where she cowered to escape my wild embraces, picked her up as if she were a stick of dry wood, and bearing the precious burden, appeared at the top of the ladder. Meanwhile the fire raged, the flames and the smoke enveloped us on all sides. "For pity's sake, madame," said I, "don't scream and kick so." My lady screamed all the louder and struggled all the worse. When half way down the ladder she said, "Young man, go back immediately, I have forgotten something very valuable to me." At these words the roof fell in, the walls crumbled away, the ladder shook, the earth opened under my feet, and I felt as if I were falling into the abyss of Tænarus.

I awoke, under an humble roof whose poor owner had received me.

I had a fracture of my shoulder, and three doctors by my side. I have known many men to die with less. As for Lady Penock, I learned with satisfaction of her escape, barring a sprained ankle; she had departed indignant at the impertinence of my conduct, and to the people who had charitably suggested to her to instal herself as a gray nun at the bedside of her preserver, she said, coloring angrily, "Oh, I should die if I were to see that young man again."

Be reassured, France has again atoned for Albion. My adventure having made some noise, a few days after the fire Providence came into my room and sat beside my bed in the shape of a noble woman named Madame de Braimes.

It appears that M. de Braimes has been, for a year past, prefect of Grenoble; that he knew my father intimately, and my name sufficed to bring these two noble beings to my side.

As soon as I could bear the motion of a carriage, they took me from Voreppe, and I am now writing to you, my dear Edgar, from the hotel of the Prefecture.

I received in Florence the last letter you directed to me at Rome. What a number of questions you ask, and how am I to answer them all?

Don't speak to me of Jerusalem, Cedron, Lebanon, Palmyra and Baalbec, or anything of the sort. Read over again Réné's Guide-book, Jocelyn's Travels, the Orientales of Olympio, and you will know as much about the East as I do, though I have been there, according to your account, for the last two years. However, I have performed all the commissions you gave me, on the eve of my departure, three years ago. I bring you pipes from Constantinople, to your mother chaplets from Bethlehem—only I bought the pipes at Leghorn, and the chaplets at Rome.

Do you remember a cold, rainy December evening in Paris, eighteen months ago, when I should have been on the borders of Afghanistan, or the shores of the Euphrates, you were walking along the quays, between eleven o'clock and midnight, walking rapidly, wrapped like a Castilian in the folds of your cloak?

Do you remember that between the Pont Neuf and the Pont Saint Michel you stumbled against a young man, enveloped likewise in a cloak, and following rapidly the course of the Seine in a direction opposite to yours? The shock was violent, and nailed us both to the spot. Do you remember that having scrutinized each other under the gaslight, you exclaimed, "Raymond," and opened your arms to embrace me; then, seeing the cold and reserved attitude of him who stood silently before you, how you changed your mind and went your way, laughing at the mistake but struck by the resemblance?

The resemblance still exists; the young man that you called Raymond, was Raymond.

One more story, and I have done. I will tell it without pride or pretence, a thing so natural, so simple, that it is neither worth boasting of nor concealing.

You know Frederick B. You remember that I have always spoken of him as a brother. We played together in the same cradle; we grew up, as it were, under the same roof. At school I prepared his lessons; out of gratitude he ate my sugar-plums. At college I performed his tasks and fought his battles. At twenty, I received a sword-thrust in my breast on his account. Later he plunged into matrimony and business, and we lost sight of, without ceasing to love each other. I knew that he prospered, and I asked nothing more. As for myself, tired of the sterile life I was leading, called fashionable life, I turned my fortune into ready money, and prepared to set out on a long journey.

The day of my departure—I had bidden you good-bye the evening before—Frederick entered my room. A year had nearly passed since we had met; I did not know that he was in Paris. I found him changed; his preoccupied air alarmed me. However, I concealed my anxiety. We cannot treat with too much reserve and delicacy the sadness of our married friends. As he talked, two big tears rolled silently down his cheeks. I had to speak.

"What is the matter?" I asked abruptly; and I pressed him with questions, tormented him until he told me all. Bankruptcy was at his door; and he spoke of his wife and children in such heart-rending terms, that I mingled my tears with his, thinking of course that I was not rich enough to give him the money he needed.

"My poor Frederic," I finally said, "is it such a very large amount?" He replied with a gesture of despair. "Come, how much?" I asked again.

"Five hundred thousand francs!" he cried, in a gloomy stupor. I arose, took him by the arm, and under the pretext of diverting him, drew him on the boulevards. I left him at the door of my notary and joined him on coming out. "Frederick," I said, giving him a line I had just written, "take that and hasten to embrace your wife and children." Then I jumped into a cab which carried me home; my journey was over. I returned from Jerusalem.

Dupe! I hear you say, Ah, no, Edgar! I am young and I understand men, but there dwell in them both the good and the beautiful, and to expect to derive any other satisfaction than that found in cultivating these qualities has always seemed to me to be an unreasonable expectation.

What! you, as a poet, enjoy the intoxication of inspiration, the feast of solitude, the silence of serene and starry nights and that does not satisfy you; you would have fortune hasten to the sound of the Muses' kisses.

"What! as a generous man, you can enjoy the delights of giving and only sow a field of benefits in the hope of reaping some day the golden harvest of gratitude!

Of what do you complain? wretched man! You are the ingrate. Besides, even with this view, be convinced, dear Edgar, that the good and the beautiful are still two of the best speculations that can be made here below, and nothing in the world succeeds better than fine verses and noble deeds. Only wicked hearts and bad poets dare to affirm the contrary. For myself, experience has taught me that self-abnegation is profit enough to him who exercises it, and disinterestedness is a blossom of luxury that well cultivated bears most savory fruit. I encountered fortune in turning my back on her. I owe to Lady Penock the touching care and precious friendship of Madame de Braimes, and if this system of remuneration continue I shall end by believing that in throwing myself into the gulf of Curtius I would fall upon a bed of roses.

The fact is, I was ruined, but whoever could have seen me at the moment would have said I was overcome with delight. I must tell you all, Edgar; I pictured to myself the transports of Frederick and his wife on seeing the abyss that was about to engulf them so easily closed; these sweet images alone did not cause my wild delight; would you believe it, the thought of my ruin and poverty intoxicated me more. I had suffered for a long time from an unoccupied youth, and was indignant at my uneventful life. At twenty I quietly assumed a position prepared for me; to play this part in the world I had taken the trouble to be born; to gather the fruits of life I had only to stretch out my hand. Irritated at the quietude of my days, wearied with a happiness that cost me nothing, I sought heroic struggles, chivalrous encounters, and not finding them in a well-regulated society, where strong interests have been substituted for strong passions, I fretted in secret and wept over my impotence.

But now my hour was come! I was about to put my will, strength and courage to the proof. I was about to wrest from study the secrets of talent. I was about to reclaim from labor the fortune I had given away, and which I owed to chance. Until that deed I had only been the son of my father, the heir of my ancestors; now I was to become the child of my own deeds. The prisoner who sees his chains fall off and sends to heaven a wild shout of liberty, does not feel a deeper joy than I felt when ready to struggle with destiny I could exclaim, "I am poor!"

I have seen everywhere *blasé* young men, old before their time, who, according to their own account, have known and exhausted every pleasure; have felt the nothingness of human things. 'Tis true these young unfortunates have tried everything but labor and devotion to some holy cause.

There remained of my patrimony fifteen thousand francs, which were laid aside to defray my travelling expenses. This, with a very moderate revenue accruing from two little farms, contiguous to the castle of my father, made up my possessions.

Putting the best face on things, supposing I might recover my fortune, an event so uncertain that it were best not to count on it, I wisely traced the line of duty with a firm hand and joyous heart.

I decided immediately that I would not undeceive my friends as to my departure, and that I would employ, in silence and seclusion, the time I was supposed to be spending abroad.

Not that it did not occur to me to proclaim boldly what I had done, for in a country where a dozen wretches are every year publicly beheaded for the sake of example, perhaps it would be well also, for example's sake, to do good publicly. To do this, however, would have been to compromise Frederick's credit, who, besides, would never have accepted my sacrifice if he could have measured its extent.

I could have retired to my estates; but felt no inclination to make an exposure of my poverty to the comments of a charitable province, nor had I taste for the life of a ruined country squire.

Besides, solitude was essential to my plans, and solitude is impossible out of Paris; one is never really lost save in a crowd. I soon found in the Masario a little room very near the clouds, but brightened by the rising sun, overlooking a sea of verdure marked here and there by a few northern pines, with their gloomy and motionless branches.

This nest pleased me. I furnished it simply, filled it with books and hung over my bed the portrait of my sainted mother, who seemed to smile on and encourage me, while you, Frederick and others believed me steaming towards the shores of the East; and here I quietly installed myself, prouder and more triumphant than a soldier of fortune taking possession of a kingdom.

Edgar, these two years I really lived ——. In that little room I spent what will remain, I very much fear, the purest, the brightest, the best period of my whole life. I am not of much account now, formerly I was nothing; the little good that is in me was developed in those two years of deep vigils. I thought, reflected, suffered and nourished myself with the bread of the strong. I initiated myself into the stern delights of study, the austere joys of poverty.

O! days of labor and privation, beautiful days! Where have you gone? Holy enchantments, shall I ever taste you again? Silent and meditative nights! when at the first glimmer of dawn I saw the angel of revery alight at my side, bend his beautiful face over me, and fold my wearied limbs in his white wings; blissful nights! will you ever return?

If you only knew the life I led through these two years! If you knew what dreams visited me in that humble nest by the dim light of the lamp, you would be jealous of them, my poet!

The days were passed in serious study. At evening I took my frugal repast, in winter, by the hearth, in summer by the open window. In December I had guests that kings might have envied. Hugo, George Sand, Lamartine, De Musset, yourself, dear Edgar. In April I had the soft breezes, the perfume of the lilacs, the song of the birds warbling among the branches, and the joyous cries of the children playing in the distant alleys, while the young mothers passed slowly through the fresh grass, their faces wreathed with sweet smiles, like the happy shadows that wander through the Elysian fields.

Sometimes on a dark night I would venture into the streets of Paris, my hat drawn over my eyes to keep out the glare of gas. On one of these solitary rambles I met you. Imagine the courage I required not to rush into your open arms. I returned frequently along the quays, listening to the confused roar, like the distant swell of the ocean, made by the great city before falling to sleep, listening to the murmurs of the river and gazing at the moon like a burning disk from the furnace, slowly rising behind the towers of Notre Dame.

Often I prowled under the windows of my friends, stopping at yours to send you a good-night.

Returning home I would rekindle my fire and begin anew my labors, interrupted from time to time by the bells of the neighboring convents and the sound of the hours striking sadly in the darkness.

O! nights more beautiful than the day. It was then that I felt germinate and flourish in my heart a strange love.

Opposite me, beyond the garden that separated us, was a window, in a story on a level with mine; it was hid during the day by the tall pines, but its light shone clear and bright through the foliage. This lamp was lit invariably at the same hour every evening and was rarely extinguished before dawn. There, I thought, one of God's poor creatures works and suffers. Sometimes I rose from my desk to look at this little star twinkling between heaven and earth, and with my brow pressed against the pane gazed sadly at it.

In the beginning it excited me to watch, and I made it a point of honor never to extinguish my lamp as long as the rival lamp was burning; at last it became the friend of my solitude, the companion of my destiny. I ended by giving it a soul to understand and answer me. I talked to it; I questioned. I sometimes said, "Who art thou?"

Now I imagined a pale youth enamored with glory, and called him my brother. Then it was a young and lovely Antigone, laboring to sustain her old father, and I called her my sister, and by a sweeter name too. Finally, shall I tell you, there were moments when I fancied that the light of our fraternal lamps was but the radiance of two mysterious sympathies, drawn together to be blended into one.

One must have passed two years in solitude to be able to comprehend these puerilities. How many prisoners have become attached to some wall-flower, blooming between the bars of their cell, like the Marvel of Peru of the garden, which closes to the beams of day to open its petals to the kisses of the evening; the flower that I loved was a star. Anxiously I watched its awakening, and could not repose until it had disappeared. Did it grow dim and flicker, I cried—"Courage and hope! God blesses labor, he keeps for thee a purer and brighter seat in heaven!"

Did I in turn feel sad, it threw out a brighter light and a voice said, "Hope, friend, I watch and suffer with thee!" No! I cannot but believe now that between that lamp and mine there passed an electric current, by which two hearts, created for each other, communicated with and understood their mutual pulsations. Of course I tried to find the house and room from whence shone my beloved light, but each day I received a new direction that contradicted the one they gave before; so I concluded that the occupant of this room had an object, like myself, in concealment, and I respected his secret.

Thus my life glided by—so much happiness lasted too short a time!

The gods and goddesses of Olympus had a messenger named Iris, who carried their billets-doux from star to star. We mortals have a fairy in our employ that leaves Iris far behind; this fairy is called the post; dwell upon the summit of Tschamalouri, and some fine morning you will see the carrier arrive with his box upon his shoulder, and a letter to your address. One evening, on returning from one of those excursions I told you of, I found at my porter's a letter addressed to me. I never receive letters without a feeling of terror. This, the only one in two years, had a formidable look; the envelope was covered with odd-looking signs, and the seal of every French consulate in the East; under this multitude of stamps was written in large characters—"In haste—very important." The square of paper I held in my hand had been in search of me from Paris to Jerusalem, and from consulate to consulate, had returned from Jerusalem to Paris, to the office of the Minister of Foreign Affairs. There they had let loose some blood-hounds of the police, who with their usual instinct followed my tracks and discovered my abode in less than a day.

I glanced first at the signature, and saw Frederick's name ; I vow, unaffectedly, that for two years I had not thought of his affairs, and his letter brought me the first news of him.

After a preamble, devoted entirely to the expression of an exaggerated gratitude, Frederick announced with a flourish of trumpets, that Fortune had made magnificent reparation for her wrongs to him ; he had saved his honor and strengthened his tottering credit. From which time forward he had prospered beyond his wildest hopes. In a few months he gained, by a rise in railroad stocks, fabulous sums. He concluded with the information that, having interested me in his fortunate speculations, my capital was doubled, and that I now possessed a clear million, which I owed to no one. At the end of this letter, bristling with figures and terms that savoured of money, were a few simple, touching lines from Frederick's wife, which went straight to my heart, and brought tears to my eyes.

When I had read the letter through, I took a long survey of my little room, where I had lived so happily ; then, sitting upon the sill of the open window, whence I could see my faithful star shine peacefully in the darkness, I remained until morning, absorbed in sad and melancholy thoughts.

Fortune has its duties as well as poverty. *Comme noblesse, fortune exige.*

If I were really so rich, I could not, ought not to live as I had done. After a few days, I went to Frederick, who believed that I had suddenly been brought from Jerusalem by his letter, and I allowed him to rest in that belief, not wishing to add to a gratitude that already seemed excessive.

Excuse the particulars, I was a veritable millionaire ; I call Heaven to witness that my first impulse was to go in search of my beloved beacon, to relieve, if possible, the unfortunate one to whom it gave light.

But then I thought so industrious a being was certainly proud, and I paused, fearing to offend a noble spirit.

One month later, a night in May, I saw extinguished one by one, the thousand lights of the neighboring houses. Two single lamps burned in the gloom; they were the two old friends. For some time I stood gazing at the bright ray shining through the foliage, and when I felt upon my brow the first chill of the morning breeze, I cried in my saddened heart,

"Farewell! farewell, little star, benign ray, beloved companion of my solitude! At this hour to-morrow, my eyes will seek but find thee not. And thou, whosoever thou art, working and suffering by that pale gleam, adieu, my sister! adieu, my brother! pursue thy destiny, watch and pray; may God shorten the time of thy probation."

I bade also to my little room, not an eternal farewell, for I have kept it since, and will keep it all my life. I do not wish that while I live strangers shall scare away such a covey of beautiful dreams as I left in that humble nest.

To see it again is one of the liveliest pleasures that my return to Paris offers. I shall find everything in the same order as when I left; but will the little star shine from the same corner of the heavens?

Thanks to Frederick's care my affairs were in order, and I set out immediately for Rome, because when one is expected from the end of the world one must at least return from somewhere.

Such is, dear Edgar, the history of my journeys and my love affairs. Keep them sacred. We are all so worthless, that, when one of us does some good by chance, he should remain silent for fear of humiliating his neighbor.

My health once established, I shall go to my mountains of Creuse and then come to you. Do not expect me until July; at that time Don Quixote will make his appearance under the apple trees of Richeport, provided, however, he is not caught up on this route by Lady Penock or some windmill.

RAYMOND DE VILLIERS.

V.

ROGER DE MONBERT *to* MONSIEUR DE MEILHAN,
Richeport,
Pont-de-l'Arche (Eure).

PARIS, 24th May, 18—.

YOUR letter did me good, my dear Edgar, because it came unexpected, from the domain of epistolary consolation. From any friend but you I would have received a sympathizing re-echo of my own accents of despair. From you I looked for a tranquillizing sedative, and you surprise me with a reanimating restorative.

Your charming philosophy has indeed invented for mortals a remedy unknown to the four faculties.

Thanks to you, I breathe freely this morning. 'Tis necessary for us to take breath during ardent crises of despair. A deep breath brings back the power of resignation to our hearts. Yet I am not duped by your too skilful friendship. I clearly perceive the interest you take in my situation in spite of your artistically labored adroitness to conceal it. This knowledge induces me to write you the second chapter of my history, quite sure that you will read it with a serious brow and answer it with a smiling pen.

Young people of your disposition, either from deep calculation or by happy instinct, substitute caprice for passion; they amuse themselves by walking by the side of love, but never meet it face to face. For them women exist, but never one woman. This system with them succeeds for a season, sometimes it lasts for ever. I have known some old men who made this scheme the glory of their lives, and who kept it up from mere force of habit till their heads were white.

You, my dear Edgar, will not have the benefit of final impenitence. At present the ardor of your soul is tempered by the suave indolence of your disposition.

Love is the most merciless and wearisome of all labors, and you are far too lazy to toil at it. When you suddenly look into the secret depths of your *self*, you will be frightened by discovering the germ of a serious passion; then you will try to escape on the wings of fancy to the realms of easy and careless pleasure. The fact of my having penetrated, unknown to you, this secret recess of your soul, makes me venture to confide my sorrows to you; continue to laugh at them, your railing will be understood, while friendship will ignore the borrowed mask and trust in the faithful face beneath.

Paris is still a desert. The largest and most populous city becomes obscure and insignificant at your feet when you view it from the heights of an all-absorbing passion. I feel as isolated as if I were on the South Sea or on the sands of Sahara. Happily our bodies assume mechanical habits that act instead of the will. Without this precious faculty of matter my isolation would lead me to a dreamy and stupid immobility. Thus, in the eyes of strangers, my life is always the same. They see no change in my manners and appearance; I keep up my acquaintances and pleasures and seek the society of my friends. I have not the heart to join a conversation, but leave it to be carried on by others. My fixed attention and absorbed manner of listening convey the idea that I am deeply interested in what is being said, and he who undertakes to relate anything to me is so satisfied with my style of listening that he prolongs to infinity his monologue. Then my thoughts take flight and travel around the world; to the seas, archipelagoes, continents and deserts I have visited. These are the only moments of relief that I enjoy, for I have the modesty to refrain from thinking of my love in the presence of others. I still possess enough innocence of heart to believe that the four letters of this sweetest of all words would be stamped on my brow in characters of fire, thus betraying a secret that indifference responds to with pitying smiles or heartless jeers.

The thousand memories sown here and there in my peregrinations pass so vividly before me, that, standing in the bright sunlight, with eyes open, I dream over again those visions of my sleepless nights in foreign lands.

Thought, ever-rebellious thought, which the most imperious will can neither check nor guide, begins to wander over the world, thus kindly granting a truce to the torments of my passions; then it works to suit my wishes, a complaisance it never shows me when I am alone. I am indebted for this relief to the officious and loquacious intervention of the first idler I meet, one whose name I scarcely know, although he calls me his friend. I always gaze with a feeling of compassionate benevolence upon the retreating steps of this unfortunate gossip, who leaves with the idea of having diverted me by his monologue to which my eyes alone have listened. As a general thing, people whom you meet have started out with one dominant idea or engrossing subject, and they imagine that the universe is disposed to attach the same importance to the matter that they themselves do. These expectations are often gratified, for the streets are filled by hungry listeners who wander around with ears outstretched, eager to share any and everybody's secrets.

A serious passion reveals to us a world within a world. Thus far, all that I have seen and heard seems to be full of error; men and things assume aspects under which I fail to recognise them. It seems as though I had yesterday been born a second time, and that my first life has left me nothing but confused recollections, and in this chaos of the past, I vainly seek for a single rule of conduct for the present. I have dipped into books written on the passions; I have read every sentence, aphorism, drama, tragedy and romance written by the sages; I have sought among the heroes of history and of the stage for the human expression of a sentiment to which my own experience might respond, and which would serve me as a guide or consolation.

I am, as it were, in a desert island where nothing betrays the passage of man, and I am compelled to dwell there without being able to trace the footsteps of those who have gone before. Yesterday I was present at the representation of the *Misanthrope.* I said to myself, here is a man in love; his character is drawn by a master hand, they say; he listens to sonnets, hums a little song, disputes with a bad author, discourses at length with his rivals, sustains a philosophical disputation with a friend, is churlish to the woman he loves, and finally is consoled by saying he will hide himself from the eyes of the world.

I would erect, at my own expense, a monument to Molière if Alceste would make my love take this form.

I have never seen an inventory of the torments of love—some of them have the most vulgar and some the most innocent names in the world. Some poet make his love-sick hero say:—

> "Un jour, Dieu, par pitié, délivra les enfers
> Des tourments que pour vous, madame, j'ai soufferts!"

I thought the poet intended to develop his idea, but unfortunately the tirade here ends. 'Tis always very vague, cloudy poetry that describes unknown torments; it seems to be a popular style, however, for all the poetry of the present day is confined to misty complaints in cloudy language. No moralist is specific in his sorrows. All lovers cry out in chorus that they suffer horribly. Each suffering deserves an analysis and a name. By way of example, my dear Edgar, I will describe one torment that I am sure you have never known or even heard of, happy mortal that you are!

The headquarters of this torment is at the office of the Poste-Restante, on Jean-Jacques-Rousseau street. The lovers in *la Nouvelle Héloïse* never mentioned this place of torture, although they wrote so many love-letters.

I have opened a correspondence with three of my servants—this torture, however, is not the one to which I allude. These three men, at this present moment, are sojourning in the three neighboring towns in which Mlle. de Châteaudun has acquaintances, relations or friends. One of these towns is Fontainebleau, where she first went when she left Paris. I have charged them to be very circumspect in obtaining all the information they can concerning her movements. Her mysterious retreat must be in one of these three localities, so I watch them all. I told them to direct all my letters to the Poste-Restante.

My porter, with the cunning sagacity of his profession, imagines he has discovered some scandalous romance, because he brings me every day a letter in the handwriting of my valet. You may imagine the complication of my torment. I am afraid of my porter, therefore I go myself to the post-office, that receptacle of all the secrets of Paris.

Usually the waiting-room is full of wretched men, each an epistolary Tantalus, who, with eyes fixed on the wooden grating, implore the clerk for a post-marked deception. 'Tis a sad spectacle, and I am sure that there is a post-office in purgatory, where tortured souls go to inquire if their deliverance has been signed in heaven.

The clerks in the post-office never seem to be aware of the impatient murmurs around them. What administrative calmness beams on the fresh faces of these distributors of consolation and of despair! In the agony of waiting, minutes lose their mathematical value, and the hands of the clock become motionless on the dial like impaled serpents. The operations of the office proceed with a slowness that seems like a miniature eternity. This anxious crowd stand in single file, forming a living chain of eager notes of interrogation, and, as fate always reserves the last link for me, I have to witness the filing-off of these troubled souls. This office brings men close together, and obliterates all social distinctions; in default of letters one always receives lessons of equality gratis.

Here you see handsome young men whose dishevelled locks and pale faces bear traces of sleepless nights—the Damocles of the Bourse, who feels the sword of bankruptcy hanging over his head—forsaken sweethearts, whose hopes wander with beating drums upon African shores—timid women veiled in black, weeping and mourning for the dead, so as to smile more effectively upon the living.

If each person were to call out the secret of his letter, the clerks themselves would veil their faces and forget the postal alphabet. A painful silence reigns over this scene of anxious waiting; at long intervals a hoarse voice calls out his Christian name, and woe to its owner if his ancestors have not bequeathed him a short or easily pronounced one.

The other day I was present at a strange scene caused by the association of seven syllables. An unhappy-looking wretch went up to the railing and gave out his name—*Sidoine Tarboriech*—these two words inflicted on us the following dialogue:—"Is it all one name?" asked the clerk, without deigning to glance at the unfortunate owner of these syllables. "Two names," said the man, timidly, as if he were fully aware of the disgrace inflicted upon him at the baptismal font. "Did you say *Antoine?*" said the clerk. "Sidoine, Monsieur." "Is it your Christian name?" "'Tis the name of my godfather, Saint Sidoine, 23 of August." "Ah! there is a Saint Sidoine, is there? Well, Sidoine . . . Sidoine—what else?" "Tarboriech." "Are you a German?" "From Toulon, opposite the Arsenal."

During this dialogue the rest of the unfortunates broke their chain with convulsive impatience, and made the floor tremble under the nervous stamping of their feet. The clerk calmly turned over with his methodically bent finger, a large bundle of letters, and would occasionally pause when the postal hieroglyphics effaced an address under a total eclipse of crests, seals and numbers recklessly heaped on; for the clerk who posts and endorses the letters takes great pains to cover the address with a cloud of ink, this little peculiarity all postmen delight in. But to return to our dialogue: "Excuse me, sir," said the clerk, "did you say your name is spelt with *Dar* or *Tar?*" "*Tar*, sir, *Tar!*"—"With a *D?*"—"No, sir, with a *T.*, *Tarboriech!*" "We have nothing for you, sir." "Oh, sir, impossible! there certainly *must* be a letter for me." "There is no letter, sir; nothing commencing with T." "Did you look for my Christian name, Sidoine?" "But, sir, we don't arrange the mail according to Christian names." "But you know, sir, I am a younger son, and at home I am called Sidoine."

This interesting dialogue was now drowned by the angry complaining of some young men, who in a state of exasperation stamped up and down the room jerking out an epigrammatic psalm of lamentations. I'll give you a few verses of it: "Heavens! some names ought to be suppressed! This is getting to be intolerable, when a man has the misfortune to be named *Extasboriech,* he ought *not* to have his letters sent to the *Poste*-Restante! If I were afflicted with such a name, I would have the Keeper of the Seals to change it."

The imperturbable clerk smiled blandly through his little barred window, and said, "Gentlemen, we must do our duty scrupulously, I only do for this gentleman what each of you would wish done for yourself under similar circumstances."

"Oh, of course!" cried out one young man, who was wildly buttoning and unbuttoning his coat as if he wanted to fight the subject through; "but we are not cursed with names so abominable as this man's!"

"Gentlemen," said the clerk, "no offensive personalities, I beg." Then turning to the miserable culprit, he continued: "Can you tell me, sir, from what place you expect a letter?" "From Lavalette, monsieur, in the province of Var." "Very good; and you think that perhaps your Christian name only is on the address—Sidoine?"

"My cousin always calls me Sidoine."

"His cousin is right," said a sulky voice in the corner.

This, my dear Edgar, is a sample of the non-classified tortures that I suffer every morning in this den of expiation, before I, the last one of all, can reach the clerk's sanctuary; once there I assume a careless air and gay tone of voice as I negligently call out my name. No doubt you think this a very simple, easy thing to do, but first listen a moment: I felt the "Star" gradually sinking under me near the Malouine Islands, the sixty-eighth degree of latitude kept me a prisoner in its sea of ice at the South Pole; I passed two consecutive days and nights on board the *Esmerelda,* between fire and inundation; and if I were to extract the quintessence of the agonies experienced upon these three occasions it could never equal the intense torture I suffer at the Poste-Restante. Three seals broken, three letters opened, three overwhelming disappointments! Nothing! nothing! nothing! Oh miserable synonym of despair! Oh cruel type of death! Why do you appear before me each day as if to warn my foolish heart that all hope is dead! Then how dreary and empty to me is this cold, unfeeling world we move in! I feel oppressed by the weight of my sorrowful yearning that hourly grows more unbearable and more hopeless; my lungs seem filled with leaden air, and all the blood in my heart stands still. In thinking of the time that must be dragged through till this same hour to-morrow, I feel neither the strength nor courage to endure it with its intolerable succession of eternal minutes. How can I bridge over this gulf of twenty-four hours that divides to-day from to-morrow? How false are all the ancient and modern allegories, invented to afflict man with the knowledge that his days are rapidly passing away! How foolish is that wisdom that mourns over our fugitive years as being nothing but a few short minutes! I would give all my fortune to be able to write the *Hora Fugit* of the poet, and offer for the first time to man these two words as an axiom of immutable truth.

There is nothing absolutely true in all the writings of the sages. Figures even, in their inexorable and systematic order, have their errors just as often as do words and apothems. An hour of pain and an hour of pleasure have no resemblance to each other save on the dial. *My* hours are weary years.

You understand then, my dear Edgar, that I write you these long letters, not to please you, but to relieve my own mind. In writing to you I divert my attention from painful contemplation, and expatriate my ideas. A pen is the only instrument capable of killing time when time wishes to kill us. A pen is the faithless auxiliary of thought; unknown to us it sometimes penetrates the secret recesses of our hearts, where we flattered ourselves the horizon of our sorrows was hid from the world.

Thus, if you discover in my letter any symptoms of mournful gayety, you may know they are purely pen-fancies. I have no connection with them except that my fingers guide the pen.

Sometimes I determine to abandon Paris and bury myself in some rural retreat, where lonely meditation may fill my sorrowing heart with the balm of oblivion; but in charity to myself I wish to avoid the absurdity of this self-deception. Nothing is more hurtful than trying a useless remedy, for it destroys your confidence in all other remedies, and fills your soul with despair. Then, again, Paris is peculiarly fitted for curing these nameless maladies—'tis the modern Thebais, deserted because 'tis crowded —silent because 'tis noisy; there, every man can pitch his tent and nurse his favorite sorrows without being disturbed by intruders. Solitude is the worst of companions when you wish to drown the past in Lethe's soothing stream. However, 'tis useless for me to reason in this apparently absurd way in order to compel myself to remain in the heart of this great city, for I cannot and must not quit Paris at present; 'tis the central point of my operations; here I can act with the greatest efficacy in the combinations of my searches—to leave Paris is to break the threads of my labyrinth. Besides, my duties as a man of the world impose cruel tortures upon me; if fate continues to work against me and I am compelled to retire from the world, the consolation of having escaped these social tortures will be mine; so you see, after all, there is a silver lining to my dark cloud. When we cannot attain good we can mitigate the evil.

Last Thursday Countess L. opened the season with an unusual event—a betrothment ball. Her select friends were invited to a sort of rehearsal of the wedding party; her beautiful cousin is to be married to our young friend Didier, whom we named Scipio Africanus. Marshal Bugeaud has given him a six-months' leave, and healed his wounded shoulder with a commander's epaulette.

Now, I know you will agree with me that my presence was necessary at this ball. I nerved myself for this new agony, and arrived there in the middle of a quadrille. Never did a comedian, stepping on the stage, study his manner and assume a gay look with more care than I did as I entered the room. I glided through the figures of the dance, and reached the further end of the ball-room which was filled with gossiping dowagers. Now I began to play my role of a happy man.

Everybody knows I am weak enough to enjoy a ball with all

the passion of a young girl, therefore I willingly joined the dancers. I selected a sinfully ugly woman, so as to direct my devotions to the antipodes of beauty—the more unlike Irene the better for me. My partner possessed that charming wit that generally accompanies ideal ugliness in a woman. We talked, laughed, danced with foolish gayety—each note of the music was accompanied by a witticism—we exchanged places and sallies at the same time—we invented a new style of conversation, very preferable to the dawdling gossip of a drawing-room. There is an exhilaration attending a conversation carried on with your feet flying and accompanied by delightful music; every eye gazed at us; every ear, in the whirl of the dance, almost touched our lips and caught what we said. Our gayety seemed contagious, and the whole room smiled approval. My partner was radiant with joy; the fast moving of her feet, the excitement of her mind, the exaltation of triumph, the halo of wit had transfigured this woman; she positively appeared handsome!

For one instant I forgot my despair in the happy thought that I had just done the noblest deed of my life; I had danced with a wall-flower, whose only crime was her ugliness, and had changed her misery into bliss by rendering her all the intoxicating ovations due only to beauty.

But alas! there was a fatal reaction awaiting me. Glancing across the room I intercepted the tender looks of two lovers, looks of mutual love that brought me back to my own misery, and made my heart bleed afresh at the thought that love like this might have been mine! What is more touchingly beautiful than the sight of a betrothed couple who exist in a little world of their own, and, ignoring the indifferent crowd around them, gaze at each other with such a wealth of love and trust in the future! I brought this image of a promised but lost happiness home with me. Oh! if I could blame Irene I would console myself by flying in a fit of legitimate anger! but this resource fails me—I can blame no one but myself. Irene knows not how dear she is to me, I only half told her of my love,—I flattered myself that I had a long future in which to prove my devotion by deeds instead of words. Had she known how deeply I loved her, she never could have deserted me.

Your unhappy friend,

ROGER DE MONBERT.

VI.

EDGAR DE MEILHAN *to the* PRINCE DE MONBERT,
St. Dominique Street (Paris).

Richeport, May 26th 18—.

DEAR ROGER:—You have understood me. I did not wish to annoy you with hackneyed condolences or sing with you an elegiac duet; but I have not the less sympathized with your sorrows; I have even evolved a system out of them. Were I forsaken, I should deplore the blindness of the unfortunate creature who could renounce the happiness of possessing me, and congratulate myself upon getting rid of a heart unworthy of me. Besides, I have always felt grateful to those benevolent beauties who take upon themselves the disagreeable task of breaking off an engagement. At first, there is a slight feeling of wounded self-love, but as I have for some time concluded that the world contains an infinity of beings endowed with charms superior to mine, it only lasts a moment, and if the scratch bleed a little, I consider myself indemnified by a tirade against woman's bad taste. Since you do not possess this philosophy, Mlle. de Chateaudun must be found, at any cost; you know my principles: I have a profound respect for any genuine passion. We will not discuss the merits or the faults of Irene; you desire her, that suffices; you shall have her, or I will lose the little Malay I learnt in Java when I went to see those dancing-girls, whose preference has such a disastrous effect upon Europeans. Your secret police is about to be increased by a new spy; I espouse your anger, and place myself entirely at the service of your wrath. I know some of the relatives of Mlle. de Chateaudun, who has connections in the neighboring departments, and in your behalf I have beaten about the chateaux for many miles around. I have not yet found what I am searching for; but I have discovered in the dullest houses a number of pretty faces who would ask nothing better, dear Roger, than to console you, that is if you are not, like Rachel, refusing to be comforted; for if there be no lack of women always ready to decoy a successful lover, some can, also, oe found disposed to undertake the cure of a profound despair; these are the services which the best friends cheerfully render. I will only permit myself to ask you one question. Are you sure, before abandoning yourself to the violence of an invisible grief, that Mlle. de Chateaudun has ever existed? If she exists, she cannot have evaporated! The diamond alone ascends entire to heaven and disappears, leaving no trace behind. One cannot abstract himself, in this way, like a quintessence from a civilized centre; in 18— the suppression of any human being seems to me impossible. Mademoiselle Irene has been too well brought up to throw herself into the water like a grisette; if she had done so, the zephyrs would have borne ashore her cloak or her umbrella; a woman's bonnet, when it comes from Beaudrand, always floats. Perhaps she wishes to subject you to some romantic ordeal to see if you are capable of dying of grief for her; do not gratify her so far. Double your serenity and coolness, and, if need be, paint like a dowager; it is necessary to sustain before these affected dames the dignity of the uglier sex of which we have the honor of forming a part. I approve the position you have taken. The Pale Faces should bear moral torture with the same impassiveness with which the Red Skins endure physical torture.

Roaming about in your interests, I had the beginning of an adventure which I must recount to you. It does not relate to a duchess, I warn you; I leave those sort of freaks to republicans. In love-making, I value beauty solely, it is the only aristocracy I look for; pretty women are baronesses, charming ones countesses; beauties become marchionesses, and I recognise a queen by her hands and not by her sceptre, by her brow and not by her crown. Such is my habit. Beyond this I am without prejudice; I do not disdain princesses provided they are as handsome as simple peasants.

I had a presentiment that Alfred intended paying me a visit, and with that wonderful acuteness which characterizes me, I said to myself: If he comes here, hospitality will force me to endure the agony of his presence as long as he pleases to impose it upon me, a torture forgotten in Dante's Hell; if I go to see him the situation is reversed. I can leave under the first indispensable pretext, that will not fail to offer itself, three days after my arrival, and I thus deprive him of all motive for invading my wigwam at Richeport. Whereupon I went to Nantes, where his relatives reside, with whom he is passing the summer.

At the expiration of four hours I suddenly remembered that most urgent business recalled me to my mother; but what was my anguish, when I saw my execrable friend accompany me to the railroad station, in a traveling suit, a cap on his head, a valise under his arm! Happily, he was going to Havre by way of Rouen, and I was relieved from all fear of invasion.

At this juncture, my dear friend, endeavor to tear yourself away, for a moment, from the contemplation of your grief, and take some interest in my story. To so distinguished a person as yourself it has at least the advantage of beginning in an entirely homely and prosaic manner. I should never have committed the error of writing you anything extraordinary; you are surfeited with the incredible; the supernatural is a twice-told tale; between you and the marvellous secret affinities exist; miracles hunt you up; you find yourself in conjunction with phenomena; what never happens has happened to you; and in the world that you, in every sense, have wandered o'er, no novelty offers itself but the commonplace.

The first time you ever attempted to do anything like other people—to marry—you failed. Your only talent is for the impossible; therefore, I hope that my recital, a little after the style of Paul de Kock's romances, an author admired by great ladies and kitchen girls, will give you infinite surprise and possess all the attraction and freshness of the unknown.

There were already two persons in the compartment into which the conductor hurried us; two women, one old and the other young.

To prevent Alfred from playing the agreeable, I took possession of the corner fronting the youngest, leaving to my tiresome friend the freezing perspective of the older woman.

You know I have no fancy for sustaining what is called the honor of French gallantry—a gallantry which consists in wearying with ill-timed attention, with remarks upon the rain and the fine weather, interlarded with a thousand and one stupid rhymes, the women forced by circumstances to travel alone.

I settled myself in my corner after making a slight bow on perceiving the presence of women in the car, one of whom evidently merited the attention of every young commercial traveler and troubadour. I set myself to examine my vis-a-vis, dividing my attention between picturesque studies and studies physiognomical.

The result of my picturesque observations was that I never saw so many poppies before. Probably they were the red sparks from the locomotive taking root and blooming along the road.

My physiognomical studies were more extended, and, without flattering myself, I believe Lavater himself would have approved them.

The cowl does not make the friar, but dress makes the woman. I shall begin by giving you an extremely detailed description of the toilet of my incognita. This is an accustomed method, which proves that it is a good one, since everybody makes use of it. My fair unknown wore neither a bark blanket fastened about her waist, nor rings in her nose, nor bracelets on her ankles, nor rings on her toes, which must appear extraordinary to you.

She wore, perhaps, the only costume that your collection lacks, that of a Parisian grisette. You, who know by heart the name of every article of a Hottentot's attire, who are strong upon Esquimaux fashions and know just how many rows of pins a Patagonian of the haut ton wears in her lower lip, have never thought of sketching such an one.

A well-approved description of a grisette should commence with her foot. The grisette is the Andalouse of Paris; she possesses the talent of being able to pass through the mire of

Lutetia on tiptoe, like a dancer who studies her steps, without soiling her white stockings with a single speck of mud. The manolas of Madrid, the cigaretas of Seville in their satin slippers are not better shod; mine—pardon the anticipation of this possessive pronoun—put forward from under the seat an irreproachable boot and aristocratically turned ankle. If she would give me that graceful buskin to place in my museum beside the shoe of Carlotta Grisi, the Princess Houn-Gin's boot and Gracia of Grenada's slipper, I would fill it with gold or sugar-plums, as she pleased.

As to her dress, I acknowledge, without any feeling of mortification, that it was of mousseline; but the secret of its making was preserved by the modiste. It was tight and easy at the same time, a perfect fit attained by Palmyre in her moments of inspiration; a black silk mantilla, a little straw bonnet trimmed plainly with ribbon, and a green gauze veil, half thrown back, completed the adornment, or rather absence of ornament, of this graceful creature.

Heavens! I had like to have forgotten the gloves! Gloves are the weak point of a grisette's costume. To be fresh, they must be renewed often, but they cost the price of two days' work. Hers were, O horror! imitation Swedish, which truth compels me to value at nineteen ha'-pennies, or ninety-five centimes, to conform to the new monetary phraseology.

A worsted work-bag, half filled, was placed beside her. What could it hold? Some circulating library novel? Do not be uneasy, the bag only contained a roll and a paper of bonbons from Boissier, dainties which play an important part in my story.

Now I must draw you an exact sketch of this pretty Parisian's face—for such she was. A Parisian alone could wear, with such grace, a fifteen-franc bonnet.

I abhor bonnets; nevertheless, on some occasions, I am forced to acknowledge that they produce quite a pleasing effect. They represent a kind of queer flower, whose core is formed of a woman's head; a full-blown rose, which, in the place of stamens and pistils, bears glances and smiles.

The half-raised veil of my fair unknown only exposed to view a chin of perfect mould, a little strawberry mouth and half of her nose, perhaps three-quarters. What pretty, delicately turned nostrils, pink as the shells of the South Sea! The upper part of the face was bathed in a transparent, silvery shadow, under which the quiver of the eyelids might be imagined and the liquid fire of her glance. As to her cheeks—you must await the succession of events if you desire more ample description; for the ears of her bonnet, drawn down by the strings, concealed their contour; what could be seen of them was of a delicate rose color. Her eyes and hair will form a special paragraph.

Now that you are sufficiently enlightened upon the subject of the perspective which your friend enjoyed on the cars between Mantes and Pont-de-l'Arche, I will pass to another exercise, highly recommended in rhetorical treatises, and describe, by way of a set-off and contrast, the female monster that served as shadow to this ideal grisette.

This frightful companion appeared very suspicious. Was she the duenna, the mother or an old relative? At any rate she was very ugly, not because her head was like a stone mask with spiral eyebrows, and lips slashed like the fossa of a heraldic dolphin, but vulgarity had stamped the mask, making its features common, coarse and dull. The habit of servile compliance had deprived them of all true expression; she squinted, her smile was vaguely stupid, and she wore an air of spurious good-nature, indicative of country birth; a dark merino dress, cloak of sombre hue, a bonnet under which stood out the many ruffles of a rumpled cap, completed the attire of the creature.

The grisette is a gay, chattering bird, which at fifteen escapes from the nest never to return; it is not her custom to drag about a mother after her, this is the special mania of actresses who resort to all sorts of tricks ignored by the proud and independent grisette. The grisette seems instinctively to know that the presence of an old woman about a young one exerts an unhealthy influence. It suggests sorcery and the witches' vigil;

snails seek roses only to spread their slime over them, and old age only approaches youth from a discreditable motive.

This woman was not the mother of my incognita; so sweet a flower could not grow upon such a rugged bush. I heard the antique say in the humblest tone, "Mlle., if you wish, I will put down the blind; the cinders might hurt you."

Doubtless she was some relative; for a grisette never has a companion, and duennas pertain exclusively to Spanish infantas.

Was my grisette simply an adventuress, graced by a hired mother to give her an air of respectability? No, there was the seal of simple honesty stamped upon her whole person; a care in the details of her simple toilet, which separated her from that venturous class. A wandering princess would not show such exactitude in her dress; she would betray herself by a ragged shawl worn over a new dress, by silk stockings with boots down at heel, by something ripped and out of order. Besides, the old woman did not take snuff nor smell of brandy.

I made these observations in less time than it takes to write them, through Alfred's inexhaustible chatter, who imagines, like many people, that you are vexed if the conversation flags an instant. Besides, between you and me, I think he wished to impress these women with an idea of his importance, for he talked to me of the whole world. I do not know how it happened, but this whirlwind of words seemed to interest my incognita, who had all along remained quietly ensconced in her corner. The few words uttered by her were not at all remarkable; an observation upon a mass of great black clouds piled up in a corner of the horizon that threatened a shower; but I was charmed with the fresh and silvery tone of her voice. The music of the words—it is going to rain—penetrated my soul like an air from Bellini, and I felt something stir in my heart, which, well cultivated, might turn into love.

The locomotive soon devoured the distance between Mantes and Pont de l'Arche. An abominable scraping of iron and twisting of brakes was heard, and the train stopped. I was terribly alarmed lest the grisette and her companion should continue their route, but they got out at the station. O Roger, wasn't I a happy dog? While they were employed in hunting up some parcel, the vehicle which runs between the station and Pont de l'Arche left, weighed down with trunks and travellers; so that the two women and myself were compelled, in spite of the weather, to walk to Pont de l'Arche. Large drops began to sprinkle the dust. One of those big black clouds which I mentioned opened, and long streams of rain fell from its gloomy folds like arrows from an overturned quiver.]

A moss-covered shed, used to put away farming implements, odd cart-wheels, performed for us the same service as the classic grotto which sheltered Eneas and Dido under similar circumstances. The wild branches of the hawthorn and sweet-briar added to the rusticity of our asylum.

My unknown, although visibly annoyed by this delay, resigned herself to her fate, and watched the rain falling in torrents. O Robinson Crusoe, how I envied you, at that moment, your famous goat-skin umbrella! how gracefully would I have offered its shelter to this beauty as far as Pont de l'Arche, for she was going to Pont de l'Arche, right into the lion's mouth. Time passed. The vehicle would not return until the next train was due, that is in five or six hours; I had not told them to come for me; our situation was most melancholy.

My infanta opened daintily her little bag, took from it a roll and some bonbons, which she began to eat in the most graceful manner imaginable, but having breakfasted before leaving Mantes, I was dying of hunger; I suppose I must have looked covetously at her provisions, for she began to laugh and offered me half of her pittance, which I accepted. In the division, I don't know how it happened, but my hand touched hers—she drew it quickly away, and bestowed upon me a look of such royal disdain that I said to myself—This young girl is destined for the dramatic profession,—she plays the Marguerites and the Clytemnestras in the provinces until she possesses *embonpoint* enough to appear at Porte Saint Martin or the Odeon. This vampire is her dresser—everything was clear.

I promised you a paragraph upon her eyes and hair; her eyes were a changeable gray, sometimes blue, sometimes green, according to the expression and the light; her chestnut locks were separated in two glossy braids, half satin, half velvet—many a great lady would have paid high for such hair.

The shower over, a wild resolution was unanimously taken to set out on foot for Pont de l'Arche, notwithstanding the mud and the puddles.

Having entered into the good graces of the infanta by speech full of wisdom and gesture carefully guarded, we set out together, the old woman following a few steps behind, and the marvellous little boot arrived at its destination without being soiled the least in the world--grisettes are perfect partridges—the house of Madame Taverneau, the post-mistress, where my incognita stopped.

You are a prince of very little penetration, dear Roger, if you have not divined that you will receive a letter from me every day, and even two, if I have to send empty envelopes or recopy the Complete Letter Writer. To whom will I not write? No minister of state will ever have so extended a correspondence.

EDGAR DE MEILHAN.

VII.

IRENE DE CHATEAUDUN *to* MME. LA VICOMTESSE DE BRAIMES,
Hotel of the Prefecture, Grenoble (Isère).

PONT DE L'ARCHE, May 29th 18—.

VALENTINE, this time I rebel, and question your infallibility.

It is useless for you to say to me, " You do not love him." I tell you I do love him, and intend to marry him. Nevertheless you excite my admiration in pronouncing against me this very well-turned sentence. " Genuine and fervid love is not so ingenuous. When you love deeply, you respect the object of your devotion and are fearful of giving offence by daring to test him.

" When you love sincerely you are not so venturesome. It is so necessary for you to trust him, that you treasure up your faith and risk it not in suspicious trifling.

" Real love is timid, it would rather err than suspect, it buries doubts instead of nursing them, and very wisely, for love cannot survive faith."

This is a magnificent period, and you should send it to Balzac; he delights in filling his novels with such very woman-like phrases.

I admit that your ideas are just and true when applied to love alone; but if this love is to end in marriage, the " test" is no longer " suspicious trifling," and one has the right to try the constancy of a character without offending the dignity of love.

Marriage, and especially a marriage of inclination, is so serious a matter, that we cannot exercise too much prudence and reasonable delay before taking the final step.

You say, " Love is timid;" well, so is Hymen. One dares not lightly utter the irrevocable promise, "Thine for life!" these words make us hesitate.

When we wish to be honorable and faithfully keep our oaths, we pause a little before we utter them.

Now I can hear you exclaim, " You are not in love; if you

were, instead of being frightened by these words, they would reassure you; you would be quick to say 'Thine for life,' and you could never imagine that there existed any other man you could love."

I am aware that this gives you weapons to be used against me; I know I am foolish! but—well, I feel that there is some one somewhere that I could love more deeply!

This silly idea sometimes makes me pause and question, but it grows fainter daily, and I now confess that it is folly, childish to cherish such a fancy. In spite of your opinion, I persist in believing that I am in love with Roger. And when you know him, you will understand how natural it is for me to love him.

I would at this very moment be talking to him in Paris but for you! Don't be astonished, for your advice prevented my returning to Paris yesterday.

Alas! I asked you for aid, and you add to my anxiety.

I left the hotel de Langeac with a joyful heart. The test will be favorable, thought I,—and when I have seen Roger in the depths of despair for a few days, seeking me everywhere, impatiently expecting me, blaming me a little and regretting me deeply, I will suddenly appear before him, happy and smiling! I will say, "Roger, you love me; I left you to think of you from afar, to question my own heart—to try the strength of your devotion; I now return without fear and with renewed confidence in myself and in you; never again shall we be separated!"

I intend to frankly confess everything to him; but you say the confession will be fatal to me. "If you intend to marry M. de Monbert, for Heaven's sake keep him in ignorance of the motive of your departure; invent an excuse—be called off to perform a duty—to nurse a sick friend; choose any story you please, rather than let him suspect you ran away to experiment upon the degree of his love."

You add, "he loves you devotedly and never will he forgive you for inflicting on him these unnecessary sufferings; a proud and deserving love never pardons suspicious and undeserved trials of its faith."

Now what can I do? Invent a falsehood? All falsehoods are stupid! Then I would have to write it, for I could not undertake to lie to his face. With strangers and people indifferent to me, I might manage it; but to look into the face of the man who loves me, who gazes so honestly into my eyes when I speak to him, who understands every expression of my countenance, who observes and admires the blush that flushes my cheek, who is familiar with every modulation of my voice, as a musician with the tones of his instrument——

Why, it is a moral impossibility to attempt such a thing! A forced smile, a false tone, would put him on his guard at once; he becomes suspicious.

At his first question my fine castle of lies vanishes into air, and I have to fall back on the unvarnished truth.

To gratify you, Valentine, I will lie, but lie at a distance. I feel that it is necessary to put many stations and provinces between my native candor and the people I am to deceive.

Why do you scold me so much? You must see that I have not acted thoughtlessly; my conduct is strange, eccentric and mysterious to no one but Roger.

To every one else it is perfectly proper. I am supposed to be in the neighborhood of Fontainebleau, with the Duchess de Langeac, at her daughter's house; and as the poor girl is very sick and receives no company, I can disappear for a short time without my absence calling forth remark, or raising an excitement in the country.

I have told my cousin a part of the truth—she understands my scruples and doubts. She thinks it very natural that I should wish to consider the matter over before engaging myself for life; she knows that I am staying with an old friend, and as I have promised to return home in two weeks, she is not a bit uneasy about me.

"My child," she said when we parted, "if you decide to marry, I will go with you to Paris; if not, you shall go with us to enjoy the waters of Aix." I have discovered that Aix is a good place to learn news of our friends in Isère.

You also reproach me for not having told Roger all my troubles; for having hidden from him what you flatteringly call "the most beautiful pages of my life."

O, Valentine! in this matter I am wiser than you, in spite of your matronly experience and acknowledged wisdom. Doubtless you understand better than I do, the serious affairs of life, but about the frivolities, I think I know best, and I tell you that courage in a woman is not an attraction in the eyes of these latter-day beaux.

Their weak minds, with an affected nicety, prefer a sighing, supplicating coquette, decked in pretty ribbons, surrounded by luxuries that are the price of her dignity; one who pours her sorrows into the lover's ear—yes! I say they prefer such a one to a noble woman who bravely faces misery with proud resignation, who refuses the favors of those she despises, and calm, strong, self-reliant, waters with her tears her hard-earned bread.

Believe me, men are more inclined to love women they can pity than women they must admire and respect; feminine courage in adversity is to them a disagreeable picture in an ugly frame; that is to say, a poorly dressed woman in a poorly furnished room. So you now see why, not wishing to disgust my future husband, I was careful that he should not see this ugly picture.

Ah! you speak to me of my dear ideal, and you say you love him? Ah! to him alone could I fearlessly read these beautiful pages of my life. But let us banish him from our minds; I would forget him!

Once I was very near betraying myself; my cousin and I called on a Russian lady residing in furnished apartments on Rivoli street.

M. de Monbert was there—as I took a seat near the fire, the Countess R. handed me a screen—I at once recognised a painting of my own. It represented Paul and Virginia gardening with Domingo.

How horrible did all three look! Time and dust had curiously altered the faces of my characters; by an inexplicable pheuomenon Virginia and Domingo had changed complexions; Virginia was a negress, and Domingo was enfranchised, bleached, he had cast aside the tint of slavery and was a pure Caucasian. The absurdity of the picture made me laugh, and M. de Monbert inquired the cause of my merriment. I showed him the screen, and he said "How very horrible!" and I was about to add "I painted it," when some one interrupted us, and so prevented the betrayal of my secret.

You will not have to scold me any more; I am going to take your advice and leave Pont de l'Arche to-day. Oh! how I wish I were in Paris this minute! I am dreadfully tired of this little place, it is so wearying to play poverty.

When I was really poor, the modest life I had to lead, the cruel privations I had to suffer, seemed to me to be noble and dignified.

Misery has its grandeur, and every sorrow has its poetry; but when the humility of life is voluntary and privations mere caprices, misery loses all its prestige, and the romantic sufferings we needlessly impose on ourselves, are intolerable, because there is no courage or merit in enduring them.

This sentiment I feel must be natural, for my old companion in misfortune, my good and faithful Blanchard, holds the same views that I do. You know how devoted she was to me during my long weary days of trouble!

She faithfully served me three years with no reward other than the approval of her own conscience. She, who was so proud of keeping my mother's house, resembling a stewardess of the olden time; when misfortune came, converted herself for my sake into maid of all work! Inspired by love for me, she patiently endured the hardships and dreariness of our sad situation; not a complaint, not a murmur, not a reproach. To see her so quietly resigned, you would have supposed that she had been both chamber-maid and cook all her life, that is if you never tasted her dishes! I shall always remember her first dinner. O, the Spartan broth of that day! She must have gotten the receipt from "The Good Lacedemonian Cook Book."

I confidently swallowed all she put before me. Strange and mysterious ragout! I dared not ask what was in it, but I vainly sought for the relics of any animal I had ever seen; what did she make it of? It is a secret that I fear I shall die without discovering.

Well, this woman, so devoted, so resigned in the days of adversity; this feminine Caleb, whose generous care assuaged my misery; who, when I suffered, deemed it her duty to suffer with me; when I worked day and night, considered it an honor to labor day and night with me—now that she knows we are restored to our fortune, cannot endure the least privation.

All day long she complains. Every order is received with imprecatory mutterings, such as "What an idiotic idea! What folly! to be as rich as Crœsus and find amusement in poverty! To come and live in a little hole with common people and refuse to visit duchesses in their castles! People must not be surprised if I don't obey orders that I don't understand."

She is stubborn and refractory. She will drive me to despair, so determined does she seem to thwart all my plans. I tell her to call me Madame; she persists in calling me Mademoiselle. I told her to bring simple dresses and country shoes; she has brought nothing but embroidered muslins, cobweb handkerchiefs and gray silk boots. I entreated her to put on a simple dress, when she came with me. This made her desperate, and through vengeance and maliciously exaggerated zeal she bundled herself up like an old witch. I tried to make her comprehend that her frightfulness far exceeded my wildest wishes; she thereupon disarmed me with this sublime reply:

"I had nothing but new hats and new shawls, and so had to *borrow* these clothes to obey Mademoiselle's orders."

Would you believe it? The proud old woman has destroyed or hidden all the old clothes that were witnesses of our past misery. I am more humble, and have kept everything. When I returned to my little garret, I was delighted to see again my modest furniture, my pretty pink chintz curtains, my thin blue carpet, my little ebony shelves, and then all the precious objects I had saved from the wreck; my father's old easy-chair, my mother's work-table, and all of our family portraits, concealed, like proud intruders, in one corner of the room, where haughty marshals, worthy prelates, coquettish marquises, venerable abbesses, sprightly pages and gloomy cavaliers all jostled together, and much astonished to find themselves in such a wretched little room, and what is worse, shamefully disowned by their unworthy descendant. I love my garret, and remained there three days before coming here; and there I left my fine princess dresses and put on my modest travelling suit; there the elegant Irene once more became the interesting widow of the imaginary Albert Guerin. We started at nine in the morning. I had the greatest difficulty in getting ready for the early train, so soon have I forgotten my old habit of early rising. When I look back and recall how for three years I arose at dawn, it looks like a wretched dream. I suppose it is because I have become so lazy.

It is distressing to think that only six months have passed since I was raised from the depths of poverty, and here I am already spoiled by good fortune!

Misfortune is a great master, but like all masters he only is obeyed when present; we work with him, but when his back is turned forget his admonitions.

We reached the depot as the train was starting, obtaining comfortable seats. I met with a most interesting adventure, that is, interesting to me; how small the world is! I had for a companion an old friend of Roger, but who fortunately did not know me; it was M. Edgar de Meilhan, the poet, whose talents I admire, and whose acquaintance I had long desired; judging from his conversation he must be quite an original character. But he was accompanied by one of those explanatory gossips who seem born to serve as cicerones to the entire world, and render useless all penetrating perspicacity.

These sort of bores are amusing to meet on a journey; rather well informed, they quote their favorite authors very neatly in order to display the extent of their information; they also have a happy way of imposing on the ignorant people, who sit around with wide-stretched mouths, listening to the string of celebrated names so familiarly repeated as to indicate a personal intimacy with each and all of them; in a word, it is a way of making the most of your acquaintance, as your witty friend M. L. would say. Now I must give you a portrait of this gentleman; it shall be briefly done.

He was an angular man, with a square forehead, a square nose, a square mouth, a square chin, a square smile, a square hand, square shoulders, square gayety, square jokes; that is to say, he is coarse, heavy and rugged. A coarse mind cultivated often appears smooth and moves easily in conversation, but a square mind is always awkward and threatening. Well, this square man evidently "made the most of his acquaintances" for my benefit, for poor little me, an humble violet met by chance on the road! He spoke of M. Guizot having mentioned this to him; of M. Thiers, who dined with him lately, having said that to him; of Prince Max de Beauvau, whom he bet with at the last Versailles races; of the beautiful Madame de Magnoncourt, with whom he danced at the English ambassador's ball; of twenty other distinguished personages with whom he was intimate, and finally he mentioned Prince Roger de Monbert, the eccentric tiger-hunter, who for the last two months had been the lion of Paris. At the name of Roger I became all attention; the square man continued:

"But you, my dear Edgar, were brought up with him, were you not?"

"Yes," said the poet.

"Have you seen him since his return?"

"Not yet, but I hear from him constantly; I had a letter yesterday."

"They say he is engaged to the beautiful heiress, Irene de Chateaudun, and will be married very soon."

"'Tis an idle rumor," said M. de Meilhan, in a dry tone that forced his dreadful friend to select another topic of conversation.

Oh, how curious I was to find out what Roger had written to

M. de Meilhan! Roger had a confidant! He had told him about me! What could he have said? Oh, this dreadful letter! What would I not give to see it! My sole thought is, how can I obtain it; unconsciously I gazed at M. de Meilhan, with an uneasy perplexity that must have astonished him and given him a queer idea of my character.

I was unable to conceal my joy, when I heard him say he lived at Richeport, and that he intended stopping at Pont de l'Arche, which is but a short distance from his estate; my satisfaction must have appeared very strange.

A dreadful storm detained us two hours in the neighborhood of the depot. We remained in company under the shed, and watched the falling rain. My situation was embarrassing; I wished to be agreeable and polite to M. de Meilhan that I might encourage him to call at Madame Taverneau's, Pont de l'Arche, and then again I did not wish to be so very gracious and attentive as to inspire him with too much assurance. It was a difficult game to play. I must boldly risk making a bad impression, and at the same time keep him at a respectful distance. Well, I succeeded in solving the problem within the pale of legitimate curiosity, offering to share with my companion in misfortune a box of bon-bons, intended for Madame Taverneau.

But what attentions he showered on me before meriting this great sacrifice! What ingenious umbrellas he improvised for me under this inhospitable shed, that grudgingly lent us a perfidious and capricious shelter! What charming seats, skilfully made of sticks and logs driven into the wet ground!

When the storm was over M. de Meilhan offered to escort us to Pont de l'Arche; I accepted, much to the astonishment of the severe Blanchard, who cannot understand the sudden change in my conduct, and begins to suspect me of being in search of adventures.

When we reached our destination, and Madam Taverneau heard that M. de Meilhan had been my escort, she was in such a state of excitement that she could talk of nothing else.

M. de Meilhan is highly thought of here, where his family have resided many years; his mother is venerated, and he himself beloved by all that know him. He has a moderate fortune; with it he quietly dispenses charity and daily confers benefits with an unknown hand. He seems to be very agreeable and witty. I have never met so brilliant a man, except M. de Monbert. How charming it would be to hear them talk together!

But that letter! What would I not give for that letter! If I could only read the first four lines! I would find out what I want to know. These first lines would tell me if Roger is really sad; if he is to be pitied, and if it is time for me to console him. I rely a little upon the indiscretion of M. de Meilhan to enlighten me. Poets are like doctors; all artists are kindred spirits; they cannot refrain from telling a romantic love affair any more than a physician can from citing his last remarkable case; the former never name their friends, the latter never betray their patients. But when we know beforehand, as I do, the name of the hero or patient, we soon complete the semi-indiscretion.

So I mercilessly slander all heiresses and capricious women of fashion that I may incite Roger's confidant to relate me my own history. I forgot to mention that since my arrival here M. de Meilhan has been every day to call on Madame Taverneau. She evidently imagines herself the object of his visits. I am of a different opinion. Indeed, I fear I have made a conquest of this dark-eyed young poet, which is not at all flattering to me. This sudden adoration shows that he has not a very elevated opinion of me. How he will laugh when he recognises this adventurous widow in the proud wife of his friend!

You reproach me bitterly for having sacrificed you to Madame Taverneau. Cruel Prefect that you are, go and accuse the government and your consul-general of this unjust preference.

Can I reach Grenoble in three hours, as I do Rouen? Can I return from Grenoble to Paris in three hours; fly when I wish, reappear when 'tis necessary? In a word have you a railway? No! Well, then, trust to my experience and believe that where locomotion is concerned there is an end to friendship, gratitude, sympathy and devotion. Nothing is to be considered but railways, roads, wagons that jolt you to death, but carry you to your destination, and stages that upset and never arrive.

We cannot visit the friends we love best, but those we can get away from with the greatest facility.

Besides, for a heroine wishing to hide herself, the asylum you offer has nothing mysterious, it is merely a Thebais of a prefecture; and there I am afraid of compromising you.

A Parisian in a provincial town is always standing on a volcano, one unlucky word may cause destruction.

How difficult it is to be a Prefect! You have commenced very properly—four children! All that is necessary to begin with. They are such convenient excuses. To be a good Prefect one must have four children. They are inexhaustible pretexts for escaping social horrors; if you wish to decline a compromising invitation, your dear little girl has got the whooping cough; when you wish to avoid dining a friend *in transitu*, your eldest son has a dreadful fever; you desire to escape a banquet unadorned by the presence of the big-wigs—brilliant idea! all four children have the measles.

Now confess you did well to have the four lovely children! Without them you would be conquered in spite of your wisdom; it requires so much skill for a Parisian to live officially in a province!

There all the women are clever; the most insignificant citizen's wife can outwit an old diplomat. What science they display under the most trying and peculiar circumstances! What profound combination in their plans of vengeance! What prudence in their malice! What patience in their cruelty! It is dreadful! I will visit you when you reside in the country, but while you reign over a prefecture, I have for you the respectful horror that a democratic mind has for all authorities.

Who is this poor convalescent whose wound caused you so much anxiety? You don't tell me his name! I understand you, Madame! Even to an old friend you must show your administrative discretion!

Is this wounded hero young? I suppose he is, as you do not say he is old. He is "about to leave, and return to his home;" "his home" is rather vague, as you don't tell me his name! Now, I am different from you; I name and fully describe every one I meet, you respond with enigmas.

I well know that your destiny is fulfilled, and that mine has all the attractiveness of a new romance. Nevertheless, you must be more communicative if you expect to be continued in office as my confidant.

Embrace for me your dear little ones, whom I insist upon regarding as your best counsellors at the prefecture, and tell my goddaughter, Irene, to kiss you for me.

IRENE DE CHATEAUDUN.

VIII.

EDGAR DE MEILHAN *to the* PRINCE DE MONBERT,
Saint Dominique street, Paris.

RICHEPORT, May 31st, 18—.

Now that you are a sort of Amadis de Gaul, striking attitudes upon a barren rock, as a sign of your lovelorn condition, you have probably forgotten, my dear Roger, my encounter upon the cars with an ideal grisette, who saved me from the horrors of starvation by generously dividing with me a bag of sugar-plums. But for this unlooked-for aid, I should have been reduced, like a famous handful of shipwrecked mariners, to feed upon my watch-chain and vest-buttons. To a man so absorbed in his grief, as you are, the news of the death from starvation of a friend upon the desert island of a railway station, would make very little impression; but I not being in love with any Irene de Chateaudun, have preserved a pleasant recollection of this touching scene, translated from the Æneid in modern and familiar prose.

I wrote immediately,—for my beauty, of an infinitely less exalted rank than yours, lodges with the post-mistress,—several fabulous letters to problematic people, in countries which do not exist, and are only designated upon the map by a dash.

Madame Taverneau has conceived a profound respect for a young man who has correspondents in unknown lands, barely sighted in 1821 at the Antarctic pole, and in 1819 at the Arctic pole, so she invited me to a little soirée musicale et dansante, of which I was to be the bright particular star. An invitation to an exclusive ball, given at an inaccessible house, never gave a woman with a doubtful past or an uncertain position, half the pleasure that I felt from the entangled sentences of Madame Taverneau in which she did not dare to hope, but would be happy if———.

Apart from the happiness of seeing Madame Louise Guérin (my charmer's name), I looked forward to an entirely new recreation, that of studying the manners of the middle class in their intimate relations with each other. I have lived with the aristocracy and with the canaille; in the highest and lowest conditions of life are found entire absence of pretension; in the highest, because their position is assured; in the lowest, because it is simply impossible to alter it. None but poets are really unhappy because they cannot climb to the stars. A half-way position is the most false.

I thought I would go early to have some talk with Louise, but the circle was already completed when I arrived; everybody had come first.

The guests were assembled in a large, gloomy room, gloriously called a drawing-room, where the servant never enters without first taking off her shoes at the door, like a Turk in a mosque, and which is only opened on the most solemn occasions. As it is doubtful whether you have ever set foot in a like establishment, I will give you, in imitation of the most profound of our novel-writers (which one? you will say; they are all profound now-a-days), a detailed description of Madame Taverneau's salon.

Two windows, hung in red calico, held up by some black ornaments, a complication of sticks, pegs and all sorts of implements on stamped copper, gave light to this sanctuary, which commanded through them an animated look-out—in the language of the commonalty—upon the scorching, noisy highway, bordered by sickly elms sprinkled with dust, from the constant passage of vehicles which shake the house to its centre; wagons loaded with noisy iron, and droves of hogs, squeaking under the drover's whip.

The floor was painted red and polished painfully bright, reminding one of a wine-merchant's sign freshly varnished; the walls were concealed under frightful velvet paper which so religiously catches the fluff and dust. The mahogany furniture stood round the room, a reproach against the discovery of America, covered with sanguinary cloth stamped in black with subjects taken from Fontaine's fables. When I say subjects I basely flatter the sumptuous taste of Madame Taverneau; it was the same subject indefinitely repeated—the Fox and the Stork. How luxurious it was to sit upon a stork's beak! In front of each chair was spread a piece of carpet, to protect the splendor of the floor, so that the guests when seated bore a vague resemblance to the bottles and decanters set round the plated centre-piece of a banquet given to a deputy by his grateful constituents.

An atrocious troubadour clock ornamented the mantel-piece representing the templar Bois-Guilbert bearing off a gilded Rebecca upon a silver horse. On either side of this frightful time-piece were placed two plated lamps under globes.

This magnificence filled with secret envy more than one housekeeper of Pont de l'Arche, and even the maid trembled as she dusted. We will not speak of the spun-glass poodles, little sugar St. Johns, chocolate Napoleons, a cabinet filled with common china, occupying a conspicuous place, engravings representing the Adieux to Fontainebleau, Souvenirs and Regrets, The Fisherman's Family, The Little Poachers, and other hackneyed subjects. Can you imagine anything like it? For my part, I never could understand this love for the common-place and the hideous. I know that every one does not dwell in Alhambras, Louvres, or Parthenons, but it is so easy to do without a clock! to leave the walls bare, to exist without Manrin's lithographs or Jazet's aquatints!

The people filling the room, seemed to me, in point of vulgarity, the queerest in the world; their manner of speaking was marvellous, imitating the florid style of the defunct Prudhomme, the pupil of Brard and St. Omer. Their heads spread out over their white cravats and immense shirt collars recalled to mind certain specimens of the gourd tribe. Some even resemble animals, the lion, the horse, the ass; these, all things considered, had a vegetable rather than an animal look. Of the women I will say nothing, having resolved never to ridicule that charming sex.

Among these human vegetables, Louise appeared like a rose

in a cabbage patch. She wore a simple white dress fastened at the waist by a blue ribbon; her hair arranged in bandeaux encircled her pure brow and wound in massive coils about her head. A Quakeress could have found no fault with this costume, which placed in grotesque and ridiculous contrast the hearselike trappings of the other women. It was impossible to be dressed in better taste. I was afraid lest my Infanta should seize this opportunity to display some marvellous toilette purchased expressly for the occasion. That plain muslin gown which never saw India, and was probably made by herself, touched and fascinated me. Dress has very little weight with me. I once admired a Granada gypsy whose sole costume consisted of blue slippers and a necklace of amber beads; but nothing annoys me more than a badly made dress of an unbecoming shade.

The provincial dandies much preferring the rubicund gossips, with their short necks covered with gold chains, to Madame Taverneau's young and slender guest, I was free to talk with her under cover of Louisa Pugett's ballads and sonatas executed by infant phenomena upon a cracked piano hired from Rouen for the occasion.

Louisa's wit was charming. How mistaken it is to educate instinct out of women! To replace nature by a schoolmistress! She committed none of those terrible mistakes which shock one; it was evident that she formed her sentences herself instead of repeating formulæ committed to memory. She had either never read a novel or had forgotten it, and unless she is a wonderful actress she remains as the great fashioner, Nature, made her—a perfect woman. We remained a greater part of the evening seated together in a corner like beings of another race. Profiting by the great interest betrayed by the company in one of those *soi-disant* innocent games where a great deal of kissing is done, the fair girl, doubtless fearing a rude salute on her delicate cheek, led me into her room, which adjoins the parlor and opens into the garden by a glass door.

On a table in the room, feebly lighted by a lamp which Louisa modestly turned up, were scattered pell-mell, screens, boxes from

Spa, alabaster paper-weights and other details of the art of illuminating, which profession my beauty practises; and which explains her occasional aristocratic airs, unbecoming an humble seamstress. A bouquet just commenced showed talent; with some lessons from St. Jean or Diaz she would easily make a good flower painter. I told her so. She received my encomiums as a matter of course, evincing none of that mock-modesty which I particularly detest.

She showed me a bizarre little chest that she was making, which at first-sight seemed to be carved out of coral; it was constructed out of the wax-seals cut from old letters pasted together. This new mosaic was very simple, and yet remarkably pretty. She asked me to give her, in order to finish her box, all the striking seals I possessed, emblazoned in figures and devices. I gave her five or six letters that I had in my pocket, from which she dexterously cut the seals with her little scissors. While she was thus engaged I strolled about the garden—a Machiavellian manœuvre, for, in order to return me my letters, she must come in search of me.

The gardens of Madame Taverneau are not the gardens of Armida; but it is not in the power of the commonalty to spoil entirely the work of God's hands; trees, by the moonbeams of a summer-night, although only a few steps from red-cotton curtains and a sanhedrim of merry tradespeople, are still trees. In a corner of the garden stood a large acacia tree, in full bloom, waving its yellow hair in the soft night-breeze, and mingling its perfume with that of the flowers of the marsh iris, poised like azure butterflies upon their long green stems.

The porch was flooded with silver light, and when Louise, having secured her seals, appeared upon the threshold, her pure and elegant form stood out against the dark background of the room like an alabaster statuette.

Her step, as she advanced towards me, was undulating and rhythmical like a Greek strophe. I took my letters, and we strolled along the path towards an arbor.

So glad was I to get away from the templar Bois-Guilbert

carrying off Rebecca, and the plated lamps, that I developed an eloquence at once persuasive and surprising. Louise seemed much agitated; I could almost see the beatings of her heart—the accents of her pure voice were troubled—she spoke as one just awakened from a dream. Tell me, are not these the symptoms, wherever you have travelled, of a budding love?

I took her hand; it was moist and cool, soft as the pulp of a magnolia flower,—and I thought I felt her fingers faintly return my pressure.

I am delighted that this scene occurred by moonlight and under the acacia's perfumed branches, for I affect poetical surroundings for my love scenes. It would be disagreeable to recall a lovely face relieved against wall-paper covered with yellow scrolls; or a declaration of love accompanied, in the distance, by the Grace de Dieu; my first significant interview with Louise will be associated in my thoughts with moonbeams, the odor of the iris and the song of the cricket in the summer grass.

You, no doubt, pronounce me, dear Roger, a pitiable Don Juan, a common-place Amilcar, for not profiting by the occasion. A young man strolling at night in a garden with a screen painter ought at least to have stolen a kiss! At the risk of appearing ridiculous, I did nothing of the kind. I love Louise, and besides she has at times such an air of hauteur, of majestic disdain that the boldest commercial traveller steeped to the lips in Pigault-Lebrun, a sub-lieutenant wild with absinthe would not venture such a caress—she would almost make one believe in virtue, if such a thing were possible. Frankly, I am afraid that I am in earnest this time. Order me a dove-colored vest, apple-green trowsers, a pouch, a crook, in short the entire outfit of a Lignon shepherd. I shall have a lamb washed to complete the pastoral.

How I reached the château, whether walking or flying, I cannot tell. Happy as a king, proud as a god, for a new love was born in my heart.

EDGAR DE MEILHAN.

IX.

IRENE DE CHATEAUDUN *to* MME. LA VICOMTESSE DE BRAIMES,
Hotel de la Préfecture, GRENOBLE (Isère).

PARIS, June 2d 18—.

IT is five o'clock, I have just come from Pont de l'Arche, and I am going to the Odeon, which is three miles from here; it seems to me that the Odeon is three miles from every spot in Paris, for no matter where you live, you are never near the Odeon!

Madame Taverneau is delighted at the prospect of treating a poor, obscure, unsophisticated widow like myself to an evening at the theatre! She has a box that she obtained, by some stratagem, the hour we got here. She seemed so hurt and disappointed when I refused to accompany her, that I was finally compelled to yield to her entreaties. The good woman has for me a restless, troublesome affection that touches me deeply. A vague instinct tells her that fate will lead us through different paths in life, and in spite of herself, without being able to explain why, she watches me as if she knew I might escape from her at any moment.

She insisted upon escorting me to Paris, although she had nothing to call her there, and her father, who is still my garret neighbor, did not expect her. She relies upon taking me back to Pont de l'Arche, and I have not the courage to undeceive her; I also dread the moment when I will have to tell her my real name, for she will weep as if she were hearing my requiem. Tell me, what can I do to benefit her and her husband; if they had a child I would present it with a handsome dowry, because parents gratefully receive money for their children, when they would proudly refuse it for themselves.

To confer a favor without letting it appear as one, requires more consideration, caution and diplomacy than I am prepared to devote to the subject, so you must come to my relief and decide upon some plan.

I first thought of making M. Taverneau manager of one of my estates—now that I have estates to be managed; but he is stupid . . . and alas, what a manager he would make! He would eat the hay instead of selling it; so I had to relinquish that idea, and as he is unfit for anything else, I will get him an office; the government alone possesses the art of utilizing fools. Tell me what office I can ask for that will be very remunerative to him—consult M. de Braimes; a Prefect ought to know how to manage such a case; ask him what is the best way of assisting a protégé who is a great fool? Let me know at once what he says.

I don't wish to speak of the subject to Roger, because it would be revealing the past. Poor Roger, how unhappy he must be! I long so to see him, and by great kindness make amends for my cruelty.

I told you of all the stratagems I had to resort to in order to find out what Roger had written to M. de Meilhan about his sorrows; well, thanks to my little sealing-wax boxes, I have seen Roger's letter! Yesterday evening, M. de Meilhan brought me some new seals, and among the letters he handed me was one from Roger! Imagine my feelings! I was so frightened when I had the letter in my hand that I dared not read it; not because I was too honorable, but too prudish; I dreaded being embarrassed by reading facts stated in that free and easy style peculiar to young men when writing to each other. The only concession I could obtain from my delicacy was to glance at the three last lines: "I am not angry with her, I am only vexed with myself," wrote the poor forsaken man. "I never told her how much I loved her; if she had known it, never would she have had the courage to desert me."

This simple honest sorrow affected me deeply; not wishing to read any more, I went into the garden to return M. de Meilhan his letters, and was glad it was too dark for him to perceive my paleness and agitation. I at once decided to return to Paris, for

I find that in spite of all my fine programmes of cruelty, I am naturally tender-hearted and distressed to death at the idea of making any one unhappy. I armed myself with insensibility, and here I am already conquered by the first groans of my victim. I would make but an indifferent tyrant, and if all the suspicious queens and jealous empresses like Elizabeth, Catharine and Christina had no more cruelty in their dispositions than I have, the world would have been deprived of some of its finest tragedies.

You may congratulate yourself upon having mitigated the severity of my decrees, for it is my anxiety to please you that has made me so suddenly change all my plans of tests and trials. You say it is undignified to act as a spy upon Roger, to conceal myself in Paris where he is anxiously seeking and waiting for me; that this ridiculous play has an air of intrigue, and had better be stopped at once or it may result dangerously . . . I am resigned—I renounce the sensible idea of testing my future husband . . . but be warned! If in the future I am tortured by discovering any glaring defects and odious peculiarities, that what you call my indiscretion might have revealed before it was too late, you will permit me to come and complain to you every day, and you must promise to listen to my endless lamentations as I repeat over and over again. O Valentine, I have learned too late what I might have known in time to save me! Valentine, I am miserable and disappointed—console me! console me!

Doubtless to a young girl reared like yourself in affluence under your mother's eye, this strange conduct appears culpable and indelicate; but remember, that with me it is the natural result of the sad life I have led for the last three years; this disguise, that I reassume from fancy, was then worn from necessity, and I have earned the right of borrowing it a little while longer from misfortune to assist me in guarding against new sorrows. Am I not justified in wishing to profit by experience too dearly bought? Is it not just that I should demand from the sad past some guarantees for a brighter future, and make my bitter sorrows the stepping-stones to a happy life? But, as I intend to follow your advice, I'll do it gracefully without again alluding to my frustrated plans.

To-morrow I return to Fontainebleau. I stayed there five days when I went back with Madame Langeac; I only intended to remain a few minutes, but my cousin was so uneasy at finding her daughter worse, that I did not like to leave before the doctor pronounced her better. This illness will assist me greatly in the fictions I am going to write Roger from Fontainebleau to-morrow. I will tell him we were obliged to leave suddenly, without having time to bid him adieu, to go and nurse a sick relative; that she is better now, and Madame de Langeac and I will return to Paris next week. In three days I shall return, and no one will ever know I have been to Pont de l'Arche, except M. de Meilhan, who will doubtless soon forget all about it; besides, he intends remaining in Normandy till the end of the year, so there is no risk of our meeting.

Oh! I must tell you about the amusing evening M. de Meilhan and I spent together at Madame Taverneau's. How we did laugh over it! He was king of the feast, although he would not acknowledge it. Madame Taverneau was so proud of entertaining the young lord of the village, that she had rushed into the most reckless extravagance to do him honor. She had thrown the whole town in a state of excitement by sending to Rouen for a piano. But the grand event of the evening was a clock. Yet I must confess that the effect was quite different from what she expected—it was a complete failure. We usually sit in the dining-room, but for this grand occasion the parlor was opened. On the mantel-piece in this splendid room there is a clock adorned by a dreadful bronze horse running away with a fierce warrior and some unheard-of Turkish female. I never saw anything so hideous; it is even worse than your frightful clock with Columbus discovering America! Madame Taverneau thought that M. de Meilhan, being a poet and an artist, would compliment her upon possessing so rare and valuable a work of art. Fortunately he said nothing—he even refrained from smiling; this showed his great generosity and delicacy, for it is only a man of refinement and delicacy that respects one's illusions—especially when they are illusions in imitation bronze!

Upon my arrival here this morning, I was pained to hear that the trees in front of my window are to be cut down; this news ought not to disturb me in the least, as I never expect to return to this house again, yet it makes me very sad; these old trees are so beautiful, and I have thought so many things as I would sit and watch their long branches waving in the summer breeze! . . . and the little light that shone like a star through their thick foliage! shall I never see it again? It disappeared a year ago, and I used to hope it would suddenly shine again. I thought: It is absent, but will soon return to cheer my solitude. Sometimes I would say: "Perhaps my ideal dwells in that little garret!" O foolish idea! Vain hope! I must renounce all this poetry of youth; serious age creeps on with his imposing escort of austere duties; he dispels the charming fancies that console us in our sorrows; he extinguishes the bright lights that guide us through darkness—drives away the beloved ideal—spreads a cloud over the cherished star, and harshly cries out: "Be reasonable!" which means: No longer hope to be happy.

Ah! Madame Taverneau calls me; she is in a hurry to start for the Odeon; it is very early, and I don't wish to go until the last moment. I have sent to the Hotel de Langeac for my letters, and must wait to glance over them—they might contain news about Roger.

I have just caught a glimpse of the two ladies Madame Taverneau invited to accompany us to the theatre. . . . I see a wine-colored bonnet trimmed with green ribbons—it is horrible to look upon! Heavens—there comes another! more intolerable than the first one! bright yellow adorned with blue feathers! . . . Mercy! what a face within the bonnet! and what a figure beneath the face! She has something glistening in her hand . . it is . . . a . . . would you believe it? a travelling-bag covered with steel beads! . . . she intends taking it to the theatre! . . . do my eyes deceive me? *can* she be filling it with oranges to carry with her? . . . she dare not disgrace us by eating oranges in a theatre. . . Oh I am lost! ruined for ever! Never—no, never will I appear in company with that steel bag of oranges and those atrocious bonnets! What *shall* I do to escape?

Alas! it is useless to rebel! I am obliged to go, but I will conceal myself in a corner of the box and no one can see me; besides this is my last day of mystery, and I may as well take advantage of it, and see the world from a plebeian stand-point—it will be my last opportunity. I dare say I shall be more amused and entertained to-night in this inelegant box than I have ever been in our splendid private ones, the Opera and the Theatre Italien! moreover, no one would dare to recognise *me* behind those dreadful bonnets! Roger himself never would have the temerity to seek me in such company. O, ye angels of mercy, pity me! Steel bag! Oranges! . . . and *such* bonnets! . . . Alas! Alas!

The letters don't come, and Madam Taverneau is so impatient that I must go at once. I want to stay at home, but she insists upon remaining with me. . . .

Four women in one box! it is a crime against society—what would my cousin say if she could see me? My next letter will give you the continuation of my romance. I will execute your commissions early in the morning.

IRENE DE CHATEAUDUN.

X.

EDGAR DE MEILHAN *to the* PRINCE DE MONBERT,
Saint Dominique Street, Paris.

RICHEPORT, June 3d, 18—.

IT seems, my dear Roger, that we are engaged in a game of interrupted addresses. For my Louise Guérin, like your Irene de Chateaudun, has gone I know not where, leaving me to struggle, in this land of apple trees, with an incipient passion which she has planted in my breast. Flight has this year become an epidemic among women.

The day after that famous soirée, I went to the post-office ostensibly to carry the letter containing those triumphant details, but in reality to see Louise, for any servant possessed sufficient intelligence to acquit himself of such a commission. Imagine my surprise and disappointment at finding instead of Madame Taverneau a strange face, who gruffly announced that the post-mistress had gone away for a few days with Madame Louise Guérin. The dove had flown, leaving to mark its passage a few white feathers in its mossy nest, a faint perfume of grace in this common-place mansion!

I could have questioned Madame Taverneau's fat substitute, but I am principled against asking questions; things are explained soon enough. Disenchantment is the key to all things. When I like a woman I carefully avoid all her acquaintance, any one who can tell me aught about her. The sound of her name pronounced by careless lips, puts me to flight; the letters that she receives might be given me open and I should throw them, unread, into the fire. If in speaking she makes any allusion to the past events of her life, I change the conversation; I tremble when she begins a recital, lest some disillusionizing incident should escape her which would destroy the impression I had formed of her. As studiously as others hunt after secrets I avoid them; if I have ever learned anything of a woman I loved, it has always been in spite of my earnest efforts, and what I have known I have carefully endeavored to forget.

Such is my system. I said nothing to the fat woman, but entered Louise's deserted chamber.

Everything was as she had left it.

A bunch of wild flowers, used as a model, had not had time to fade; an unfinished bouquet rested on the easel, as if awaiting the last touches of the pencil. Nothing betokened a final departure. One would have said that Louise might enter at any moment. A little black mitten lay upon a chair; I picked it up—and would have pressed it to my lips, if such an action had not been deplorably rococo.

Then I threw myself into an old arm-chair, by the side of the bed—like Faust in Marguerite's room—lifting the curtains with as much precaution as if Louise reposed beneath. You are going to laugh at me, I know, dear Roger, but I assure you, I have never been able to gaze upon a young girl's bed without emotion.

That little pillow, the sole confidant of timid dreams, that narrow couch, fitted like a tomb for but one alabaster form, inspired me with tender melancholy. No anacreontic thoughts came to me, I assure you, nor any disposition to rhyme in *ette*, herbette, filette, coudrette. The love I bear to noble poesy saved me from such an exhibition of bad taste.

A crucifix, over which hung a piece of blessed box, spread its ivory arms above Louise's untroubled slumber. Such simple piety touched me. I dislike bigots, but I detest atheists.

Musing there alone it flashed upon me that Louise Guérin had never been married, in spite of her assertion. I am disposed to doubt the existence of the late Albert Guérin. A sedate and austere atmosphere surrounds Louise, suggesting the convent or the boarding-school.

I went into the garden; the sunbeams checkered the steps of the porch; the wilted iris drooped on its stem, and the acacia flowers strewed the pathway. Apropos of acacia flowers, do you know, that fried in batter, they make excellent fritters?

Finding myself alone in the walks where I had strolled with her, I do not know how it happened, but I felt my heart swell, and I sighed like a young abbé of the 17th century.

I returned to the château, having no excuse for remaining longer, vexed, disappointed, wearied, idle—the habit of seeing Louise every day had grown upon me.

And habit is everything to poor humanity, as that graceful poet Alfred de Musset says. My feet only know the way to the post-office; what shall I do with myself while this visit lasts? I tried to read, but my attention wandered; I skipped the lines, and read the same paragraph over twice; my book having fallen down I picked it up and read it for one whole hour upside down, without knowing it—I wished to make a monosyllabic sonnet—extremely interesting occupation—and failed. My quatrains were tedious, and my tercets entirely too diffuse.

My mother begins to be uneasy at my dullness; she has asked twice if I were sick—I have fallen off already a quarter of a pound; for nothing is more enraging than to be deserted at the most critical period of one's infatuation! Ixion of Normandy, my Juno is a screen-painter, I open my arms and clasp only a cloud! My position, similar to yours, cannot, however, be compared with it — mine only relates to a trifling flirtation, a thwarted fancy, while yours is a serious passion for a woman of your own rank who has accepted your hand, and therefore has no right to trifle with you,—she must be found, if only for vengeance!

Remorse consumes me because of my sentimental stupidity by moonlight. Had I profited by the night, the solitude and the occasion, Louise had not left me; she saw clearly that I loved her, and was not displeased at the discovery. Women are strange mixtures of timidity and rashness.

Perhaps she has gone to join her lover, some saw-bones, some counting-house Lovelace, while I languish here in vain, like Celadon or Lygdamis of cooing memory.

This is not at all probable, however, for Madame Taverneau would not compromise her respectability so far as to act as chaperon to the loves of Louise Guérin. After all, what is it to me? I am very good to trouble myself about the freaks of a prudish screen-painter! She will return, because the hired piano has not been sent back to Rouen, and not a soul in the house knows a note of music but Louise, who plays quadrilles and waltzes with considerable taste, an accomplishment she owes to her mistress of painting, who had seen better days and possessed some skill.

Do not be too much flattered by this letter of grievances, for I only wanted an excuse to go to the post-office to see if Louise has returned—suppose she has not! the thought drives the blood back to my heart.

Isn't it singular that I should fall desperately in love with this simple shepherdess—I who have resisted the sea-green glances and smiles of the sirens that dwell in the Parisian ocean? Have I escaped from the Marquise's Israelite turbans only to become a slave to a straw bonnet? I have passed safe and sound through the most dangerous defiles to be worsted in open country; I could swim in the whirlpool, and now drown in a fish-pond; every celebrated beauty, every renowned coquette finds me on my guard. I am as circumspect as a cat walking over a table covered with glass and china. It is hard to make me pose, as they say in a certain set; but when the adversary is not to be feared, I allow him so many advantages that in the end he subdues me.

I was not sufficiently on my guard with Louise at first.

I said to myself: "She is only a grisette"—and left the door of my heart open—love entered in, and I fear I shall have some trouble in driving him out.

Excuse, dear Roger, this nonsense, but I must write you something. After all, my passion is worth as much as yours. Love is the same whether inspired by an empress or a rope-dancer, and I am just as unhappy at Louise's disappearance as you are at Irene's.

EDGAR DE MEILHAN.

XI.

ROGER DE MONBERT *to* MONSIEUR DE MEILHAN,
Pont de l'Arche (Eure).

PARIS, June 3d 18—.

SHE is in Paris !

Before knowing it I felt it. The atmosphere was filled with a voice, a melody, a brightness, a perfume that murmured : Irene is here !

Paris appears to me once more populated ; the crowd is no longer a desert in my eyes ; this great dead city has recovered its spirit of life ; the sun once more smiles upon me ; the earth bounds under my feet ; the soft summer air fans my burning brow, and whispers into my ear that one adored name—Irene !

Chance has a treasure-house of atrocious combinations. Chance ! The cunning demon ! He calls himself Chance so as to better deceive us. With an infernal skilfulness he feigns not to watch us in the decisive moments of our lives, and at the same time leads us like blind fools into the very path he has marked out for us.

You know the two brothers Ernest and George de S. were planted by their family in the field of diplomacy : they study Eastern languages and affect Eastern manners. Well, yesterday we met in the Bois de Boulogne, they in a calash, and I on horseback—I am trying riding as a moral hygiene—as the carriage dashed by they called out to me an invitation to dinner ; I replied, "Yes," without stopping my horse. Idleness and indolence made me say "Yes," when I should have said, "No ;" but *Yes* is so much easier to pronounce than *No*, especially on horseback. *No* necessitates a discussion ; *Yes* ends the matter, and economizes words and time.

I was rather glad I had met these young sprigs of diplomacy. They are good antidotes for low spirits, for they are always in a hilarious state and enjoy their youth in idle pleasure, knowing they are destined to grow old in the soporific dulness of an Eastern court.

I thought we three would be alone at dinner; alas! there were five of us.

Two female artistes who revelled in their precocious emancipation; two divinities worshipped in the temple of the grand sculptors of modern Athens; the Scylla and Charybdis of Paris.

I am in the habit of bowing with the same apparent respect to every woman in the universe. I have bowed to the ebony women of Senegal; to the moon-colored women of the Southern Archipelago; to the snow-white women of Behring's Strait, and to the bronze women of Lahore and Ceylon. Now it was impossible for me to withdraw from the presence of two fair women whose portraits are the admiration of all connoisseurs who visit the Louvre. Besides, I have a theory: the less respectable a woman is, the more respect we should show her, and thus endeavor to bring her back to virtue.

I remained and tried to add my fifth share of antique gayety to the feast. We were Praxiteles, Phidias and Scopas; we had inaugurated the modest Venus and her sister in their temples, and we drank to our model goddesses in wines from the Ionian Archipelago.

That evening, you may remember, Antigone was played at the Odeon in the Faubourg Saint-Germain.

I have another theory: in any action, foolish or wise, either carry it through bravely when once undertaken, or refrain from undertaking it. I had not the wisdom to refrain, therefore I was compelled to imitate the folly of my friends; at dessert I even abused the invitation, and too often sought to drown sorrow in the ruby cup.

We started for the Odeon. Our entrance at the theatre caused quite an excitement. The ladies, cavalierly suspended on the arms of the two future Eastern ambassadors, sailed in with a conscious air of epicurean grace and dazzling beauty. The classic ushers obsequiously threw open the doors, and led us to our box. I brought up the procession, looking as insolent and proud as I did the day I entered the ruined pagoda of Bangalore to carry off the statue of Sita.

The first act was being played, and the Athenian school preserved a religious silence in front of the proscenium. The noise we made by drawing back the curtain of our box, slamming the door and loudly laughing, drowned for an instant the touching strains of the tragic choir, and centred upon us the angry looks of the audience.

With what cool impertinence did our divinities lean over the seats and display their round white arms, that have so often been copied in Parian marble by our most celebrated sculptors! Our three intellectual faces, wreathed in the silly smiles of intoxication, hovered over the silken curls of our goddesses, thus giving the whole theatre a full view of our happiness!

Occasionally a glimmer of reason would cross my confused brain, and I would soliloquize: Why am I disgracing myself in this way before all these people? What possesses me to act in concert with these drunken fools and bold women? I must rush out and apologize to the first person I meet!

It was impossible for me to follow my good impulse—some unseen hand held me back—some mysterious influence kept me chained to the spot. We are influenced by magic, although magicians no longer exist!

Between the acts, our two Greek statues criticised the audience in loud tones, and their remarks, seasoned with attic salt, afforded a peculiar supplement to the choir of Antigone.

"Those four women on our right must be sensible people," said our blonde statue; "they have put their show-piece in front. I suppose she is the beauty of the party; did you ever behold such dreadful bonnets and dresses? They must have come from the Olympic Circus. If I were disfigured in that way, I would be a box-opener, but never would be seen in one!"

"I think I have seen them before," said the bronze statue; they hire their bonnets from the fish-market—disgusting creatures that they are!"

"What do the two in the corner look like, my angel?"

"I see nothing but a shower of curls; I suppose *she* found it more economical to curl her hair than to buy a bonnet. Every time I stretch my neck to get a look at her, she hides behind those superb bonnets."

"Which proves," said Ernest, "that she is paradoxically ugly."

"I pity them, if they are seeking four husbands," said George; "and if they are married—I pity their four husbands."

Whilst my noisy companions were trying to discover their ideal fright in the corner of the box on our right, I felt an inexplicable contraction of my heart—a chill pass through my whole body; my silly gayety was by some unseen influence suddenly changed into sadness—I felt my eyes fill with tears. The only way I could account for this revulsion in my feelings was the growing conviction that I was disgracing myself in a den of malefactors of both sexes. My fit of melancholy was interrupted very opportunely by the choir chanting the hymn of Bacchus, that antique wonder, found by Mendelssohn in the ruins of the Temple of Victory.

When the play was over, I timidly proposed that we should remain in our box till the crowd had passed out; but our Greek statues would not hear to it, as they had determined upon a triumphal exit. I was obliged to yield.

The bronze statue despotically seized my arm, and dragged me toward the stair. I felt as if I had a cold lizard clinging to me. I was seized with that chilly sensation always felt by nervous people when they come in contact with reptiles.

I recalled the disastrous day that I was shipwrecked on the island of Eaei-Namove, and compelled to marry Dai-Natha, the king's daughter, in order to escape the unpleasant alternative of being eaten alive by her father. On the staircase of the Odeon I regretted Dai-Natha.

In the midst of the dense crowd that blockaded the stairway, I heard a frightened cry that made the blood freeze in my veins. There was but one woman in the world blest with so sweet a voice—musical even when raised in terror.

If I were surrounded by crashing peals of thunder, rushing waters and yells of wild beasts, I still could recognise, through the din of all this, the cry of a beloved woman. I am gifted with that marvellous perception of hearing, derived from the sixth sense, the sense of love.

Irene de Chateaudun had uttered that cry of alarm—*Take care, my dear!* she had exclaimed with that accent of fright that it is impossible to disguise—in that tone that will be natural in spite of all the reserve that circumstances would impose, *Take care, my dear!*

Some one near me said that a door-keeper had struck a lady on the shoulder with a panel of a portable door which he was carrying across the passage-way. By standing on my toes I could just catch a glimpse of the board being balanced in the air over every one's head. My eyes could not see the woman who had uttered this cry, but my ears told me it was Irene de Chateaudun.

The crowd was so dense that some minutes passed before I could move a step towards the direction of the cry, but when I had finally succeeded in reaching the door, I flung from me the hateful arm that clung to mine, and rushing into the street, I searched through the crowd and looked in every carriage and under every lady's hood to catch a glimpse of Irene, without being disconcerted by the criticisms that the people around indulged in at my expense.

Useless trouble! I discovered nothing. The theatre kept its secret; but that cry still rings in my ears and echoes around my heart.

This morning at daybreak I flew to the Hotel de Langeac. The porter stared at me in amazement, and answered all my eager inquiries with a stolid, short *no*. The windows of Irene's room were closed and had that deserted appearance that proved the absence of its lovely occupant—windows that used to look so bright and beautiful when I would catch glimpses of a snowy little hand arranging the curtains, or of a golden head gracefully bent over her work, totally unconscious of the loving eyes feasting upon her beauty—oh! many of my happiest moments have been spent gazing at those windows, and now how coldly and silently they frowned upon my grief!

The porter lies! The windows lie! I exclaimed, and once more I began to search Paris.

This time I had a more important object in view than trying to fatigue my body and divert my mind. My eyes are multiplied to infinity; they questioned at once every window, door, alley, street, carriage and store in the city. I was like the miser who accused all Paris of having stolen his treasure.

At three o'clock, when all the beauty and fashion of Paris was promenading on Paix aux Panoramas street, I was stopped on the corner and button-holed by one of those gossiping friends whom fiendish chance always sends at the most trying moments in life in order to disgust us with friendship. . . A dazzling form passed before me. . . Irene alone possesses that graceful ease, that fairy-like step, that queenly dignity—I could recognise her among a thousand—it was useless for her to attempt disguising her exquisite elegance beneath a peasant dress—besides I caught her eye, so all doubts were swept away; several precious minutes were lost in trying to shake off my vexatious friend. I abruptly bade him good-day and darted after Irene, but she has the foot of a gazelle, and the crowd was so compact that in spite of my elbowing and föot-crushing, I made but little headway.

Finally, through an opening in the crowd, I saw Mlle. de Chateaudun turn the corner and enter that narrow street near the Café Vernon. This time she cannot possibly escape me—she is in a long, narrow street, with deserted galleries on either side—circumstances are propitious to a meeting and explanation—in a minute I am in the narrow street a few yards behind Irene. I prepare my mind for this momentous conversation which is to decide my fate. I firmly clasp my arms to still the violent throbbings of my heart. I am about to be translated to heaven or engulfed by hell.

She rapidly glanced at a Chinese store in front of her and,

without showing any agitation, quietly opened the door and went in. Very good, thought I, she will purchase some trifle and be out in a few minutes. I will wait for her.

Five feet from the store I assumed the attitude of the god Terminus; by the way, this store is very handsomely ornamented, and far surpasses in its elegant collection of Chinese curiosities the largest store of the sort in Hog Lane in the European quarter of Canton.

Another of those kind friends whom chance holds in reserve for our annoyance, came out of a bank adjoining the store, and inferring from my statue-like attitude that I was dying of ennui and would welcome any diversion, rushed up to me and said:

"Ah! my dear cosmopolitan, how are you to-day? Don't you want to accompany me to Brussels? I have just bought gold for the journey; gold is very high, fifteen per cent."

I answered by one of those listless smiles and unintelligible monosyllables which signifies in every language under the sun, don't bore me.

In the meantime I remained immovable, with my eyes fastened on the Chinese store. I could have detected the flight of an atom.

My friend struck the attitude of the Colossus of Rhodes, and supporting his chin upon the gold head of his cane which he held in the air clenched by both hands, thus continued: "I did a very foolish thing this morning. I bought my wife a horse, a Devonshire horse, from the Crémieux stables. . . . That reminds me, my dear Roger, you are the very man to decide a knotty question for me. I bet D'Allinville thirty louis that . . what would *you* call a lady's horse?"

For some moments I preserved that silence which shows that we are not in a humor for talking; but friends sent by ingenious Chance understand nothing but the plainest language, so my friend continued his queries:

"What would you call a lady's horse?"

"I would call it a horse," said I, with indifference.

"Now, Roger, I believe you are right; D'Allinville insists that a lady's horse is a palfrey."

"In the language of chivalry he is right."

"Then I have lost my bet?"

"Yes."

"My dear Roger, this question has been worrying me for two days."

"You are very fortunate to have nothing worse than a term of chivalry to annoy you. I would give all the gold in that broker's office if my troubles were as light as yours."

"I am afraid you *are* unhappy, . . . you have been looking sad for some time, Roger, . . . come with me to Brussels. . . . We can make some splendid speculations there. Now-a-days if the aristocracy don't turn their attention to business once in a while, they will be completely swept out by the moneyed scum of the period. Let us make a venture: I hear of twenty acres of land for sale, bordering on the Northern Railroad—there is a clear gain of a hundred thousand francs as soon as the road is finished; I offer you half—it is not a very risky game, nothing more than playing lansquenet on a railroad!"

No signs of Irene. My impatience was so evident that this time my obtuse friend saw it, and, shaking me by the hand, said:

"Good-bye, my dear Roger, why in the world did you not tell me I was *de trop?* Now that I see there is a fair lady in the case I will relieve you of my presence. Adieu! adieu!"

He was gone, and I breathed again.

By this time my situation had become critical. This Chinese door, like that of Acheron, refused to surrender its prey. Time was passing. I had successively adopted every attitude of feverish expectation; I had exhausted every pose of a museum of statues, and saw that my suspicious blockade of the pavement alarmed the store-keepers. The broker adjoining the Chinese store seemed to be putting himself on the defensive, and meditating an article for the *Gazette des Tribunaux.*

I now regretted the departure of my speculating friend; his

presence would at least have given my conduct an air of respectability,—would have legalized, so to speak, my odd behavior. This time chance left me to my own devices.

I had held my position for two hours, and now, as a regard for public opinion compelled me to retire, and I had no idea of doing so until I had achieved a victory, I determined to make an attack upon the citadel containing my queen of love and beauty. Irene had not left the store, for she certainly had no way of escaping except by the door which was right in front of my eyes—she must be all this time selecting some trifle that a man could purchase in five minutes,—it takes a woman an eternity to buy anything, no matter how small it may be! My situation had become intolerable—I could stand it no longer; so arming myself with superhuman courage, I bravely opened the shop-door and entered as if it were the breach of a besieged city.

I looked around and could see nothing but a confused mingling of objects living and dead; I could only distinguish clearly a woman bowing over the counter, asking me a question that I did not hear. My agitation made me deaf and blind.

"Madame," I said, "have you any . . . Chinese curiosities?"

"We have, monsieur, black tea, green tea, and some very fine Pekin."

"Well, madame, . . . give me some of all."

"Do you want it in boxes, monsieur?"

"In boxes, madame, if you choose."

I looked all around the room and saw nobody but two old women standing behind another counter—no signs of Irene.

I paid for my tea, and while writing down my address, I questioned the saleswoman:

"I promised my wife to meet her here at three o'clock to select this tea—not that my presence was necessary, as her taste is always mine--but she requested me to come, and I fear I have made a mistake in the hour, my watch has run down and I had no idea it was so late—I hope she did not wait for me? has she been here?" Thereupon I gave a minute description of

Irene de Chateaudun, from the color of her hair to the shade of her boot.

"Yes, monsieur, she was here about three o'clock, it is now five; she was only here a few minutes—long enough to make a little purchase."

"Yes, . . . I gasped out, . . . I know, but I thought I saw her . . . did she not come in . . . that door?"

"Yes, sir, she entered by that door and went out by the opposite one, that one over there," said she, pointing to a door opening on New Vivienne street.

I suppressed an oath, and rushed out of the door opening on this new street, as if I expected to find Mlle. de Chateaudun patiently waiting for me to join her on the pavement. My head was in such a whirl that I had not the remotest idea of where I was going, and I wandered recklessly through little streets that I had never heard of before—it made no difference to me whether I ran into Scylla or Charybdis—I cared not what became of me.

Like the fool that repeats over and over again the same words without understanding their meaning, I kept saying: "The fiend of a woman! the fiend of a woman!" At this moment all my love seemed turned to hate! but when this hate had calmed down to chill despair, I began to reflect with agonizing fear that perhaps Irene had seen me at the Odeon with those dreadful women. I felt that I was ruined in her eyes for ever! She would never listen to my attempt at vindication or apologies—women are so unforgiving when a man strays for a moment from the path of propriety, and they regard little weaknesses in the light of premeditated crimes, too heinous for pardon—Irene would cry out with the poet:

"Tu te fais criminel pour te justifier!"

You are fortunate, my dear Edgar, in having found the woman you have always dreamed of and hoped for; you will have all the charms of love without its troubles; it is folly to believe that love is strengthened by its own torments and stimulated by sorrows. A storm is only admired by those on shore; the suffering sailors curse the raging sea and pray for a calm.

Your letter, my dear Edgar, is filled with that calm happiness that is the foundation of all true love; in return, I can only send you an account of my despair. Friendship is often a union of these two contrasts.

Enjoy your happy lot, my friend; your reputation is made. You have a good name, an enviable and an individual philosophy, borrowed neither from the Greeks nor the Germans. Your future is beautiful; cherish the sweetest dreams; the woman you love will realize them all.

Night is a bad counsellor, so I dare not make any resolutions, or come to any decision at this dark hour. I shall wait for the sun to enlighten my mind.

In my despair I have the mournful consolation of knowing that Irene is in Paris. This great city has no undiscovered secrets; everything and every person hid in its many houses is obliged sooner or later to appear in the streets. I form the most extravagant projects; I will buy, if necessary, the indiscretion of all the discreet lips that guard the doors; I shall recruit an army of salaried spies. On the coast of the Coromandel there is a tribe of Indians whose profession is to dive into the Gulf of Bengal, that immense bathing-tub of the sun, and search for a beautiful pearl that lies buried among the coral beds at the bottom of the ocean. It is a pearl of great price, as valuable as the finest diamond. . . . Irene is my pearl of great price, and I will search for and find her in this great ocean of men and houses called Paris. . . . After thinking and wondering till I am dizzy and sick at heart, I have come to the conclusion that Irene is acting in this manner to test my love—this thought consoles me a little, and I try to drown my sorrow in the thought of our mutual happiness, when I shall have triumphantly passed through the ordeal.

The most charming of women is willing to believe that everybody loves except her lover.

ROGER DE MONBERT.

XII.

IRENE DE CHATEAUDUN *to* MME. LA VICOMTESSE DE BRAIMES,
Grenoble, (Isère).

PARIS, June 2d—Midnight.

OH! How indignant I am! How angry and mortified are my feelings! Good Heavens! how his shameful conduct makes me hate and despise him! . . . I will try to be calm—to collect my scattered thoughts and give you a clear account of what has just occurred—tell you how all of my plans are destroyed—how I am once more alone in this cruel world, more sad, more discouraged and more hopeless than I ever was in my darkest days of misery and poverty . . . . but I cannot be calm—it is impossible for me to control my indignation when I think of the shameful behavior of this man—of his gross impertinence—his insolent duplicity . . . . Well, I went to the Odeon; M. de Monbert was there, I saw him, he certainly made no attempt to conceal his presence; you know he plumes himself upon being open and frank—never hides anything from the world—wishes people to see him in his true character, &c., precisely what I saw to-night. Yes, Valentine, there he was as tipsy as a coachman—with those little hair-brained de S.'s, the eldest simply tipsy as a lord, the young one, George, was drunk, very drunk. This is not all, the fascinating Prince was escort to two fashionable beauties, two miserable creatures of distressing notoriety, two of those shameless women whom we cannot fail to recognise on account of their scandalous behavior in public; sort of market-women disguised as fashion-plates—half apple-venders, half coquettes, who tap men on the cheek with their scented gloves and intersperse their conversation with dreadful oaths from behind their bouquets and Pompadour fans! . . . these creatures talked in shrill tones, laughed out loud enough to be heard by every one around—joined in the chorus of the Choir of Antigone with the old men of Thebes! . . .

People in the gallery said : "they must have dined late," that was a charitable construction to put upon their shameful conduct—I thought to myself, this is their usual behavior—they are always thus.

I must tell you, so you can better appreciate my angry mortification, that just as we were stepping into the carriage the servant handed me the letters that I had sent him to bring from the Hotel de Langeac. Among the number was one from M. de Monbert, written several days after I had left Paris; this letter is worthy of being sent to Grenoble; I enclose it. While reading it, my dear Valentine, don't forget that I read it at the theatre, and my reading was constantly interrupted by the vulgar conversation and noisy laughter of M. de Monbert and his choice companions, and that each high-flown sentence of this hypocritical note had at the same time a literal and free translation in the scandalous remarks, bursts of laughter, and stupid puns of the despicable man who had written it.

I confess that this flow of wit interfered with my perusal of these touching reproaches; the brilliant improvisations of the orator prevented me from becoming too much affected by the elegiacs of the writer.

Here is the note that I was trying to decipher through my tears when Monsieur de Monbert swaggered into the theatre.

"Is this a test of love—a woman's vengeance or an idle caprice, Mademoiselle? My mind is not calm enough to solve the enigma. Be merciful and drive me not to madness! Tomorrow may be too late—then your words of reason might be responded to by the jargon of insanity! Beware! and cast aside your cloak of mystery before the sun once more goes down upon my frenzy. All is desolation and darkness within and without—nothing appears bright to my eyes, and my soul is wrapped in gloom. In your absence I cease to live, but it seems as if my deep love gives me still enough strength to hold a wandering pen that my mind no longer guides. With my love I gave you my soul and mind—what remains to me would excite your pity. I implore you to restore me to life.

"You cannot comprehend the ecstasy of a man who loves you, and the despair of a man who loses you. Before knowing you I never could have imagined these two extremes, separated by a whole world and brought together in one instant. To be envied by the angels—to breathe the air of heaven—to seek among the divine joys for a name to give one's happiness, and suddenly, like Lucifer, to be dashed by a thunderbolt into an abyss of darkness, and suffer the living death of the damned !

"This is your work !

"No, it cannot be a jest, it is not a vengeance ; one does not jest with real love, one does does not take vengeance on an innocent man ; then it must be a test ! a test ! ah well, it has been borne long enough, and my bleeding heart cries out to you for mercy. If you prolong this ordeal, you will soon have no occasion to doubt my love ! . . . your grief will be remorse.

ROGER."

Yes, you are right this time, my dear Prince ; my sorrow is remorse, deep remorse ; I shall never forgive myself for having been momentarily touched by your heartrending moans and for having shed real tears over your dramatic pathos.

I was seated in the corner of our box, trembling with emotion and weeping over these tender reproaches—yes, I wept !—he seemed so sad, so true to me—I was in an humble frame of mind, thoroughly convinced by this touching appeal that I had been wicked and unjust to doubt so faithful a heart. I was overcome by the magnitude of my offence—at having caused this great despair by my cruelty. Each word of this elaborate dirge was a dagger to my heart ; I credulously admired the eloquence and simplicity of the style ; I accepted as beautiful writing all these striking images—these antitheses full of passion and pretension : "*Reason responded to by insanity.*" "*The power of love that gives him strength to hold a pen. Extremes separated by a whole world and brought together in an instant, and this living death that he suffers, this name for his past happiness that had to be sought for among the joys of heaven !*"

I accepted as gospel truth all these high-flown fictions, and was astonished at nothing until I came to the *Lucifer* part; that, I confess, rather startled me—but the finishing tirade composed me. I thought it fascinating, thrilling, heart-rending! In my enthusiastic pity I was, by way of expiation, admiring the whole letter when I was disturbed by a frightful noise made by people entering the adjoining box. I felt angry at their insulting my sadness with their heartless gayety. I continue to read, admire and weep—my neighbors continue to laugh and make a noise. Amidst this uproar I recognise a familiar voice—I listen—it is certainly the Prince de Monbert—I cannot be mistaken. Probably he has come here with strangers—he has travelled so much that he is obliged to do the honors of Paris to grand ladies who were polite to him abroad—but from what part of the world could these grand ladies have come? They seem to be indulging in a queer style of conversation. One of them boldly looked in our box, and exclaimed, "Four women! Four monsters!" I recognised her as a woman I had seen at the Versailles races—all was explained.

Then they played a sort of farce for their own pleasure, to the great annoyance of the audience. I will give you a sample of it, so you can have an idea of the wit and good taste displayed by these gentlemen. The most intoxicated of the young men asked, between two yawns, who were the authors of *Antigone?* "Sophocles," said M. de Monbert. "But there are two, are there not?" "Two *Antigones?*" said the Prince laughing; "yes, there is Ballanche's." "Ah, yes! Ballanche, that is his name," cried out the ignorant creature; "I knew I saw two names on the hand-bill! Do you know them?"

"I am not acquainted with Sophocles," said the Prince, becoming more and more jovial, "but I know Ballanche; I have seen him at the Academy."

This brilliant witticism was wonderfully successful; they all clapped so loud and laughed so hilariously that the audience became very angry, and called out, "Silence!" "Silence!" For a moment the noisy were quiet, but soon they were worse than ever, acting like maniacs. At the end of each scene, little

George de S., who is a mere school-boy, cried out in deafening tones: "Bravo! Ballanche!" then turning to the neighboring boxes he said: "My friends, applaud; you must encourage the author;" and the two bold women clapped their hands and shrieked out, "Let us encourage Ballanche! Bravo! Ballanche!" It was absurd

Madame Taverneau and her friends were indignant; they had heard the compliment bestowed upon us—"Four women. Four monsters!" This rapid appreciation of our elegant appearance did not make them feel indulgent towards our scandalous neighbors. Near us were several newspaper men who gave the names of the Prince de Monbert, the Messrs. de S., and their two beauties. These journalists spoke with bitter contempt of what they called the young lions of the Faubourg Saint-Germain, of the rude manners of the aristocracy, of the ridiculous scruples of those proud legitimists, who feared to compromise themselves in the interests of their country, and yet were compromised daily by a thousand extravagances; then they related falsehoods that were utterly without foundation, and yet were made to appear quite probable by the disgraceful conduct of the young men before us. You may imagine how cruelly I suffered, both as a fiancée and as a legitimist. I blushed for our party in the presence of the enemy; I felt the insult offered to me personally less than I did the abuse brought upon our cause. In listening to those deserved sneers I detested Messrs. de S. as much as I did Roger. I decided during this hour of vexation and shame that I would rather always remain simple Madame Guérin than become the Princess de Monbert.

What do you think of this despair, the result of champagne? Ought I not to be touched by it? How sweet it is to see one's self so deeply regretted!

It is quite poetical and even mythological; Ariadne went no further than this. She demanded of Bacchus consolation for the sorrows caused by love. How beautifully *he* sang the hymn to Bacchus in the last act of Antigone! He has a fine tenor voice; until now I was not aware of his possessing this gift

How happy he seemed among his charming companions! Valentine, was I not right in saying that the trial of discouragement is infallible? In love despair is a snare; to cease to hope is to cease to feign; a man returns to his nature as soon as hypocrisy is useless. The Prince has proved to me that he prefers low society, that it is his natural element; that he had completely metamorphosed himself so as to appear before us as an elegant, refined, dignified gentleman!

Oh! this evening he certainly was sincere; his real character was on the surface; he made no effort to restrain himself; he was perfectly at home, in his element; and one cannot disguise his delight at being in his element. There is a carelessness in his movements that betrays his self-satisfaction; he struts and spreads himself with an air of confidence; he seems to float in the air, to swim on the crest of the wave. . . . People can conceal their delight when they have recognised an adored being among a crowd . . . can avoid showing that a piece of information casually heard is an important fact that they have been trying to discover for weeks; . . . can hide sudden fear, deep vexation, great joy; but they cannot hide this agreeable impression, this beatitude that they feel upon suddenly returning to their element, after long days of privation and constraint. Well, my dear, the element of Monsieur de Monbert is low company. I take credit to myself for not saying anything more.

I have often observed these base proclivities in persons of the same high condition of life as the Prince. Men brought up in the most refined and cultivated society, destined to fill important positions in life, take the greatest pleasure in associating with common people; they impose elegance upon themselves as a duty, and indulge in vulgarity as a recreation; they have a spite against these charming qualities they are compelled to assume, and indemnify themselves for the trouble of acquiring them by rendering them mischievously useless when they seek low society and attempt to shine where their brilliancy is unappreciated. This low tendency of human nature explains the eternal struggle between nature and education; explains the taste, the passion of intelligent distinguished men for bad company; the more reserved and dignified they are in their manners, the more they seek the society of worthless men and blemished women. Another reason for this low proclivity is the vanity of men; they like to be admired and flattered, although they know their admirers are utterly worthless and despicable.

All these turpitudes would be unimportant if our poor nobility were still triumphantly occupying their rightful position; but while they are struggling to recover their prestige what can be done with such representatives? Oh, I hated those little fools who by their culpable folly compromised so noble a cause! Can they not see that each of their silly blunders furnishes an arm against the principles they defend, against their party, against us all? They are at war with a country that distrusts their motives and detests and envies their advantages . . . and they amuse themselves by irritating the country by their aggressive hostility and blustering idleness. By thus displaying their ill manners and want of sense, it seems as if they wished to justify all the accusations of their enemies and gain what they really deserve, a worse reputation than they already bear. They are accused of being ignorant . . . they are illiterate! They are accused of being impudent. . . They are insolent! They are accused of being beasts. . . They show themselves to be brutes! And yet not much is exacted of them, because they are known to be degenerate. Only half what is required from others is expected from them. They are not asked for heroism or talent, or genius; they are only expected to behave with dignity, they cannot even assume it! They are not asked to add to the lustre of their names, they are only entreated to respect them—and they drag them in the mire! Ah, these people make me die of shame and indignation.

It is from this nursery of worthless, idle young fops that I, Irene de Chateaudun, will be forced to choose a husband. No, never will I suffer the millions that Providence has bestowed upon me to be squandered upon ballet-dancers and the scum of Paris! If it be absolutely necessary that my fortune should be enjoyed by women, I will bestow it upon a convent, where I will retire for the rest of my life; but I certainly would prefer becoming the wife of a poor, obscure, but noble-minded student, thirsting for glory and ambitious of making illustrious his plebeian name, seeking among the dust of ages for the secret of fame . . . than to marry one of the degenerate scions of an old family, who crawl around crushed by the weight of their formidable name; these little burlesque noblemen who retain nothing of their high position but pride and vanity; who can neither think, act, work nor suffer for their country; these disabled knights who wage war against bailiffs and make their names notorious in the police offices and tap-rooms of the Boulevard.

It is glorious to feel flowing in one's veins noble, heroic blood, to be intoxicated with youthful pride when studying the history of one's country, to see one's school-mates forced to commit to memory as a duty, the brilliant record of the heroic deeds of our ancestors! To enter upon a smooth path made easy and pleasant for us by those gone before; to be already armed with the remembrance of noble deeds, laden with generous promises; to have praiseworthy engagements to fulfil, grand hopes to realize; to have in the past powerful protectors, inspiring models that one can invoke in the hour of crisis like exceptional patrons, like saints belonging exclusively to one's own family; to have one's conduct traced out by masters of whom we are proud; to have nothing to imagine—nothing to originate, no good example to set, nothing to do but to nobly continue the work grandly commenced, to keep up the tradition, to follow the old routine—it is especially glorious when the tradition is of honor, when the routine is of glory.

But who comprehends these sentiments now? Who dares utter these noble words without an ironical smile? Only a few helpless believers like myself who still energetically but vainly protest against these degradations. Some go to Algeria to prove their hereditary bravery and obtain the Cross of Honor they are deprived of here; others retire to their châteaux and study the fine arts, thus enjoying the only generous resource of discouraged souls; surrounded by the true and the beautiful, they try to forget an ungrateful and degenerate party. Others, disciples of Sully, temper their strength by hard work in the fruitful study of sacred science, and become enthusiastic, absorbed husbandmen, in order to conceal their misanthropy. But what can they do? Fight all alone for a deserted cause? What can the best officers accomplish without soldiers?

You see, Valentine, I forget my own sorrows in thinking of our common woes; when I reflect upon the sad state of public affairs, I find Roger doubly culpable. Possessing so brilliant a mind, such superb talents, he could by his influence bring these young fools back to the path of honor. How unpardonable it is in him to lead them further astray by his dangerous example?

Oh, Valentine! I feel that I am not fitted to live in times like these. Everything displeases me. The people of past ages seemed unintelligent, impracticable; the people of the present day are coarse and hypocritical—the former understand nothing, the latter pervert everything. The former had not the attainments that I require, the latter have not the delicacy that I exact. The world is ugly; I have seen enough of it. It is sad to think of one so young as I, just entering upon life, having my head weighed down by the cares and disappointments of sixty years! For a blonde head this weight is very heavy!

What! in this grand world, not one noble being, not one elevated soul possessed of high aspirations and a holy respect for love!

For a young woman to own millions and be compelled to hoard them because she has no one to bestow them upon! To be rich, young, free, generous, and forced to live alone because no worthy partner can be found! . .

Valentine, is not this a sad case?

Now my anger is gone—I am only sad, but I am mortally sad. . . . I know not what to do. . . . Would I could fly to your arms! Ah! mother! my mother! why am I left to struggle all alone in this unfeeling world!

IRENE DE CHATEAUDUN.

XIII.

EDGAR DE MEILHAN *to the* PRINCE DE MONBERT,
Saint Dominique Street, Paris.

RICHEPORT, June 8th 18—.

SHE is here! Sound the trumpets, beat the drums!

The same day that you found Irene, I recovered Louise!

In making my tenth pilgrimage from Richeport to Pont de l'Arche, I caught a glimpse from afar of Madame Taverneau's plump face encased in a superb bonnet embellished with flaming ribbons! The drifting sea-weed and floating fruit which were the certain indication to Christopher Columbus of the presence of his long-dreamed-of land, did not make his heart bound with greater delight than mine at the sight of Madame Taverneau's bonnet! For that bonnet was the sign of Louise's return.

Oh! how charming thou didst appear to me then, frightful tulle cabbage, with thy flaunting strings like unto an elephant's ears, and thy enormous bows resembling those pompons with which horses' heads are decorated! How much dearer to me wert thou than the diadem of an empress, a vestal's fillet, the ropes of pearls twined among the jetty locks of Venice's loveliest patricians, or the richest head-dress of antique or modern art!

Ah, but Madame Taverneau was handsome! Her complexion, red as a beet, seemed to me fresh as a new-blown rose,—so the poets always say,—I could have embraced her resolutely, so happy was I.

The thought that Madame Taverneau might have returned alone flashed through my mind ere I reached the threshold, and I felt myself grow pale, but a glance through the half-open door drove away my terror. There, bending over her table, was Louise, rolling grains of rice in red sealing-wax in order to fill the interstices between the seals that she had gotten from me, and among which figured marvellously well your crest so richly and curiously emblazoned.

A slender thread of light falling upon the soft contour of her features, carved in cameo their pure and delicate outline. When she saw me a faint blush brightened her pallor like a drop of crimson in a cup of milk; she was charming, and so distinguished-looking that, putting aside the pencils, the vase of flowers, the colors and the glass of clear water beside her, I should never have dreamt that a simple screen-painter sat before me.

Isn't it strange, when so many fashionable women in the highest position look like apple-sellers or old-clothes women in full dress, that a girl in the humblest walks of life should have the air of a princess, in spite of her printed cotton gown!

With me, dear Roger, Louise Guérin the grisette has vanished; but Louise Guérin, a charming and fascinating creature whom any one would be proud to love, has taken her place. You know that with all my oddities, my wilfulness, my *Huronisms* as you call them, the slightest equivocal word, the least approach to a bold jest, uttered by feminine lips shocks me. Louise has never, in the many conversations that I have had with her, alarmed my captious modesty; and often the most innocent young girls, the virtuous mothers of a family, have made me blush up to my eyes. I am by no means so prudish; I discourse upon Trimalcion's feast and the orgies of the twelve Cæsars, but certain expressions, used by every one, never pass my lips; I imagine that I see toads and serpents drop from the tongues of those who speak them: only roses and pearls fall from Louise's lips. How many women have fallen in my eyes from the rank of a goddess to the condition of a fishwoman, by one word whose ignominy I might try in vain to make them understand!

I have told you all this, my dear Roger, so that you may see how from an ordinary railway adventure, a slight flirtation, has resulted a serious and genuine love. I treat myself and things with rough frankness, and closely scan my head and heart, and arrive at the same result—I am desperately in love with Louise. The result does not alarm me; I have never shrunk from happiness. It is my peculiar style of courage.

which is rarer than you imagine; I have seen men who would seek the bubble reputation even in the cannon's mouth, who had not the courage to be happy!

Since her return Louise appears thoughtful and agitated; a change has come over the spirit of her dream. It is evident that her journey has thrown new light upon her situation. Something important has taken place in her life. What is it? I neither know nor care to know. I accept Louise as I find her with her present surroundings. Perhaps absence has revealed to her, as it has to me, that another existence is necessary to her. This at least is certain, she is less shy, less reserved, more confiding; there is a tender grace in her manner unfelt before. When we walk in the garden, she leans upon my arm, instead of touching it with the tips of her fingers. Now, when I am with her, her cold reserve begins to thaw, and instead of going on with her work, as formerly, she rests her head on her hand and gazes at me with a dreamy fixedness singular to behold. She seems to be mentally deliberating something, and trying to come to a conclusion. May Eros, with his golden arrows, grant that it prove favorable to me! It will prove so, or human will has no power, and the magnetic fluid is an error!

We are sometimes alone, but that cursed door is never shut, and Madame Taverneau paces up and down outside, coming in at odd moments to enliven the conversation with a witticism, in which exercise the good woman, unhappily, thinks she excels. She fears that Louise, who is not accustomed to the usages of society, may tire me. I am neither a Nero nor a Caligula, but many a time have I mentally condemned the honest post-mistress to the wild beasts of the Circus!

To get Louise away from this room, whose architecture is by no means conducive to love-making, I contrived a boating party to the Andelys, with the respectable view of visiting the ruins of Richard Cœur-de-Lion's fortress. The ascent is extremely rough, for the donjon is poised, like an eagle's nest, upon the summit of a steep rock; and I counted upon Madame Taverneau, strangled in her Sunday stays, breathless, perspiring, red as a lobster put on hot-water diet, taking time half-way up the ascent to groan and fan herself with her handkerchief.

Alfred stopped by on his way from Havre, and for once in his life was in season. I placed the rudder in his hands, begging at the same time that he would spare me his fascinating smiles, winks and knowing glances. He promised to be a stock and kept his word, the worthy fellow!

A fresh breeze sprang up in time to take us up the river. We found Louise and Madame Taverneau awaiting us upon the pier, built a short time since in order to stem the rush of water from the bridge.

Proud of commanding the embarkation, Alfred established himself with Madame Taverneau, wrapped in a yellow shawl with a border of green flowers, in the stern. Louise and I, in order to balance the boat, seated ourselves in the bows.

The full sail made a sort of tent, and isolated us completely from our companions. Louise, with only a narrow canvas shaking in the wind between her and her chaperon, feeling no cause for uneasiness, was less reserved; a third party is often useful in the beginning of a love idyl. The most prudish woman in the world will grant slight favors when sure they cannot be abused.

Our boat glided through the water, leaving a fringe of silver in its wake. Louise had taken off her glove, and, leaning over the side, let the water flow in crystal cascades through her ivory fingers; her dress, which she gathered round her from the too free gambols of the wind, sculptured her beauty by a closer embrace. A few little wild flowers scattered their restless leaves over her bonnet, the straw of which, lit up by a bright sun-ray, shed around her a sort of halo. I sat at her feet, embracing her with my glance; bathing her in magnetic influences; surrounding her with an atmosphere of love! I called to my assistance all the powers of my mind and heart to make her love me and promise to be mine!

Softly I whispered to myself: "Come to my succor, secret forces of nature, spring, youth, delicate perfumes, bright rays! Let soft zephyrs play around her pure brow; flowers of love, intoxicate her with your searching odors; let the god of day mingle his golden beams with the purple of her veins; let all living, breathing things whisper in her ear that she is beautiful, only twenty, that I am young and that I love her!" Are poetical tirades and romantic declarations absolutely necessary to make a lovely woman rest her blushing brow upon a young man's shoulder?

My burning gaze fascinated her; she sat motionless under my glance. I felt my hope sparkle in my eyes; her eyelids slowly drooped; her arms sank at her side; her will succumbed to mine; aware of her growing weakness, she made a final effort, covered her eyes with her hand, and remained several minutes in that attitude in order to recover from the radiations of my will.

When she had, in a measure, recovered her self-possession, she turned her head towards the river-bank and called my attention to the charming effect of a cottage embosomed in trees, from which rickety steps, moss-grown and picturesquely studded with flowers, led down to the river. One of Isabey's delicious water-colors, dropped here without his signature. Louise—for art, no matter how humble, always expands the mind—has a taste for the beauties of nature, wanting in nearly her whole sex. A flower-stand filled with roses best pleases the majority of women, who cultivate a love of flowers in order to provoke anacreontic and obsolete comparisons from their antiquated admirers.

The banks of the Seine are truly enchanting. The graceful hills are studded with trees and waving corn-fields; here and there a rock peeps picturesquely forth; cottages and distant châteaux are betrayed by their glittering slate roofs; islets as wild as those of the South Sea rise on the bosom of the waters like verdure-clad rafts, and no Captain Cook has ever mentioned these Otaheites a half-day's journey from Paris.

Louise intelligently and feelingly admired the shading of the foliage, the water rippled by a slight breeze, the rapid flight of the kingfisher, the languid swaying to and fro of the water-lily, the little forget-me-nots opening their timid blue eyes to the morning sun, and all the thousand and one beauties dotted along the river's bank. I let her steep her soul in nature's loveliness, which could only teach her to love.

In about four hours we reached the Andelys, and after a light lunch of fresh eggs, cream, strawberries and cherries, we began the ascent to the fortress of the brave king Richard.

Alfred got along famously with Madame Taverneau, having completely dazzled her by an account of his high social acquaintance. During the voyage he had repeated more names than can be found in the Royal Almanac. The good post-mistress listened with respectful deference, delighted at finding herself in company with such a highly connected individual. Alfred, who is not accustomed, among us, to benevolent listeners, gave himself up to the delight of being able to talk without fear of interruption from jests and ironical puns. They had charmed each other.

The stronghold of Richard Cœur-de-Lion recalls, by its situation and architecture, the castles of the Rhine. The stone-work is so confounded with the rock that it is impossible to say where nature's work ends or man's work begins.

We climbed, Louise and I, in spite of the steep ascent, the loose stones, over the ramparts fallen to decay, the brushwood and all sorts of obstacles, to the foot of the mass of towers built one within another, which form the donjon-keep. Louise was obliged more than once, in scrambling up the rocks, to give me her hand and lean upon my shoulder. Even when the way was less rugged, she did not put aside her unconstrained and confiding manner; her timid and intense reserve began to soften a little.

Madame Taverneau, who is not a sylph, hung with all her weight to Alfred's arm, and what surprises me is that she did not pull it off.

We made our way through the under-brush, masses of rubbish and crumbling walls, to the platform of the massive keep, from whence we saw, besides the superb view, far away in the distance, Madame Taverneau's yellow shawl, shining through the foliage like a huge beetle.

At this height, so far above the world, intoxicated by the fresh air, her cheek dyed a deeper red, her hair loosened from its severe fastenings, Louise was dazzlingly and radiantly beautiful; her bonnet had fallen off and was only held by the ribbon strings; a handful of daisies escaped from her careless grasp.

"What a pity," said I, "that I have not a familiar spirit at my service! We should soon see the stones replaced, the towers rise from the grass where they have slept so long, and raise their heads in the sunlight; the drawbridge slide on its hinges, and men-at-arms in dazzling cuirasses pass and repass behind the battlements. You should sit beside me as my chatelaine, in the great hall, under a canopy emblazoned with armorial bearings, the centre of a brilliant retinue of ladies in waiting, archers and varlets. You should be the dove of this kite's nest!"

This fancy made her smile, and she replied: "Instead of amusing yourself in rebuilding the past, look at the magnificent scene stretched out before you."

In fact, the sky was gorgeous; the sun was sinking behind the horizon, in a hamlet of clouds, ruined and abandoned to the fury of the flames of sunset; the darkened hills were shrouded in violet tints; through the light mists of the valley the river shone at intervals like the polished surface of a Damascus blade. The blue smoke ascended from the chimneys of the village of Andelys, nestling at the foot of the mountain; the silvery tones of the bells ringing the Angelus came to us on the evening breeze; Venus shone soft and pure in the western sky. Madame Taverneau had not yet joined us; Alfred's fascinations had made her forget her companion.

Louise, uneasy at being so long separated from her chaperon, leaned over the edge of the battlement. A stone, which only needed the weight of a tired swallow to dislodge it, rolled from under Louise's foot, who, terribly frightened, threw herself in my arms. I held her for a moment pressed to my heart. She was very pale; her head was thrown back, the dizziness of lofty heights had taken possession of her.

"Do not let me fall; my head whirls!"

"Fear not," I replied; "I am holding you, and the spirit of the gulf shall not have you."

"Ouf! What an insane idea, to climb like cats over this old pile of stones!" cried Alfred, who had finally arrived, dragging after him Madame Taverneau, who with her shawl looked like a poppy in a corn-field. We left the tower and gained our boat. Louise threw me a tearful and grateful glance, and seated herself by Madame Taverneau. A tug-boat passed us; we hailed it; it threw us a rope, and in a few hours we were at Pont de l'Arche.

This is a faithful account of our expedition; it is nothing, and yet a great deal. It is sufficient to show me that I possess some influence over Louise; that my look fascinates her, my voice affects her, my touch agitates her; for one moment I held her trembling against my heart; she did not repulse me. It is true that by a little feminine Jesuitism, common enough, she might ascribe all this to vertigo, a sort of vertigo common to youth and love, which has turned more heads than all the preci pices of Mount Blanc!

What a strange creature is Louise! An inexplicable mixture of acute intelligence and virgin modesty, displaying at the same time an ignorance and information never imagined. These piquant contrasts make me admire her all the more. The day after to-morrow Madame Taverneau is going on business to Rouen. Louise will be alone, and I intend to repeat the donjon scene, with improvements and deprived of the inopportune appearance of Madame Taverneau's yellow shawl and the luckless Alfred's green hunting-dress. What delicious dreams will visit me to-night in my hammock at Richeport!

My next letter will begin, I hope, with this triumphant line of the Chevalier de Bertin:

"Elle est à moi, divinités du Pinde!"

Good-bye, my dear Roger. I wish you good luck in your search. Since you have once seen Irene, she cannot wear Gyges' ring. You may meet her again; but if you have to make your way through six Boyars, three Moldavians, eleven bronze statues, ten check-sellers, crush a multitude of King Charles spaniels, upset a crowd of fruit-stands, go straight as a bullet towards your beauty; seize her by the tip of her wing, politely but firmly, like a gendarme; for the Prince Roger de Monbert must not be the plaything of a capricious Parisian heiress.

EDGAR DE MEILHAN.

XIV.

IRENE DE CHATEAUDUN *to* MME. LA VICOMTESSE DE BRAIMES,
Hotel de la Prefecture, Grenoble (Isere).

PONT DE L'ARCHE, June 18th 18—.

I HAVE only time to send you a line with the box of ribbons. The trunk will go to-morrow by the stage. I would have sent it before, but the children's boots were not done. It is impossible to get anything done now—the storekeepers say they can't get workmen, the workmen say they can't get employment. Blanchard will be in Paris to superintend its packing. If you are not pleased with your things, especially the blue dress and mauve bonnet, I despair of ever satisfying you. I did not take your sashes to Mlle. *Vatelin.* It was Prince de Monbert's fault; in passing along the Boulevards I saw him talking to a gentleman—I turned into Panorama street—he followed me, and to elude him I went into the Chinese store. M. de Monbert remained outside; I bought some tea, and telling the woman I would send for it, went out by the opposite door which opens on Vivienne street. The Prince, who has been away from Paris for ten years, was not aware of this store having two exits, so in this way I escaped him. This hateful prince is also the cause of my returning here. The day after that wretched evening at the Odeon, I went to inquire about my cousin. There I found that Madame de Langeac had left Fontainebleau and gone to Madame de H.'s, where they are having private theatricals. She returns to Paris in ten days, where she begs me to wait for her. I also heard that M. de Monbert had had quite a scene with the porter on the same morning—insisting that he had seen me, and that he would not be put off by lying servants any longer; his language and manner quite shocked the household. The prospect of a visit from him filled me with fright. I returned to my garret—Madame Taverneau was anxiously waiting for my return, and carried me off without giving me any time for reflection; so I am here once more.

Perhaps you think that in this rural seclusion, under the shade of these willows, I ought to find tranquillity? Just the reverse. A new danger threatens me; I escape from a furious prince, to be ensnared by a delirious poet. I went away leaving M. de Meilhan gracious, gallant, but reasonable; I return to find him presuming, passionate, foolish. It makes me think that absence increases my attractiveness, and separation clothes me with new charms.

This devotion is annoying, and I am determined to nip it in the bud; it fills me with a horrible dread that in no way resembles the charming fear I have dreamed of. The young poet takes a serious view of the flattery I bestowed upon him only in order to discover what his friend had written about me; he has persuaded himself that I love him, and I despair of being able to dispel the foolish notion.

I have uselessly assumed the furious air of an angry Minerva, the majestic deportment of the Queen of England opening Parliament, the prudish, affected behavior of a school-mistress on promenade; all this only incites his hopes. If it were love it might be seductive and dangerous, but it is nothing more than magnetism. . . . You may laugh, but it is surely this and nothing else; he acts as if he were under some spell of fascination; he looks at me in a malevolent way that he thinks irresistible. . . . But I find it unendurable. I shall end by frankly telling him that in point of magnetism I am no longer free . . . "that I love another," as the vaudeville says, and if he asks who is this other, I shall smilingly tell him, "it is the famous disciple of Mesmer, Dr. Dupotet."

Yesterday his foolish behavior was very near causing my death. Alarmed by an embarrassing tête-à-tête in the midst of an old castle we were visiting, I mounted the window-sill in one of the towers to call Madame Taverneau, whom I saw at the foot of the hill; the stone on which I stood gave way, and if M. de Meilhan had not shown great presence of mind and caught me, I would have fallen down a precipice forty feet deep! Instant death would have been the result. Oh! how frightened I was! I tremble yet. My terror was so great that I would have fainted if I had had a little more confidence; but another fear made me recover from this. Fortunately I am going away from here, and this trifling will be over.

Yes, certainly I will accompany you to Geneva. Why can't we go as far as Lake Como? What a charming trip to take, and what comfort we will enjoy in my nice carriage! You must know that my travelling-carriage is a wonder; it is being entirely renovated, and directly it is finished, I will jump in it and fly to your arms. Of course you will ask what I am to do with a travelling-carriage—I who have never made but one journey in my life, and that from the Marais to the Faubourg Saint Honoré? I will reply, that I bought this carriage because I had the opportunity; it is a chef-d'œuvre. There never was a handsomer carriage made in London. It was invented—and you will soon see what a splendid invention it is—for an immensely rich English lady who is always travelling, and who is greatly distressed at having to sell it, but she believes herself pursued by an audacious young lover whom she wishes to get rid of, and as he has always recognised her by her carriage, she parts with it in order to put him off her track. She is an odd sort of woman whom they call Lady Penock; she resembles Levassor in his English rôles; that is to say, she is a caricature. Levassor would not dare to be so ridiculous.

Good-bye, until I see you. When I think that in one month we shall be together again, I forget all my sorrows.

IRENE DE CHATEAUDUN.

XV.

Roger de Monbert *to* Monsieur de Meilhan,
Pont-de-l'Arche (Eure).

Paris, June 19th 18—.

It is useless to slander the police; we are obliged to resort to them in our dilemmas; the police are everywhere, know everything, and are infallible. Without the police Paris would go to ruin; they are the hidden fortification, the invisible rampart of the capital; its numerous agents are the detached forts. Fouché was the Vauban of this wonderful system, and since Fouché's time, the art has been steadily approaching perfection. There is to-day, in every dark corner of the city an eye that watches over our fifty-four gates, and an ear that hears the pulsations of all the streets, those great arteries of Paris.

The incapacity of my own agents making me despair of discovering anything; I went to the Polyphemus of Jerusalem street, a giant whose ever open eye watches every Ulysses. They told me in the office—Return in three days.

Three centuries that I had to struggle through! How many centuries I have lived during the last month!

The police! Why did not this luminous idea enter my mind before?

At this office of public secrets they said to me: Mlle. de Chateaudun left Paris five days ago. On the 12th she passed the night at Sens; she then took the route to Burgundy; changed horses at Villevallier, and on the 14th stopped at the château of Madame de Lorgeville, seven miles from Avallon.

The particularity of this information startled me. What wonderful clock-work! What secret wheels! What intelligent mechanism! It is the machine of Marly applied to a human river. At Rome a special niche would have been devoted to the goddess of Police.

What a lesson to us! How circumspect it should make us! Our walls are diaphanous, our words are overheard; our steps are watched . . . everything said and done reaches by secret informers and invisible threads the central office of Jerusalem street. It is enough to make one tremble !!!

At the château of Mad. de Lorgeville !

I walked along repeating this sentence to myself, with a thousand variations: At the château of Mad. de Lorgeville.

After a decennial absence, I know nobody in Paris—I am just as much of a stranger as the ambassador of Siam . . . Who knows Mad. de Lorgeville ? M. de Balaincourt is the only person in Paris who can give me the desired information—he is a living court calendar. I fly to see M. de Balaincourt.

This oracle answers me thus: Mad. de Lorgeville is a very beautiful woman, between twenty-four and twenty-six years of age. She possesses a magnificent *mezzo-soprano* voice, and twenty thousand dollars income. She learnt miniature painting from Mad. Mirbel, and took singing lessons from Mad. Damoveau. Last winter she sang that beautiful duo from Norma, with the Countess Merlin, at a charity concert.

I requested further details.

Madame de Lorgeville is the sister of the handsome Léon de Varèzes.

Oh ! ray of light ! glimmer of sun through a dark cloud !

The handsome Léon de Varèzes ! The ugly idea of troubadour beauty ! A fop fashioned by his tailor, and who passes his life looking at his figure reflected in four mirrors as shiny and cold as himself !

I pressed M. de Balaincourt's hand and once again plunged into the vortex of Paris.

If the handsome Léon were only hideous I would feel nothing but indifference towards him, but he has more sacred rights to my hatred, as you will see.

Three months ago this handsome Léon made a proposal of marriage to Mlle. de Chateaudun—she refused him. This is evidently a preconcerted plan ; or it is a ruse. The handsome Léon had a lady friend well known by everybody but himself, and he has deferred this marriage in order to gild, after the manner of Ruolz, his last days of bachelorhood; meanwhile Mlle. de Chateaudun received her liberty, and during this truce I have played the rôle of suitor. Either of these conjectures is probable—both may be true—one is sufficient to bring about a catastrophe!

This fact is certain, the handsome Léon is at the waters of Ems enjoying his expiring hours of single-blessedness in the society of his painted friend, and his family are keeping Mlle. de Chateaudun at the Château de Lorgeville till the season at Ems is over. In a few days the handsome Léon, on pretence of important business, will leave his Dulcinea, and, considering himself freed from an unlawful yoke, will come to the Chateau de Lorgeville to offer his innocent hand and pure homage to Mlle. de Chateaudun. In whatever light the matter is viewed, I am a dupe—a butt! I know well that people say: "*Prince Roger is a good fellow.*" With this reputation a man is exposed to all the feline wickedness of human nature, but when once aroused "the good fellow" is transformed, and all turn pale in his presence.

No, I can never forgive a woman who holds before me a picture of bliss, and then dashes it to the ground—she owes me this promised happiness, and if she tries to fly from me I have a right to cry "stop thief."

Ah! Mlle. de Chateaudun, you thought you could break my heart, and leave me nothing to cherish but the phantom of memory! Well! I promise you another ending to your play than you looked for! We will meet again!

Stupid idiot that I was, to think of writing her an apology to vindicate my innocent share of the scene at the Odeon! Vindication well spared! How she would have laughed at my honest candor! . . . She shall not have an opportunity of laughing! Dear Edgar, in writing these disconsolate lines I have lost the calmness that I had imposed upon myself when I began my letter. I feel that I am devoured by that internal demon that bears a woman's name in the language of love—jealousy! Yes, jealousy fills my soul with bitterness, encircles my brow with a band of iron, and makes me feel a frenzied desire to murder some fellow-being! During my travels I lost the tolerant manners of civilization. I have imbibed the rude cruelty of savages—my jealousy is filled with the storms and fire of the equator.

What do you pale effeminate young men know of jealousy? Is not your professor of jealousy the actor who dashes about on the stage with a paste-board sword?

I have studied the monster under other masters; tigers have taught me how to manage this passion.

Dear Edgar, once night overtook us amidst the ruins of the fort that formerly defended the mouth of the river Caveri in Bengal. It was a dark night illumined by a single star like the lamp of the subterranean temple of Elephanta. But this lone star was sufficient to throw light upon the formidable duel that took place before us upon the sloping bank of the ruined fort.

It was the season of love . . . how sweet is the sound of these words!

A tawny monster with black spots, belonging to the fair sex of her noble race, was calmly quenching her thirst in the river Caveri—after she had finished drinking she squatted on her hind feet and stretched her forepaws in front of her breast—sphinx-like—and luxuriously rubbed her head in and out among the soft leaves scattered on the riverside.

At a little distance the two lovers watched—not with their eyes but with their nostrils and ears, and their sharp growl was like the breath of the khamsin passing through the branches of the euphorbium and the nopal. The two monsters gradually reached the paroxysm of amorous rage; they flattened their ears, sharpened their claws, twisted their tails like flexible steel, and emitted sparks of fire from eyes and skin.

During this prelude the tigress stretched herself out with stoical indifference, pretending to take no interest in the scene

—as if she were the only animal of her race in the desert. At intervals she would gaze with delight at the reflected image of her grace and beauty in the river Caveri.

A roar that seemed to burst from the breast of a giant crushed beneath a rock, echoed through the solitude. One of the tigers described an immense circle in the air and then fell upon the neck of his rival. The two tawny enemies stood up on their hind legs, clenching each other like two wrestlers, body to body, muzzle to muzzle, teeth to teeth, and uttering shrill, rattling cries that cut through the air like the clashing of steel blades. Ordinary huntsmen would have fired upon this monstrous group. We judged it more noble to respect the powerful hate of this magnificent love. As usual the aggressor was the strongest; he threw his rival to the ground, crushed him with his whole weight, tore him with his claws, and then fastening his long teeth in his victim's throat, laid him dead upon the grass—uttering, as he did so, a cry of triumph that rang through the forest like the clarion of a conqueror.

The tigress remained in the same spot, quietly licking her paw, and when it was quite wet rubbed it over her muzzle and ears with imperturbable serenity and charming coquetry.

This scene contained a lesson for both sexes, my dear Edgar. When nature chooses our masters she chooses wisely.

Heaven preserve you from jealousy! I do not mean to honor by this name that fickle, unjust, common-place sentiment that we feel when our vanity assumes the form of love. The jealousy that gnaws my heart is a noble and legitimate passion. Not to avenge one's self is to give a premium of encouragement to wicked deeds. The forgiveness of wrongs and injuries puts certain men and women too much at their ease. Vengeance is necessary for the protection of society.

Dear Edgar, tell me of your love; fear not to wound me by a picture of your happiness; my heart is too sympathetic for that. Tell me the traits that please you most in the object of your tenderness. Let your soul expand in her sweet smiles—

revel in the intoxicating bliss of those long happy talks filled with the enchanting grace and music of a first love.

After reading my letter, remove my gloomy picture from your mind—forget me quietly; let not a thought of my misery mar your present happiness.

I intend to honor the handsome Léon by devoting my personal attention to his future fate.

ROGER DE MONBERT.

XVI.

EDGAR DE MEILHAN *to the* PRINCE DE MONBERT,
St. Dominique Street (Paris).

RICHEPORT, June 23d 18—.

YOU place a confidence in the police worthy the prince you are, dear Roger; you rely upon their information with a faith that surprises and alarms me. How do you expect the police to know anything concerning honest people? Never having watched them, being too much occupied with scoundrels, they do not know how to go about it. Spies and detectives are generally miserable wretches, their name even is a gross insult in our language; they are acquainted with the habits and movements of thieves, whose dens and haunts they frequent; but what means have they of fathoming the whimsical motives of a high-born young girl? Their forte is in making a servant drunk, bribing a porter, following a carriage or standing sentinel before a door. If Mademoiselle de Chateaudun has gone away to avoid you, she will naturally suppose that you will endeavor to follow her. Of course, she has taken every precaution to preserve her incognita—changing her name, for instance—which would be sufficient to mystify the police, who, until applied to by you, have had no object in watching her movements. The proof that the police are mistaken is the exactitude of the information that they have given you. It is too much like the depositions of witnesses in a criminal trial, who say: "Two years ago, at thirty-three minutes and five seconds after nine o'clock in the evening, I met, in the dark, a slender man, whose features I could not distinguish, who wore olive-green pantaloons, with a brownish tinge." I am very much afraid that your expedition into Burgundy will be of none avail, and that, haggard-eyed and morose, you will drop in upon a quiet family utterly amazed at your domiciliary visit.

My dear Prince, endeavor to recollect that you are not in India; the manners of the Sunda Isles do not prevail here, and

I feared from your letter some desperate act which would put you in the power of your friends, the police. In Europe we have professors of æsthetics, Sanscrit, Slavonic, dancing and fencing, but professors of jealousy are not authorized. There is no chair in the College of France for wild beasts; lessons expressed in roarings and in blows from savage paws do very well for the fabulous tiger city of Java legends. If you are jealous, try to deprive your rival of the railroad grant which he was about to obtain, or ruin him in his electoral college by spreading the report that, in his youth, he had written a volume of sonnets. This is constitutional revenge which will not bring you before the bar of justice. The courts now-a-days are so tricky that they might give you some trouble even for suppressing such an insipid fop as Léon de Varèzes. Tigers, whatever you may say, are bad instructors. With regard to tigers, we only tolerate cats, and then they must have velvet paws.

These counsels of moderation addressed to you, I have profited by myself, for, in another way, I have reached a fine degree of exasperation. You suspect, of course, that Louise Guérin is at the bottom of it, for a woman is always at the bottom of every man's madness. She is the leaven that ferments all our worst passions.

Madame Taverneau set out for Rouen; I went to see Louise, my heart full of joy and hope. I found her alone, and at first thought that the evening would be decisive, for she blushed high on seeing me. But who the deuce can count upon women! I left her the evening before, sweet, gentle and confiding; I found her cold, stern, repelling and talking to me as if she had never seen me before. Her manner was so convincing that nothing had passed between us, that I found it necessary to take a rapid mental survey of all the occurrences of our expedition to the Andelys to prove to myself that I was not somebody else. I may have a thousand faults, but vanity is not among them. I rarely flatter myself, consequently I am not prone to believe that every one is thunder-struck, in the language of the writers of the past century, on beholding me. My interpretation of glances, smiles, tones of the voice are generally very faithful; I do not pass over expressions that displease me. I put this interpretation upon Louise's conduct. I do not feel an insuperable dislike to M. Edgar de Meilhan. Sure of the meaning of my text, I acted upon it, but Louise assumed such imposing and royal airs, such haughty and disdainful poses, that unless I resorted to violence I felt I could obtain nothing from her. Rage, instead of love, possessed me; my hands clenched convulsively, driving the nails into my flesh. The scene would have turned into a struggle. Fortunately, I reflected that such emphasized declarations of love, with the greater part of romantic and heroic actions, were not admitted in the Code.

I left abruptly, lest the following elegant announcement should appear in the police gazettes: "Mr. Edgar de Meilhan, landed proprietor, having made an attack upon Madame Louise Guérin, screen-painter, &c."—for I felt the strongest desire to strangle the object of my devotion, and I think I should have done so had I remained ten minutes longer.

Admire, dear Roger, the wisdom of my conduct, and endeavor to imitate it. It is more commendable to control one's passions than an army, and it is more difficult.

My wrath was so great that I went to Mantes to see Alfred! To open the door of paradise and then shut it in my face, spread before me a splendid banquet and prevent me from sitting down to it, promise me love and then offer me prudery, is an infamous, abominable and even indelicate act. Do you know, dear Roger, that I just escaped looking like a goose; the rage that possessed me gave a tragic expression to my features, which alone saved me from ridicule! Such things we never forgive a woman, and Louise shall pay me yet!

I swear to you that if a woman of my own rank had acted thus towards me, I should have crushed her without mercy; but Louise's humble position restrained me. I feel a pity for the weak which will be my ruin; for the weak are pitiless towards the strong.

Poor Alfred must be an excellent fellow not to have thrown

me out of the window. I was so dull with him, so provoking, so harsh, so scoffing, that I am astonished that he could endure me for two minutes. My nerves were in such a state of irritation that I beheaded with my whip more than five hundred poppies along the road. I who never have committed an assault upon any foliage, whose conscience is innocent of the murder of a single flower! For a moment I had a notion to ask a catafalque of the romantic Marquise. You may judge from that the disordered state of my faculties and my complete moral prostration.

At last, ashamed of abusing Alfred's hospitality in such a manner, and feeling incapable of being anything else than irritable, cross-grained and intractable, I returned to Richeport, to be as gloomy and disagreeable as I pleased.

Here, dear Roger, I pause—I take time, as the actors say; it is worth while. As fluently as you may read hieroglyphics, and explain on the spot the riddles of the sphinx, you can never guess what I found at Richeport, in my mother's room! A white black-bird? a black swan? a crocodile? a megalonyx? Priest John or the amorabaquin? No, something more enchantingly improbable, more wildly impossible. What was it? I will tell you, for a hundred million guesses would never bring you nearer the truth.

Near the window, by my mother's side, sat a young woman, bending over an embroidery frame, threading a needle with red worsted. At the sound of my voice she raised her head and I recognised—Louise Guérin!

At this unexpected sight, I stood stupified, like Pradon's Hippolyte.

To see Louise Guérin quietly seated in my mother's room, was as electrifying as if you, on going home some morning, were to find Irene de Chateaudun engaged in smoking one of your cigars. Did some strange chance, some machiavellian combination introduce Louise at Richeport? I shall soon know.

What a queer way to avoid men, to take up one's abode among them! Only prudes have such ideas. At any rate it is a gross insult to my powers of fascination. I am not such a patriarch as all that! My head still counts a few hairs, and I can walk very well without a cane!

What does it matter, after all? Louise lives under the same roof with me, my mother treats her in the most gracious manner, like an equal. And, indeed, one would be deceived by her; she seems more at her ease here than at Madame Taverneau's, and what would be a restraint on a woman of her class, on the contrary gives her more liberty. Her manners have become charming, and I often ask myself if she is not the daughter of one of Madame de Meilhan's friends. With wonderful tact she immediately put herself in unison with her surroundings; women alone can quickly become acclimated in a higher sphere. A man badly brought up always remains a booby. Any danseuse taken from the foot-lights of the Opera by the caprice of a great lord, can be made a fine lady. Nature has doubtless provided for these sudden elevations of fortune by bestowing upon women that marvellous facility of passing from one position to another without exhibiting surprise or being thrown out of their element. Put Louise into a carriage having a countess's crown upon the panel of the door, and no one would doubt her rank. Speak to her, and she would reply as if she had had the most brilliant education. The auspicious opening of a flower transplanted into a soil that suits it, shone through Louise's whole being. My manner towards her partakes of a tenderer playfulness, a more affectionate gallantry. After all, Richeport is better than Pont de l'Arche, for there is nothing like fighting on your own ground.

Come then, my friend, and be a looker-on at the courteous tournay. We expect Raymond every day; we have all sorts of paradoxes to convert into truths; your insight into such matters might assist us. *A bientôt.*

EDGAR DE MEILHAN.

XVII.

IRENE DE CHATEAUDUN *to* MME. LA VICOMTESSE DE BRAIMES,
Hotel of the Prefecture, Grenoble (Isère).

RICHEPORT, June 29th 18—.

I AM at Richeport, at Madame de Meilhan's house! . . . This astonishes you, . . . so it does me; you don't understand it, . . . neither do I. The fact is, that when you can't control events, the best thing to be done is to let events control you.

On Sunday I went to hear mass in the beautiful church at Pont de l'Arche, a splendid ruin that looks like a heap of stony lacework, lovely guipure torn to pieces; while I was there a lady came in and sat beside me; it was Madame de Meilhan. I recognised her at once, having been accustomed to seeing her every Sunday at mass. As it was late, and the services were almost ended, I thought it very natural that she should sit by me to avoid walking the length of the aisle to reach her own pew, so I continued to read my prayers without paying any attention to her, but she fastened her eyes upon me in such a peculiar way that I, in my turn, felt compelled to look up at her, and was startled by the alteration of her face; suddenly she tottered and fell fainting on Madame Taverneau's shoulder. She was taken out of the church, and the fresh air soon restored her to consciousness. She seemed agitated when she saw me near her, but the interest I showed in her sickness seemed to reassure her; she gracefully thanked me for my kind attention, and then looked at me in a way that was very embarrassing. I invited her to return with me to Madame Taverneau's and rest herself; she accepted the offer, and Madame Taverneau carried her off with great pomp. There Madame de Meilhan explained how she had walked alone from Richeport in spite of the excessive heat, at the risk of making herself ill, because her son had taken the coachman and horses and left home suddenly that morning without saying where he was going. As she said this she looked at me significantly. I bore these questioning looks with proud calmness. I must tell you that the evening before, M de Meilhan had called on me during the absence of Madame Taverneau and her husband. The danger of the situation inspired me. I treated him with such coldness, I reached a degree of dignity so magnificent that the great poet finally comprehended there are some glaciers inaccessible, even to him. He left me, furious and disconsolate, but I do him the justice to say that he was more disconsolate than furious. This real sorrow made me think deeply. If he loved me seriously, how culpable was my conduct! I had been too coquettish towards him; he could not know that this coquetry was only a ruse; that while appearing to be so devoted to him my whole mind was filled with another. Sincere love should always be respected; one is not compelled to share it, but then one has no right to insult it.

The uneasiness of Madame de Meilhan; her conduct towards me—for I was certain she had purposely come late to mass and taken a seat by me for the purpose of speaking to me and finding out what sort of a person I was—the uneasiness of this devoted mother was to me a language more convincing of the sincerity of her son's sentiments than all the protestations of love he could have uttered in years. A mother's anxiety is an unmistakable symptom; it is more significant than all others. The jealousy of a rival is not so certain an indication; distrustful love may be deceived, but maternal instinct *never* is. Now, to induce a woman of Madame de Meilhan's spirit and character to come agitated and trembling to see me, . . . why, I can say it without vanity, her son must be madly in love, and she wished at all costs either to destroy or cure this fatal passion that made him so unhappy.

When she arose to leave, I asked permission to walk back with her to Richeport, as she was not well enough to go so far alone; she eagerly accepted my offer, and as we went along, conversing upon indifferent subjects, her uneasiness gradually disappeared; our conversation seemed to relieve her mind of its heavy burden.

It happened that truth spoke for itself, as it always does, but unfortunately is not always listened to. By my manners, the tone of my voice, my respectful but dignified politeness—which in no way resembled Mad. Taverneau's servile and obsequious eagerness to please, her humble deference being that of an inferior to a superior, whilst mine was nothing more than that due to an old lady from a young one—by these shades insignificant to the generality of people, but all revealing to an experienced eye, Mad. de Meilhan at once divined everything, that is to say, that I was her equal in rank, education and nobility of soul; she knew it, she felt it. This fact admitted, one thing remained uncertain; why had I fallen from my rank in society? Was it through misfortune or error? This was the question she was asking herself.

I knew enough of her projects for the future, her ambition as a mother, to decide which of the two suppositions would alarm her most. If I were a light, trifling woman, as she every now and then seemed to hope, her son was merely engaged in a flirtation that would have no dangerous result; if on the contrary I was an honorable woman, which she evidently feared might be the case, her son's future was ruined, and she trembled for the consequences of this serious passion. Her perplexity amused me. The country around us was superb, and as we walked along I went into ecstasies over the beauty of the scenery and the lovely tints of the sky; she would smile and think: "She is only an artist, an adventuress—I am saved; she will merely be Edgar's friend, and keep him all the winter at Richeport." Alas! it is a great pity that she is not rich enough to spend the winter in Paris with Edgar; she seems miserable at being separated from him for months at a time.

At a few yards from the châteaux a group of pretty children chasing a poor donkey around a little island attracted my attention.

" That island formerly belonged to the Richeport estate," said Mad. de Meilhan; "so did those large meadows you see down below; the height of my ambition is to buy them back, but to do this Edgar must marry an heiress."

This word troubled me, and Mad. de Meilhan seemed annoyed. She evidently thought: "She is an honest woman, and wants to marry Edgar, I fear." I took no notice of her sudden coldness of manner, but thought to myself: How delightful it would be to carry out these ambitious plans, and gratify every wish of this woman's heart! I have but to utter one word, ana not only would she have this island and these meadows, but she would possess all this beautiful forest. Oh! how sweet would it be to feel that you are a small Providence on earth, able to penetrate and instantly gratify the secret wishes of people you like! Valentine, I begin to distrust myself; a temptation like this is too dangerous for a nature like mine; I feel like saying to this noble, impoverished lady: here, take these meadows, woods and islands that you so tenderly sigh for—I could also say to this despairing young poet: here, take this woman that you so madly love, marry her and be happy . . . without remembering that this woman is myself; without stopping to ask if this happiness I promise him will add to my own.

Generosity is to me dangerously attractive! How I would love to make the fortune of a noble poet! I am jealous of these foreigners who have lately given us such lessons in generosity. I would be so happy in bestowing a brilliant future upon one who chose and loved me in my obscurity, but to do this love is necessary, and my heart is broken—dead! I have no love to give.

Then again, M. de Meilhan has so much originality of character, and I admit only originality of mind. He puts his horse in his chamber, which is an original idea, to be sure; but I think horses had better be kept in the stable, where they would certainly be more comfortable. And these dreadful poets are such positive beings! Poets are not poetical, my dear. . . . . Edgar has become romantic since he has been in love with me, but I think it is an hypocrisy, and I mistrust his love.

Edgar is undeniably a talented, superior man, and captivating, as the beautiful Marquise de R. has proved; but I fail to recognise in his love the ideal I dreamed of. It is not the expression of an eye that he admires, it is the fine shape of the lids, limpid pupils; it is not the ingenuous grace of a smile that pleases him, it is the regularity of the lines, the crimson of the lips; to him beauty of soul adds no charm to a lovely face. Therefore, this love that a word of mine can render legitimate, frightens me as if it were a guilty passion; it makes me uneasy and timid. I know you will ridicule me when I say that upon me this passionate poet has the same effect as women abounding in imagination and originality of mind have upon men, who admire but never marry them. He has none of that affectionate gravity so necessary in a husband. On every subject our ideas differ; this different way of seeing things would cause endless disputes between us, or what is sadder yet, mutual sacrifices. Everybody adores the charming Edgar, I say Edgar, for it is by this name I daily hear him praised. I wish I could love him too! He was astonished to find me at his mother's house yesterday. Since my first visit to Richeport, Mad. de Meilhan would not allow a single day to pass without my seeing her; each day she contrived a new pretext to attract me; a piece of tapestry work to be designed, a view of the Abbey to be painted, a new book to read aloud or some music to try; the other evening it was raining torrents when I was about leaving and she insisted upon my staying all night; now she wishes me to remain for her birthday, which is on the 5th; she continues to watch me closely. Mad. Taverneau has been questioned—the mute, Blanchard, has been tortured. . . Mad. Taverneau replied that she had known me for three years and that during this time I had never ceased to mourn for the late Albert Guérin; in her zeal she added that he was a very deserving young man! My good Blanchard contented herself with saying that I was worth more than Mad. de Meilhan and all of her family put together. While they study me I study them. There is no danger in my remaining at Richeport. Edgar respects his mother—she watches over me. If necessary, I will tell her everything. . . She speaks kindly of Mlle. de Chateaudun—she defends me. . . How I laughed to myself this morning! I heard that M. de Monbert had secretly applied to the police to discover my whereabouts and the police sent him to join me at Burgundy! . . What could have made any one think I was there? At whose house will he go to seek me? and whom will he find instead of me? However, I may be there before long if my cousin will travel by way of Macon. She will not be ready to start before next week.

Oh! I am so anxious to see you again! Do not go to Geneva without me.

IRENE DE CHATEAUDUN.

XVIII.

Roger de Monbert *to* Monsieur Edgar de Meilhan,
Pont de l'Arche (Eure).

Paris, July 2d 18—.

Do you believe, my dear Edgar, that it is easy to live when the age of love is passed? Verily one must be able to love his whole lifetime if he wishes to live an enchanted life, and die a painless death. What a seductive game! what unexpected luck! How many moments delightfully employed! Each day has its particular history; at night we delight in telling it over to ourselves, and indulge in the wildest conjectures as to what will be the events of each to-morrow. The reality of to-day defeats the anticipations of yesterday. We hope one moment and despair the next—now dejected, now elated. We alternate between death and blissful life.

The other morning at nine o'clock we stopped at the stage-office at Sens for ten minutes. I went into the hotel and questioned everybody, and found they had seen many young ladies of the age, figure and beauty of Mlle. de Chateaudun.

Happy people they must be!

However, I only asked all these questions to amuse myself during the ten minutes' relay. My mind was at rest—for the police are infallible; everything will be explained at the Château de Lorgeville. I stopped my carriage some yards from the gate, got out and walked up the long avenue, being concealed by the large trees through which I caught glimpses of the château.

It was a large symmetrical building—a stone quadrangle, heavily topped off by a dark slate roof, and a dejected-looking weathercock that rebelled against the wind and declined to move.

All the windows in the front of the house were tear-stained at the base by the winter rains.

A modern entrance, with double flights of steps decorated by four vases containing four dead aloe-stems buried in straw, betrayed the cultivated taste of the handsome Léon.

I expected to see the shadow of a living being. . . . No human outline broke the tranquil shade of the trees.

An accursed dog, man's worst enemy, barked furiously, and made violent efforts to break his rope and fly at me. . . . I hope he is tied with a gordian knot if he wishes to see the setting sun!

Finally a gardener enjoying a sinecure came to enliven this landscape without a garden; he strolled down the avenue with the nonchalance of a workman paid by the handsome Léon.

I am able to distinguish among the gravest faces those that can relax into a smile at the sight of gold. The gardener passed before me, and after he had bestowed upon me the expected smile, I said to him:

"Is this Mad. de Lorgeville's château?"

He made an affirmative sign. Once more I bowed to the genius of the Jerusalem street goddess.

I said to the gardener in a solemn tone: "Here is a letter of the greatest importance; you must hand it to Mlle. de Chateaudun when she is alone." I then showed him my purse and said: "After that, this money is yours."

"The sweet young lady!" said the gardener, walking off towards the château with the gold in one hand, the letter in the other, and the purse in his eye—"The good young lady! it is a long time since she has received a love-letter."

I said to myself, The handsome Léon does not indulge in letter-writing—he has a good reason for that.

The following is the letter carried by the gardener to the chateau:—

"Mademoiselle,—

"Desperate situations justify desperate measures. I am willing to believe that I am still, by your desire, undergoing a terrible ordeal, but I judge myself sufficiently tried.

"I am ready for everything except the misery of losing you My last sane idea is uttered in this warning.

"I must see you; I must speak to you.

"Do not refuse me a few moments' conversation—Mademoiselle, in the name of Heaven save me! save yourself!

"There is in the neighborhood of the château some farm-house, or shady grove. Name any spot where I can meet you in an hour. I am awaiting your answer. . . . After an hour has passed I will wait for nothing more in this world."

The gardener walked along with the nonchalance of the man of the Georgics, as if meditating upon the sum of happiness contained in a piece of gold. I looked after him with that resignation we feel as the end of a great trial approaches.

He was soon lost to view, and in the distance I heard a door open and shut.

In a few minutes Mlle. Chateaudun would be reading my letter. I read it over in my own mind, and rapidly conjectured the impression each word would make upon her heart.

Through the thick foliage where I was concealed, I had a confused view of one wing of the chateau; the wall appeared to be covered with geeen tapestry torn in a thousand places. I could distinguish nothing clearly at a distance of twenty yards. Finally I saw approaching a graceful figure clad in white—and through the trees I caught sight of a blue scarf—a muslin dress and blue scarf—nothing more, and yet my heart stood still! My sensations at this moment are beyond analyzation. I felt an emotion that a man in love will comprehend at once. . . . A muslin dress fluttering under the trees where the fountains ripple and the birds sing! Is there a more thrilling sight?

I stood with one foot forward on the gravel-path, and with folded arms and bowed head I waited. I saw the scarf fringe before seeing the face. I looked up, and there stood before me a lovely woman . . . but it was not Irene! . . .

It was Mad. de Lorgeville. She knew me and I recognised her, having known her before her marriage. She still possessed the beauty of her girlhood, and marriage had perfected her loveliness by adorning her with that fascinating grace that is wanting even in Raphael's madonnas.

A peal of merry laughter rooted me to the spot and changed the current of my ideas. The lady was seized with such a fit of gayety that she could scarcely speak, but managed to gasp out my name and title in broken syllables. Like a great many men, I can stand much from women that I am not in love with. . . . I stood with arms crossed and hat off, waiting for an explanation of this foolish reception. After several attempts, Mad. de Lorgeville succeeded in making her little speech. After this storm of laughter there was still a ripple through which I could distinguish the following words, although I did not understand them :—

"Excuse me, monsieur, . . . but if you knew . . . when you see . . . but she must not see my foolish merriment, . . . she cherishes the fancy that she is still young, . . . like all women who are no longer so, . . . give me your arm, . . . we were at table . . . we always keep a seat for a chance visitor . . . One does not often meet with an adventure like this except in novels. . . ."

I made an effort to assume that calmness and boldness that saved my life the day I was made prisoner on the inhospitable coast of Borneo, and the old Arab king accused me of having attempted the traffic of gold dust—a capital crime—and said to the fair young châtelaine :

"Madame, there is not much to amuse one in the country; gayety is a precious thing; it cannot be bought; happy is he who gives it. I congratulate myself upon being able to present it to you. Can you not give me back half of it, madame?"

"Yes, monsieur, come and take it yourself," said Madame de Lorgeville; "but you must use it with discretion before witnesses."

"I can assure you, madame, that I have not come to your château in search of gayety. Allow me to escort you to the door and then retire."

"You are my prisoner, monsieur, and I shall not grant your request. The arrival of the Prince de Monbert is a piece of good fortune. My husband and I will not be ungrateful to the good genius that brought you here. We shall keep you."

"One moment, madame," said I, stopping in front of the château; "I accept the happiness of being retained by you; but will you be good enough to name the persons I am to meet here?"

"They are all friends of M. de Monbert."

"Friends are the very people I dread, madame."

"But they are all women."

"Women I dread most of all."

"Ah! monsieur, it is quite evident that you have been among savages for ten years."

"Savages are the only beings I am not afraid of!"

"Alas! monsieur, I have nothing in that line to offer you. This evening I can show you some neighbors who resemble the tribes of the Tortoise of the Great Serpent—these are the only natives I can dispose of. At present you will only see my husband, two ladies who are almost widows, and a young lady" . . . . here Mad. de Lorgeville was seized with a new fit of laughter . . . finally she continued: "A young lady whose name you will know later."

"I know it already, madame."

"Perhaps you do . . . to-morrow our company will be increased by two persons, my brother." . .

"The handsome Léon!"

"Ah you know him! . . . My brother Léon and his wife." . . .

I started so violently that I dropped Mad. de Lorgeville's arm—she looked frightened, and I said in a painfully constrained voice:

"And his wife . . . . Mad. de Varèzes? . . . . Ah! I did not know that M. de Varèzes was married."

"My brother was married a month ago," said Mad. Lorgeville. "He married Mlle. de Bligny."

"Are you certain of that, madame?"

This question was asked in a voice and accompanied by an expression of countenance that would have made a painter or musician desperate, even were they Rossini or Delacroix.

Mad. de Lorgeville, alarmed a second time by my excited manner, looked at me with commiseration, as if she thought me crazy! Certainly neither my face nor manner indicated sanity.

"You ask if I am sure my brother is married!" said Mad. de Lorgeville with petrified astonishment. "You are surely jesting?"

"Yes, madame, yes," said I, with an exuberance of gayety, "it is a joke . . . . I understand it all . . . I comprehend everything . . . that is to say—I understand nothing . . . but your brother, the excellent Léon de Varèzes, is married—that is all I wanted to know. . . What a very handsome young man he is! . . I suppose, madame, that you opened my note without reading the address . . . or did Mlle. de Chateaudun send you here to meet me?"

"Mlle. de Chateaudun is not here . . . . excuse this silly laughter . . . . the gardener gave your note to one of my guests . . . . a young lady of sixty-five summers . . . Who by the strangest coincidence is named Mlle. de Chantverdun . . . Now you can account for my amusement . . . Mlle. de Chantverdun is a canoness. She read your letter, and wished for once in her life to enjoy uttering a shriek of alarm and faint at the sight of a love letter; so come monsieur," said Mad. de Lorgeville, smilingly leading me towards the house, "come and make your excuses to Mlle. de Chantverdun, who has recovered her senses and sent me to her rendezvous."

Involuntarily, my dear Edgar, I indulged in this short monologue after the manner of the old romancers: O tender love! passion full of intoxication and torment! love that kills and resuscitates! What a terrible vacuum thou must leave in life, when age exiles thee from our heart! Which means that I was resuscitated by Mad. de Lorgeville's last words!

In a few minutes I was bowing with a moderate degree of respect before Mlle. de Chantverdun, and making her such adroit excuses that she was enchanted with me. Happiness had restored my presence of mind—my deferential manner and apologies delighted the poor old-young lady. I made her believe that this mistake was entirely owing to a similarity of names, and that the age of Mlle. de Chantverdun was an additional point of resemblance.

This distinction was difficult to manage in its exquisite delicacy; my skilfulness won the approbation of Mad. de Lorgeville.

We passed a charming afternoon. I had recovered my gayety that trouble had almost destroyed, and enjoyed myself so much that sunset found me still at the château. Dear Edgar, this time I am not mistaken in my conjectures. Mlle. de Chateaudun is imposing a trying ordeal upon me—I am more convinced of it than ever; it is the expiation before entering Paradise. Hasten your love affairs and prepare for marriage—we will have a double wedding, and we can introduce our wives on the same day. This would be the crowning of my dearest hopes—a fitting seal to our life-long friendship!

Roger de Monbert.

XIX.

IRENE DE CHATEAUDUN *to* MME. LA VICOMTESSE DE BRAIMES,
Hotel de la Prefecture, Grenoble (Isère).

RICHEPORT, July 6th 18—.

IT is he! Valentine, it is he! I at once recognised him, and he recognised me! And our future lives were given to each other in one of those looks that decide a life. What a day! how agitated I still am! My hand trembles, my heart beats so violently that I can scarcely write. . . It is one o'clock; I did not close my eyes last night and I cannot sleep to-night. I am so excited, my mind so foolishly disturbed, that sleep is a state I no longer comprehend; I feel as if I could never sleep again. Many hours will have to pass before I can extinguish this fire that burns my eyes, stop this whirl of thoughts rushing through my brain; to sleep, I must forget, and never, never can I forget his name, his voice, his face! My dear Valentine, how I wished for you to-day! How proud I would have been to prove to you the realization of all my dreams and presentiments!

Ah! I knew I was right; such implicit faith could not be an error; I was convinced that there existed on earth a being created for me, who would some day possess and govern my heart! A being who had always possessed my love, who sought me, and called upon me to respond to his love; and that we would end by meeting and loving in spite of all obstacles. Yes, often I felt myself called by some superior power. My soul would leave me and travel far away in response to some mysterious command. Where did it go? Then I was ignorant, now I know—it went to Italy, in answer to the gentle voice, to the behest of Raymond! I was laughed at for what was called my romantic idea, and I tried to ridicule it myself. I fought against this fantasy. Alas! I fought so valiantly against it that it was almost destroyed. Oh! I shudder when I think of it. . . A few moments more . . . and I would have been irrevocably engaged; I would no longer have been worthy of this love for which I had kept myself irreproachable, in spite of all the temptations of misery, all the dangers of isolation, and the long-hoped-for day of blissful meeting, would have been the day of eternal farewell! This averted misfortune frightened me as if it were still menacing. Poor Roger! I heartily pardon him now; more than that, I thank him for having so quickly disenchanted me.

Edgar! . . . Edgar! . . . I hate him when I remember that I tried to love him; but no, no, there never was anything like love between us! Heavens! what a difference! . . . And yet the one of whom I speak with such enthusiasm . . . I saw yesterday for the first time . . . I know him not . . . I know him not . . . and yet I love him! . . . Valentine, what will you think of me?

This most important day of my life opened in the ordinary way; nothing foreshadowed the great event that was to decide my fate, that was to throw so much light upon the dark doubts of my poor heart. This brilliant sun suddenly burst upon me unheralded by any precursory ray.

Some new guests were expected; a relative of Madame de Meilhan, and a friend of Edgar, whom they call Don Quixote. This struck me as being a peculiar nickname, but I did not ask its origin. Like all persons of imagination, I have no curiosity; I at once find a reason for everything; I prefer imagining to asking the wherefore of things; I prefer suppositions to information. Therefore I did not inquire why this friend was honored with the name of Don Quixote. I explained it to myself in this wise: A tall, thin young man, resembling the Chevalier de la Mancha, and who perhaps had dressed himself like Don Quixote at the carnival, and the name of his disguise had clung to him ever since; I fancied a silly, awkward youth, with an ugly yellow face, a sort of solemn jumping-jack, and I confess to no desire to make his acquaintance. He disturbed me in one respect, but I was quickly reassured. I am always afraid of being recognised by visitors at the château, and have to exercise a great deal of ingenuity to find out if we have ever met. Before appearing before them, I inquire if they are fashionable people, spent last winter in Paris, &c.? I am told Don Quixote is almost a savage; he travels all the time so as to sustain his character as knight-errant, and that he spent last winter in Rome. . . . This quieted my fears . . . I did not appear in society until last winter, so Don Quixote never saw me; knowing we could meet without the possibility of recognition, I dismissed him from my mind.

Yesterday, at three o'clock, Madame de Meilhan and her son went to the depot to meet their guests. I was standing at the front door when they drove off, and Madame de Meilhan called out to me: "My dear Madame Guérin, I recommend my bouquets to you; pray spare me the eternal *soucis* with which the cruel Etienne insists upon filling my rooms; now I rely upon you for relief."

I smiled at this pun as if I had never heard it before, and promised to superintend the arrangement of the flowers. I went into the garden and found Etienne gathering *soucis*, more *soucis*, nothing but *soucis*. I glanced at his flower-beds, and at once understood the cause of his predilection for this dreadful flower; it was the only kind that deigned to bloom in his melancholy garden. This is the secret of many inexplicable preferences.

I thought with horror that Madame de Meilhan would continue to be a prey to *soucis* if I did not come to her rescue, so I said: "Etienne, what a pity to cull them all! they are so effective in a garden; let us go look for some other flowers—it is a shame to ruin your beautiful beds!" The flattered Stephen eagerly followed me to a corner of the garden where I had admired some superb catalpas. He gathered branches of them, with which I filled the Japanese vases on the mantel, and ornamented the corners of the parlor, thus converting it into a flowery grove. I also arranged some Bengal roses and dahlias that had escaped Etienne's culture, and with the addition of some asters and a very few *soucis* I must confess, I was charmed with the result of my labors. But I wanted some delicate flowers for the pretty vase on the centre table, and remembering that an old florist, a friend of Madame

Taverneau and one of my professed admirers, lived about a mile from the château, I determined to walk over and describe to him the dreadful condition of Madame de Meilhan, and appeal to him for assistance. Fortunately I found him in his green-house, and delighted him by repeating the pun about filling the house with *soucis*. Provincials have a singular taste for puns ; I never make them, and only repeat them because I love to please. The old man was fascinated, and rewarded my flattery by making me up a magnificent bouquet of rare, unknown, nameless, exquisite flowers that could be found nowhere else ; my bouquet was worth a fortune, and what fortune ever exhaled such perfume? I started off triumphant. I tell you all this to show how calm and little inclined I was to romance on that morning.

I walked rapidly, for we can hardly help running when in an open field and pursued by the arrows of the sun ; we run till we are breathless, to find shelter beneath some friendly tree.

I had crossed a large field that separates the property of the florist from Madame de Meilhan's, and entered the park by a little gate ; a few steps off a fountain rippled among the rocks—a basin surrounded by shells received its waters. This basin had originally been pretentiously ornamented, but time and vegetation had greatly improved these efforts of bad taste. The roots of a grand weeping willow had pitilessly unmasked the imposture of these artificial rocks, that is, they have destroyed their skilful masonry ; these rocks, built at great expense on the shore, have gradually fallen into the very middle of the water, where they have become naturalized ; some serve as vases to clusters of beautiful iris, others serve as resting-places for the tame deer that run about the park and drink at the stream ; aquatic plants, reeds and entwined convolvulus have invaded the rest ; all the pretentious work of the artist is now concealed ; which proves the vanity of the proud efforts of man. God permits his creatures to cultivate ugliness in their cities only ; in his own beautiful fields he quickly destroys their miserable attempts. Vainly, under pretext of a fountain, do they heap up in the woods and valleys masonry upon masonry, rocks upon rocks ; vainly do they lavish money upon their gingerbread work about the limpid brooks; the water-nymph smilingly watches their labor, and then in her capricious play amuses herself by changing their hideous productions into charming structures; their den of a farmer-general into a poet's nest; and to effect this miracle only three things are necessary—three things that cost nothing, and which we daily trample under foot—flowers, grass and pebbles. . . . Valentine, I know I have been talking too long about this little lake, but I have an excuse: I love it much! You shall soon know why. . . .

I heard the purling of the water, and could not resist the seductive freshness of its voice; I leaned over the rocks of the fountain, took off my glove and caught in the hollow of my hand the sparkling water that fell from the cascade, and eagerly drank it. As I was intoxicating myself with this innocent beverage, I heard a footstep on the path; I continued to drink without disturbing myself, until the following words made me raise my head:

"Excuse me, *mademoiselle*, but can you direct me where to find Mad. de Meilhan?"

He called me *Mademoiselle*, so I must be recognised; the idea made me turn pale; I looked with alarm at the young man who uttered these words, I had never seen him before, but he might have seen me and would betray me. I was so disconcerted that I dropped half of my flowers in the water; the current was rapidly whirling them off among the crevices of the rocks, when he jumped lightly from stone to stone, and rescuing the fugitive flowers, laid them all carefully by the others on the side of the fountain, bowed respectfully and retraced his steps down the walk without renewing his unanswered question. I was, without knowing why, completely reassured; there was in his look such high-toned loyalty, in his manner such perfect distinction, and a sort of precaution so delicately mysterious, that I felt confidence in him. I thought, even if he does know my name it will make no difference—for he would never mention having met me—my secret is safe with a man of his character! You need not laugh at me for prematurely deciding upon his character, . . . for my surmises proved correct!

The dinner hour was drawing near, and I hurried back to the château to dress. I was compelled, in spite of myself, to look attractive, on account of having to put on a lovely dress that the treacherous Blanchard had spread out on the bed with the determination that I should wear it; protesting that it was a blessed thing she had brought this one, as there was not another one fit for me to appear in before Mad. de Meilhan's guests. It was an India muslin trimmed with twelve little flounces edged with exquisite Valenciennes lace; the waist was made of alternate tucks and insertion, and trimmed with lace to match the skirt. This dress was unsuitable to the humble Madame Guérin—it would be imprudent to appear in it. How indignant and angry I was with poor Blanchard! I scolded her all the time she was assisting me to put it on! Oh! since then how sincerely have I forgiven her! She had brought me a fashionable sash to wear with the dress, but I resisted the temptation, and casting aside the elegant ribbon, I put on an old lilac belt and descended to the parlor where the company were assembled.

The first person I saw, on entering the room, was the young man I had met by the fountain. His presence disconcerted me. Mad. de Meilhan relieved my embarrassment by saying: "Ah! here you are! we were just speaking of you. I wish to introduce to you my dear Don Quixote." I turned my head towards the other end of the room where Edgar was talking to several persons, thinking that Don Quixote was one of the number; but Mad. de Meilhan introduced the young man of the fountain, calling him M. de Villiers: he was Don Quixote.

He addressed some polite speech to me, but this time he called me madame, and in uttering this word there was a tone of sadness that deeply touched me, and the earnest look with which he regarded me I can never forget—it seemed to say, I know your history, I know you are unhappy, I know this unhappiness is unjustly inflicted upon you, and you arouse my tenderest sympathy. I assure you, my dear Valentine, that his look expressed all this, and much more that I refrain from telling you, because I know you will laugh at me.

Madame de Meilhan having joined us, he went over to Edgar.

"What do you think of her?" asked Edgar, who did not know that I was listening.

"Very beautiful."

"She is a companion, engaged by my mother to stay here until I marry."

The hidden meaning of this jesting speech seemed to disgust M. de Villiers; he cast upon his friend a severe and scornful look that clearly said: You conceited puppy! I think, but am not certain, this look also signified: Would-be Lovelace! Provincial Don Juan, &c.

At dinner I was placed opposite him, and all during the meal I was wondering why this handsome, elegant, distinguished-looking young man should be nicknamed Don Quixote. Thoughtful observation solved the enigma. Don Quixote was ridiculed for two things: being very ugly and being too generous. And I confess I felt myself immediately fascinated by his captivating characteristics.

After dinner we were on the terrace, when he approached me and said with a smile:

"I am distressed, madame, to think that without knowing you, I must have made a disagreeable impression."

"I confess that you startled me."

"How pale you turned! . . . perhaps you were expecting some one!" . . He asked this question with a troubled look and such charming anxiety that I answered quickly—too quickly, perhaps:

"No, monsieur, I did not expect any one.'

"You saw me coming up the walk?"

"Yes, I saw you coming."

"But was there any reason why I should have caused you this sudden fright! . . some resemblance, perhaps?—no?—It is strange . . I am puzzled."

"And I am also very much puzzled, monsieur."

"About me! . . . What happiness!"

"I wish to know why you are called Don Quixote?"

"Ah! you embarrass me by asking for my great secret, Madame, but I will confide it to you, since you are kind enough to be interested in me. I am called Don Quixote because I am a kind of a fool, an original, an enthusiastic admirer of all noble and holy things, a dreamer of noble deeds, a defender of the oppressed, a slayer of egotists; because I believe in all religions, even the religion of love. I think that a man ought to respect himself out of respect to the woman who loves him; that he should constantly think of her with devotion, avoid doing anything that could displease her, and be always, even in her absence, courteous, pleasing, amiable, I would even say *loveable*, if the word were admissible; a man who is beloved is, according to my ridiculous ideas, a sort of dignitary; he should thenceforth behave as if he were an idol, and deify himself as much as possible. I also have my patriotic religion; I love my country like an old member of the National Guard. . . . My friends say I am a real Vaudeville Frenchman. I reply that it is better to be a real Vaudeville Frenchman than an imitation of English jockeys, as they are; they call me knight-errant because I reprove them for speaking coarsely of women. I advise them to keep silent and conceal their misdeeds. I tell them that their boasted preferences only prove their blindness and bad taste; that I am more fortunate than they; all the women of my acquaintance are good and perfect, and my greatest desire in life is to be worthy of their friendship. I am called Don Quixote because I love glory and all those who have the ambition to seek it; because in my eyes there is nothing true but the hopeful future, as we are deceived at every step we take in the present. Because I understand inexplicable disinterestedness, generous folly; because I can understand how one can live for an idea and die for a word; I can sympathize with all who struggle and suffer for a cherished belief; because I have the courage to turn my back upon those whom I despise and am eccentric enough to always speak the truth; I assert that nobody is worth the hypocrisy of a falsehood; because I am an incorrigible, systematic, insatiable dupe; I prefer going astray, making a mistake by doing a good deed, rather than being always distrustful and suspicious; while I see evil I believe in good; doubtless the evil predominates and daily increases, but then it is cultivated, and if the same cultivation were bestowed upon the good perfection would be attained. Finally, madame, and this is my supreme folly, I believe in happiness and seek it with credulous hope; I believe that the purest joys are those which are most dearly bought; but I am ready for any sacrifice, and would willingly give my life for an hour of this sublime joy that I have so long dreamed of and still hope to possess. . . Now you know why I am called Don Quixote. To be a knight-errant in the present day is rather difficult; a certain amount of courage is necessary to dare to say to unbelievers: I believe; to egotists, I love; to materialists, I dream; it requires more than courage, it requires audacity and insolence. Yes, one must commence by appearing aggressive in order to have the right to appear generous. If I were merely loyal and charitable, my opinions would not be supported; instead of being called *Don Quixote*, I would be called *Grandison* . . . and I would be a ruined man! Thus I hasten to polish my armor and attack the insolent with insolence, the scoffers with scoffing; I defend my enthusiasm with irony; like the eagle, I let my claws grow in order to defend my wings." . . Here he stopped. . . "Heavens!" he exclaimed, "how could I compare myself to an eagle; I beg your pardon, madame, for this presumptuous comparison. . . . You see to what flights your indulgence leads me" . . . and he laughed at his own enthusiasm, . . but I did not laugh, my feelings were too deeply stirred.

Valentine, what I repeat to you is very different from his way of saying it. What eloquence in his noble words, his tones of voice, his sparkling eyes! His generous sentiments, so long restrained, were poured forth with fire; he was happy at finding himself at last understood, at being able for once in his life to see appreciated the divine treasures of his heart, to be able to impart all his pet ideas without seeing them jeered at and their name insulted! Sympathy inspired him with confidence in me. With delight I recognised myself in his own description. I saw with pride, in his profound convictions, his strong and holy truths, the poetical beliefs of my youth, that have always been treated by every one else as fictions, and foolish illusions; he carried me back to the happy days of my early life, by repeating to me, like an echo of the past, those noble words that are no longer heard in the present—those noble precepts—those beautiful refrains of chivalry in which my infancy was cradled . . . . As I listened I said to myself: how my mother would have loved him! and this thought made my eyes fill with tears. Ah! never, never did such an idea cross my mind when I was with Edgar, or near Roger. . . Now you must acknowledge, my dear Valentine, that I am right when I say that: It is he! It is he!

We had been absorbed an hour in these confidential reveries, forgetting the persons around us, the place we were in, who we were ourselves, and the whole world!

The universe had disappeared, leaving us only the delicate perfume of the orange blossoms around us, and the soft light of the stars peeping forth from the sky above us.

We returned to the parlor and I was seated near the centre-table, when Edgar came up to me and said:

"What is the matter with you this evening? You seem depressed; are you not well?"

"I have a slight cold."

"What a tiresome general--he continued—he monopolizes all my evening, . . . a tiresome hero is *so* hard to entertain!"

I forgot to tell you we had a general to dinner.

"Raymond, come here . . . it is your turn to keep the warrior awake." . . M. de Villiers approached the table and began to examine the bouquet I had brought. "Ah! I recognise these flowers!" he looked at me and I blushed. "I do too," said Edgar, without taking in the true sense of the words, and he pointed to the prettiest flowers in the bouquet, and said: "these are the flowers of the *pelargonium diadematum coccineum.*" I exclaimed at the dreadful name. M. de Villiers repeated: "*Pelargonium diadematum coccineum!*" in an undertone, with a most fascinating smile, and said: "Oh! I did not mean that!" . . . I could not help looking at him and smiling in complicity; now why should Edgar be so learned?

I suppose you think it very childish to write you these particulars, but the most trifling details of this day are precious to me, and I must confide them to some one. Towards midnight we separated, and I rejoiced at being alone with my happiness. The emotion I felt was so lively that I hastened to carry it far away from everybody, even from him, its author. I wished for solitude that I might ask myself what had caused this agitation—nothing of importance had occurred this day, no word of engagement for the future had been made, and yet my whole life wore a different aspect . . . my usually calm heart was throbbing violently—my mind always so uneasy was settled; who had thus changed my fate? . . . A stranger . . . and what had he done to merit this sudden preference? He had picked up some flowers. . . But this stranger wore on his brow the aureola of the dreamed-of ideal, his musical voice had the imperative accent of a master, and from the first moment he looked at me, there existed between us that mysterious affinity of fraternal instincts, that spontaneous alliance of two hearts suddenly mated, unfailing gratitude, irresistible sympathy, mutual echo, reciprocal exchange, quick appreciation, ardent and sublime harmony, that creates in one moment—the poets are right—that creates in one moment eternal love!

To restore my tranquillity, I sat down to write to you, but had not the courage to put my thoughts on paper, and I remained there all night, trembling and meditative, oppressed by this powerful emotion; I did not think, I did not pray, I did not live; I loved, and absorbed in loving, taking no note of time, I sat there till daybreak; at five o'clock I heard a noise of rakes and scythes in the garden, and wishing to cool my hot eyes with a breath of fresh air, I descended to the terrace.

Everybody was asleep in the château and all the blinds closed, but I opened the glass door leading into the garden, and after walking up and down the gravel-path, crossed the bridge over the brook, and went by way of the little thicket where I had rested yesterday; I was led by some magnetic attraction to the covered spring; I did not go up the poplar-walk, but took a little by-path seldom used by any one, and almost covered with grass; I reached the spring, and suddenly . . . before me . . . I saw him . . . Valentine! . . . he was there alone, . . . sitting on the bench by the fountain, with his beautiful eyes fastened on the spot where he had seen me the day before! And oh, the sad wistfulness of his look went straight to my heart! I stood still, happy, yet frightened; I wished to flee; I felt that my presence was a confession, a proof of his empire; I was right when I said he called me and I obeyed the call! . . . He looked up and saw me, . . . and oh, how pale he turned, . . . he seemed more alarmed than I had been the day previous! His agitation restored my calmness; it convinced me that during these hours of separation our thoughts had been the same, and that our love was mutual. He arose and approached me, saying:—

"This is your favorite place, madame, and I will not intrude any longer, but before I go you can reward this great sacrifice by a single word: confess frankly that you are not astonished at finding me here?" I was silent, but my blushes answered for me. As he stood there looking at me I heard a noise near us; it was only a deer coming to drink at the spring; but I trembled so violently that M. de Villiers saw by my alarm that it would distress me to be found alone with him; he was moving away, when I made a sign for him to remain, which meant: Stay, and continue to think of me. . . . I then quickly returned to the château. I have seen him since; we passed the day together, with Madame de Meilhan and her son, playing on the piano, or entertaining the country neighbors, but under it all enjoying the same fascinating preoccupation, an under-current of bliss, a secret intoxication. Edgar is uneasy and Madame de Meilhan is contented; the serious love of her son alarmed her; she sees with pleasure an increasing rivalry that may destroy it. I know not what is about to happen, but I dread anything unpleasant occurring to interrupt my sweet contentment; any explanations, humiliations, adieux, departures—a thousand annoyances, . . . but it matters not, I am happy, I am in love, and I know there is nothing so satisfying, so sweet as being in love!

This time I say nothing of yourself, my dear Valentine, of yourself, nor of our old friendship, but is not each word of this letter a proof of tender devotion? I confide to you every thought and emotion of my heart—so foolish that one would dare not confess them to a mother. Is not this the same as saying to you: You are the beloved sister of my choice?

Give my dear little goddaughter Irene a kiss for me. Oh, I am so glad she is growing prettier every day!

Irene de Chateaudun.

XX.

ROGER DE MONBERT *to* MONSIEUR EDGAR DE MEILHAN,
Richeport, Pont de l'Arche (Eure).

Paris, July 8th 18—.

DEAR EDGAR,—Stupidity was invented by our sex. When a woman deceives or deserts us,—synonymous transgressions,—we are foolish enough to prolong to infinity our despair, instead of singing with Metastasio—

"Grazie all' inganni tuoi
Al fin respir' o Nice!"

Alas! such is man! Women have more pride. If I had deserted Mlle. de Chateaudun she certainly would not have searched the highways and byways to discover me. I fear there is a great deal of vanity at the bottom of our manly passions. Vanity is the eldest son of love. I shall develop this theory upon some future occasion. One must be calm when one philosophizes. At present I am obliged to continue in my folly, begging reason to await my return.

In the intense darkness of despair, one naturally rushes towards the horizon where shines some bright object, be it lighthouse, star, phosphorus or jack-o'-lantern. Will it prove a safe haven or a dangerous rock? Fate,—Chance,—to thee we trust!

My faithful agents are ever watchful. I have just received their despatches, and they inspire me with the hope that at last the thick mist is about to be dispersed. I will spare you all the minute details written by faithful servants, who have more sagacity than epistolary style, and give you a synopsis:—Mlle. de Chateaudun left for Rouen a month ago. She engaged two seats in the car. She was seen at the depot—her maid was with her. There is no longer any doubt—Irene is at Rouen; I have proofs of it in my hand.

An old family servant, devoted to me, is living at Rouen. I will make his house the centre of my observations, and will not compromise the result by any negligence or recklessness on my part.

The inexorable logic of victorious combinations will be revealed to me on the first night of my solitude. I am about to start; address me no longer at Paris. Railways were invented for the benefit of love affairs. A lover laid the first rail, and a speculator laid the last. Happily Rouen is a faubourg of Paris! This advantage of rapid locomotion will permit me to pass two hours at Richeport with you, and have the delight of pressing Raymond's hand. Two hours of my life gained by losing them with my oldest and best friend. I will be overjoyed to once more see the noble Raymond, the last of knight-errants, doubtless occupied in painting in stone-color some old manor where Queen Blanche has left traditions of the course of true love.

How dreadful it is, dear Edgar, to endeavor to unravel a mystery when a woman is at the bottom of it! Yes, Irene is at Rouen, I am convinced of that fact. Rouen is a large city, full of large houses, small houses, hotels and churches; but love is a grand inquisitor, capable of searching the city in twenty-four hours, and making the receiver of stolen property surrender Mlle. de Chateaudun. Then what will happen? Have I the right to institute a scheme of this strange nature about a young woman? Is she alone at Rouen? And if misfortune does not mislead me by these certain traces, is there anything in reserve for me worse than losing her?

Oh! if such be the case, then is the time to pray God for strength to repeat the other two verses of the poet:—

"Col mio rival istesso,
Posso di te parlar!"

Farewell, for a short time, dear Edgar. I fly to fathom this mystery.

ROGER DE MONBERT.

XXI.

RAYMOND DE VILLIERS *to* MME. LA VICOMTESSE DE BRAIMES,
Hotel of the Prefecture, Grenoble (Isere).

RICHEPORT, July 6th, 18—.

MADAME: Need I tell you that I left your house profoundly touched by your goodness, and bearing away in my heart one of the most precious memories that shall survive my youth? What can I tell you that you have not already learnt from my distress and emotion at the hour of parting? Tears came to my eyes as I pressed M. de Braimes's hand, that loyal hand which had so often pressed my father's, and when I turned back to get one last look at you, surrounded by your beautiful children, who waved me a final adieu, I felt as if I had left behind me the better part of myself; for a moment I reproached you for having cured me so quickly. My friends have nicknamed me Don Quixote, I do not exactly know why; but this I do know, that with the prospect of a reward like unto that which you have offered me, any one would accept the office of redresser of wrongs and slayer of giants, even at the risk of having to jump into the fire occasionally to save a Lady Penock.

More generous than the angels, you have awarded me, on earth, the palm which is reserved for martyrs in heaven. You appeared before me like one of those benevolent fairies which exorcise evil genii. 'Tis true that you do not wear the magic ring, but your wit alleviates suffering and proclaims a truce to pain. Till now I have laughed at the stoics who declare that suffering is not an evil; seated at my pillow, one smile from you converted me to their belief. Hitherto I have believed that patience and resignation were virtues beyond my strength and courage; without an effort, you have taught me that patience is sweet and resignation easy to attain. I have been persuaded that health is the greatest boon given to man: you have proved its fallacy. And M. de Braimes has shown himself your faithful accomplice, not to speak of your dear little ones, who, for a month past, have converted my room into a flower-garden and a bird-cage, where they were the sweetest flowers and the gayest birds. Finally, as if my life, restored by your tender care, was not enough, you have added to it the priceless jewel of your friendship. A thousand thanks and blessings! With you happiness entered into my destiny. You were the dawn announcing a glorious sunrise, the prelude to the melodies which, since yesterday, swell in my bosom. If I take pleasure in recognising your gentle influence in the secret delight that pervades my being, do not deprive me of the illusion. I believe, with my mother, in mysterious influences. I believe that, as there are miserable beings who, unwittingly, drag misfortune after them and sow it over their pathway, there are others, on the other hand, who, marked by the finger of God, bear happiness to all whom they meet. Happy the wanderer who, like me, sees one of those privileged beings cross his path! Their presence, alone, brings down blessings from heaven and the earth blossoms under their footsteps.

And really, madame, you do possess the faculty of dissipating fatal enchantments. Like the morning star, which disperses the mighty gatherings of goblins and gnomes, you have shone upon my horizon and Lady Penock has vanished like a shadow. Thanks to you, I crossed France with impunity from the borders of Isère to the borders of the Creuse, and then to the banks of the Seine, without encountering the implacable islander who pursued me from the fields of Latium to the foot of the Grande Chartreuse. I must not forget to state that at Voreppe, where I stopped to change horses, the keeper of the ruined inn, recognising my carriage, politely presented me with a bill for damages; so much for a broken glass, so much for a door beaten in, so much for a shattered ladder. I commend to M. de Braimes this brilliant stroke of one of his constituents; it is an incident forgotten by Cervantes in the history of his hero.

In spite of my character of knight-errant, I reached my dear mountains without any other adventure. I had not visited them for three years, and the sight of their rugged tops rejoiced my heart. You would like the country; it is poor, but poetic. You would enjoy its green solitudes, its uncultivated fields, its silent valleys and little lakes enshrined like sheets of crystal in borders of sage and heather. Its chief charm to me is its obscurity; no curiosity-hunter or ordinary tourist has ever frightened away the dryads from its chestnut groves or the naiads from its fresh streams. Even a flitting poet has scarcely ever betrayed its rural mysteries. My château has none of the grandeur that you have, perhaps, ascribed to it. Picture to yourself a pretty country-house, lightly set on a hill-top, and pensively overlooking the Creuse flowing at its feet under an arbor of alder-bushes and flowering ash. Such as it is, imbedded in woods which shelter it from the northern blasts and protect it from the heats of the summer solstice; there—if the hope that inspires me is not an illusion of my bewildered brain; if the light that dazzles me is not a chance spark from chimerical fires, there, among the scenes where I first saw the light, I would hide my happiness. You see, madame, that my hand trembles as I write. One evening you and I were walking together, under the trees in your garden; your children played about us like young kids upon the green sward. As we walked we talked, and insensibly began to speak of that vague need of loving which torments our youth. You said that love was a grave undertaking, and that often our whole life depended upon our first choice. I spoke of my aspirations towards those unknown delights, which haunted me with their seductive visions as Columbus was haunted by visions of a new world. Gravely and pensively you listened to me, and when I began to trace the image of the oft-dreamed-of woman, so vainly sought for in the ungrateful domain of reality, I remember that you smiled as you said: "Do not despair, she exists; you will meet her some day." Were you speaking earnestly then? Is it she? Keep still, do not even breathe, she might fly away.

After a few days spent in revisiting the scenes of my childhood, and breathing afresh the sweet perfumes still hovering around infancy's cradle, I left for Paris, where I scarcely rested

The manner in which I employed the few hours passed in that hot city would doubtless surprise you, madame. My carriage rolled rapidly through the wealthy portion of the city, and following my directions was soon lost in the gloomy solitude of the Marais.

I alighted in the wilderness of a deserted street before a melancholy and dejected-looking house, and as I raised the heavy latch of the massive door, my heart beat as if I were about to meet, after a long absence, an aged mother who wept for my return, or a much-loved sister. I took a key from its nail in the porter's lodge and began to climb the stair, which, viewed from below, looked more picturesque than inviting, particularly when one proposed to ascend to the very top. Fortunately, I am a mountaineer; I bounded up that wide ladder with as light a step as if it had been a marble stairway, with richly wrought balustrade. At the end of the ascent I hurriedly opened a door, and, perfectly at home, entered a small room. I paused motionless upon the threshold, and glanced feelingly around. The room contained nothing but a table covered with books and dust, a stiff oak arm-chair, a hard and uninviting-looking lounge, and on the mantel-piece, in two earthen vases, designed by Ziegler, the only ornaments of this poor retreat, a few dry, withered asters. No one expected me, I expected no one. There I remained until evening, waiting for nightfall, thinking the sun would never set and the day never end. Finally, as the night deepened, I leaned on the sill of the only window, and with an emotion I cannot describe, watched the stars peep forth one by one. I would have given them all for a sight of the one star which will never shine again. Shall I tell you about it, madame, and would you comprehend me? You know nothing of my life; you do not know that, during two years, I lived in that garret, poor, unknown, with no other friend than labor, no other companion than the little light which appeared and disappeared regularly every evening through the branches of a Canada pine. I did not know then, neither do I know now, who watched by that pale gleam, but I felt for it a nameless affection, a mysterious tenderness. On leaving my retreat, I sent it, through the trees, a long farewell, and the not seeing it on my return distressed me as the loss of a brother. What has become of you, little shining beacon, who illumined the gloom of my studious nights? Did a storm extinguish you? or has God, whom I invoked for you, granted my prayer, and do you shine with a less troubled ray in happier climes? It is a long story; and I know a fresher and a more charming one, which I will speedily tell you.

I took the train the next day (that was yesterday) for Richeport, where M. de Meilhan had invited me to meet him. You know M. de Meilhan without ever having seen him. You are familiar with his verses and you like them. I profess to love the man as much as his talents. Our friendship is of long standing; I assisted at the first lispings of his muse; I saw his young glory grow and expand; I predicted from the first the place that he now holds in the poetic pleiad, the honor of a great nation. To hear him you would say that he was a pitiless scoffer; to study him you would soon find, under this surface of rancorless irony, more candor and simplicity than he is himself aware of, and which few people possess who boast of their faith and belief. He has the mind of a sceptic and the believing soul of a neophyte.

In less than three hours I reached Pont de l'Arche. Railroads have been much abused; it is charitable to presume that those honest people who do so have no relatives, friends nor sweethearts away from them. M. de Meilhan and his mother were waiting for me at the depot; the first delights of meeting over—for you must remember that I have not seen my poet for three years—I leave you to imagine the peals of laughter that greeted the mention of Lady Penock's formidable name. Edgar, who knew of my adventure and was excited by the joy of seeing me again, amused himself by startling the echoes with loud and repeated "Shockings!" We drove along in an open carriage, laughing, talking, pressing each other's hands, asking question upon question, while Madame de Meilhan, after having shared our gayety, seemed to watch with interest the exhibition of our mutual delight. This scene had the most beautiful surroundings in the world; an exquisite country, which in order to be fully appreciated, visited, described, sung of in prose and verse, should be fifteen hundred miles from France.

My mind is naturally gay, my heart sad. When I laugh, something within me suffers and repines; it is by no means rare for me to pass suddenly and without transition from the wildest gayety to the profoundest sadness and melancholy. On our arrival at Richeport we found several visitors at the châteaux, among the number a general, solemnly resigned to the pleasures of a day in the country. To escape this illustrious warrior, who was engaged upon the battle of Friedland, Edgar made off between two cavalry charges and carried me into the park, where we were soon joined by Madame de Meilhan and her guest, the terrible general at the head.

Interrupted for a moment by the skilful retreat of the young poet, the battle of Friedland began again with redoubled fury. The paths of the park are narrow; the warrior marched in front with Edgar, who wiped the drops from his brow and exhausted himself in vain efforts to release his arm from an iron grasp; Madame de Meilhan and those who accompanied her represented the corps d'armée; I formed the rear guard; balls whistled by, battalions struggled, we heard the cries of the wounded and were stifled by the smell of powder; wishing to avoid the harrowing sight of such dreadful carnage, I slackened my pace and was agreeably surprised to find, at a turn in the path, that I had deserted my colors; I listened and heard only the song of the bulfinch; I took a long breath and breathed only the odor of the woods; I looked above the birches and aspens for a cloud of smoke which would put me upon the track of the combatants; I saw only the blue sky smiling through the trees; I was alone; by one of those reactions of which I spoke, I sank insensibly into a deep revery.

It was intensely hot; I threw myself upon the grass, under the shadow of a thick hedge, and there lay listening to nature's faint whispers, and the beating of my own heart. The joy that I had just felt in meeting Edgar again, made the void in my heart, which friendship can never fill, all the more painful; my senses, subdued by the heat, chanted in endless elegies the serious and soothing conversation that we had had one evening under your lindens. Whether I had a presentiment of some approaching change in my destiny, or whether I was simply overcome by the heat, I know not, but I was restless; my restlessness seemed to anticipate some indefinite happiness, and from afar the wind bore to me in warm puffs the cheering refrain: "She exists, she exists, you will find her!"

I at last remembered that I had only been Madame de Meilhan's guest a few hours, and that my abrupt disappearance must appear, to say the least, strange to her. On the other hand, Edgar, whom I had treacherously abandoned in the greatest danger, would have serious grounds of complaint against me. I arose, and driving away the winged dreams that hovered around me, like a swarm of bees round a hive, prepared to join my corps, with the cowardly hope that when I arrived, the engagement might be over and the victory won. Unfortunately, or rather fortunately, I was unacquainted with the windings of the park, and wandered at random through its verdant labyrinths, the sun pouring down upon my devoted head until I heard the silvery murmur of a neighboring stream, babbling over its pebbly bed. Attracted by the freshness of the spot, I approached and in the midst of a confusion of iris, mint and bindweed, I saw a blonde head quenching its thirst at the stream. I could only see a mass of yellow hair wound in heavy golden coils around this head, and a little hand catching the water like an opal cup, which it afterwards raised to two lips as fresh as the crystal stream which they quaffed. Her face and figure being entirely concealed by the aquatic plants which grew around the spring, I took her for a child, a girl of twelve or more, the daughter perhaps of one of the persons whom I had left upon the battle-field of Friedland. I advanced a few steps nearer, and in my softest voice, for I was afraid of frightening her, said: "Mademoiselle, can you tell me if Madame de Meilhan is near here?" At these words I saw a young and beautiful creature, tall, slender, erect, lift herself like a lily from among the reeds, and trembling and pale, examine me with the air of a startled gazelle. I stood mute and motionless, gazing at her. Surely she possessed the royal beauty of the lily. An imagination enamored of the melodies of the antique muse would have immediately taken her for the nymph of that brook. Like two blue-bells in a field of ripe grain, her large blue eyes were as limpid as the stream which reflected the azure of the sky. On her brow sat the pride of the huntress Diana. Her attitude and the expression of her face betrayed a royalty which desired to conceal its greatness, a strange mixture of timorous boldness and superb timidity—and over it all, the brilliancy of youth—a nameless charm of innocence and childishness tempered in a charming manner the dignity of her noble presence.

I turned away, charmed and agitated, not having spoken a word. After wandering about sometime longer I finally discovered the little army corps, marching towards the château, the general always ahead. As I had anticipated, the battle was about over, a few shots fired at the fugitives were alone heard. Edgar saw me in the distance, and looked furious. "Ah traitor!" said he, "you have lagged behind! I am riddled with balls; I have six bullets in my breast." "Monsieur," cried the general, "at what juncture did you leave the combat?" "You see," said Edgar to me, "that the torture is about to commence again." "General," observed Madame de Meilhan, "I think that the munitions are exhausted and dinner is ready." "Very well," gravely replied the hero, "we will take Lubeck at dessert." "Alas! we are taken;" said Edgar, heaving a sigh that would have lifted off a piece of the Cordilleras.

M. de Meilhan left the group of promenaders and joined me; we walked side by side. You can imagine, madame, how anxious I was to question Edgar; you can also comprehend the feeling of delicacy which restrained me. My poet worships beauty; but it is a pagan worship of color and form. The result is, a certain boldness of detail not always excusable by grace of expression, in his description of a beautiful woman; too lively an enthusiasm for the flesh; too great a satisfaction in drawing lines and contours not to shock the refined. A woman poses before him like a statue or rather like a Georgian in a slave-market, and from the manner in which he analyzes and dissects her, you would say that he wanted either to sell or buy her. I allude now to his speech only, which is lively, animated but rather French its picturesque crudity. As a poet he sculptures like Phidias, and his verse has all the dazzling purity of marble.

I preferred to apply to Madame de Meilhan. On our return to the château I questioned her, and learned that my beautiful unknown was named Madame Louise Guérin. At that word "Madame" my heart contracted. Wherefore? I could not tell. Afterwards I learned that she was a widow and poor, that she lived by the labor of those pretty fingers which I had seen dabbling in the water. Further than that, Madame de Meilhan knew nothing, her remarks were confined to indulgent suppositions and benevolent comments. A woman so young, so beautiful, so poor, working for her livelihood, must be a noble and pure creature. I felt for her a respectful pity, which her appearance in the drawing-room in all the magnificence of her beauty, grace and youth, changed into extravagant admiration. Our eyes met as if we had a secret between us; she appeared, and I yielded to the charm of her presence. Edgar observed that she was his mother's companion, who would remain with her until he married. The wretch! if he had not written such fine verses, I would have strangled him on the spot. I sat opposite her at dinner, and could observe her at my ease. She appeared like a young queen at the board of one of her great vassals. Grave and smiling, she spoke little, but so to the point, and in so sweet a voice, that I cherished in my heart every word that fell from her lips, like pearls from a casket. I also was silent and was astonished, that when she did not speak, any one should dare to open his lips before her. Edgar's witty sallies seemed to be in the worst possible taste, and twenty times I was on the point of saying to him: "Edgar, do you not see that the queen is listening to you?"

At dessert, as the general was preparing to manœuvre the artillery of the siege, every one rose precipitately, to escape the capture and pillage of Lubeck. Edgar rushed into the park, the guests dispersed; and while Madame de Meilhan, bearing with heroic resignation the inconveniences attached to her dignity as mistress of the house, fought by the general's side like Clorinde by the side of Argant, I found myself alone, with the young widow, upon the terrace of the château. We talked, and a powerful enchantment compelled me to surrender my soul into her keeping. I amazed myself by confiding to her what I had never told myself.

My most cherished and hidden feelings were drawn irresistibly forth from the inmost recesses of my bosom. When I spoke, I seemed to translate her thoughts; when she in turn replied, she paraphrased mine. In less than an hour I learned to know her. She possessed, at the same time, an experimental mind, which could descend to the root of things, and a tender and inexperienced heart which life had never troubled. Theoretically she was governed by a lofty and precocious reason ripened by misfortune; practically, she was swayed by the dictates of an innocent and untried soul. Until now, she has lived only in the activity of her thoughts; the rest of her being sleeps, seeks or awaits. Who is she? She is not a widow. Albert Guérin is not her name; she has never been married. Where Madame de Meilhan hesitates, I doubt, I decide. How does it happen that the mystery with which she is surrounded has to me all the prestige and lustre of a glowing virtue? How is it that my heart rejoices at it when my prudence should take alarm? Another mystery, which I do not undertake to explain. All that I know is, that she is poor, and that if I had a crown I should wish to ennoble it by placing it upon that lovely brow.

Do not tell me that this is madness; that love is not born of a look or a word, that it must germinate in the heart for a season before it can bear fruit. Enthusiasts live fast. They reach the same end as reason, and by like paths; only reason drags its weary length along, while enthusiasm flies on eagle's wing. Besides, this love has long since budded; it only sought a heart to twine itself around. Is it love? I deceive myself perhaps. Whence this feeling that agitates me? this intoxication that has taken possession of me? this radiance that dazzles me? I saw her again, and the charm increased. How you would love her! how my mother would have loved her!

In the midst of these preoccupations I have not forgotten, madame, the instructions that you gave me. That you are interested in Mademoiselle de Chateaudun's destiny suffices to interest me likewise. The Prince de Monbert is expected here; I can therefore send you, in a few days, the information you desire taken on the spot. It has been ten years since I have seen the Prince; he has a brilliant mind and a loyal heart, and he has, in his life, seen more tigers and postilions than any other man in France. I will scrupulously note any change that ten years' travel may have brought about in his manner of thinking and seeing; but I believe that I can safely declare beforehand, that nothing can be found in his frank nature to justify the flight of the strange and beautiful heiress.

Accept, madame, my respectful homage.

RAYMOND DE VILLIERS.

XXII.

ROGER DE MONBERT *to* M. LE COMTE DE VILLIERS,
Pont de l'Arche (Eure).

Rouen, July 10th 18—.

VERY rarely in life do we receive letters that we expect; we always receive those that we don't expect. The expected ones inform us of what we already know; the unexpected ones tell us of things entirely new. A philosopher prefers the latter—of which I now send you one.

I passed some hours at Richeport with you and Edgar, and there I made a discovery that you must have made before me, and a reflection that you will make after me. I am sixty years old in my feelings—travel ages one more than anything else—you are twenty-five, according to your baptismal register. How fortunate you are to have some one able to give you advice! How unfortunate I am that my experience has been sad enough to enable me to be that one to give it! But I have a vague presentiment that my advice will bring you happiness, if followed. We should never neglect a presentiment. Every man carries in him a spark of Heaven's intelligence—it is often the torch that illumines the darkness of our future. This is called presentiment.

Read attentively, and do not disturb yourself about the end. I must first explain by what means of observation I made my discovery. Then the dénoûement will appear in its proper place, which is not at the beginning.

The following is what I saw at the Château de Richeport. You did not see it, because you were an actor. I was merely a spectator, and had that advantage over you.

You, Edgar, and myself were in the parlor at noon. It is the hour in the country when one takes shelter behind closed blinds to enjoy a friendly chat. One is always sad, dreamy, meditative at this hour of a lovely summer-day, and can speak carelessly of indifferent things, and at the same time have every thought concentrated upon one beloved object. These are the mysteries of the *Démon de Midi*, so much dreaded by the poet-king.

There was in one corner of the room a little rosewood-table, so frail that it could be crushed by the weight of a man's hand. On this table was a piece of embroidery and a crystal vase filled with flowers. Suspended over this table was a copy of Camille Roqueplan's picture: "*The Lion in Love.*" In the recess near the window was a piano open, and evidently just abandoned by a woman; the little stool was half-overturned by catching in the dress of some one suddenly rising, and the music open was a soprano air from *Puritani*:—

"Vien diletto, in ciel e luna,
Tutto tace intorno. . . ."

You will see how by inductions I reached the truth. I don't know the woman of this piano; I nevertheless will swear she exists. Moreover, I know she is young, pretty, has a good figure, is graceful and easy in her manner, and is adored by some one in the château. If any ordinary woman had left her embroidery on the table, if she had upset the stool in leaving the piano, two idle nervous young men like yourselves would from curiosity and ennui have examined the embroidery, disarranged the vase of flowers, picked up the stool, and closed the piano. But no hand dared to meddle with this holy disorder under pretext of arranging it. These evidences, still fresh and undisturbed, attest a respect that belongs only to love.

This woman, to me unknown, is then young and pretty, since she is so ardently loved, and by more than one person, as I shall proceed to prove. She has a commanding figure, because her embroidery is fine. I know not if she be maid or wife, but this I do know, if she is not married, the vestiges that she left in the parlor indicate a great independence of position and character. If she is married, she is not governed by her husband, or indeed she may be a widow.

Allow me to recall your conversation with Edgar at dinner. Hitherto I have remarked that in all discussions of painting, music, literature and love, your opinions always coincided with Edgar's; to hear you speak was to hear Edgar, and *vice versa.* In opinions and sentiments you were twin-brothers. Now listen how you both expressed yourselves before me on that day.

"I believe," said Edgar, "that love is a modern invention, and woman was invented by André Chénier, and perfected by Victor Hugo, Dumas and Balzac. We owe this precious conquest to the revolution of '89. Before that, love did not exist; Cupid with his bow and quiver reigned as a sovereign. There were no women, there were only *beauties.*

"O, miracle des belles,
Je vous enseignerais un nid de tourterelles."

"These two lines have undergone a thousand variations under the pens of a thousand poets. Women were only commended for their eyes—very beautiful things when they *are* beautiful, but they should not be made the object of exclusive admiration. A beauty possessing no attraction but beautiful eyes would soon lose her sway over the hearts of men. Racine has used the words *eye* and *eyes* one hundred and sixty-five times in *Andromache.* Woman has been deprived of her divine crown of golden or chestnut hair; she has been dethroned by having it covered with white powder. We have avenged woman for her long neglect; we have preserved the *eyes* and added all the other charms. Thus women love us poets; and in our days Orpheus would not be torn to pieces by snowy hands on the shores of the Strymon."

"Ah! that is just like you, Edgar," you said, with a sad laugh and a would-be calm voice. "At dessert you always give us a dish of paradoxes. I myself greatly prefer Montmorency cherries."

Some minutes after Edgar said:

"The other day I paid a visit to Delacroix. He has commenced a picture that promises to be superb; my dear traveller, Roger, it will possess the sky you love—pure indigo, the celestial carpet of the blue god."

"I abhor blue," you said; "I dread ophthalmia. Surfeit of blue compels the use of green spectacles. I adore the skies of

Hobbema and Backhuysen ; one can look at them with the naked eye for twenty years, and yet never need an oculist in old age."

After some rambling conversation you uttered an eulogy on a sacred air of Palestrina that you heard sung at the Conservatory concert. When you had finished, Edgar rested his elbows on the table, his chin on his hand, and let fall from his lips the following words, warmed by the spiritual fire of his eyes.

" I have always abhorred church-music," said he. " Sacred music is proscribed in my house as opium is in China. I like none but sentimental music All that does not resemble in some way the *Amor possente nome* of Rossini must remained buried in the catacombs of the piano. Music was only created for women and love. Doubtless simplicity is beautiful, but it so often only belongs to simple people.

" Art is the only passion of a true artist. The music of Palestrina resembles the music of Rossini about as much as the twitter of the swallow resembles the song of the nightingale."

It was evident to me, my young friend, that neither of you expressed your genuine convictions and true opinions. You were sitting opposite, and yet neither looked at the other while speaking. You both were handsome and charming, but handsome and charming like two English cocks before a fight. What particularly struck me was that neither of you ever said : " What is the matter with you to-day, my friend ? you seem to delight in contradicting me." Edgar did not ask you this question, nor did you ask it of him. You thought it useless to inquire into the cause of these half-angry contradictions ; you both knew what you were about. You and Edgar both love the same woman. It is the woman who suddenly retreated from the piano. Perhaps she left the house after some disagreeable scene between you two in her presence.

I watched all your movements when we three were together in the parlor. The tone of your voices, naturally sonorous, sounded harsh and discordant ; you held in your hand a branch of *hibiscus* that you idly pulled to pieces. Edgar opened a magazine and read it upside downwards ; it was quite evident that you were a restraint upon each other, and that I was a restraint upon you both.

At intervals Edgar would cast a furtive glance at the open piano, at the embroidery, and the vase of flowers; you unconsciously did the same; but your two glances never met at the same point; when Edgar looked at the flowers, you looked at the piano; if either of you had been alone, you would have never taken your eyes off these trifles that bore the perfumed impression of a beloved woman's hand, and which seemed to retain some of her personality and to console you in her absence.

You were the last comer in the house adorned by the presence of this woman; you are also the most reasonable, therefore your own sense and what is due to friendship must have already dictated your line of conduct—let me add my advice in case your conscience is not quite awake—fly! fly! before it is too late—linger, and your self-love, your interested vanity, will no longer permit you to give place to a friend who will have become a rival. Passion has not yet taken deep root in your heart; at present it is nothing more than a fancy, a transitory preference, a pleasant employment of your idle moments.

In the country, every young woman is more or less disposed to break the hearts of young men, like you, who gravitate like satellites. Women delight in this play—but like many other tragic plays, it commences with smiles but terminates in tears and blood! Moreover, my young friend, in withdrawing seasonably, you are not only wise, you are generous!

I know that Edgar has been for a long time deeply in love with this woman; you are merely indulging in a rural flirtation, a momentary caprice. In a little while, vain rivalry will make you blind, embitter your disposition, and deceive you as to the nature of your sentiments—believing yourself seriously in love you will be unable to withdraw. To-day your pride is not interested; wait not until to-morrow. Edgar is your friend, you must respect his prerogatives. A woman gave you a wise example to follow—she suddenly withdrew from the presence of you both when she saw a threatening danger.

A pretty woman is always dangerous when she comes to inaugurate the divinity of her charms in a lonely château, in the presence of two inflammable young men. I detect the cunning of the fair unknown: she lavishes innocent smiles upon both of you—she equally divides her coquetries between you; she approaches you to dazzle—she leaves you to make herself regretted; she entangles you in the illusion of her brilliant fascination; she moves to seduce your senses; she speaks to charm your soul; she sings to destroy your reason.

Forget yourself for one instant, my young friend, on this flowery slope, and woe betide you when you reach the bottom! Be intoxicated by this feast of sweet words, soft perfumes and radiant smiles, then send me a report of your soul's condition when you recover your senses! At present, in spite of your skirmishes of wit, you are still the friend of Edgar . . . hostility will certainly come. Friendship is too feeble a sentiment to struggle against love. This passion is more violent than tropical storms—I have felt it—I am one of its victims now! There lives another woman—half siren, half Circe—who has crossed my path in life, as you well know. If I had collected in my house as many friends as Socrates desired to see in his, and all these friends were to become my rivals, I feel that my jealousy would fire the house, and I would gladly perish in the flames after seeing them all dead before my eyes.

Oh, fatal preoccupation! I only wished to speak of your affairs, and here I am talking of my own. The clouds that I heap upon your horizon roll back towards mine.

In exchange for my advice, render me a service. You know Madame de Braimes, the friend of Mlle. de Chateaudun. Madame de Braimes is acquainted with everything that I am ignorant of, and that my happiness in life depends upon discovering. It is time for the inexplicable to be explained. A human enigma cannot for ever conceal its answer. Every trial must end before the despair of him who is tried. Madame de Braimes is an accomplice in this enigma; her secret now is a burden on her lips, she must let it fall into your ear, and I will cherish a life-long gratitude to you both.

Any friend but you would smile at this apparently strange language—I write you a long chapter of psychological and moral inductions to show my knowledge about the management of love affairs and affairs otherwise—I divine all your enigmas; I illuminate the darkness of all your mysteries, and when it comes to working on my own account, to be perspicacious for my own benefit, to make discoveries about my own love affair, I suddenly abdicate, I lose my luminous faculties, I put a band over my eyes, and humbly beg a friend to lend me the thread of the labyrinth and guide my steps in the bewildering darkness. All this must appear singular to you, to me it is quite natural. Through the thousand dark accidents that love scatters in the path of life, light can only reach us by means of a friend. We ourselves are helpless; looking at others we are lynx-eyed, looking at ourselves we are almost blind. It is the optical nerve of the passions. It is mortifying to thus sacrifice the highest prerogatives of man at the feet of a woman, to feel compelled to yield to her caprices and submit to the inexorable exigencies of love. The artificial life I am leading is odious to me. Patience is a virtue that died with Job, and I cannot perform the miracle of resuscitating it.

Take my advice—be prudent—be wise—be generous—leave Richeport and come to me; we can assist and console each other; you can render me a great service, I will explain how when we meet—I will remain here for a few days; do not hesitate to come at once—Between a friend who fears you and a friend who loves you and claims you—can you hesitate?

ROGER DE MONBERT.

XXIII.

IRENE DE CHATEAUDUN *to* MME. LA VICOMTESSE DE BRAIMES,
Grenoble (Isere).

Pont de l'Arche, July 15th 18—.

COME to my help, my dear Valentine—I am miserable. Each joyless morning finds me more wretched than I was the previous night. Oh! what a burden is life to those who are fated to live only for life itself! No sunshine gilds my horizon with the promises of hope—I expect nothing but sorrow. Who can I trust now that my own heart has misled me? When error arose from the duplicity of others I could support the disenchantment—the deceptive love of Roger was not a bitter surprise, my instinct had already divined it; I comprehended a want of congeniality between us, and felt that a rupture would anticipate an alliance; and while thinking I loved him, I yet said to myself: This is not love.

But now I am my own deceiver—and I awaken to lament the self-confidence and assurance that were the source of my strength and courage. With flattering ecstasy I cried: It is he! . . . Alas! he replied not: It is she! And now he is gone—he has left me! Dreadful awakening from so beautiful a dream!

Valentine, burn quickly the letter telling you of my ingenuous hopes, my confident happiness—yes, burn the foolish letter, so there will remain no witness of my unrequited love! What! that deep emotion agitating my whole being, whose language was the tears of joy that dimmed my eyes, and the counted beatings of my throbbing heart—that master-passion, at whose behest I trembled while blushes mantled and fled from my cheek, betraying me to him and him to me; the love whose fire I could not hide—the beautiful future I foresaw—that world of bliss in which I began to live—this pure love that gave an impetus to life—this devotion that I felt was reciprocated. . . . All, all was but a creation of my fancy. . . . and all has vanished

. . . here I am alone with nothing to strengthen me but a memory . . . the memory of a lost illusion. . . . Have I a right to complain? It is the irrevocable law—after fiction, reality—after a meteor, darkness—after the mirage, a desert!

I loved as a young heart full of faith and tenderness never oved before—and this love was a mistake; he was a stranger to me—he did not love me, and I had no excuse for loving him; he is gone, he had a right to go, and I had no right to detain him—I have not even the right to mourn his absence. Who is he? A friend of Madame de Meilhan, and a stranger to me! . . He a stranger! . . . to me! . . . No, no, he loves me, I know he does . . . but why did he not tell me so! Has some one come between us? Perhaps a suspicion separates us. . . . Oh! he may think I am in love with Edgar! horrible idea! the thought kills me. . . . I will write to him; would you not advise it? What shall I tell him? If he were to know who I am, doubtless his prejudices against me would be removed. Oh! I will return to Paris—then he will see that I do not love Edgar, since I leave him never to return where he is. Yet he could not have been mistaken concerning the feelings existing between his friend and myself; he must have seen that I was perfectly free: independence cannot be assumed. If he thought me in love with another, why did he come to bid me good-bye? why did he come alone to see me? and why did he not allude to my approaching return to Paris?—why did he not say he would be glad to meet me again? How pale and sad he was! and yet he uttered not one word of regret—of distant hope! The servant said: "Monsieur de Villiers wishes to see madame, shall I send him away as I did Monsieur de Meilhan?" I was in the garden and advanced to meet him. He said: "I return to Paris to-morrow, madame, and have come to see if you have any commands, and to bid you good-bye."

Two long days had passed since I last saw him, and this unexpected visit startled me so that I was afraid to trust my voice to speak. "They will miss you very much at Richeport," he added, "and Madame de Meilhan hopes daily to see you return." I hastily said: "I cannot return to her house, I am going away from here very soon." He did not ask where, but gazed at me in a strange, almost suspicious way, and to change the conversation, said: "We had at Richeport, after you left, a charming man, who is celebrated for his wit and for being a great traveller—the Prince de Monbert." . . . He spoke as if on an indifferent subject, and Heaven knows he was right, for Roger at this moment interested me very, very little. I waited for a word of the future, a ray of hope to brighten my life, another of those tender glances that thrilled my soul with joy . . . but he avoided all allusion to our past intercourse; he shunned my looks as carefully as he had formerly sought them. . . . I was alarmed. . . . I no longer understood him. . . . I looked around to see if we were not watched, so changed was his manner, so cold and formal was his speech. . . . Strange! I was alone with him, but he was not alone with me; there was a third person between us, invisible to me, but to him visible, dictating his words and inspiring his conduct.

"Shall you remain long in Paris?" I asked, trembling and dismayed. "I am not decided at present, madame," he replied. Irritated by this mystery, I was tempted for a moment to say: "I hope, if you remain in Paris for any length of time, I shall have the pleasure of seeing you at my cousin's, the Duchess de Langeac," and then I thought of telling him my story. I was tired of playing the rôle of adventuress before him . . . but he seemed so preoccupied, and inattentive to what I said, he so coldly received my affectionate overtures, that I had not the courage to confide in him. Would not my confidence be met with indifference? One thing consoled me—his sadness; and then he had come, not on my account, but on his own; nothing obliged him to make this visit; it could only have been inspired by a wish to see me. While he remained near me, in spite of his strange indifference, I had hope; I believed that in his farewell there would be one kind word upon which I could live till we should meet again. . . I was mistaken . . . he bowed and left me . . . left me without a word . . . ! Then I felt that all was lost, and bursting into tears sobbed like a child. Suddenly the servant opened the door and said: "The gentleman forgot Madame de Meilhan's letters." At that moment he entered the room and took from the table a packet of letters that the servant had given him when he first came, but which he had forgotten when leaving. At the sight of my tears he stood still with an agitated, alarmed look upon his face; he then gazed at me with a singular expression of cruel joy sparkling in his eyes. I thought he had come back to say something to me, but he abruptly left the room. I heard the door shut, and knew it had shut off my hopes of happiness.

The next day, at the risk of meeting Edgar with him, I remained all day on the road that runs along the Seine. I hoped he would go that way. I also hoped he would come once more to see me . . . to bring him back I relied upon my tears—upon those tears shed for him, and which he must have understood . . . he came not! Three days have passed since he left, and I spend all my time in recalling this last interview, what he said to me, his tone of voice, his look. . . . One minute I find an explanation for everything, my faith revives . . . he loves me! he is waiting for something to happen, he wishes to take some step, he fears some obstacle, he waits to clear up some doubts . . . a generous scruple restrains him. . . . The next minute the dreadful truth stares me in the face. I say to myself: "He is a young man full of imagination, of romantic ideas . . . we met, I pleased him, he would have loved me had I belonged to his station in life; but everything separates us; he will forget me." . . . Then, revolting against a fate that I can successfully resist, I exclaim: "I *will* see him again. . . I am young, free, and beautiful—I must be beautiful, for he told me so—I have an income of a hundred thousand pounds . . . . With all these blessings it would be absurd for me not to be happy. Besides, I love him deeply, and this ardent love inspires me with great confidence . . . it is impossible that so much love should be born in my heart for no purpose." . . . Sometimes this confidence deserts me, and I despairingly say: "M. de

Villiers is a loyal man, who would have frankly said to me: 'I love you, love me and let us be happy.'" . . . Since he did not say that, there must exist between us an insurmountable obstacle, a barrier of invincible delicacy; because he is engaged he cannot devote his life to me, and he must renounce me for ever. M. de Meilhan comes here every day; I send word I am too sick to see him; which is the truth, for I would be in Paris now if I were well enough to travel. I shall not return by the cars, I dread meeting Roger. I forgot to tell you about his arrival at Richeport; it is an amusing story; I laughed very much at the time; *then* I could laugh, now I never expect to smile again.

Four days ago, I was at Richeport, all the time wishing to leave, and always detained by Mad. de Meilhan; it was about noon, and we were all sitting in the parlor—Edgar, M. de Villiers, Mad. de Meilhan and myself. Ah! how happy I was that day. . . How could I foresee any trouble? . . . They were listening to an air I was playing from Bellini. . . A servant entered and asked this simple question: "Does madame expect the Prince de Monbert by the twelve o'clock train?" . . . . . At this name I quickly fled, without stopping to pick up the piano stool that I overturned in my hurried retreat. I ran to my room, took my hat and an umbrella to hide my face should I meet any one, and walked to Pont de l'Arche. Soon after I heard the Prince had arrived, and dinner was ordered for five o'clock, so he could leave in the 7.30 train. Politeness required me to send word to Mad. de Meilhan that I would be detained at Pont de l'Arche. To avoid the entreaties of Edgar I took refuge at the house of an old fishwoman, near the gate of the town. She is devoted to me, and I often take her children toys and clothes. At half-past six, the time for Roger to be taken to the depot, I was at the window of this house, which was on the road that led to the cars—presently I heard several familiar voices. . . . I heard my name distinctly pronounced. . . . "Mlle. de Chateaudun." . . . I concealed myself behind the half-closed blinds, and attentively listened: "She is at Rouen," said the Prince.

. . . "What a strange woman," said M. de Villiers: "Ah! this conduct is easily explained," said Edgar, "she is angry with him." "Doubtless she believes me culpable," replied the Prince, "and I wish at all costs to see her and justify myself." In speaking thus, they all three passed under the window where I was. I trembled—I dared not look at them. . . . When they had gone by, I peeped through the shutter and saw them all standing still and admiring the beautiful bridge with its flower-covered pillars, and the superb landscape spread before them. Seeing these three handsome men standing there, all three so elegant, so distinguished! A wicked sentiment of female vanity crossed my mind; and I said to myself with miserable pride and triumph: "All three love me. . . All three are thinking of me!" . . . Oh! I have been cruelly punished for this contemptible vanity. Alas! one of the three did not love me—and he was the one I loved—one of them did not think of me, and he was the one that filled my every thought. Another sentiment more noble than the first, saddened my heart. I said: "Here are three devoted friends . . . perhaps they will soon be bitter enemies . . . and I the cause." O Valentine! you cannot imagine how sad and despondent I am. Do not desert me now that I most need your comforting sympathy! Burn my last letter, I entreat you.

IRENE DE CHATEAUDUN.

XXIV.

EDGAR DE MEILHAN *to* MADAME GUERIN,
Pont de l'Arche (Eure).

RICHEPORT, July 10th 18—.

THREE times have I been to the post-office since you left the château in such an abrupt and inexplicable manner. I am lost in conjecture about your sudden departure, which was both unnecessary and unprepared. It is doubtless because you do not wish to tell me the reason that you refuse to see me. I know that you are still at Pont de l'Arche, and that you have never left Madame Taverneau's house. So that when she tells me in a measured and mysterious tone that you have been absent for some time; looking at the closed door of your room, behind which I divine your presence, I am seized with an insane desire to kick down the narrow plank which separates me from you. Fits of gloomy passion possess me which illogical obstacles and unjust resistance always excite.

What have I done? What can you have against me? Let me at least know the crime for which I am punished. On the scaffold they always read the victim his sentence, equitable or otherwise. Will you be more cruel than a hangman? Read me my sentence. Nothing is more frightful than to be executed in a dungeon without knowing for what offence.

For three days—three eternities—I have taxed my memory to an alarming extent. I have recalled everything that I have said for the last two weeks, word by word, syllable for syllable, endeavoring to give to each expression its intonation, its inflection, its sharps and flats. Every different signification that the music of the voice could give to a thought, I have analyzed, debated, commented upon twenty times a day. Not a word, accent nor gesture has enlightened me. I defy the most embittered and envious spirit to find anything that could offend the most susceptible pride, the haughtiest majesty. Nothing has occurred in my familiar intercourse with you that would alarm a sensitive plant or a mimosa. Therefore, such cannot be the motive for your panic-stricken flight. I am young, ardent, impetuous; I attach no importance to certain social conventionalities, but I feel confident that I have never failed in a religious respect for the holiness of love and modesty. I love you—I could never, wilfully, have offended you. How could my eyes and lips have expressed what was neither in my head nor in my heart? If there is no fire without smoke, as a natural consequence there can be no smoke without fire!

It is not that—Is it caprice or coquetry? Your mind is too serious and your soul too honest for such an act; and besides, what would be your object? Such feline cruelties may suit blasé women of the world who are roused by the sight of moral torture; who give, in the invisible sphere of the passions, feasts of the Roman empresses, where beating hearts are torn by the claws of the wild beasts of the soul, unbridled desires, insatiate hate and maddened jealousy, all the hideous pack of bad passions. Louise, you have not wished to play such a game with me. It would be unavailing and dangerous.

Although I have been brought up in what is called the world, I am still a savage at heart. I can talk as others do of politics, railroads, social economy, literature. I can imitate civilized gesture tolerably well; but under this white-glove polish I have preserved the vehemence and simplicity of barbarism. Unless you have some serious, paramount reason, not one of those trivial excuses with which ordinary women revenge themselves upon the lukewarmness of their lovers—do not prolong my punishment a day, an hour, a minute—speak not to me of reputation, virtue or duty. You have given me the right to love you—by the light of the stars, under the sweet-scented acacias, in the sunlight at the window of Richard's donjon which opens over an abyss. You have conferred upon me that august priesthood. Your hand has trembled in mine. A celestial light, kindled by my glance, has shone in your eyes. If only for a moment, your soul was mine—the electric spark united us.

It may be that this signifies nothing to you. I refuse to acknowledge any such subtle distinctions—that moment united us for ever. For one instant you wished to love me; I cannot divide my mind, soul and body into three distinct parts; all my being worships you and longs to obtain you. I cannot graduate my love according to its object. I do not know who you are. You might be a queen of earth or the queen of heaven; I could not love you otherwise.

Receive me. You need explain nothing if you do not wish; but receive me; I cannot live without you. What difference does it make to you if I see you?

Ah! how I suffered, even when you were at the château! What evil influence stood between us? I had a vague feeling that something important and fatal had happened. It was a sort of presentiment of the fulfilment of a destiny. Was your fate or mine decided in that hour, or both? What decisive sentence had the recording angel written upon the ineffaceable register of the future? Who was condemned and who absolved in that solemn hour?

And yet no appreciable event happened, nothing appeared changed in our life. Why this fearful uneasiness, this deep dejection, this presentiment of a great but unknown danger? I have had that same instinctive perception of evil, that magnetic terror which slumbering misers experience when a thief prowls around their hidden treasure; it seemed as if some one wished to rob me of my happiness.

We were embarrassed in each other's presence; some one acted as a restraint upon us. Who was it? No one was there but Raymond, one of my best friends, who had arrived the evening before and was soon to depart in order to marry his cousin, young, pretty and rich! It is singular that he, so gentle, so confiding, so unreserved, so chivalrous, should have appeared to me sharp, taciturn, rough, almost dull,—and my feelings towards him were full of bitterness and spite. Can friendship be but lukewarm hate? I fear so, for I often felt a savage desire to quarrel with Raymond and seize him by the throat. He talked of a blade of grass, a fly, of the most indifferent object, and I felt wounded as if by a personality. Everything he did offended me; if he stood up I was indignant, if he sat down I became furious; every movement of his seemed a provocation; why did I not perceive this sooner? How does it happen that the man for whom I entertain such a strong natural aversion should have been my friend for ten years? How strange that I should not have been aware of this antipathy sooner!

And you, ordinarily so natural, so easy in your manners, became constrained; you scarcely answered me when he was present. The simplest expression agitated you; it seemed as if you had to give an account to some one of every word, and that you were afraid of a scolding, like a young girl who is brought by her mother into the drawing-room for the first time.

One evening, I was sitting by you on the sofa, reading to you that sublime elegy of the great poet, La Tristesse d'Olympio; Raymond entered. You rose abruptly, like a guilty child, assumed an humble and repentant attitude, asking forgiveness with your eyes. In what secret compact, what hidden covenant, had you failed?

The look with which Raymond answered yours doubtless contained your pardon, for you resumed your seat, but moved away from me so as not to abuse the accorded grace; I continued to read, but you no longer listened—you were absorbed in a delicious revery through which floated vaguely the lines of the poet. I was at your feet, and never have I felt so far away from you. The space between us, too narrow for another to occupy, was an abyss.

What invisible hand dashed me down from my heaven? Who drove me, in my unconsciousness, as far from you as the equator from the pole? Yesterday your eyes, bathed in light and life, turned softly towards me; your hand rested willingly in mine. You accepted my love, unavowed but understood; for I hate those declarations which remind one of a challenge. If one has need to say that he loves, he is not worth loving; speech is intended for indifferent beings; talking is a means of keeping silent; you must have seen, in my glance, by the trembling of my voice, in my sudden changes of color, by the impalpable caress of my manner, that I love you madly.

It was when Raymond looked at you that I began to appreciate the depth of my passion. I felt as if some one had thrust a red-hot iron into my heart. Ah! what a wretched country France is! If I were in Turkey, I would bear you off on my Arab steed, shut you up in a harem, with walls bristling with cimetars, surrounded by a deep moat; black eunuchs should sleep before the threshold of your chamber, and at night, instead of dogs, lions should guard the precincts!

Do not laugh at my violence, it is sincere; no one will ever love you like me. Raymond cannot—a sentimental Don Quixote, in search of adventures and chivalrous deeds. In order to love a woman, he must have fished her out of the spray of Niagara; or dislocated his shoulder in stopping her carriage on the brink of a precipice; or snatched her out of the hands of picturesque bandits, costumed like Fra Diavolo; he is only fit for the hero of a ten-volume English novel, with a long-tailed coat, tight gray pantaloons and top-boots. You are too sensible to admire the philanthropic freaks of this modern paladin, who would be ridiculous were he not brave, rich and handsome; this moral Don Juan, who seduces by his virtue, cannot suit you.

When shall I see you? Our moments of happiness in this life are so short; I have lost three days of Paradise by your persistence in concealing yourself. What god can ever restore them to me?

Louise, I have only loved, till now, marble shadows, phantoms of beauty; but what is this love of sculpture and painting compared with the passion that consumes me? Ah! how bittersweet it is to be deprived at once of will, strength and reason, and trembling, kneeling, vanquished, to surrender the key of one's heart into the hands of the beautiful victor! Do not, like Elfrida, throw it into the torrent!

EDGAR DE MEILHAN.

XXV.

RAYMOND DE VILLIERS *to* MME. LA VICOMTESSE DE BRAIMES,
Hotel of the Prefecture, Grenoble (Isère).

ROUEN, July 12th 18—

MADAME:—If you should find in these hastily written lines expressions of severity that might wound you in one of your tenderest affections, I beg you to ascribe them to the serious interest with which you have inspired me for a person whom I do do not know. Madame, the case is serious, and the comedy, performed for the gratification of childish vanity, might, if prolonged, end in a tragedy. Let Mademoiselle de Chateaudun know immediately that her peace of mind, her whole future is at stake. You have not a day, not an hour, not an instant to lose in exerting your influence. I answer for nothing; haste, O haste! Your position, your high intelligence, your good sense give you, necessarily, the authority of an elder sister or a mother over Mademoiselle de Chateaudun; exercise it if you would save that reckless girl. If she acts from caprice, nothing can justify it; if she is playing a game it is a cruel one, with ruin in the end; if she is subjecting M. de Monbert to a trial, it has lasted long enough.

I accompanied M. de Monbert to Rouen; I lived in daily, hourly intercourse with him, and had ample opportunities for studying his character; he is a wounded lion. Never having had the honor of meeting Mademoiselle de Chateaudun, I cannot tell whether the Prince is the man to suit her; Mademoiselle de Chateaudun alone can decide so delicate a question. But I do assert that M. de Monbert is not the man to be trifled with, and whatever decision Mademoiselle de Chateaudun may come to, it is her duty and due to her dignity to put an end to his suspense.

If she must strike, let her strike quickly, and not show herself more pitiless than the executioner, who, at least, puts a speedy end to his victim's misery. M. de Monbert, a gentleman in the higheat acceptation of the word, would not be what he now is, if he had been treated with the consideration that his sincere distress so worthy of pity, his true love so worthy of respect, commanded. Let her not deceive herself; she has awakened, not one of those idle loves born in a Parisian atmosphere, which die as they have lived, without a struggle or a heart-break, but a strong and deep passion that if trifled with may destroy her. I acknowledge that there is something absurd in a prince on the eve of marrying a young and beautiful heiress finding himself deserted by his fiancée with her millions; but when one has seen the comic hero of this little play, the scene changes. The smile fades from the lips; the jest is silent; terror follows in the footsteps of gayety, and the foolish freak of the lovely fugitive assumes the formidable proportions of a frightful drama. M. de Monbert is not what he is generally supposed to be, what I supposed him before seeing him after ten years' separation. His blood has been inflamed by torrid suns; he has preserved, in a measure, the manners and fierce passions of the distant peoples that he has visited; he hides it all under the polish of grace and elegance; affable and ready for anything, one would never suspect, to see him, the fierce and turbulent passions warring in his breast; he is like those wells in India, which he told me of this morning; they are surrounded by flowers and luxuriant foliage; go down into one of them and you will quickly return pale and horror-stricken. Madame, I assure you that this man suffers everything that it is possible to suffer here below. I watch his despair; it terrifies me. Wounded love and pride do not alone prey upon him; he is aware that Mademoiselle de Chateaudun may believe him guilty of serious errors; he demands to be allowed to justify himself in her eyes; he is exasperated by the consciousness of his unrecognised innocence. Condemn him, if you will, but at least let him be heard in his own defence. I have seen him writhe in agony and give way to groans of rage and despair. When calm, he is more terrible to contemplate; his silence is the pause before a tempest. Yesterday, on returning, discouraged, after a whole day spent in fruitless search, he took my hand and raised it abruptly to his eyes. "Raymond," said he, "I have never wept," and my hand was wet. If you love Mademoiselle de Chateaudun, if her future happiness is dear to you, if her heart can only be touched through you, warn her, madame, warn her immediately; tell her plainly what she has to expect; time presses.

It is a question of nothing less than anticipating an irreparable misfortune. There is but one step from love to hate; hate which takes revenge is still love. Tell this child that she is playing with thunder; tell her the thunder mutters, and will soon burst over her head. If Mademoiselle de Chateaudun should have a new love for her excuse, if she has broken her faith to give it to another, unhappy, thrice unhappy she! M. de Monbert has a quick eye and a practised hand; mourning would follow swiftly in the wake of her rejoicing, and Mademoiselle de Chateaudun might order her widow's weeds and her bridal robes at the same time.

This, madame, is all that I have to say. The foolish rapture with which my last letter teemed is not worth speaking of. A broken hope, crushed, extinguished; a happiness vanished ere fully seen! During the four days that I was at Richeport, I began to remark the existence between M. de Meilhan and myself of a sullen, secret, unavowed but real irritation, when a letter from M. de Monbert solved the enigma by convincing me that I was in the way under that roof. Fool, why did I not see it myself and sooner? Blind that I was, not to perceive from the first that this young man loved that woman! Why did I not instantly divine that this young poet could not live unscathed near so much beauty, grace and sweetness? Did I think, unhappy man that I am, that she was only fair to me; that I alone had eyes to admire her, a heart to worship and understand her? Yes, I did think it; I believed blindly that she bloomed for me alone; that she had not existed before our meeting; that no look, save mine, had ever rested upon her;

that she was, in fact, my creation; that I had formed her of my thoughts, and vivified her with the fire of my dreams. Even now, when we are parted for ever, I believe, that if God ever created two beings for each other, we are those two beings, and if every soul has a sister spirit, her soul is the sister spirit of mine. M. de Meilhan loves her; who would not love her? But what he loves in her is visible beauty: the slope of her shoulders, the perfection of her contours. His love could not withstand a pencil-stroke which might destroy the harmony of the whole. Beautiful as she is, he would desert her for the first canvas or the first statue he might encounter. Her rivals already people the galleries of the Louvre; the museums of the world are filled with them. Edgar feels but one deep and true love; the love of Art, so deep that it excludes or absorbs all others in his heart. A fine prospect alone charms him, if it recalls a landscape of Ruysdael or of Paul Huet, and he prefers to the loveliest model, her portrait, provided it bears the signature of Ingres or Scheffer. He loves this woman as an artist; he has made her the delight of his eyes; she would have been the joy of my whole life. Besides, Edgar does not possess any of the social virtues. He is whimsical by nature, hostile to the proprieties, an enemy to every well-beaten track. His mind is always at war with his heart; his sincerest inspirations have the scoffing accompaniment of Don Juan's romance. No, he cannot make the happiness of this Louise so long sought for, so long hoped for, found, alas! to be irremediably lost. Louise deceives herself if she thinks otherwise. But she does not think so. What is so agonizing in the necessity that separates us, is the conviction that such a separation blasts two destinies, silently united. I do not repine at the loss of my own happiness alone, but above all, over that of this noble creature. I am convinced that when we met, we recognised each other; she mentally exclaimed, "It is he!" when I told myself, "It is she!" When I went to bid her farewell, a long, eternal farewell, I found her pale, sad; the tears rolled, unchecked, down her cheeks. She loves me, I know it; I feel it; and still I must depart! she wept.

and I was forced to be silent! One single word would have opened Paradise to us, and that word I could not utter! Farewell, sweet dream, vanished for ever! And thou, stern and stupid honor, I curse thee while I serve thee, and execrate while I sacrifice all to thee. Ah! do not think that I am resigned; do not believe that pride can ever fill up the abyss into which I have voluntarily cast myself; do not hope that some day I shall find self-satisfaction as a recompense for my abnegation. There are moments when I hate myself and rebel against my own imbecility. Why depart? What is Edgar to me? still less, what interest have I in his love episodes? I love; I feel myself loved in return; what have I to do with anything else?

Contempt for my cowardly virtue is the only price that I have received for my sacrifice, and I twit myself with this thought of Pascal: "Man is neither an angel nor a brute, and the misfortune is that when he wishes to make himself an angel, he becomes a brute!" Be silent, my heart! At least it shall never be said that the descendant of a race of cavaliers entered his friend's house to rob him of his happiness.

I am sad, madame. The bright ray seen for a moment, has but made the darkness into which I have fallen, more black and sombre; I am unutterably sad! What is to become of me? Where shall I drag out my weary days? I do not know. Everything wearies and bores me, or rather all things are indifferent to me. I think I will travel. Wherever I go, your image will accompany me, consoling me, if I can be consoled. At first I thought that I would carry you my heart to comfort; but my unhappiness is dear to me, and I do not wish to be cured of it.

I press M. de Braimes's hand, and clasp your charming children warmly to my heart.

RAYMOND DE VILLIERS.

XXVI.

EDGAR DE MEILHAN *to the* PRINCE DE MONBERT,
Poste Restante (Rouen).

Richeport, July 23d 18—.

I AM mad with rage, wild with grief! That Louise! I do not know what keeps me from setting fire to the house that conceals her! I must go away; I shall commit some insane act, some crime, if I remain! I have written her letter after letter; I have tried in every way to see her; all my efforts unavailing! It is like beating your head against a wall! Coquette and prude!—appalling combination, too common a monstrosity, alas!

She will not see me! all is over! nothing can overcome her stupid, obstinacy which she takes for virtue. If I could only have spoken to her once, I should have said—I don't know what, but I should have found words to make her return to me. But she entrenches herself behind her obstinacy; she knows that I would vanquish her; she has no good arguments with which to answer me; for I love her madly, desperately, frantically! Passion is eloquent. She flies from me! O perfidy and cowardice! she dare not face the misery she has caused, and veils her eyes when she strikes!

I am going to America. I will dull my mental grief by physical exhaustion; I will subdue the soul through the body; I will ascend the giant rivers whose bosoms bloom with thousands of islands; penetrate into the virgin forests where no trapper has yet set his foot; I will hunt the buffalo with the savage, and swim upon that ocean of shaggy heads and sharp horns; I will gallop at full speed over the prairie, pursued by the smoke of the burning grass. If the memory of Louise refuses to leave me, I will stop my horse and await the flames! I will carry my love so far away that it must perforce leave me.

I feel it, my life is wrecked for ever!—I cannot live in a world where Louise is not mine! Perhaps the young universe may contain a panacea for my anguish! Solitude shall pour its balm in my wound; once away from this civilization which stifles me, nature will cradle me in her motherly arms; the elements will resume their empire over me; ocean, sky, flowers, foliage will draw off the feverish electricity that excites my nerves; I will become absorbed in the grand whole, I will no longer live; I will vegetate and succeed in attaining the content of the plant that opens its leaves to the sun. I feel that I must stop my brain, suspend the beating of my heart, or I shall go raving mad.

I shall sail from Havre. A year from now write to me at the English fort in the Rocky Mountains, and I will join you in whatever corner of the globe you have gone to bury your despair over the loss of Irene de Chateaudun!

EDGAR DE MEILHAN

XXVII.

EDGAR DE MEILHAN *to* MADAME GUERIN,

Pont-de-l'Arche (Eure).

RICHEPORT, July 23d 18—.

LOUISE, I write to you, although the resolution that I have taken should, no doubt, be silently carried out; but the swimmer struggling with the waves in mid-ocean cannot help, although he knows it is useless, uttering a last wild cry ere he sinks forever beneath the flood. Perhaps a sail may appear on the desert horizon and his last despairing shout be heard! It is so hard to believe ourselves finally condemned and to renounce all hope of pardon! My letter will be of no avail, and yet I cannot help sending it.

I am going to leave France, change worlds and skies. My passage is taken for America. The murmur of ocean and forest must soothe my despair. A great sorrow requires immensity. I would suffocate here. I should expect, at every turn, to see your white dress gleaming among the trees. Richeport is too much associated with you for me to dwell here longer; your memory has exiled me from it for ever. I must put a huge impossibility between myself and you; six thousand miles hardly suffice to separate us.

If I remained, I should resort to all manner of mad schemes to recover my happiness; no one gives up his cherished dream with more reluctance than I, especially when a word could make it a reality.

Louise, Louise, why do you avoid me and close your heart against me! You have not understood, perhaps, how much I love you? Has not my devotion shone in my eyes? I have not been able, perhaps, to convey to you what I felt? You have no more comprehended my adoration than the insensate idol the prayers of the faithful prostrated before it.

Nevertheless, I was convinced that I could make you happy;

I thought that I appreciated the longings of your soul, and would be able to satisfy them all.

What crime have I committed against heaven to be punished with this biting despair? Perhaps I have failed to appreciate some sincere affection, repulsed unwittingly some simple, tender heart that your coldness now avenges; perhaps you are, unconsciously, the Nemesis of some forgotten fault.

How fearful it is to suffer from rejected love! To say to oneself: "The loved one exists, far from me, without me; she is young, smiling, lovely—to others; my despair is only an annoyance to her, I am necessary to her in nothing; my absence leaves no void in her life; my death would only provoke from her an expression of careless pity; my good and noble qualities have made no impression upon her; my verses, the delight of other young hearts, she has never read; my talents are as destructive to me as if they were crimes; why seek a hell in another world; is it not here?

And besides, what infinite tenderness, what perpetual care, what timid and loving persistence, what obedience to every unexpressed wish, what prompt realization of even the slightest fancy! for what! for a careless glance, a smile that the thought of another brings to her lips! How can it be helped! he who is not beloved is always in the wrong.

I go away, carrying the iron in my wound; I will not drag it out, I prefer to die with it. May you live happy, may the fearful suffering that you have caused me never be expiated. I would have it so; society punishes murder of the body, heaven punishes murders of the soul. May your hidden assassination escape Divine vengeance as long as possible.

Farewell, Louise, farewell.

EDGAR DE MEILHAN.

XXVIII.

IRENE DE CHATEAUDUN *to* MME. LA VICOMTESSE DE BRAIMES,
Hotel de la Prefecture, Grenoble (Isère).

PARIS, July 27th 18—.

VALENTINE, I am very uneasy. Why have I not heard from you for a month? Are you in any trouble? Is one of your dear children ill? Are you no longer at Grenoble? Have you taken your trip without me? The last would be the most acceptable reason for your silence. You have not received my letters, and ignorance of my sorrows accounts for your not writing to console me. Yet never have I been in greater need of the offices of friendship. The resolution I have just taken fills me with alarm. I acted against my judgment, but I could not do otherwise. I was influenced by an agonized mother, whose hallowed grief persuaded me against my will to espouse her interests. Why have I not a friend here to interpose in my behalf and save me from myself? But, after all, does it make any difference what becomes of me? Hope is dead within me. I no longer dream of happiness. At last the sad mystery is explained. . . . M. de Villiers is not free; he is engaged to his cousin. . . . Oh, he does not love her, I am sure, but he is a slave to his plighted troth, and of course she loves him and will not release him. . . . Can he, for a stranger, sacrifice family ties and a love dating from his childhood? Ah! if he really loved me, he would have had the courage to make this sacrifice; but he only felt a tender sympathy for me, lively enough to fill him with everlasting regret, not strong enough to inspire him with a painful resolution. Thus two beings created for each other meet for a moment, recognise one another, and then, unwillingly, separate, carrying in their different paths of life a burden of eternal regrets! And they languish apart in their separate spheres, unhappy and attached to nothing but the memory of the past—made wretched for life by the accidents of a day!

They are as the passengers of different ships, meeting for an hour in the same port, who hastily exchange a few words of sympathy, then pass away to other latitudes, under other skies—some to the North, others to the South, to the land of ice—to the cradle of the sun—far, far away from each other, to die. Is it then true that I shall never see him again? Oh, my God! how I loved him! I can never forgive him for not accepting this love that I was ready to lavish upon him.

I will now tell you what I have resolved to do. If I waver a moment I shall not have the courage to keep my promise. Madame de Meilhan is coming after me; I could not, after causing her such sorrow, resist the tears of this unhappy mother. She was in despair; her son had suddenly left her, and in spite of the secrecy of his movements, she discovered that he was at Havre and had taken passage there for America, on the steamer Ontario. She hoped to reach Havre in time to see her son, and she relied upon me to bring him home. I am distressed at causing her so much uneasiness, but what can I say to console her? I will at best be generous; Edgar's sorrow is like my own; as he suffers for me, I suffer for another; I cannot see his anguish, so like my own, without profound pity; this pity will doubtless inspire me with eloquence enough to persuade him to remain in France and not break his mother's heart by desertion. Besides, I have promised, and Madame de Meilhan relies upon me. How beautiful is maternal love! It crushes the loftiest pride, it overthrows with one cry the most ambitious plans; this haughty woman is subjugated by grief; she calls me her daughter; she gladly consents to this marriage which, a short time ago, she said would ruin her son's prospects, and which she looked upon with horror; she weeps, she supplicates. This morning she embraced me with every expression of devotion and cried out: "Give me back my son! Oh, restore to me my son! . . . You love him, . . . he loves you, . . . he is handsome, charming, talented. . . . I shall never see him again if you let him go away; tell him you love him; have you the cruelty to deprive me of my only son?" What could I say? how could I make an idolizing mother understand that I did not love her son? . . . If I had dared to say, "It is not he that I love, it is another," . . . she would have said: "It is false; there is not a man on earth preferable to my son." She wept over the letter that Edgar wrote me before leaving. Valentine, this letter was noble and touching. I could not restrain my own tears when I read it. Finally, I was forced to yield. I am to accompany Madame de Meilhan to Havre; I hope we will reach there before the steamer leaves! . . . Edgar will not go to America, . . . and I! . . . Oh, why is he the one to love me thus? . . . She has come for me! Adieu; write to me, my dear Valentine, . . . I am so miserable. If you were only here! What will become of me? Adien!

IRENE DE CHATEAUDUN.

XXIX.

IRENE DE CHATEAUDUN *to* MME. LA VICOMTESSE DE BRAIMES,
Hotel de la Prefecture, Grenoble (Isère).

Paris, Aug. 2d 18—.

IT is fortunate for me to-day, my dear Valentine, that I have the reputation of being a truthful person, professing a hatred of falsehood, otherwise you would not believe the strange facts that I am about to relate to you. I now expect to reap the fruits of my unvarying sincerity. Having always shown such respect for truth, I deserve to be believed when I assert what appears to be incredible.

What startling events have occurred in a few hours! My destiny has been changed by my peeping through a hole!! Without one word of comment I will state exactly what happened, and you must not accuse me of highly coloring my pictures; they are lively enough in themselves without any assistance from me. Far from adding to their brilliancy, I shall endeavor to tone them down and give them an air of probability. We left Pont de l'Arche the other day with sad and anxious hearts; during the journey Mad. de Meilhan, as if doubting the strength of my resolution and the ardor of my devotion, dilated enthusiastically upon the merits of her son. She boasted of his generosity, of his disinterestedness and sincerity; she mentioned the names of several wealthy young ladies whom he had refused to marry during the last two or three years. She spoke of his great success as a poet and a brilliant man. She impressed upon me that a noble love could exercise such a happy influence upon his genius, and said it was in my power to make him a good and happy man for life, by accepting this love, which she described to me in such touching language, that I felt moved and impressed, if not with love, at least with tender appreciation. She said Edgar had never loved any one as he had loved me—this passion had changed all his ideas—he lived for me alone. To indu/e him to listen to any one it was necessary to bring my name in the conversation so as to secure his ear; he spent his days and nights composing poems in my honor. He should have returned to Paris in response to the beautiful Marquise de R.'s sighs and smiles, but he never had the courage to leave me; for me he had pitilessly sacrificed this woman, who was lovely, witty and the reigning belle of Paris. She mournfully told me of the wild foolish things he would do upon his return to Richeport, after having made fruitless attempts to see me at Pont de l'Arche; his cruelty to his favorite horse, his violence against the flowers along the path, that he would cut to pieces with his whip; his sullen, mute despair; his extravagant talk to her; her own uneasiness; her useless prayers; and finally this fatal departure that she had vainly endeavored to prevent. She saw that I was affected by what she said, she seized my hand and called down blessings upon me, thanking me a thousand times passionately and imperiously, as if to compel me to accede to her wishes.

I sorrowfully reflected upon all this trouble that I had caused, and was frightened at the conviction that I had by a few engaging smiles and a little harmless coquetry inspired so violent a passion. Thinking thus, I did justice to Edgar, and acknowledged that some reparation was due to him. He must have taken all these deceptive smiles to himself; when I first arrived at Pont de l'Arche, I had no scruples about being attractive, I expected to leave in a few days never to return again. Since then I had without pity refused his love, it is true; but could he believe this proud disdain to be genuine, when, after this decisive explanation, he found me tranquilly established at his mother's house? And there could he follow the different caprices of my mind, divine those temptations of generosity which first moved me in his favor, and then discover this wild love that was suddenly born in my soul for a phantom that I had only seen for a few hours? . . . . Had he not, on the contrary, a right to believe that I loved him, and to exclaim against the infamy, cruelty and perfidy of my refusing to see him, and my endeavors to convince him that I cared nothing for him? He was right to accuse me, for appearances were all against me—my own conduct condemned me. I must acknowledge myself culpable, and submit to the sentence that has been pronounced against me. I resigned myself sadly to repair the wrong I had committed. One hope still remained to me: Edgar brought back by me would be restored to his mother, but Edgar would cease to love me when he knew my real name. There is a difference between loving an adventuress, whose affections can be trifled with, and loving a woman of high birth and position, who must be honorably sought in marriage. Edgar has an invincible repugnance to matrimony; he considers this august institution as a monstrous inconvenience, very immoral, a profane revelation of the most sacred secrets of life; he calls it a public exhibition of affection; he says no one has a right to proclaim his preference for one woman. To call a woman: my wife! what revolting indiscretion! To call children: my children! what disgusting fatuity! In his eyes nothing is more horrible than a husband driving in the Champs Elysées with his family, which is tantamount to telling the passers-by: This woman seated by my side is the one I have chosen among all women, and to whom I am indebted for all pleasure in life; and this little girl who resembles her so much, and this little boy, the image of me, are the bonds of love between us. The Orientals, he added, whom we call barbarians, are more modest than we; they shut up their wives; they never appear in public with them, they never let any one see the objects of their tenderness, and they introduce young men of twenty, not as their sons, but as the heirs of their names and fortunes.

Recalling these remarkable sentiments of M. de Meilhan, I said to myself: he will never marry. But Mad. de Meilhan, who was aware of her son's peculiar thoeries, assured me that they were very much modified, and that one day in speaking of me, he had angrily exclaimed: "Oh! I wish I were her husband, so I could shut her up, and prevent any one seeing her!" Now I understand why a man marries! This was not very reassuring, but I devoted myself like a victim, and for a victim there is no half sacrifice. Generosity, like cruelty, is absolute.

After a night of anxious travel, we reached Havre at about ten in the morning. We drove rapidly to the office of the American steamers. Madame de Meilhan rushed frantically about until she found the sleepy clerk, who told her that M. de Meilhan had taken passage on the *Ontario*.

"When does this vessel leave?"

"I cannot tell you," said the gaping clerk.

We ran to the pier and tremblingly asked: "Can you tell us if the American vessel *Ontario* sails to-day?"

The old sailor replied to us in nautical language which we could not understand. Another man said: "The *Ontario* is pretty far out by this time! We ran to the other end of the pier and found a crowd of people watching a cloud that was gradually disappearing in the distance. "I see nothing now," said one of the people. But *I* saw a little . . . little smoke . . . and I could distinctly see a flag with a large O. on it. . . . Madame de Meilhan, pale and breathless, had not the strength to ask the name of the fatal vessel that was almost out of sight . . . I could only gasp out the word "*Ontario?*" . . .

"Precisely so, madame, but don't be uneasy . . . it is a fast vessel, and your friends will land in America before two weeks are passed. You look astonished, but it is the truth, the *Ontario* is never behind time! Madame de Meilhan fell fainting in my arms. She was lifted to our carriage and soon restored to consciousness, but was so overcome that she seemed incapable of comprehending the extent of her misfortune. We drove to the nearest hotel, and I remained in her room silently weeping and reproaching myself for having destroyed the happiness of this family.

During these first moments of stupor Madame de Meilhan showed no indignation at my presence; but no sooner had she recovered the use of her senses than she burst into a storm of abuse; calling me a detestable intriguer, a low adventuress who, by my stage tricks, had turned the head of her noble son; I would be the cause of his death—that fatal country would never give back her son; what a pity to see so superior a man, a pride and credit to his country, perish, succumb, to the snares of an obscure prude, who had not the sense to be his mistress, who was incapable of loving him for a single day; an ambitious schemer, who had determined to entrap him into marriage, but unhesitatingly sacrificed him to M. de Villiers as soon as she found M. de Villiers was the richer of the two, . . . and many other flattering accusations she made, that were equally ill-deserved. I quietly listened to all this abuse, and went on preparing a glass of *eau sucrée* for the poor weeping fury, whose conduct inspired me with generous pity. When she had finished her tirade, I silently handed her the orange water to calm her anger, and I looked at her . . . my look expressed such firm gentle pride, such generous indulgence, such invulnerable dignity, that she felt herself completely disarmed. She took my hand and said, as she dried her tears: "You must forgive me, I am *so* unhappy!" Then I tried to console her; I told her I would write to her son, and she would soon have him back, as my letter would reach New York by the time he landed, and then it would only take him two weeks to return. This promise calmed her; then I persuaded her to lie down and recover from the fatigue of travelling all night. When I saw her poor swollen eyelids fairly closed, I left her to enjoy her slumbers and retired to my own room. I rested awhile and then rang to order preparations for our departure; but instead of the servant answering the bell, a pretty little girl, about eight years old, entered my room; upon seeing me she drew back frightened.

"What do you want, my child?" I said, drawing her within the door.

"Nothing, madame," she said.

"But you must have come here for something?"

"I did not know that madame was in her room."

"What did you come to do in here?"

"I came, as I did yesterday, to see."

"To see what?"

"In there . . . the Turks . . . "

"The Turks? What! am I surrounded by Turks?"

"Oh! they are not in the little room adjoining yours; but through this little room you can look into the large saloon where they all stay and have music . . . will madame permit me to pass through?"

"Which way?"

"This way. There is a little door behind this toilet-table; I open it, go in, get up on the table and look at the Turks."

The child rolled aside the toilet-table, entered the little room, and in a few minutes came running back to me and exclaimed:

"Oh! they are so beautiful! does not madame wish to see them?"

"No."

In a short time she returned again.

"The musicians are all asleep," she said . . . "but, madame, the Turks are crazy—they don't sleep—they don't speak—they make horrible faces--they roll their eyes—they have such funny ways—one of them looks like my uncle when he has the fever—Oh! that one must be crazy, madame— . . . look, he is going to dance! now he is going to die!"

The absurd prattle of the child finally aroused my curiosity. I went into the little room, and, mounting the table beside her, looked through a crevice in the wooden partition and clearly saw everything in the large saloon. It was hung up to a certain height with rich Turkish stuffs. The floor was covered by a superb Smyrna carpet. In one recess of the room the musicians were sleeping with their bizarre musical instruments tightly clasped in their arms. A dozen Turks, magnificently dressed, were seated on the soft carpet in Oriental fashion, that is to say, after the manner of tailors. They were supported by piles of cushions of all sizes and shapes, and seemed to be plunged in ecstatic oblivion.

One of these dreamy sons of Aurora attracted my attention by his brilliant costume and flashing arms. By the pale light of the exhausted lamps and the faint rays of dawning day, almost obscured by the heavy drapery of the windows, I could scarcely distinguish the features of this splendid Mussulman, at the same time I thought I had seen him before. I had seen but few pachas during my life, but I certainly had met this one somewhere. I looked attentively and saw that his hands were whiter than those of his compatriots—this was a suspicious fact. After closely watching this doubtful infidel, this amateur barbarian, I began to suspect civilization and Europeanism. . . . One of the musicians asleep near the window, turned over and his long guitar—a *guzla*, I think it is called—caught in the curtain and drew it a little open; the sunlight streamed in the room and an accusing ray fell upon the face of the spurious young Turk. . . . It was Edgar de Meilhan! A little cup filled with a greenish conserve rested on a cushion near by. I remembered that he had often spoken to me of the wonderful effects of hashish, and of the violent desire he had of experiencing this fascinating stupefaction; he had also told me of one of his college friends who had been living in Smyrna for some years; an original, who had taken upon himself the mission of re-barbarizing the East. This friend had sent him a number of Indian poinards and Turkish pipes, and had promised him some tobacco and hashish. This modern and amateur Turk was named Arthur Granson. . . . I asked the innkeeper's little daughter if she knew the name of the man who had hired the saloon? She said yes, that he was named Monsieur Granson. . . . This name and this meeting explained everything.

O Valentine! I will be sincere to the end, . . . and confess that Edgar was wonderfully handsome in this costume! . . . the magnificent oriental stuff, the Turkish vest, embroidered in gold and silver, the yatagans, pistols and poinards studded with jewels, the turban draped with inimitable art—all these things gave him a majestic, superb, imposing aspect! . . . which at first astonished me, . . . for we are all children when we first see beautiful objects, . . . but he had a stupid look. . . . No, never did a sultan of the opera, throwing his handkerchief to his bayadère . . . a German prince of the gymnasium complimented by his court—a provincial Bajazet listening to the threatening declarations of Roxana—never did they display in the awkwardness of their rôles, in the stiffness of their movements, an attitude more absurdly ridiculous, an expression of countenance more ideally stupid. It is difficult to comprehend how a brilliant mind could so completely absent itself from its dwelling-place without leaving on the face it was wont to animate, a single trace, a faint ray of intelligence! Edgar had his eyes raised to the ceiling, . . . and for an instant I think I caught his look, . . . but Heavens! what a look! May I never meet such another! I shall add one more incident to my recital —important in itself but distasteful to me to relate—I will tell it in as few words as possible: Edgar was leaning on two piles of cushions; he seemed to be absorbed in the contemplation of invisible stars; he was awake, but a beautiful African slave, dressed like an Indian queen, was sleeping at his feet!

This strange spectacle filled my heart with joy. Instead of being indignant, I was delighted at this insult to myself. Edgar evidently forgot me, and truly he had a right to forget me; I was not engaged to him as I had been to Roger. A young poet has a right to dress like a Turk, and amuse himself with his friends, to suit his own fancy; but a noble prince has no right to scandalize the public when the dignity of his rank has to be striven after and recovered; when the glory of his name is to be kept untarnished. Oh! this disgusting sight gave rise to no angry feeling in my bosom. I at once comprehended the advantages of the situation. No more sacrifice, no more remorse, no more hypocrisy! I was free; my future was restored to me. Oh, the good Edgar! Oh, the dear poet! How I loved him . . . for not loving me!!

I told the little girl to run quickly and bring me a servant. When the man came I handed him six louis to sharpen his wits, and then solemnly gave him my orders: "When they ring for you in that saloon, do you tell that young Turk with a red vest on . . . you will remember him?" "Yes, madame." "You will tell him that the countess his mother is waiting here for him, in room

No. 7, at the end of the corridor." "Ah! the lady who was weeping so bitterly?" "The same one." "Madame may rely upon me."

I then paid my bill, and, inquiring the quickest way of leaving Havre, I fled from the hotel. Walking along Grande Rue de Paris, I saw with pleasure that the city was filled with strangers, who had come to take part in the festivities that were taking place at Havre, and that I could easily mingle in this great crowd and leave the town without being observed. Uneasy and agitated, I hurried along, and just as I was passing the theatre I heard some one call me. Imagine my alarm when I distinctly heard some one call: "Mlle. Irene! Mlle. Irene!" I was so frightened that I could scarcely move. The call was repeated, and I saw my faithful Blanchard rushing towards me, breathless and then I recognised the supplicating voice . . . I turned around and weeping, she exclaimed: "I know everything, Mlle., you are going to America! Take me with you. This is the first time I have ever been separated from you since your birth!" I had left the poor woman at Pont de l'Arche, and she, thinking I was going to America, had followed me. "Be quiet and follow me," said I, forgetting to tell her that I was not going to America. I reached the wharf and jumped into a boat; the unhappy Blanchard, who is a hydrophobe, followed me. "You are afraid?" said I. "Oh, no, Mlle., I am afraid on the Seine, but at sea it is quite a different thing." The touching delicacy of this ingenious conceit moved me to tears. Wishing to shorten the agony of this devoted friend, I told the oarsman to row us into the nearest port, instead of going further by water, as I had intended, in order to avoid the Rouen route and the Prince, the steamboat and M. de Meilhan. As soon as we landed I sent my faithful companion to the nearest village to hire a carriage. "I must be in Paris, to-morrow," said I. "Then we are not going to America?" "No." "So much the better," said she, as she trotted off in high glee to look for a carriage. I remained alone, gazing at the ocean. Oh! how I enjoyed the sight! How I would love to live on this charming, terrible azure desert! I was so absorbed in admiration that I soon forgot my worldly troubles and the vain tribulations of my obscure life. I was intoxicated by its wild perfume, its free, invigorating air! I breathed for the first time! With what delight I let the sea-breeze blow my hair about my burning brow! How I loved to gaze on its boundless horizon! How much—laugh at my vanity—how much I felt at home in this immensity! I am not one of those modest souls that are oppressed and humiliated by the grandeur of Nature; I only feel in harmony with the sublime, not through myself, but through the aspirations of my mind. I never feel as if there was around me, above me, before me, too much air, too much height, too much space. I like the boundless, luminous horizon to render solitude and liberty invisible to my eyes.

I know not if every one else is impressed as I was upon seeing the ocean for the first time. I felt released from all ties, purified of all hatred, and even of all earthiy love; I was freed, calm, strong, armed, ready to brave all the evils of life, like a being who had received from God a right to disdain the world. The ocean and the sky have this good effect upon us—they wean us from worldly pleasures.

Upon reaching Paris, I went at once to your father's to inquire about you, and had my uneasiness about you set at rest. You must have left Geneva by this time; I hope soon to receive a letter from you. I am not staying with my cousin. I am living in my dear little garret. I wish a long time to elapse before I again become Mlle. de Chateaudun. I wish time to recover from the rude shocks I have had. What do you think of my last experience? What a perfect success was my theory of discouragement! Alas! too perfect. First trial: Western despair and champagne! Second trial: Eastern despair and hashisch!—Not to speak of the consolatory accessories, snowy-armed beauties and ebony-armed slaves! I would be very unsophisticated indeed if I did not consider myself sufficiently enlightened. I implore you not to speak to me of your hero whom you wish me to marry; I am determined never to marry. I shall love an image, cherish a star. The little light has returned. I see it shining as I write to you. Yes, these poetic loves are all-sufficient for my wounded soul. One thing disturbs me; they have cut down the large trees in front of my window. To-morrow, perhaps, I shall at last see the being that dwells in this fraternal garret. . . . Valentine—suppose it should be my long-sought ideal! . . . I tremble! perhaps a third disenchantment awaits me. . . . Good-night, my dear Valentine, I embrace you. I am very tired, but very happy . . . it is so delightful to be relieved of all uneasiness, to feel that you are not compelled to console any one.

IRENE DE CHATEAUDUN.

XXX.

EDGAR DE MEILHAN *to the* PRINCE DE MONBERT,
Poste Restante (Rouen).

PARIS, July 27th 18—.

MY dear Roger, at the risk of bringing down upon my head the ridicule merited by men who fire a pistol above their heads after having left on their table the night before the most thrilling adieux to the world, I must confess that I have not gone; you have a perfect right to drive me out of Europe; I promised to go to America, and you can compel me to fulfil my promise; be clement, do not overpower me with ridicule; do not riddle me with the fire of your mocking artillery; my sorrow, even though I remain in the old world, is none the less crushing.

I must tell you how it all happened.

As all my life I have never been able to comprehend the division of time, and it's a toss-up whether I distinguish day from night, I turned my back on the best hotel in Havre, and stopped at one nearest the wharf, from whence I could see the smoke-stacks of the Ontario, about to sail for New York. I was leaning on the balcony, in the melancholy attitude of Raphael's portrait, gazing at the swell of the ocean, with that feeling of infinite sadness which the strongest heart must yield to in the presence of that immensity formed of drops of bitter water, like human tears. I followed, listlessly, with my eyes the movements of a strange group which had just landed from the Portsmouth packet. They were richly-dressed Orientals, followed by negro servants and women enveloped in long veils.

One of these Turks looked up as he passed under my window, saw me, and exclaimed in very correct French, with a decided Parisian accent: "Why, it's Edgar de Meilhan!" and, regardless of Oriental dignity, he dashed into the inn, bounded into my room, rubbed my face against his crisp black beard, punched me in the stomach with the carved hilts of a complete collection of yataghans and kandjars, and finally said, seeing my uncertainty: "Why! don't you know me, your old college chum, your playmate in childhood, Arthur Granson! Does my turban make such a change in me? So much the better! Or are you mean enough to stick to the letter of the proverb which pretends that friends are not Turks? By Allah and his prophet Mahomet, I shall prove to you that Turks are friends."

During this flood of words I had in truth recognised Arthur Granson, a good and odd young fellow, whom I am very fond of, and who would surely please you, for he is the most paradoxical youth to be found in the five divisions of the globe. And, what is very rare, he acts out his paradoxes, a whim which his great independence of character and above all a large fortune permit him to indulge, for gold is liberty; the only slaves are the poor.

"This much is settled, I will install myself here with my living palette of local colors;" and without giving me time to answer him, he left me to give the necessary orders for lodging his suite.

When he returned, I said to him: "What does this strange masquerade mean? The carnival has been over for some time, and will not return immediately, as we are hardly through the summer." "It is not a masquerade," replied Arthur, with a dogmatic coolness and transcendental gravity which at any other time would have made me laugh. "It is a complete system, which I shall unfold to you."

Whereupon my friend, taking off his Turkish slippers, crossed his legs on the divan in the approved classic attitude of the Osmanli, and running his fingers through his beard, spoke as follows:

"During my travels I have observed that no people appreciate the peculiar beauties of the country they inhabit. No one admires his own physiognomy; every one would like to resemble some one else. Spaniards and Turks make endless excuses for being handsome and picturesque. The Andalusian apologizes to you for not wearing a coat and round hat. The Arnaout, whose costume is the most gorgeous and elegant that has ever been worn by the human form divine, sighs as he gazes at your overcoat, and consults with himself upon the advisability of shooting you to get possession of it, in the first mountain gorge where he may meet you alone or poorly attended. Civilization is the natural enemy of beauty. All its creations are ugly. Barbarism—or rather relative barbarism—has found the secret of form and color. Man living so near to Nature imitates her harmony, and finds the types of his garments and his utensils in his surroundings. Mathematics have not yet developed their straight lines, dry angles and painful aridity. Now-a-days, picturesque traditions are lost, the long pantaloon has invaded the universe; frightful fashion-plates circulate everywhere; now, I refuse to believe that man's taste has become perverted to such a degree that if he were shown costumes combining elegance with richness, he would not prefer them to hideous modern rags. Having made these judicious and profound reflections, I felt as if I had been enlightened from above, and the secret of my earthly mission revealed to me; I had come into the world to preach costume, and, as you see, I preach it by example. Reflecting that Turkey is the country most menaced by the overcoat and stove-pipe hat, I went to Constantinople to bring about a reaction in favor of the embroidered vest and the turban. My grave studies upon the subject, my fortune and my taste have enabled me to attain the *ne plus ultra* of style.

"I doubt whether a Sultan ever possessed so splendid or so characteristic a wardrobe. I discovered among the bazaars of the cities least infected by the modern spirit, some tailors with a profound contempt for Frank fashions, who, with their tremulous hands, performed marvels of cutting and embroidery. I will show you caftans braided in a miserable little out-of-the-way village of Asia Minor, by some poor devils whom you would not trust with your dog, which surpass, in intricacy of design, the purest arabesques of the Alhambra, and in color, the most gorgeous peacock tails of Eugene Delacroix or Narciso Ruy Diaz de la Pena, a great painter, who out of commiseration for the commonalty only makes use of a quarter of his name.

"I am happy to say that my apostleship has not been without fruit. I have brought back to the dolman more than one young Osmanli about to rig himself out at Buisson's; I have saved more than one horse of the Nedji race from the insult of an English saddle; more than one tipsy Turk addicted to champagne has returned to opium at my suggestion. Some Georgians who were about to be admitted to the balls of the European embassies are indebted to me for being shut up closer than ever. I impressed upon these degenerate Orientals the disastrous results of such a breach of propriety. I persuaded the Sultan Abdul Medjid to give up the idea of introducing the guillotine into his empire. Without flattering myself, I think I have done a great deal of good, and if there were only a few more gay fellows like myself we should prevent people from making guys of themselves—And what are you doing, my dear Edgar?" "I am going to America, and I am waiting for the Ontario to get up steam." "That's a good idea! You can become a savage and resuscitate the last Mohican of Fenimore Cooper. I already see you, with a blue turtle on your breast, eagle's feathers in your scalp, and moccasins worked with porcupine quills. You will be very handsome; with your sad air you will look as if you were weeping over your dead race. If I had not been away for four years, I would accompany you, but I was in such a hurry to put my affairs in order, that I have returned to France by way of England, in order to avoid the quarantine. I will admit you to my religion; you shall become my disciple; I preserve barbaric costumes, you shall preserve savage costumes. It is not so handsome, but it is more characteristic. There were some Indians on our steamer; I studied them; they are the people to suit you. But, before your departure, we will indulge in an Eastern orgie in the purest style." "My dear Granson, I am not in a humor to take part in an orgie, even though it be an Eastern orgie; I am desperately sad." "Very well; I see that you are; some heart sorrow; you

Occidentals are always in a state of torment about some woman; which would never occur if they were all shut up; it is dangerous to let such animals wander about. I am delighted that you are so sad and melancholy. I can now prove to you the superior efficacy of my exhilarating means. I found at Cairo, in the Teriaki Square, opposite the hospital for the insane—wasn't it a profoundly philosophical idea to establish in such a place dealers in happiness?—an old scamp, dry as a papyrus of the time of Amenoteph, shrivelled as the beards of the Pschent of the goddess Isis; this cabalistic druggist possessed the true receipt for the preparation of hashisch; besides, he seemed old enough to have gotten it direct from the Old Man of the Mountain, if he were not himself the Prince of Assassins who lived in the time of Saint Louis; this skeleton in a parchment case furnished me with a quantity of paradise, under the guise of green paste, in little Japanese cups done up in silver wire. I intend to initiate you into these hypercelestial delights. I shall give you a box of happiness, which will make you forget all the false coquettes in the world."

Without listening to my repeated refusals, Granson begged me to call him henceforth Sidi-Mahmoud; had his room spread with Persian rugs, ottomans piled up in every direction, the walls cushioned to lean against, and perfumes scattered about; three or four dusky musicians placed themselves in a convenient recess with taraboucks, rebeks and guzlas—an Ethiopean, naked to the waist, served us the precious drug on a red lacquered waiter.

To accommodate Granson I swallowed several spoonfuls of this greenish confection, which, at first, seemed to be flavored with honey and pistachio. I had dressed myself—for Granson is one of those obstinate idiots that one is compelled to yield to in order to get rid of—in an Anatolian costume of fabulous richness, my friend insisting that when one ascends to Paradise he should not be annoyed by the slope of his sleeves.

In a few moments I felt a slight warmth in my stomach—my body threw off sparks and flared up like a bank-bill in the flame of a candle; I was subject to no law of nature; weight, bulk, opacity had entirely disappeared. I retained my form, but it became transparent; flexible, fluid objects passed through me without inconveniencing me in the least; I could enlarge or decrease myself to suit any place I wished to occupy. I could transport myself at will from one place to another. I was in an impossible world, lighted by a gleam of azure grotto, in the centre of a bouquet of fire-works formed of everchanging sheafs, luminous flowers with gold and silver foliage, and calices of rubies, sapphires and diamonds; fountains of melted moonbeams, throwing their spray over crystal vases, which sang with voices like a harmonica the arias of the greatest singers. A symphony of perfumes followed this first enchantment, which vanished in a shower of spangles at the end of a few seconds; the theme was a faint odor of iris and acacia bloom which pursued, avoided, crossed and embraced each other with delicious ease and grace. If anything in this world can give you an approximative idea of this exquisitely perfumed movement, it is the dance for the piccolos in the Almée of Felicien David.

As the movement increased in sweetness and charm, the two perfumes took the shape of the flowers from which they emanated; two irises and two bunches of acacia bloomed in a marvellously transparent onyx vase; soon the irises scintillated like two blue stars, the acacia flowers dissolved into a golden stream, the onyx vase assumed a female shape, and I recognised the lovely face and graceful form of Louise Guérin, but idealized, passed to the state of Beatrice; I am not certain that there did not rise from her white shoulders a pair of angel's wings—she gazed so sadly and kindly at me that I felt my eyes fill with tears—she seemed to regret being in heaven; from the expression of her face one might have thought that she accused me, and at the same time entreated my forgiveness.

I will not take you through the various windings of this marvellous open-eyed dream; the monotonous harmony of the tarabouck and the rebek faintly reached my ear, and served as rhythm to this wonderful poem, which will, henceforth, make Homer, Virgil, Ariosto and Tasso as wearisome to read as a table of logarithms. All my senses had changed places; I saw music and heard colors; I had new perceptions, as the denizens of a planet superior to ours must have; at will, my body was composed of a ray, a perfume or a sweet savor; I experienced the ecstasy of the angels fused in divine light, for the effect of hashisch bears no resemblance whatever to that of wine and alcohol, by the use of which the people of the North debase and stupefy themselves; its intoxication is purely intellectual.

Little by little order was established in my brain. I began to observe objects around me

The candles had burned down to the socket; the musicians slept, tenderly embracing their instruments. The handsome negress lay at my feet. I had taken her for a cushion. A pale ray of light appeared on the horizon; it was three o'clock in the morning. All at once a smoke-stack, puffing forth black smoke, crossed the bar; it was the *Ontario* leaving its moorings.

A confusion of voices was heard in the next room; my mother, having in some way learnt of my projected exile, had broken through Granson's orders to admit no one, and was calling for me.

I was rather mortified at being caught in such an absurd dress; but my mother observed nothing; she had but one thought, that I was about to leave her for ever. I do not remember what she said, such things cannot be written, the endearments she bestowed upon me when I was only five or six years old; finally she wept. I promised to stay and return to Paris. How can you refuse your mother anything when she weeps? Is she not the only woman whom we can never reproach?

After all, as you have said, Paris is the wildest desert; there you are completely alone. Indifferent and unknown people may value sands and swamps.

If my sorrow prove too tenacious, I shall ask my friend

Arthur Granson for the address of the old Teriaki, and I shal send to Cairo for some boxes of forgetfulness. We will shar them together if you wish. Farewell, dear Roger, I am your mind and heart.

EDGAR DE MEILHAN.

XXXI.

RAYMOND DE VILLIERS *to* MME. LA VICOMTESSE DE BRAIMES,
Hotel of the Prefecture, Grenoble (Isere).

PARIS, July 30th 18—.

O DAY of bliss unutterable! I have found her, it is she! As you have opened your heart to my sadness, madame, open it to my joy. Forget the unhappy wretch who, a few days ago, abandoned himself to his grief, who even yesterday bade an eternal farewell to hope. That unfortunate has ceased to exist; in his place appears a young being intoxicated with love, for whom life is full of delight and enchantment. How does it happen that my soul, which should soar on hymns of joy, is filled with gloomy forebodings? Is it because man is not made for great felicity, or that happiness is naturally sad, nearer akin to tears than to laughter, because it feels its fragility and instinctively dreads the approaching expiation?

After having vainly searched for Mademoiselle de Chateaudun within the walls of Rouen, M. de Monbert decided, on receipt of some new information, to seek her among the old châteaux of Brittany. My sorrow, feeding upon itself, counselled me not to accompany him. The fact is that I could be of no earthly use in his search. Besides, I thought I perceived that my presence embarrassed him. To tell the truth, we were a constraint upon each other. Every sorrowful heart willingly believes itself the centre of the universe, and will not admit the existence, under heaven, of any other grief than its own. I let the Prince depart, and set out alone for Paris. One last hope remained; I persuaded myself that if Louise had not loved M. de Meilhan she would have left Richeport at the same time that I did.

I got out at Pont de l'Arche, and prowled like a felon about the scenes where happiness had come to me.

I wandered about for an hour, when I saw the letter-carrier coming to the post-office for the letters to be delivered at the neighboring châteaux. Paler and more tremulous than the silvery foliage of the willows on the river shore, I questioned him and learned that Madame Guérin was still at Richeport. I went away with death in my heart; in the evening I reach Paris.

Resolved to see no one in that city, and only intending to pass a few days in solitude and silence, I sought no other abode than the little room which I had occupied in less fortunate but happier times. I wished to resume my old manner of living; but I had no taste for anything. When one goes in pursuit of happiness, the way is smiling and alluring, hope brightens the horizon; when we have clutched it and then let it escape, everything becomes gloomy and disenchanted; for it is a traveller whom we do not meet twice upon our road. I tried to study, which only increased my weariness. What was the use of knowledge and wisdom? Life was a closed book to me. I tried the poets, who added to my sufferings, by translating them into their passionate language. Thus, reason is baffled by the graceful apparition of a lovely blonde, who glided across my existence like a gossamer over a clear sky, and banished repose for ever from my heart! My eyes had scarcely rested upon the angle of my dreams ere she took flight, leaving on my brow the shadow of her wings! She was only a child, and that child had passed over my destiny like a tempest! She rested for a moment in my life, like a bird upon a branch, and my life was broken! In fact I lost all control over myself. Young, free and rich, I was at a loss to know what to do. What was to become of me? Turn where I would, I still saw nothing around me but solitude and despair. During the day I mingled with the crowd and wandered about the streets like a lost soul; returning at night overcome, but not conquered by fatigue. Burning sleeplessness besieged my pillow, and the little light no longer shone to comfort and encourage me. I no longer heard, as before, a caressing voice speaking to me through the trees of the garden. "Courage, friend! I watch and suffer with thee." Finally, one night I saw the star peep forth and shine. Although I had no heart for such fancies, still I felt young and joyous again, on seeing it. As before, I gazed at it a long time. Was it the same, that, for two years, I had seen burn and go out regularly at the same hour? It might be doubted; but I did not doubt it for a moment, because I took pleasure in believing it. I felt less isolated and gained confidence, now that my star had not deserted me. I called it my martyr when I spoke to it: "Whence comest thou? Hast thou too suffered? Hast thou mourned my absence a little?" And, as before, I thought it answered me in the silence of the night. Towards morning I slept, and in a dream, I saw, as through a glass, Louise watching and working in a room as poor as mine, by the light of the well-beloved ray. She looked pale and sad, and from time to time stopped her work to gaze at the gleam of my lamp. When I awoke, it was broad day; and I went out to kill time.

On the boulevard I met an old friend of my father's; he was refined, cultivated and affectionate. He had come from our mountains, to which he was already anxious to return, for in their valleys he had buried himself. My dejected air and sorrowful countenance struck him. He gained my confidence, and immediately guessed at my complaint. "What are you doing here?" he asked; "it is an unwholesome place for grief. Return to our mountains. Your native air will do you good. Come with me; I promise you that your unhappiness will not hold out against the perfume of broom and heather." Then he spoke with tender earnestness of my duties. He did not conceal from me the obligations my fortune and the position left me by my father, laid me under to the land where I was born; I had neglected it too long, and the time had now come when I ought to occupy myself seriously with its needs and interests. In short, he made me blush for my useless days, and led me, gently and firmly, back to reality. At night-fall I returned to my little chamber, not consoled but stronger, and decided to set out on the morrow for the banks of the Creuse. I did not expect to be cured, but it pleased me to mingle the thought of Louise with the benefits that I could bestow, and to bring down blessings upon the name which I had longed to offer her.

I immediately remarked on entering, that my little beacon shone with unaccustomed brilliancy. It was no longer a thread of light gleaming timidly through the foliage, but a whole window brightly illuminated, and standing out against the surrounding darkness. Investigating the cause of this phenomonon, I discovered that, during the day, the trees had been felled in the garden, and peering out into the gloom, I preceived, stretched along the ground, the trunk of the pine which, for two years, had hid from me the room where burned the fraternal light. Before departing, I should at least catch a glimpse of the mysterious being, who, probably unconsciously, had occupied so many of my restless thoughts. I could not control a sad smile at the thought of the disenchantment that awaited me on the morrow. I passed in review the faces which were likely to appear at that window, and as the absurd is mixed with almost every situation in life, I declare that this bewildering question occurred to me: "Suppose it should be Lady Penock?"

I slept little, and arose at day-break. I was restless without daring to acknowledge to myself the cause. It would have mortified me to have to confess that there was room beside my grief for a childish curiosity, a poetical fancy. What is man's heart made of? He bemoans himself, wraps a cere-cloth around him and prepares to die, and a flitting bird or a shining light suffices to divert him. I watched the sun redden the house-tops. Paris still slept; no sound broke the stillness of the slumbering city, but the distant roll of the early carts over the stones. I looked long at the dear garret, which I saw for the first time in the eye of day. The window had neither shutter nor blind, but a double rose-colored curtain hung before it, mingling its tint with that of the rising sun. That window, with neither plants nor running vines to ornament it, had an air of refinement that charmed me. The house itself looked honest. I wrote several letters to shorten the slow hours which wearied my patience. Every shutter that opened startled me, and sent the blood quickly back to my heart. My reason revolted against such childishness; but in spite of it, something within me refused to laugh at my folly.

After some hours, I caught a glimpse of a hand furtively drawing aside the rose-colored curtains. That timid hand could only belong to a woman; a man would have drawn them back unceremoniously. She must, likewise, be a young woman; the shade of the curtains indicated it. Evidently, only a young woman would put pink curtains before a garret-window. Whereupon I recalled to mind the little room where I had bade adieu to Louise before leaving Richeport. I lived over again the scene in that poetic nook; again I saw Louise as she appeared to me at that last interview, pale, agitated, shedding silent tears which she did not attempt to conceal.

At this remembrance my grief burst all bounds, and spent itself in imprecations against Edgar and against myself. I sat a long time, with my face buried in my hands, in mournful contemplation of an invisible image. Ah! unhappy man, I exclaimed, in my despair, why did you leave her? God offered you happiness and you refused it! She stood there, before you, trembling, desperate, her eyes bathed in tears, awaiting but one word to sink in your arms, and that word you refused to utter, cowardly fleeing from her! It is now your turn to weep, unfortunate wretch! Your life, which has but begun, is now ended, and you will not even have the supreme consolation of melancholy regrets, for the sting of remorse will for ever remain in your wound; you will be pursued to your dying day by the phantom of a felicity which you would not seize!

When I raised my head, the garret-window had noiselessly opened, and there, standing motionless in a flood of sunshine, her golden hair lifted gently by the morning breeze, was Louise gazing at me.

Madame, try to imagine what I felt; as for me, I shall never be able to give it expression. I tried to speak, and my voice died away on my lips; I wished to stretch out my arms towards the celestial vision, they seemed to be made of stone and glued to my side; I wished to rush to her, my feet were nailed to the floor. However, she still stood there smiling at me. Finally, after a desperate effort, I succeeded in breaking the charm which bound me, and rushed from my room wild with delight, mad with happiness. I was mad, that's the word. Holy madness! cold reason should humble itself in the dust before thee! As quick as thought, by some magic, I found myself before Louise's door. I had recognised the house so long sought for before. I entered without a question, guided alone by the perfume that ascended from the sanctuary; I took Louise's hands in mine, and we stood gazing silently at each other in an ecstasy of happiness fatally lost and miraculously recovered; the ecstasy of two lovers, who, separated by a shipwreck, believing each other dead, meet, radiant with love and life, upon the same happy shore.

"Why, it was you!" she said at last, pointing to my room with a charming gesture.

"Why, it was you!" I exclaimed in my turn, eagerly glancing at a little brass lamp which I had observed on a table covered with screens, boxes of colors and porcelain palettes.

"You were the little light!"

"You were my evening star!"

And we both began to recite the poem of those two years of our lives, and we found that we told the same story. Louise began my sentences and I finished hers. In disclosing our heart secrets and the mysterious sympathy that had existed between us for two years, we interrupted each other with expressions of astonishment and admiration. We paused time and time again to gaze at each other and press each other's hands, as if to assure ourselves that we were awake and it was not all a dream. And every moment this gay and charming refrain broke in upon our ecstasy:

"So you were the brother and friend of my poverty!"

"So you were the sister and companion of my solitude!"

We finally approached in our recollections, through many windings, our meeting upon the banks of the Seine, under the shades of Richeport.

"What seems sad to me," she said with touching grace, "is that after having loved me without knowing me, you should have left me as soon as you did know me. You only worshipped your idle fancies, and, had I loved you then," she continued, "I should have been forced to be jealous of this little lamp."

I told her what inexorable necessity compelled me to leave Richeport and her. Louise listened with a pensive and charming air; but when I came to speak of Edgar's love, she burst out laughing and began to relate, in the gayest manner, some story or other about Turks, which I failed to understand.

"M. de Meilhan loves you, does he not?" I asked finally, with a vague feeling of uneasiness.

"Yes, yes," she cried, "he loves me to—madness!"

"He loves you, since he is jealous."

"Yes, yes," she cried again, "jealous as a—Mussulman." And then she began to laugh again.

"Why," I again asked, "if you did not love him, did you stay at Richeport two or three days after I left?"

"Because I expected you to return," she replied, laying aside her childish gayety and becoming grave and serious.

I told her of my love. I was sincere, and therefore should have been eloquent. I saw her eyes fill with tears, which were not this time tears of sorrow. I unfolded to her my whole life; all that I had hoped for, longed for, suffered down to the very hour when she appeared to me as the enchanting realization of my youthful dreams.

"You ask me," she said, "to share your destiny, and you do not know who I am, whence I come, or whither I go."

"You mistake, I know you," I cried; "you are as noble as you are beautiful; you come from heaven, and you will return to it. Bear me with you on your wings."

"Sir, all that is very vague," she answered, smilingly.

"Listen," said I. "It is true that I do not know who you are; but I know, I feel that falsehood has never profaned those lips, nor perverted the brightness of those eyes. Here is my hand;

it is the hand of a gentleman. Take it without fear or hesitation, that is all I ask."

"M. de Villiers, it is well," she said placing her little hand in mine. "And now," she added, "do you wish to know my life?"

"No," I replied, "you can tell me of it when you have given it to me."

"But—"

"I have seen you," said I; "you can tell me nothing. I feel that there is a mystery in your existence, but I also feel that that mystery is honorable, that you could only conceal a treasure."

At these words an indefinable smile played around her lips.

"At least," she cried, "you know certainly that I am poor?"

"Yes," I answered, "but you have shown yourself worthy of fortune, and I, on my part, hope that I have proved myself not altogether unworthy of poverty."

The day glided imperceptibly by, enlivened with tender communings. I examined in all its details the room which my thoughts had so often visited. It required considerable self-control to repress the inclination to carry to my lips the little lamp which had brought me more delight than Aladdin's ever could have done. I spoke of you, madame, mingling your image with my happiness in order to complete it. I told Louise how you would love her, that she would love you too; she replied that she loved you already. At evening we parted, and our joyous lamps burned throughout the night.

In the midst of my bliss, I do not forget, madame, the interests that are dear to you. Have you written to Mademoiselle de Chateaudun as I begged you to do? Have you written with firmness? Have you told your young friend that her peace and future are at stake? Have you pointed out to her the storm ready to burst over her head? When I left M. de Monbert he was gloomy and irritated. Let Mademoiselle Chateaudun take care!

Accept the expression of my respectful homage.

RAYMOND DE VILLIERS.

XXXII.

IRENE DE CHATEAUDUN *to* MME. LA VICOMTESSE DE BRAIMES,
Hotel of the Prefecture, Grenoble (Isere).

PARIS, Aug. 5th 18—.

ALL of your letters have reached me at once. I received two yesterday and one this morning, the latter being written first and dated at Berne. Ah! if it had reached me in due time, what distress I would have been spared! What! he wrote you, "I love her," and said nothing to me! When he left me you know how unhappy he was, and I, who was made so miserable by his departure, I thought he was indifferent!

When I told you that I was about to sacrifice myself to console Madame de Meilhan, you must have thought me insane; I can see by your letter from Geneva, which I received yesterday, that you were dreadfully alarmed about me. Cursed journey! Cursed mail! A letter lost might have destroyed my happiness for ever! This letter was delayed on the road several days, and, during these several days, I suffered more torture than I ever felt during the most painful moments of my life. These useless sorrows, that I might so easily have avoided, render me incredulous and trembling before this future of promised happiness. I have suffered so much that joy itself finds me fearful; and then this happiness is so great that it is natural to receive it with sadness and doubt.

He told you of his delirious joy, on recognising me at the window; but he did not tell you, he could not tell you, of my uneasiness, of my dreadful suspicions, my despair when I saw him in this garret.

Our situations were not the same; what astonished and delighted him, also astonished and delighted me, but at the same time filled me with alarm. He believed me to be poor, discovered me in an attic; it was nothing to be surprised at; the only wonderful thing about it was that my garret should be immediately opposite the house where he lived. . . . I knew he was wealthy; I knew he was the Count de Villiers; I knew he was of an old and noble family; I knew from his conversation that he had travelled over Italy in a manner suitable to his rank; I found him in Richeport, elegant and generous; he possesses great simplicity of manner, it is true, but it is the lordly simplicity of a great man. . . . In fact, everything I knew about him convinces me that his proper place was not a garret, and that if I saw him there, I did not see him in his own house.

Remember, Valentine, that for two months I have lived upon deceptions; I have been disillusioned; I have inspired the most varied and excessive griefs; I have studied the most picturesque consolations; I have seen myself lamented at the Odeon, by one lover in a box with painted women, . . . and at Havre by another in a tavern with a slave. . . . I might now see myself lamented at Paris by a third in a garret with a grisette! Oh! torture! in this one instant of dread, all the arrows of jealousy rankled in my heart. Oh! I could not be indignant this time, I could not complain, I could only die. . . . And I think that if I had not seen the pure joy beaming in his eyes, lighting up his noble countenance; if I had not instantly divined, comprehended everything, I believe I would have dashed myself from the window to escape the strange agony that made my heart cold and my brain dizzy—agony that I could not and would not endure. But he looked too happy to be culpable; he made a sign, and I saw that he was coming over to see me. I waited for him—and in what a state! My hair was disarranged, and I called Blanchard to assist me in brushing it; my voice was so weak she came running to me frightened, thinking me ill. . . . a thousand confused thoughts rushed through my brain; one thing was clear: I had found him again, I was about to see him!

When I was dressed—oh! that morning little did I think I would need a becoming dress, . . . I sat on the sofa in my poor little parlor, and there, pale with emotion, scarcely daring to breathe, I listened with burning impatience to the different noises about the house. In a few moments I heard a knock, the door open, a voice exclaim, "You, Monsieur le Comte!" He did not wait to be announced, but came in at once to the parlor where I was. He was so joyous at finding me, and I so delighted at seeing him, that for the first blissful moments of our meeting neither of us thought explanations necessary; his joy proved that he was free to love me, and my manner showed that I might be everything to him. When he found his voice, he said to me: "What! were you this cherished star that I have loved for two years?"

Then I remembered my momentary fears, and said: "What! were you the mysterious beacon? Why were you living there? Why did the Comte de Villiers dwell in a garret?"

Then, dear Valentine, he told me his noble history; he confessed, rather unwillingly, that he had been poor like myself; very poor, because he had given all his fortune to save the honor of a friend, M. Frederick de B. . . . . Oh! how I wept, while listening to this touching story, so full of sublime simplicity, generous carelessness and self-sacrifice! This would have made me adore him if I had not already madly loved him. While he was telling me, I was thinking of the unfortunate Frederick's wife, of her anxiety, of the torture she suffered, as a wife and a mother, when she believed her husband lost and her children ruined; of her astonishment and wild joy when she saw them all saved; of her deep, eternal gratitude! and I had but one thought, I said to myself: "How I would like to talk with this woman of Raymond!"

I wished in turn to relate my own history; he refused to listen to me, and I did not insist. I wished to be generous, and let him for some time longer believe me to be poor and miserable. He was so happy at the idea of enriching and ennobling me, that I had not the courage to disenchant him.

However, yesterday, I was obliged to tell him everything; in his impatience to hasten our marriage he had devoted the morning to the drawing up of his papers, contracts and settlements; for two days he had been tormenting me for my family papers in order to arrange them, and to find the register of my birth, which was indispensable when he appeared before the mayor. I had always put off giving it to him, but yesterday he entreated me so earnestly, that I was compelled to assent. In order to prepare him for the shock, I told him my papers were in my secretary, and that if he would come into my room he could see them. At the sight of the grand family pictures covering the walls of my retreat, he stood aghast; then he examined them with uneasiness. Some of the portraits bore the names and titles of the illustrious persons they represented. Upon reading the name, Victor Louis de Chateaudun, Marechal de France, he stopped motionless and looked at me with a strange air; then he read, beneath the portrait of a beautiful woman, the following inscription: "Marie Felicité Diane de Chateaudun, Duchesse de Montignan," and turning quickly towards me, with a face deadly pale, he exclaimed: "Louise?" "No, not Louise, but Irene!" I replied; and my voice rang with ancestral pride when I thus appeared before him in my true character.

For a moment he was silent, and a bitter, sad expression came over his countenance, that frightened me. Then I thought, it is nothing but envy; it is hard for a man who knows he is generous to be outdone in generosity. It is disappointing, when he thinks he is bestowing everything, to find he is about to receive millions; it is cruel, when he dreams of making a sacrifice like the hero of a novel, to find himself constrained to destroy all the romance by conducting the affair on a business basis. But Raymond was more than sad, and his almost severe demeanor alarmed my love, as well as my dignity . . . he crossed to the other side of the room and sat down. I followed him, trembling with agitation, and my eyes filled with tears.

"You no longer love me," I said.

"I dare not love the fiancée of my friend."

"Don't mention M. de Monbert, nor your scruples, he would not understand them."

"But he told you he loved you, Mlle., why did you leave him so abruptly?"

"I distrusted this love and wished to test it."

"What is the result of the test?"

"He does not love me, and I despise him."

"He does love you, and you ought to respect him."

Then, in order to avoid painful explanations and self-justification, I handed him a long letter I had written to my cousin, in which I related, without telling her of my disguise, that I had seen the Prince de Monbert at the theatre, described the people whom he was with, and my disgust at his conduct. I begged her to read this letter to the Prince himself, who is with her now—he has followed her to one of her estates in Brittany; he would see from the decided tone of my letter, that my resolution was taken, that I did not love him, and that the best thing he could do was to forget me.

I had written this letter yesterday, under your inspiration, and to ward off the imaginary dangers you feared. Rely upon it, my dear Valentine, M. de Monbert knows that he has acted culpably towards me; he might, perhaps, endeavor to prevent my marriage, but when he knows I am no longer free, he will be compelled to resign himself to my loss; don't be alarmed, I know of two beautiful creatures whom he will allow to console him. A man really unhappy would not have confided the story of his disdained love to all his friends, valets and the detectives; he would not hand over to idle gossip a dear and sacred name; a man who has no respect for his love, does not love seriously; he deserves neither regard nor pity. I will write to him myself to-morrow, if you desire it; but as to a quarrel, what does he claim? I have never given him any rights; if he threatens to provoke my husband to a duel, I have only to say: "Take for your seconds Messrs. Ernest and George de S., who were intoxicated with you at the Odeon," and he will blush with shame, and instantly recognise how odious and ridiculous is his anger.

I left Raymond alone in my room reading this letter, and I returned to the saloon to weep bitterly. I could not bear to see him displeased with me; I knew he would accuse me of being trifling and capricious—the idea of having offended him pierced my heart with anguish. I know not if the letter justified me in his eyes, whether he thought it honest and dignified, but as soon as he had finished reading it he called me: "Irene," he said, and I trembled with sweet emotion on hearing him, for the first time, utter my real name; I returned to the next room, he took my hand and continued: "Pardon me for believing, for a moment, that you were capricious and trifling, and I forgive you for having made me act an odious part towards one of my friends."

Then he told me in a tender voice that he understood my conduct, and that it was right; that when one is not sure of loving her intended, or of being loved by him, she has a right to test him, and that it was only honest and just. Then he smilingly asked me if I did not wish to try him, and leave him a month or two to see if I was beloved by him.

"Oh! no," I cried, "I believe in you. I do not wish to leave you. Oh! how can true lovers live apart from each other? How can they be separated for a single day?"

I recalled what you told me when I abandoned M. de Monbert, and acknowledged that you were right when you said: "Genuine love is confiding, it shuns doubt because it cannot endure it."

This sad impression that he felt upon learning that Louise Guérin was Irene de Chateaudun, was the only cloud that passed over our happiness. Soon joy returned to us lively and pure—and we spoke of you tenderly; he was the poor wounded man that gave you so much uneasiness; he was the model husband you had chosen for me, and whom I refused with such proud scorn!

Ah! my good Valentine, how I thank you for having nursed him as a sister; how noble and charming you were to him; I would like to reward you by having you here to witness our happiness. And you must thank the esteemed M. de Braimes for me, and my beautiful Irene, who taught him to love my name, and brought him a bouquet every morning; and your handsome Henri, the golden-haired angel, who brought him his little doves in your work-basket to take care of, while he studied his lessons. Embrace for me these dear children he caressed, who cheered his hours of suffering, whom I so love for his sake and yours.

Will you not let me show my appreciation of my little god-daughter by rendering her independent of future accidents, enabling her without imprudence to marry for love?

I am so happy in loving that I can imagine it to be the only source of joy to others; yet this happiness is so great that I find myself asking if my heart is equal to its blessings; if my poor reason, wearied by so many trials, will have sufficient strength to support these violent emotions; if happiness has not, like misery, a madness. I endeavor when alone to calm my excited mind; I sit down and try to quietly think over my past life with that inflexibility of judgment, that analyzing pedantry, of which you have so often accused me.

You remember, Valentine, more than once you have told me you saw in me two persons, a romantic young girl and a disenchanted old philosopher. . . . Ah! well, to-day the romantic young girl has reached the most thrilling chapter of her life; she feels her weak head whirl at the prospect of such intoxicating bliss, and she appeals to the old philosopher for assistance. She tells him how this bliss frightens her; she begs him to reassure her about this beautiful future opening before her, by proving to her that it is natural and logical; that it is the result of her past life, and finally that however great it may be, however extraordinary it may seem, it is possible, it is lasting, because it is bought at the price of humiliation, of sorrow, of trials!

Yes, I confess it, these happy events appear to be so strange, so impossible, that I try to explain them, to calmly analyze them and believe in their reality.

I recall one by one all my impressions of the last four years, and exert my mind to discover in the strangeness, in the fatality, in the excessive injustice of my past misfortunes, a natural explanation for extraordinary and incredible events of the present. The reverses themselves were romantic and improbable, therefore the reparations and consolations should in their turn be equally romantic. Is it an ordinary thing for a young girl reared like myself in Parisian luxury, belonging to an illustrious family, to be reduced to the sternest poverty, and through family pride and dignity to conceal her name? Is not such dignity, assailed by fate, destined sooner or later to vindicate itself?

You see that through myself I would have been restored to my rank. M. de Meilhan wished to marry me without fortune or name. . . . Yesterday, M. de Villiers knew not who I was; my uncle's inheritance has therefore been of no assistance to me. I believe that native dignity will always imperceptibly assert itself. I believe in the logic of events; order has imperious laws; it is useless to throw statues to the ground, the time always comes when they are restored to their pedestals. From my rank I fell unjustly, unhappily. I must be restored to it justly. Every glaring injustice has a natural consequent, a brilliant reparation. I have suffered extraordinary misfortune; I have a right to realize ideal happiness. At twenty, I lost in one year my noble and too generous father and my poor mother; it is only just that I should have a lover to replace these lost ones.

As to these violent passions which you pretend I have inspired, but which are by no means serious, I examine them calmly and find in the analysis an explanation of many of the misfortunes, many of the mistakes of poor women, who are accused of inconstancy and perfidy, and who are, on the contrary, only culpable through innocence and honest faith. They believe they love, and engage themselves, and then, once engaged, they discover that they are not in love. Genuine love is composed of two sentiments; we experience one of these when we believe we love; we are uneasy, agitated by an imperfect sentiment that seeks completion; we struggle in its feeble ties; we are neither bound nor free; not happy, nor at liberty to seek happiness at another source. . . . . The old philosopher speaks—hear him.

There are two kinds of love, social love and natural love; voluntary love and involuntary love. An accomplished and deserving young man loves a woman; he loves her, and deserves to be loved in return; she wishes to love him, and when alone thinks of him; if his name is mentioned, she blushes; if any one says in her presence, "Madame B. used to be in love with him," she is disturbed, agitated. These symptoms are certain proofs of the state of her heart, and she says to herself, "I love Adolphe," just as I said, "I love Roger." . . . But the voice of this man does not move her to tears; his fiery glances do not make her turn pale or blush; her hand does not tremble in the presence of his. . . . She only feels for him social love; there exists between them a harmony of ideas and education, but no sympathy of nature.

The other love is more dangerous, especially for married women, who mistake remorse for that honest repugnance necessarily inspired in every woman of refined mind and romantic imagination.

I frankly confess that if I had been married, if I had no longer control of my actions, I should have thought I was in love with Edgar. . . . I should have mistaken for an odious and culpable passion, the fearful trouble, insupportable uneasiness that his love caused me to feel. But my vigilant reason, my implacable good faith watched over my heart; they said: "Shun Roger;" they said: "Fear Edgar. . . . If I had married Roger, woe to me! Conventional love, leaving my heart all its dreams, would have embittered my life. . . . But if, more foolish still, I had married Edgar, woe, woe to me! because one does not sacrifice with impunity to an incomplete love all of one's theories, habits and even weaknesses and early prejudices.

What enlightened me quickly upon the unreality of this love was the liberty of my position. Why being free should I fear a legitimate love? Strange mystery! wonderful instinct! With Roger, I sadly said to myself: "I love him, but it is not with love." . . . With Edgar, I said in fright: "This is love, yet I do not love him." And then when Raymond appeared, my heart, my reason, my faith at the first glance recognised him, and without hesitation, almost without prudence, I cried out, "It is he . . . I love him." . . . Now this is what I call real love, ideal love, harmony of ideas and sympathy of hearts.

Oh! it does me good to be a little pedantic; I am so excited, it calms me; I am not so afraid of going crazy when I adopt the sententious manner. Ah! when I can laugh I am happy. Anything that for a moment checks my wild imagination, reassures me.

This morning we laughed like two children! You will laugh too; when I write one name it will set you off; he said to me, "I must go to my coachmaker's and see if my travelling carriage needs any repairs." I said, "I have a new one; I will send for it, and let you see it." In an hour my carriage was brought into the court-yard. With peals of laughter he recognised Lady Penock's carriage. "Lady Penock! What! do you know Lady Penock? Are you the audacious young lover who pursued her until she was compelled to sell me her carriage." "Yes, I was the man." Ah! how gay we were; he was the hero of Lady Penock, his was the little light, he was the wounded man, he was the husband selected for me! Ah! it all makes me dizzy; and we shall set off to travel in this carriage.

Ah! Lady Penock, you must pardon him.

IRENE DE CHATEAUDUN.

XXXIII.

EDGAR DE MEILHAN *to the* PRINCE DE MONBERT,

Porte Restante (Rouen).

PARIS, Aug. 11th 18—.

HERE I am in Paris, gloomy, with nothing to do, not knowing how to fill up the void in my life, discontented with myself, ridiculous in my own eyes, alike in my love and in my despair. I have never felt so sad, so wretched, so cast-down. My days and nights are passed in endless self-accusation : one by one I revise every word and action relating to Louise Guérin. I compose superb sentences which I had forgotten to pronounce, the effect of which would have been irresistible. I tell myself: "On such a day, you were guilty of a stupid timidity, which would have made even a college-boy laugh." It was the moment for daring. Louise, unseen, threw you a look which you were too stupid to understand. The evening that Madame Taverneau was at Rouen, you allowed yourself to be intimidated like a fool, by a few grand airs, an affectation of virtue over which the least persistence would have triumphed. Your delicacy ruined you. A little roughness doesn't hurt sometimes, especially with prudes. You have not profited by a single one of your advantages ; you let every opportunity pass." In short, I am like a general who has lost a battle, and who, having retired to his tent, in the midst of a field strewn with the dead and the dying marks out, too late, a strategic plan which would have infallibly gained him the victory !

What a pitiless monster an unsatiated desire is, tearing your heart with its sharp claws and piercing beak for want of other prey ! The punishment of Prometheus pales beside it, for the arrows of Hercules cannot reach this unseen vulture ! "This is my first unsuccessful love ; the first falcon that has returned to me without bringing the dove in his talons ; I am devoured by an inexpressible rage ; I pace my room like a wild beast, uttering inarticulate cries ; I do not know whether I love or hate

Louise the most, but I should take infinite delight in strangling her with her blonde tresses and trampling her, affrighted and suppliant, under my feet.

My good Roger, I weary you with my lamentations; but whom can we weary, if not our friends? When will you return to Paris? Soon, I hope, since you have ceased writing to me.

I have gone back to the lady with the turban, passing nearly every evening in the catafalque, which she calls her drawing-room. This lugubrious habitation suits my melancholy. She finds me more gloomy, more Giaour-like, more Lara-like than usual; I am her hero, her god! or rather her demon, for she has now taken to the sorceries of the satanic school! I assure you that she annoys me inexpressibly, and yet I feel a sort of pleasure in being admired by her. It consoles my vanity for Louise's disdain, but not my heart. Alas! my poor heart, which still bleeds and suffers. I caught a glimpse of Paradise through a half-open door. The door is shut, and I weep upon the threshold!

If Louise were dead, I might be calm; but she exists, and not for me—that thought makes life insupportable. I can think of nothing else, and I scarcely know whether the words I write to you make any sense. I leave my letter unfinished. I will finish it this evening if I can succeed in diverting myself, for a moment, from this despair which possesses me.

Roger, something incredible has happened, overturning every calculation, every prevision. I am stupefied, benumbed—I was at the Marquise's, where it was darker than usual. One solitary lamp flickered in a corner, dozing under a huge shade. A fat gentleman, buried in an easy-chair, drowsily retailed the news of the day.

I was not listening to him; I was thinking of Louise's little white couch, from which I had once lifted the snowy curtain, with that sorrowful intensity, those poignant regrets which torture rejected lovers. Suddenly a familiar name struck my ear—the name of Irene de Chateaudun. I became attentive—"She is to be married to-morrow," continued the well-posted gentleman, "to—wait a minute, I get confused about names and dates; with that exception, my memory is excellent—a young man, Gaston, Raymond, I am not certain which, but his first name ends in *on* I am sure."

I eagerly questioned the fat man; he knew nothing more; hastily returning to my rooms I sent Joseph out to obtain further information.

My servant, who is quick and intelligent, and merits a master more given to intrigue and gallantry than I, went to the twelve mayors' offices. He brought me a list of all the banns that had been published.

The news was true; Irene de Chateaudun marries Raymond. What does that signify? Irene your fiancée, Raymond our friend! What comedy of errors is being played here? This, then, was the motive of these flights, these disappearances. They were laughing at you. It seems to me rather an audacious proceeding. How does it happen that Raymond, who knew of your projected marriage with Mademoiselle de Chateaudun, should have stepped in your shoes? This comes of deeds of prowess à la Don Quixote, and rescues of old Englishwomen.

Hasten, my friend, by railroad, post-horses, in the stirrup, on hippogriff's wing; what am I talking about? You will scarcely receive my letter ere the marriage has taken place. But I will keep watch for you. I will acquit myself of your revenge, and Mademoiselle Irene de Chateaudun shall not become Madame Raymond de Villiers until I have whispered that in her ear which will make her paler than her marriage veil. As to Raymond, I am not astonished at what he has done; I felt towards him at Richeport a hate which never deceives me and which I always feel towards cowards and hypocrites; he talked too much of virtue not to be a scoundrel. I would I had the power to raze out from my life the time that I loved him. It is impossible to oppose this revolting marriage. How is it possible that Irene de Chateaudun, who was to enjoy the honor of being your wife, whom you had represented to me as a woman of high intelligence and lofty culture, could have allowed herself to be impressed, after having known you, by the jeremiads of this sentimental sniveller? Since Eve, women have disliked all that is noble, frank and loyal; to fall is an unconquerable necessity of their nature; they have always preferred, to the voice of an honorable man, the perfidious whisper of the evil spirit, which shows its painted face among the leaves and wraps its slimy coils around the fatal tree.

EDGAR DE MEILHAN.

XXXIV.

RAYMOND DE VILLIERS *to* MME. LA VICOMTESSE DE BRAIMES,
Hotel de la Prefecture, Grenoble (Isère).

Paris, Aug. 11th 18—.

THIS is probably the last letter that I shall ever write to you. Do not pity me, my fate is more worthy of envy than of pity. I never knew, I never dreamed of anything more beautiful. It has been said time and again that real life is tame, spiritless and disenchanted by the side of the fictions of the poets. What a mistake! There is a more wonderful inventor than any rhapsodist, and that inventor is called reality. It wears the magic ring, and imagination is but a poor magician compared with it. Madame, do not write to Mademoiselle de Chateaudun. Since you have not done so my letters must necessarily have miscarried. Blessed be the happy chance which prevented you from following my advice! What did I say to you? I was a fool. Be careful not to alarm my darling. The man has lived long enough upon whom she has bestowed her love for one single day. Do not write, it is too late; but admire the decrees of fate. The diamond that I had sought with the Prince de Monbert, I have unwittingly found; I assisted in searching for it, while it was hid, unknown to me, in my heart. Louise is Irene. Madame Guérin is Mademoiselle de Chateaudun. If you could have seen her delight in revealing her identity! I saw her joyful and triumphant as if her love were not the most precious gift she could bestow. When she proclaimed herself, I felt an icy chill pass through me; but I thanked God for the bliss which I shall not survive, so great that death must follow after.

"Do you not love me well enough," she said, "to pardon me my fortune?"

How was she to know that in revealing herself she had signed my death-warrant?

She spoke, laughingly, of M. de Monbert, as she had done

of Edgar; to excuse herself she related a story of disenchantment which you already know, madame. It would have been honorable in me, at this juncture, to have undeceived Irene and enlightened her upon the Prince's passion. I did so, but feebly. When happiness is offered us loaded with ball, we have no longer the right to be generous.

We are to be married privately to-morrow, without noise or display. A plain-looking carriage will wait for us on the Place de la Madeleine; immediately on leaving the church we shall set out for Villiers. M. de Meilhan is at Richeport. M. de Monbert is in Brittany. Eight days must elapse before the news can reach them. Thus I have before me eight days of holy intoxication. What man has ever been able to say as much?

Recall to mind the words of one of your poet friends; It is better to die young and restore to God, your judge, a heart pure and full of illusions. Your poet is right; only it is more ecstatic to die in the arms of happiness, and to be buried with the flower of a love which has not yet faded.

My love would never have followed the fatal law of commonplace affection; years would never have withered it in their passage. But what signifies its duration, if we can crowd eternity into an hour? What signifies the number of days if the days are full?

Nevertheless, I cannot refrain from regretting an existence which promises so much beauty. We would have been very happy in my little château on the Creuse. I was born for fireside joys, the delights of home. I already saw my beautiful children playing over my green lawns, and pressing joyfully around their mother. What exquisite pleasure to be able to initiate into the mysteries of fortune the sweet and noble being whom I then believed to be poor and friendless! I would take possession of her life to make a long fête-day of it. What tender care would I not bestow upon so dear and charming a destiny! Downy would be her nest, warm the sun that shone upon her, sweet the perfumes that surrounded her, soft the breezes that fanned her cheek, green and velvety the turf under her delicate feet! But a truce to such sweet dreams. I know M. de Monbert; what I have seen of him is sufficient. M. de Meilhan, too, will not disappoint me. I shall not conceal myself; in eight days these two men will have found me. In eight days they will knock at my door, like two creditors, demanding restitution, one of Louise, the other of Irene. If I were to descend to justification, even if I were to succeed in convincing them of my loyalty and uprightness, their despair would cry out all the louder for vengeance. Then, madame, what shall I do? Shall I try to take the life of my friends after having robbed them of their happiness? Let them kill me; I shall be ready; but they shall see upon my lips, growing cold in death, the triumphant smile of victorious love; my last sigh, breathing Irene's name, will be a cruel insult to these unhappy men, who will envy me even in the arms of death.

I neither believe nor desire that Irene should survive me. My soul, in leaving, will draw hers after it. What would she do here below, without me? You will see, that feeling herself gently drawn upward, she will leave a world that I no longer inhabit. I repeat, that I would not have her live on earth without me. But sorrow does not always kill; youth is strong, and nature works miracles. I have seen trees, struck by lightning, still stand erect and put forth new leaves. I have seen blasted lives drag their weary length to a loveless old age. I have seen noble hearts severed from their mates, slowly consumed by the weariness of widowhood and solitude. If we could die when we have lost those we love, it would be too sweet to love. Jealous of his creature, God does not always permit it. It is a grace which he accords only to the elect. If, by a fatality not without precedent, Irene should have the strength and misfortune to survive me, to you, madame, do I confide her. Care for her, not with the hope of consoling her, but to banish all bitterness from her regrets. Picture my death to her, not as the expiation of the innocent whim of her youth, but as that of a happiness too great to go unchecked. Tell her that there are great joys as well as great sorrows, and that when they have outweighed the human measure of happiness, the heart which holds them must break and grow still. Tell her, ah! above all, tell her that I have dearly loved her, and if I carry her whole life away with me, I leave her mine in exchange. Finally, madame, tell her that I died blessing her, regretting that I had but one life to lay down as the price of her love.

While I write, I see her at her window, smiling, radiant, beautiful, beaming with happiness, resplendent with life and youth.

Farewell, madame; an eternal farewell!

RAYMOND DE VILLIERS.

XXXV.

EDGAR DE MEILHAN *to the* PRINCE DE MONBERT,
Poste-Restante (Rouen).

Paris, August 12th 18—.

WHAT I wrote you yesterday was very infamous and incredible. You think that is all; well, no! you have only half of the story. My hand trembles with rage so that I can scarcely hold my pen. What remains to be told is the acme of perfidy; a double-dyed treason; we have been made game of, you as a plighted husband, I as a lover. All this seems as incoherent to you as a dream. What can I have in common with Irene whom I have never seen? Wait, you shall see!

My faithful Joseph discovered that the marriage was to take place at the Church of the Madeleine, at six o'clock in the morning.

I was so agitated, so restless, so tormented by gloomy presentiments that I did not go to bed. At the given hour I went out wrapped in my cloak. Although it is summer-time I was cold; a slight feverish chill ran through me. The catastrophe to come had already turned me pale.

The Madeleine stood out faintly against the gray morning sky. The livid figures of some revellers, surprised by the day, were seen here and there on the street corners. The stir of the great city had not yet begun. I thought I had arrived too soon, but a carriage with neither crest nor cipher, in charge of a servant in quiet livery, was stationed in one of the cross-streets that run by the church.

I ascended the steps with uncertain footing, and soon saw, in one of those spurious chapels, which have been stuck with so much trouble in that counterfeit Greek temple, wax lights and the motions of the priest who officiated.

The bride, enveloped in her veil, prostrated before the altar, seemed to be praying fervently; the husband, as if he were not the most contemptible of men, stood erect and proud, his face beaming with joy. The ceremony drew to a close, Irene raised her head, but I was so placed as not to be able to distinguish her features.

I leaned against a column in order to whisper in Irene's ear, as she passed, a word as cutting as the crystal poniards of the bravos of Venice, which break in the wound and slay without a drop of blood. Irene advanced buoyantly along, leaning on Raymond's arm, with an undulating, rhythmical grace, as if her feet trod the yielding clouds, instead of the cold stones of the aisle. She no longer walked the earth, her happiness lifted her up; the ardor of her delight made me comprehend those assumptions of the Saints, who soared in their ecstasy above the floors of their narrow cells and caverns; she felt the deep delight of a woman who sacrifices herself.

When she reached the column that concealed me, an electrical current doubtless warned her of my presence, for she shuddered as if struck by an unseen arrow, and quickly turned her head; a stray sunbeam lit up her face, and I recognised in Irene de Chateaudun, Louise Guérin; in the rich heiress, the screen-painter of Pont de l'Arche!

Irene and Louise were the same person!

We have been treated as Cassandras of comedy; we have played in all seriousness the scene between Horace and Arnolphe. We have confided to each other our individual loves, hopes and sorrows. It is very amusing; but, contrary to custom, the tragedy will come after the farce, and we will play it so well that no one will be tempted to laugh at our expense; we will convert ridicule into terror. Ah! Mademoiselle Irene de Chateaudun, you imagined that you could amuse yourself with two such men as the Prince de Monbert and Edgar de Meilhan! that there it would end, and you had only to say to them: "I love another better!" And you, Master Raymond, thought that your virtuous reputation would make your perfidy appear like an act of devotion! No, no, in the drama where the great lady was an adventuress, the artless girl a fast woman, the hero a traitor, the lover a fool, and the betrothed husband a Geronte, the rôles are to be changed.

A hoarse cry escaped me, Irene clung convulsively to Raymond's arm, and precipitately left the church. Raymond, without understanding this sudden flight, yielded to it and rapidly descended the steps. The carriage was in waiting; they got into it; the coachman whipped up his horses and soon they were out of sight.

Irene, Louise, whatever may be your name or your mask, you shall not long remain Madame de Villiers; a speedy widowhood will enable you to begin your coquetries again. I regret to be compelled to strike you through another, for *you* merit death.

EDGAR DE MEILHAN.

XXXVI.

ROGER DE MONBERT *to* MONSIEUR LE COMTE DE VILLIERS,

Au Château de Villiers (Creuse).

August 16th 18—.

MONSIEUR,—

I take pleasure in sending you, by way of apologue, an anecdote, which you may read with profit.

During my travels I met with an estimable man, a Creole of the colony of Port Natal, by the name of Smollet.

I sometimes hunted in the neighborhood of his place, and on two occasions demanded his hospitality. He received me in a dubious manner, admitted me to his table, scarcely spoke to me; served me with Constantia wine, refused to accept my proffered hand, and surrendered me his own couch to rest my wearied limbs upon. From Port Natal I wrote this savage two notes of thanks, commencing: *My dear friend*—in writing, I could not confer on him a title of rank, so I gave him one of affection: *My dear friend.* My letters were ignored—as I had asked nothing, there was nothing to answer. One evening I met the Creole walking up the avenue of Port Natal, and advanced towards him, and held out my hand in a friendly way. Once more he declined to accept it. My vexation was apparent: "Monsieur," said the savage, "you appear to be an honest, sincere young man, very unlike a European. I must enlighten and warn your too unsuspecting mind. You have several times called me *your dear friend.* Doing this might prove disastrous to you, and then I would be in despair. I am not your friend; I am the friend of no one. . . . Avoid me, monsieur; shun my neighborhood, shun my house. Withdraw the confidence, that with the carelessness of a traveller you have reposed in me. . . . Adieu!" This *adieu* was accompanied by a sinister smile and a savage look that were anything but reassuring to me. I afterwards discovered that the Creole Smollet was a professional bandit!!

I hope, Monsieur de Villiers, that the application of this apologue will not escape you. At all events, I will add a few lines to enlighten your unsophisticated mind. You have always been my friend, monsieur. You have never disclaimed this relation; you have always pressed my hand when we met. Your professed friendship justified my confidence, and it would have been ungrateful in me to have esteemed you less than I did the savage. You and Mad. de Braimes have cunningly organized against me a plot of the basest nature. Doubtless you call it a happy combination of forces—I call it a perfidious conspiracy. I imagine I hear you and Mad. de Braimes at this very moment laughing at your victim as you congratulate yourselves on the success of your machinations. It affords me pleasure to think that one of these two friends is, perhaps, a man. Were they both women I could not demand satisfaction. You deserve my gratitude for your great kindness in assisting me when I most needed a friend. When I sought Mlle. de Chateaudun with a foolish, blind anxiety, you charitably aided me in my efforts to find her. You were my guide, my compass, my staff; you led me over roads where Mlle. de Chateaudun never thought of going; your guidance was so skilful that at the end of my searches you alone found what we had both been vainly seeking. You must have been delighted and entertained at the result, monsieur! Did Mad. de Braimes laugh very much? Truly, monsieur, you are old beyond your years, and your education was not confined to Greek and Latin; your talent for acting has been cultivated by a profound study of human nature. You play high comedy to perfection, and you should not let your extreme modesty prevent your aspiring to a more brilliant theatre. It is a pity that your fine acting should be wasted upon me alone. You deserve a larger and more appreciative audience! You do not know yourself. I will hold a mirror before your eyes; you can affect astonishment, disinterestedness, magnanimity, and a constellation of other virtues, blooming like flowers in the gardens of the golden age. You are a perfected comedian. If you really possessed all the virtues you assume, you would, like Enoch, excite the jealousy of Heaven, and be translated to your proper sphere A man of your transcendent virtue would be a moral scourge in our corrupt society. He would, by contrast, humiliate his neighbors. In these degenerate days such a combination of gifts is antagonistic to nature.

Do relieve our anxiety by accepting the title of comedian. Acknowledge yourself to be an actor, and our anxious fears are quieted.

I would have my mind set at rest upon one more point. Courage is another virtue that can be assumed by a coward, and it would afford me great pleasure to see you act the part of a *brave* comedian.

While waiting for your answer I feel forced to insult you by thinking that this last talent is wanting in your rich repertory. Be kind enough to deny this imputation, and prove yourself to be a thoroughly accomplished actor.

Your admiring audience,

ROGER DE MONBERT.

XXXVII.

EDGAR DE MEILHAN *to the* COUNT DE VILLIERS,

Château de Villiers, via Guéret (Creuse).

PARIS, Aug. 16th 18—.

NOBLE hidalgo, illustrious knight of la Mancha; you who are so fond of adventures and chivalric deeds, I am about to make you a proposition which, I hope, will suit your taste: a fight with sharp weapons, be it lance, or axe, or dagger; a struggle to the death, showing neither pity nor quarter. I know beforehand what you are going to say: Your native generosity will prevent you from fighting a duel with your friend. In the first place, I am not your friend; traitors have not that honor. Do not let that scruple stop you, refined gentleman.

Your mask has fallen off, dear Tartuffe with the fine feelings. We now know to what figures you devote yourself. Before dragging English women out of the flames you are well aware of their social position. You save friends from bankruptcy at a profit of eighty per cent., and when you make love to a grisette, you have her crest and the amount of her income in your pocket. In coming to my house, you knew that Louise was Irene. Madame de Braimes had acquainted you with all the circumstances during your interesting convalescence. All this may seem very natural to others and to a virtuous mortal, a Grandison like yourself. But I think differently; to me your conduct appears cowardly, base and contemptible. I should not be able to control myself, but would endeavor to make you comprehend my opinion of you, by slapping you in the face, wherever I met you. I hope that you will spare me such a disagreeable alternative by consenting to *pose* for a few moments before my sword or pistol, as you please. Allow me to entreat you not to exhibit any grandeur of soul, by firing in the air, it would not produce the slightest effect upon me, for I should kill you like a dog. Your presence upon the earth annoys me, and I do not labor for morality in deeds myself

EDGAR DE MEILHAN.

XXXVIII.

COMTE DE VILLIERS *to* MESSRS. ROGER DE MONBERT *and* EDGAR DE MEILHAN,

VILLIERS, Aug 18th 18—.

LET us drop such language unworthy of you and of me. We are gentlemen, of military descent; our fathers when they did each other the honor that you offer me, challenged, but did not insult each other. If the affair were equal, if I had only one to contend with, perhaps I might attempt to bring him to reason There are two of you; come on, I await you.

COMTE DE VILLIERS

XXXIX.

VILLIERS, August 21st 18—.

FOR two days I have been trying to answer your letter, my dear Valentine, but I am so uneasy, nervous and excited that I dare not commit to paper my wild and troubled thoughts; I am still sane enough to accuse myself of madness, but dread to prove it. Were I to write down all the strange ideas that rush through my mind, and then read them over, conviction of insanity would stare me in the face.

I was right when I told you it was a risk to accept such a wealth of happiness; my sweet enchantment is disturbed by dark threatening clouds—danger lurks in the air—the lightest word fills me with uneasiness—a letter written in a strange hand—an unexpected visitor, who leaves Raymond looking preoccupied—everything alarms me, and he gently chides me and asks why I look so sad. I say because I am too happy; but he thinks this a poor reason for my depression, and to divert my thoughts he walks with me through the beautiful valleys and tells me of his youth and the golden dreams of his early manhood, and assures me that his dreams of happiness are realized beyond his most exalted hopes—that he did not believe the angels would permit so perfect a being as myself to dwell on earth—that to be loved by me for a day, for an hour, he would willingly give up his life, and that such a sacrifice was a small price for such a love. I dared not mar his happiness by giving expression to my sad fears. His presence allays my apprehensions; he has so much confidence in the future that I cannot help being inspired with a portion of it; thus, when he is near me, I feel happy and reassured, but if he leaves me for a moment I am beset by myriads of terrible threatening phantoms. I accuse myself of having been imprudent and cruel; I fear I have not, as you say, inspired two undying passions, two life-long devotions, but exasperated two vindictive men. I well know that M. de Monbert did not love me, and yet I fear his unjust resentment. I recall

Edgar's absurd breach of faith, and Edgar, whose image had until now only seemed ridiculous, Edgar appears before my troubled vision furious and threatening. I am haunted by a vague remembrance: The day of my wedding, after the benediction, as we were leaving the chapel, I was terribly frightened —in the silent gloom of the immense church I heard a voice, an angry stifled voice, utter my name . . . the name I bore at Pont de l'Arche—Louise! . . . I quickly turned around to see whence came this voice that could affect me so powerfully at such a moment! I could discover no one. . . . Louise! . . . Many women are called Louise, it is a common name—perhaps it was some father calling his daughter, or some brother his sister. There was nothing remarkable in the calling of this name, and yet it filled me with alarm. I recalled Edgar's looks on that evening he was so angry with me; the rage gleaming in his eyes; the violent contraction of his features, his voice terrible and stifled like the voice in the church, and I was now convinced that his love was full of haughty pride, selfishness and hatred. But I said to myself, if it had been he, he would have followed me and looked in our carriage—I would have seen him in the church, or on the portico outside. . . . Besides, why should he have come? . . . he had given up seeing me; he could easily have found me had he so desired; he knew where Madame Taverneau's house was in Paris, and he knew that I lived with her; if he had hoped to be received by me, he would have simply called to pay a visit. . . . Finally, if he was at this early hour—six in the morning—in the church, at so great a distance from where I live, it was not to act as a spy upon me. The man who called Louise was not Edgar—it could not have been Edgar. This reflection reassured me. I questioned Raymond; he had seen no one, heard no one. I remembered that M. de Meilhan was not in Paris, and tried to convince myself that it was foolish to think of him any more. But yesterday I learned in a letter from Madame Taverneau—who as yet knows nothing of my marriage or departure from Paris, and will not know, until a year has elapsed, of the fortune I have settled upon her—I learned that M. de Meilhan left Havre and came direct to Paris. His mother did not tell him that I had gone with her to bring him home. When she found that her own influence was sufficient to detain him in France, she was silent as to my share in the journey. I thank her for it, as I greatly prefer he should remain ignorant of the foolish idea I had of sacrificing myself at his shrine in order to make his mother happy. But what alarms me is that she keeps him in Paris because she knows that he will learn the truth at Richeport, and because she hopes that the gayeties around him will more quickly make him forget this love that so interfered with her ambitious projects. So Edgar *was* in Paris the day of my wedding . . . and perhaps . . . but no, who could have told him anything? . I lived three miles from the parish where I was married. . . . It could not have been he . . . and yet I fear that man. . . . I remember with what bitterness and spite he spoke to me of Raymond, in a letter, filled with unjust reproaches, that he wrote me three days after my departure from Richeport. In this letter, which I immediately burned, he told me that M. de Villiers was engaged to be married to his cousin. O how wretched this information made me! It had been broken off years ago, but M. de Villiers thought the engagement still existed; he spoke of it as a tie that would prevent his friend from indulging in any pretensions to my favor; and yet what malevolence there was in his praise of him, what jealous fear in his insolent security! How ingenuously he said: "Since I have no cause to fear him, why do I hate him?" I now remember this hatred, and it frightens me. Aided by Roger he will soon know all; he will discover that Irene de Chateaudun and Louise Guérin are the same person, and then two furious men will demand an explanation of my trifling with their feelings and reproach me with the duplicity of my conduct. . . . Valentine, do you think they could possibly act thus? Valentine! do you think these two men, who have so shamefully insulted my memory, so grossly betrayed me and proved themselves disgracefully faithless, would dare lay any claims to my love? Alas! in spite of the absurdity of such a supposition, Heaven knows they are fully capable of acting thus; men in love have such relaxed morality, such elastic consciences!

Under pretext of imaginary ungovernable passions, they indulge, without compunction, in falsehood, duplicity and the desecration of every virtue! . . . and yet think a pure love can condone and survive such unpardonable wrongs. They lightly weigh the tribute due to the refinement of a woman's heart. Their devotion is characterized by a singular variety. The loyal love of noble women is sacrificed to please the whims of those unblushing creatures who pursue such men with indelicate attentions and enslave them by flattering their inordinate vanity, and they, to preserve their self-love unhurt, pierce and mortally wound the generous hearts that live upon their affection and revere their very names—these they strike without pity and without remorse. And then when the tender love falls from these broken hearts, like water from a shattered vase, never to be recovered, they are astonished, uneasy, . . . they have broken the heart filled with love, and now, with stupid surprise and pretended innocence, they ask what has become of the love! . . . they cowardly murdered it, and are indignant that it dared to die beneath their cruel blows. But why dwell upon Edgar and his anger and hatred, of Roger and his fury? Fate needs not these terrible instruments to destroy our happiness; the slightest accident, the most trifling imprudence can serve its cruelty; every thing will assist it in taking vengeance upon a man revelling in too much love, too much love. The cold north wind blowing at night upon his heated brow may strike him with the chill of death; the bridge may perfidiously break beneath his feet and cast him in the surging torrent below; a lofty rock, shivered by the winter frost, may fall upon him and crush him to atoms; his favorite horse may be frightened at a shadow and hurl him over the threatening precipice . . . that child playing in front of my window might carelessly strike him on the temple with one of those pebbles and kill him. . . .

Oh! Valentine, I am not laboring under an illusion. I see

danger; the world revolts against pure, unalloyed happiness; society pursues it as an offence; nature curses it because of its perfection; to her every perfect thing seems a monstrosity not to be borne—directly she suspects its existence, she gives the alarm and the elements unite in conspiring against this happiness; the thunder-bolt is warned and holds itself in readiness to burst over the radiant brow. With human beings all the evil passions are simultaneously aroused: secret notice, unknown voices warn the envious people of every nation that there is somewhere a great joy to be disturbed; that in some corner of the earth two beings exist who sought and found each other—two hearts that love with ideal equality and intoxicating harmony. . . Chance itself, that careless railer, is overbearing and jealous towards them; it is angry with these two beings who voluntarily sought and conscientiously chose each other without waiting for it to confer happiness upon them—it discovers their names, that never knows the name of any one, and pursues them with its animosity; it recovers its sight in order to recognise and strike them. I feel that we are too happy! Death stares us in the face! My soul shudders with fear! On earth we are not allowed to taste of supreme delight—pure, unalloyed happiness—to feel at once that ecstasy of soul and delirium of passion—that pride of love and loftiness of a pure conscience . . . burning joys are only permitted to culpable love. When two unfortunate beings, bound by detested ties, meet and mutually recognise the ideals of their dreams, they are allowed to love each other because they have met too late, because this immense joy, this finding one's ideal, is poisoned by remorse and shame. Their criminal happiness can remain undisturbed because it is criminal; it has the conditions of life, frailty and misery; it bears the impress of sin, therefore it belongs to a common humanity. . . . But find ideal bliss in a legitimate union, find it in time to welcome it without shame and cherish it without remorse; be happy as a lover and honored as a wife; to experience the wild ardor of love and preserve the charming freshness of purity—to delight in obeying the equitable law of the most harmonious love by being alternately a slave and a queen; to call upon him who calls upon you; seek him who seeks you; love him who loves you—in a word, to be the idol of your idol! . . . it is too much, it surpasses human happiness, it is stealing fire from heaven—it is, I tell you, incurring he punishment of death!

In my enthusiasm I already stand upon the boundary of the true world—I have a glimpse of paradise; earth recedes from my gaze; I understand and expect death, because life has bid me a last farewell—the exaltation that I feel belongs to the future of the blessed; it is a triumphant dying—that final and supremely happy thought that tells me my soul is about to take its flight.

Oh! merciful God! my brain is on fire! and why do I write you these incoherent thoughts! Valentine, you see all excessive emotions are alike; the delirium of joy resembles the frenzy of despair. Having attained the summit of happiness, what do we see at our feet? . . . a yawning abyss! . . . we have lost the steep path by which we so painfully reached the top; once there, we have no means of gradually descending the declivity . . . from so great a height we cannot walk, we fall!

There is but one way of preserving happiness—abjure it—never welcome it; sometimes it delights in visiting ungrateful people. Vainly do I seek to reassure myself by expiation, by sacrifices; during these eight days I have been lavishly giving gold in the neighborhood, I have endowed all the children, fed the poor, enriched the hospitals; I would willingly ruin myself by generous charity, by magnificent donations—I would cheerfully give my entire fortune to obtain rest and peace for my troubled mind.

Every morning I enter the empty church and fervently pray that God will permit me by some great sacrifice to insure my happiness. I implore him to inflict upon me hard trials, great humiliations, intense pain, sufferings beyond any strength, but to have mercy upon my poor heart and spare me Raymond . . . to leave me a little longer Raymond. . . .

Raymond and his love!

But these tears and prayers will be vain—Raymond himself, without understanding his presentiments, instinctively feels that his end is approaching. His purity of soul, his magnanimity, the unexampled disinterestedness of his conduct, are indications—these sublime virtues are symptoms of death—this generosity, this disinterestedness are tacit adieux. Raymond possesses none of the weaknesses of men destined for a long life; he has indulged in none of the wicked passions of the age—he has kept himself apart, observing but not sharing the actions of men. He regards life as if he were a pilgrim, and takes no part in any of its turmoils—he has not bargained for any of its disenchantments; his great pride, his life-long, unbending loyalty have concealed a mournful secret; he has stood aloof because he was convinced of his untimely end. He feels self-reliant because he will only have a short time to struggle; he is joyous and proud, because he looks upon the victory as already won. . . I weep as I admire him. .

Alas! am I to regard with sorrow and fear these noble qualities—these seductive traits that won my love? Is it because he deserves to be loved more than any being on earth has ever been loved, that I tremble for him! Valentine, does not such an excess of happiness excite your pity?

Ever since early this morning, I have been suffering torment—Raymond left me for a few hours—he went to Guéret; one of his cousins returning from the waters of Néris was to pass through there at ten o'clock, and requested him to meet her at the hotel. Nothing is more natural, and I have no reason to be alarmed—yet this short absence disturbs me as much as if it were to last years—it makes me sad—it is the first time we have been separated so long a time during these eight blissful days.

Ah! how I love him, and how heavy hangs time on my hands during his absence!

One thought comforts me in my present state of exaltation; I am unequal to any great misfortune. . . . A fatal piece of news, a painful sight, a false alarm. . . . a certain dreaded name mingled with one that I adore—ah! a false report, although immediately contradicted, would kill me on the spot—I could not live the two minutes it would require to hear the denial—the truth happily demonstrated. This thought consoles me—if my happiness is to end, I shall die with it.

Valentine, it is two o'clock! Oh! why does Raymond not return? My heart sinks—my hand trembles so that I can scarcely hold the pen—my eyes grow dim. . . . What can detain him? He left at eight, and should have returned long ago. I know well that the relative he went to see might have been delayed on the road—she may have mistaken the time, women are so ignorant about travelling—they never understand the time-tables.

All this tells me I am wrong to be uneasy—and yet . . I shudder at every sound . . . . his horse is so fiery . . . . I am astonished that Raymond did not let me read his relative's letter; he said he had left it on his table . . . but I looked on the table and it was not there. I wished to read the letter so as to find out the exact time he was to be at Guéret, and then I could tell when to expect him home.

But this relative is the mother of the girl he was to have married . . . . perhaps she still loves him . . . . is she with her mother? . . . . Ah! what an absurd idea! I am so uneasy that I divert my mind by being jealous—to avoid thinking of possible dangers, I conjure up impossible ones. . . . . Oh! my God! it is not his love I doubt . . . his love equals mine—it is the intensity of his love that frightens me—it is in this love so pure, so perfect, so divine—in this complete happiness that the danger lies. Is it not sinful to idolize one of God's creatures, when this adoration is due to God alone—to devote one's whole existence to a human being, for his sake to forget everything else? This is the sin before Heaven. . .

Oh! if I could only see him, and once more hear his voice! That blessed voice I love so much! How miserable I am! . . . What agony I suffer! . . . I stifle . . my brain whirls—my mind is so confused that I cannot think . . . this torture is worse than death. . . And then if he should suddenly appear before me, what joy ! . . . . Oh ! I don't wish him to enter the room at once—I would like one minute to prepare myself for the happiness of seeing him . . . . one single moment. . . . If he were to abruptly enter, I would become frantic with joy as I embraced him !

My dear Valentine, what a torment is love ! . . . . It is utterly impossible for me to support another hour of this agitation. I am sure I have a fever—I shiver with cold—I burn—my brain is on fire. . . . . .

As I write this to you, seated at the window, I eagerly watch the long avenue by which he must return. . . I write a word . . . a whole line so as to give him time to approach, hoping I will see him coming when I raise my eyes—. . After writing each line I look again . . . . nothing appears in the distance; I see neither his horse nor the cloud of dust that would announce his approach. The clock strikes! three o'clock ! . . . Valentine ! it is fearful . . . hope deserts me . . . all is lost . . . I feel myself dying . . . Instinct tells me that some dreadful tragedy, ruinous to me, is now enacting on this earth. . Ah ! my heart breaks . . . I suffer torture. . . . Raymond ! Raymond ! Valentine ! my mother ! help ! . . help ! . . . I see a horse rushing up the avenue . . . but it is not Raymond's . . . ah ! it *is* his . . . but . . . I don't see Raymond . . . . the saddle is empty . . . God !

This unfinished letter of the Comtesse de Villiers to Madame de Braimes bore neither address nor signature.

XL.

ROGER DE MONBERT *to* MONSIEUR EDGAR DE MEILHAN,
Hotel de Bellevue, Bruxelles (Belgique).

YOU are now at Brussels, my dear Edgar, at least for my own peace of mind I hope so. Although I fear not for you the rigors of the law, still I am anxious to know that you are on a safe and hospitable shore.

Criminal trials, even when they have a favorable issue, are injurious. In your case it is necessary to keep concealed, await the result of public opinion, and let future events regulate your conduct. Besides, as there is no law about duelling, you must distrust the courts of justice. The day will come when some jury, tired of so many acquittals, will agree upon a conviction. Your case may be decided by this jury—so it is only prudent for you to disappear, and abide the issue.

Things have entirely changed during my ten years' absence; all this is new to me. Immediately after the duel I obeyed your instructions, and went to see your lawyer, Delestong. With the exception of a few omissions, I was obliged to relate everything that happened. I must tell you exactly what I said and what I left unsaid, so that if we are summoned before the court our testimony shall not conflict.

It was unnecessary to relate what passed between us before the duel, so I merely said we had drawn lots as to who should be the avenger, and who the second; nor did I deem it proper to explain the serious causes of the duel, as it would have resulted in a long story, and the bringing in of women's names at every turn, an unpardonable thing in a man. I simply said the cause was serious, and of a nature to fully justify a deadly meeting; that we, Monsieur de Meilhan and myself, left Guéret at six o'clock in the morning; when three miles from the town, we left the high-road of Limoges and entered that part of the woods called the Little Cascade, where we dismounted and awaited the arrival of M. de Villiers, who, in a few minutes, rode up to us, accompanied by two army-officers as seconds. We exchanged bows at a distance of ten feet, but nothing was said until the elder of the officers advanced towards me, shook my hand, and drawing me aside, began: "We military men dare not refuse to act on this occasion as seconds when summoned by a brave man, but we always come with the hope of effecting a reconciliation. These young men are hot-headed. There is some pretty woman at the root of the difficulty, and they are acting the rôles of foolish rivals. The day has passed for men to fight about such silly things; it is no longer the fashion. Now, cannot we arrange this matter satisfactorily, without injuring the pride of these gentlemen?"

"Monsieur," I replied, "it is with profound regret that I decline making any amicable settlement of this affair. Under any other circumstances I would share your peaceable sentiments; as it is, we have come here with a fixed determination. If you knew—"

"Do tell me the provocation—I am very anxious to learn it," said the officer, interrupting me, eagerly.

"You ask what is impossible," I replied; "nothing could alter our determination. We fully made up our minds before coming here."

"That being the case, monsieur," said he, "my friend and I will withdraw; we decline to countenance a murder."

"If you retire, captain," I responded, pressing his hand, "I will also leave, and not be answerable for the result—and what will be the consequence? I can assure you, upon my honor, that these gentlemen will fight without seconds."

The officer bowed and waved his hand, in sign of forced acquiescence. After a short pause, he continued: "We have entered upon a very distasteful affair, and the sooner it is ended the better. Have they decided upon the weapons?"

"They have decided, monsieur, to draw lots for the choice of arms," I replied.

"Then," he cried, "there has been no insult given or received; they are both in the right and both in the wrong."

"Exactly so, captain."

"I suppose we will have to consent to it. Let us draw for the weapons, since it is agreed upon."

The lot fell on the sword.

"With this weapon," I said, "all the disadvantages are on the side of M. de Meilhan; the skilful fencing of his adversary is celebrated among amateurs. He is one of Pons's best scholars."

"Have you brought a surgeon?" said the captain.

"Yes, monsieur, we left Dr. Gillard in a house near by."

As you see, dear Edgar, I shall lay great stress upon the disadvantages you labored under in using the sword; and, when necessary, I shall express in eloquent terms the agony I felt when I saw your hand, more skilful in handling the pen than the sword, hesitatingly grasp the hilt.

I finished my deposition in these words: "When the distance had been settled, by casting lots, we handed our principals two swords exactly alike; one of the adverse seconds and myself stood three steps off with our canes raised in order to separate them at all risk, if necessary, in obedience to the characteristically French injunction of the duelling code as laid down by M. Chateunvillard.

"At the given signal the swords were bravely crossed; Edgar, with the boldness of heroic inexperience, bravely attacked his adversary. Raymond, compelled to defend himself, was astonished. At this terrible moment, when thought paralyzes action, he was absorbed in thought. The contest was brief. Edgar's sword, only half parried, pierced his rival's heart. The surgeon came to gaze upon a lifeless corpse.

"Edgar mounted his horse, rode off and I have not seen him since. Those who remained rendered the last offices to the dead."

I am obliged to write you these facts, my dear Edgar, not for information, but to recall them to you in their exact order; and especially, I repeat, in order to avoid contradiction on the witness-stand. Now I must write you of what you are ignorant.

I had a duty to fulfil, much more terrible than yours, and I was obliged to recall our execrable oath in order to renew courage and strength to keep my promise.

Before we had cast lots for the leading part in this duel, we swore to go ourselves to the house of this woman and announce to her the issue of the combat, if it proved favorable to us. In the delirium of angry excitement, filling our burning hearts at the moment, this oath appeared to be the most reasonable thing in the world. Our blood boiled with such violent hatred against him and her that it seemed just for vengeance, with refined cruelty, to step over a corpse and pursue its work ere its second victim had donned her widow's robes.

Edgar! Edgar! when I saw that blood flowing, when I saw life and youth converted into an inanimate mass of clay, when you left me alone on this inanimate theatre of death, my feelings underwent a sudden revolution; this moment seemed to age me a half a century, and without lessening my hatred, only left me a confused perception of it, with a vague memory full of disenchantment and sadness.

The crime was great, it is true, but what a terrible expiation! What hellish torture heaped upon him at once! To lose all at the point of the sword, all!—youth, fortune, love, wife, celestial joys, beautiful nature and the light of the sun!

However, dear Edgar, I remembered our solemn promise; and as you were not here to release me, I was obliged to fulfil it to the letter. And then again, shall I say it, this humane consideration did not extend to the offending woman; my heart was still filled with a sentiment that has no name in the language of the passions!—A mixture of hatred, love, jealousy, scorn and despair.

She was not dead! A man had been sacrificed as a victim upon the altar of this goddess: that was all.

Do not women require amusement of this sort?

She would live; to-day, she would weep; to-morrow, seek the common path of consolation. One victim is not enough to gratify her cruel vanity! She must be quickly consoled, that she might be ready to receive fresh sacrifices in her temple.

My heart filled with angry passions awakened by these thoughts, I spurred my horse, and hastened in the direction of the house that had been described to me the day before. I soon recognised the picturesque spot, where this accursed house lay concealed in the midst of beautiful trees and smiling waters.

An electric shock must have communicated to you, dear Edgar, the oppression of heart I felt at the sight of the landscape. There was the history of love in every tree and flower. There was an ineffable record in the hedges of the valleys; loving caresses in the murmur of the water-lilies; ecstasies of lovers in the quivering of the leaves; divine intoxication in the exhalations of the wild flowers, and in the lights, shadows and gentle breezes under the mysterious alcoves of the trees. Oh! how happy they must have been in this paradise! The whole air was filled with the life of their love and happiness! There must have been present a supernatural and invisible being, who was a jealous witness of this wedded bliss, and who made use of your sword to destroy it! So much happiness was an offence before heaven. We have been the blind instrument of a wrathful spirit. But what mattered death after such a day of perfect bliss! After having tasted the most exquisite tenderness in the world! When looking at the proud young husband sitting in this flowery bower, with the soft starlight revealing his happy face as he tenderly and hopefully gazed on his lovely bride, who would not have exclaimed with the poet,

"My life for a moment of bliss like this."

Who would not have welcomed your sword-thrust as the price of a moment's duration of such divine joy?

The survivors are the unfortunate ones, because they saw but could not taste this happiness.

Infernal Tantalus of the delights of Paradise, because their dream has become the reality of another, and lawful vengeance leaves them a satisfaction poisoned by remorse!

Come with me, dear Edgar, in my sad pilgrimage to this accursed house, and with me behold the closing scene. I left the shade of the woods and approached the lawn, that, like an immense terrace of grass and flowers, spread before the house. I saw many strange things, and with that comprehensive, sweeping glance of feverish excitement; two horses covered with foam, their saddles empty and bridles dragging, trampled down the flower-borders. One horse was Raymond's, returned riderless! Doubtless brought home by the servant who had accompanied him.

Not a face was visible, in the sun, the shade, the orchard, on the steps, or at the windows. I observed in the garden two rakes lying on some beautiful lilies; they had not been carefully laid down, but dropped in the midst of the flowers, on hearing some cry of distress from the house.

One window was open; the rich curtains showed it to be the room of a woman; the carelessly pushed open blinds proved that an anxious watcher had passed long hours of feverish expectation at the window. A desolate silence reigned around the house; this silence was fearful, and at an hour of the day when all is life and animation, in harmony with the singing birds and rippling waters.

I ascended the steps, mechanically noticing the beautiful flowers clustering about the railing; flowers take a part in every catastrophe of life. On the threshold, I forgot myself to think of you, to live with your spirit, to walk with your feet, for my own resolution would have failed me at this fatal moment.

In the vestibule I looked through a half-open folding-door, and, in the funereal darkness, saw some peasantry kneeling and praying. No head was raised to look at me. I slowly entered the room with my eyes downcast, and lids swollen with tears I forcibly restrained. In a recess, lying on a sofa, was something white and motionless, the sight of which froze my blood. . . . It was—I cannot write her name, Edgar—it was she. My troubled gaze could not discover whether dead or living. She seemed to be sleeping, with her hair lying carelessly about the pillow, in the disorder of a morning repose

Near by was a young man-servant, his vest spotted with blood; with face buried in his hands he was weeping bitterly.

Near her head a window was raised to admit the fresh air. This window opened on an inner courtyard, very gloomy on account of the masses of leaves that seemed to drop from the walls and fill it with sombreness.

Two men dressed in black, with faces more melancholy-looking than their garments, were in this courtyard, talking in low tones; through the window I could only see their heads and shoulders. I merely glanced at them; my eyes, my sorrow, my hatred, my love were all concentrated upon this woman. Absorbed by a heart-rending gaze, an instinct rather than idea rooted me to the spot.

I waited for her to recover her senses, to open her eyes, not to add to her anguish by a word or look of mine, but to let her see me standing there, a living, silent accusation. Some farmer-boys entered with lighted candles, a cross and basin of holy-water. In the disorder of my mind, I understood nothing, but slowly walked out on the terrace, with the vague idea of breathing a little fresh air and returning.

The serenity of the sky, the brightness of the sun, the green trees, the fragrant flowers, the songs of the birds, offered an ironical contrast to the scene of mourning. Often does nature refuse to countenance human sorrows, because they are ungrateful to her goodness. She creates the wonders of heaven to make us happy; we evoke the secrets of hell to torture our souls and bodies. Nature is right to scorn our self-inflicted sorrows.

You see, my dear Edgar, that I make you share all of my torments, all of my gloomy reflections. I make you live over this hour, minute by minute, agony on agony, as I suffered it myself.

I stood aside under a tree, waiting I know not for what; one of the men in black, I had seen from the window, came down the steps of the terrace and advanced towards me. I made some confused remark; the situation supplied it with intelligence.

"You are a relation, a friend, an acquaintance?" he said, inquiringly.

"Yes, monsieur."

"It is a terrible misfortune," he added, clasping his hands and bowing his head; "or rather say two terrible misfortunes in one day; the poor woman is also dead." . . .

Like one in a dream I heard the latter remark, and I now transcribe it to you as my impression of something that occurred long, long ago, although I know it took place yesterday.

"Yes, dead," he went on to say; "we were called in too late. Bleeding would have relieved the brain. It was a violent congestion; we have similar cases during our practice. An immense loss to the community. A woman who was young, beautiful as an angel, and charity itself. . . . Dead!"

He looked up, raised his hand to heaven, and walked rapidly away.

I am haunted by a memory that nothing can dispel. This spectre doubtless follows you too, dear Edgar. It is a mute, eloquent image fashioned in the empty air, like the outline of a grave; a phantom that the sun drives not away, pursuing me by day and by night. It is Raymond's face as he stood opposite to you on the field of death, his brow, his eye, his lips, his whole bearing breathing the noblest sentiments that were ever buried in an undeserved grave. This heroic young man met us with the fatal conviction that his last hour had come; he felt towards us neither hatred nor contempt; he obeyed the inexorable exigencies of the hour, without accusation, without complaint.

The silence of Raymond clothed in sublime delicacy his friendship for us, and his love for her. His manner expressed neither the resignation that calls for pity nor the pride that provokes passion; his countenance shone with modest serenity, the offspring of a grand resolve.

In a few days of conjugal bliss he had wandered through the flowery paths of human felicity; he had exhausted the measure of divine beatitude allotted to man on earth, and he stood nerved for the inevitable and bloody expiation of his happiness.

All this was written on Raymond's face.

Edgar! Edgar! we were too relentless. Why should honor, the noblest of our virtues, be the parent of so much remorse?

Adieu.

ROGER DE MONBERT.

XLI.

EDGAR DE MEILHAN *to the* PRINCE DE MONBERT,
St. Dominique Street, Paris (France).

Do not be uneasy, dear Roger; I have reached the frontier without being pursued; the news of the fatal duel had not yet spread abroad. I thank you, all the same, for the letter which you have written me, and in which you trace the line of conduct I should pursue in case of arrest. The moment a magistrate interferes, the clearest and least complicated affair assumes an appearance of guilt. However, it would have been all the same to me if I had been arrested and condemned. I fled more on your account than on my own. No human interest can ever again influence me; Raymond's death has ended my life!

What an inexplicable enigma is the human heart! When I saw Raymond facing me upon the ground, an uncontrollable rage took possession of me. The heavenly resignation of his face seemed infamous and finished hypocrisy. I said to myself: "He apes the angel, the wretch!" and I regretted that custom interposed a sword between him and my hatred. It seemed so coldly ceremonious, I would have liked to tear his bosom open with my nails and gnaw his heart out with my teeth. I knew that I would kill him; I already saw the red lips of his wound outlined upon his breast by the pale finger of death. When my steel crossed his, I attempted neither thrusts nor parries. I had forgotten the little fencing I knew. I fought at random, almost with my eyes shut; but had my adversary been St. George or Grisier, the result would have been the same.

When Raymond fell I experienced a profound astonishment; something within me broke which no hand will ever be able to restore! A gulf opened before me which can never be filled! I stood there, gloomily gazing upon the purple stream that flowed from the narrow wound, fascinated in spite of myself by this spectacle of immobility succeeding action, death succeeding life, without shade or transition; this young man, who a moment before was radiant with life and hope, now lay motionless before me, as impossible to resuscitate as Cheops under his pyramid. I was rooted to the spot, unconsciously repeating to myself Lady Macbeth's piteous cry: "Who would have thought the man to have had so much blood in him?"

They led me away; I allowed them to put me into the carriage like a thing without strength or motion. The excitement of anger was succeeded by an icy calmness; I had neither memory, thought nor plans; I was annihilated; I would have liked to stop, throw myself on the ground and lie there for ever. I felt no remorse, I had not even the consciousness of my crime; the thought that I was a murderer had not yet had time to fix itself in my mind; I felt no connection whatever with the deed that I had done, and asked myself if it was I, Edgar de Meilhan, who had killed Raymond! It seemed as if I had been only a looker-on.

As to Irene, the innocent cause of this horrible catastrophe, I scarcely thought of her; she only appeared to me a faint phantom seen in another existence! My love, my longings, my jealousy had all vanished. One drop of Raymond's warm blood had stilled my mad vehemence. She is dead, poor darling, it is the only happiness that I could wish her; her death lessens my despair. If she lived, no torture, no penance could be fierce enough to expiate my crime! No hermit of the desert would lash his quivering flesh more pitilessly than I!

Rest in peace, dear Louise, for you will always be Louise to me, even in heaven, which I shall never reach, for I have killed my brother and belong to the race of Cain; I do not pity thee, for thou hast clasped in thy arms the dream of thy heart. Thou hast been happy; and happiness is a crime punishable on earth by death, as is genius and divinity.

You will forgive me! for I caught a glimpse of the angel through the woman. I also sought my ideal and found it. O beautiful loving being! why did your faith fail you, why did you doubt the love you inspired! Alas! I thought you a faithless coquette; you were conscientious; your heart was a treasure that you could not reclaim, and you wished to bestow it worthily! Now I know all; we always know all when it is too late, when the seal of the irreparable is fixed upon events! You came to Havre, poor beauty, to find me, and fled believing yourself deceived; you could not read my despair through my fictitious joy; you took my mask for my real countenance, the intoxication of my body for the oblivion of my soul! In the midst of my orgie, at the very moment when my foot pressed on the Ethiop's body, your azure eyes illumined my dream, your blonde tresses rippled before me like golden waters of Paradise; thoughts of you filled my mind like a vase with divine essence! never have I loved you better; I loved you better than the condemned man, standing on the last step of the scaffold, loves life, than Satan loves heaven from the depths of hell! My heart, if opened, would have exhibited your name written in all its fibres, like the grain of wood which runs through the whole tree. Every particle of my being belonged to you; thoughts of you pervaded me, in every sense, as light passes through the air. Your life was substituted for mine; I no longer possessed either free will or wish.

For a moment you paused upon the brink of the abyss, and started back affrighted; for no woman can gaze, unflinchingly, into the depths of man's heart; precipices always have frightened you—dear angel, as if you had not wings! If you had paused an instant longer, you would have seen far, far in the gloom in a firmament of bright stars, your adored image.

Vain regrets! useless lamentation! The damp and dark earth covers her delicate form! Her beautiful eyes, her pure brow, her fascinating smile we shall never see again—never—never—if we live thousands of years. Every hour that passes but widens the distance between us. Her beauty will fade in the tomb, her name be lost in oblivion! For soon we shall have disappeared, pale forms bending over a marble tomb!

It is very sad, sinister and terrible, but yet it is best so. See her in the arms of another: Roger! what have we done to God to be damned alive! I can pity Raymond, since death separates him from Louise. May he forgive me! He will, for he was a grand, a noble, a perfect friend. We both failed to appreciate him, as a matter of course; folly and baseness are alone comprehended here below!

We ran a desperate race for happiness! One alone attained it—dead!

EDGAR DE MEILHAN.

THE END.

www.ingramcontent.com/pod-product-compliance
Lightning Source LLC
LaVergne TN
LVHW010221110826
845151LV00004B/1169

* 9 7 8 1 4 2 5 5 2 7 4 3 3 *